The Private Eye Writers of America Presents:

Fifty Shades of Grey Fedora

Edited by Robert J. Randisi

Fifty Shades of Grey Fedora © 2015 by Robert J. Randisi
Contributors retain the rights to their individual pieces of work.

All Rights Reserved. No part of this book may be reproduced or transmitted in any form or by any means, electronic or mechanical, including photocopying, without permission in writing from the publisher.

For more information contact:
Riverdale Avenue Books
5676 Riverdale Avenue
Riverdale, NY 10471.

www.riverdaleavebooks.com

Design by www.formatting4U.com
Cover by Scott Carpenter

Digital ISBN 9781626011533
Print ISBN 9781626011526

First Edition February 2015

Table of Contents

"Quarryville" by Michael Bracken

"Natural Death" by Max Allan Collins

"I Wish I Had Your Job," by Ted Fitzgerald

"The Policy" by Carolina Garcia-Aguilera

"The Naked and the Dead" by Parnell Hall

"Emily's Tears" by David Housewright

"Love for Bail" by Jerry Keannealy

"The Fedora" by Terrill Lee Lankford

"On The Job" by Dick Lochte

"Professor Oryfys and the Case for Climax Change" by John Lutz

"Just Tell Me What You Want" by Christine Matthews

"Digger Redux" by Warren Murphy

"A Concrete Garterbelt" by M. Ruth Myers

"Family Affair" by Sara Paretsky

"Bulletville" by Gary Phillips

"Last Tango in Flatbush" by Robert J. Randisi

"Take Off Your Clothes" by Justin Scott

Fifty Shades of Grey Fedora

INTRODUCTION

Are there actually Fifty Shades?

If this anthology is any indication, inviting mystery writers to contribute "sex," or even "erotic" stories to a private eye anthology is opening the door for many different shades of black and white and everything in between.

The 17 authors whose talents are combined here have produced everything from "innuendo" and "tease," to full blown "sex," or "erotica." Yes, everything is here from the chaste kiss and missionary position to bondage, erotic lactation, and silk fetish.

It's been awhile since we published a Private Eye Writers of America original anthology, so we're hoping that the contents herein will make up for the wait. The business of publishing has changed drastically over the past half dozen years. With the advent of epublishing, Kindles and Nooks, things are different for the readers as well as the writers, but a good story is still a good story, and that's all we've tried to produce here.

Well, almost all...

Robert J. Randisi,
Clarksville, Mo

QUARRYVILLE, TEXAS
By Michael Bracken

I drove into Quarryville, a dried-out scab of a town in West Texas, and tried to rent a room at the motel. The horse-faced woman behind the counter insisted that all six rooms were occupied despite there being no vehicles in the parking lot other than mine. Rather than argue with her, I scooped some faded brochures from the counter rack and returned with them to my SUV.

After driving into the sun all afternoon, I was hot, tired, and covered in a thin film of sweat. I had hoped to clean up at the motel before I met my client, a woman who wanted to find out why her brother had committed suicide and why no one in town would talk to her about it, but that was no longer an option. I chewed on a breath mint, checked the directions I'd received during our telephone conversation the previous evening, and drove to her home.

The town I passed through continued to exist because entropy had yet to run its course. Through the first half of the previous century Quarryville had shipped granite east to Dallas, but after the quarry closed in the early 1950s, the town began a long, slow slide into oblivion. Many of the storefronts along Main Street were boarded up, and the rest might as well have been. Only a pawnshop, the ubiquitous Dairy Queen, and a Texaco that still offered full service and had a sign announcing "Mechanic on Duty" showed signs of life. Even the Quarryville Bank & Trust, the largest, most imposing structure downtown, appeared to be more mausoleum than active financial institution.

My client lived on the other side of the railroad tracks in a pale yellow bungalow on a street lined with single-family homes constructed for quarry employees during the town's heyday. The only house on the block with central air conditioning rather than window units, my client's home was also one of the few that was both occupied and without a "For Sale" sign sprouting from the yard. The street lacked curbs, so I parked my SUV where the chip seal road fought a losing battle against her encroaching lawn. The grass had steadily invaded the chip seal until a yearlong, statewide drought had joined the battle.

I crossed the dying lawn, climbed three steps to the porch, and leaned into the bell. Chimes sounded somewhere inside and a moment later the door opened to reveal Donna Devonshire standing on the other side of the screen. An attractive woman who had recently stepped over to my side of fifty, she wore a thin, scoop-front cotton dress that flowed over her body. Her weight had settled mostly around her hips, but ample breasts gave her an hourglass figure so unlike the apple- and pear-shaped women I had dated since my divorce several years earlier. Her shoulder-length auburn hair had been pulled into a ponytail, and she had a fine spray of freckles across the bridge of her nose that she didn't bother to hide with make-up. Cool air wafted around her and through the screen, carrying an aroma of vanilla and cinnamon that reminded me of my first crush, a young widow for whom I had mown the lawn when I was a teenager.

As I examined my client, she examined me in return, and she smiled at what she saw. "You must be the dick I hired."

Without waiting for confirmation, my client pushed open the screen. "Come in."

I followed her into the sparsely furnished house, through the living room to the eat-in kitchen. She offered me sweet tea and we sat at the kitchen table. I showed her my I.D. and slid one of my business cards across to her. My name—Studebaker Johnson—along with my cellphone number and license number were printed on the face of the card.

We shared small talk about the weather—Quarryville had not received a measureable amount of rain in two hundred and twelve days and a mere fraction of an inch during the one rain that bisected the ongoing drought—and about my drive from Waco. Because my day rate included travel time, my expenses included mileage, and my bank account suffered from anemia, I'd had no qualms accepting a job so far from home. My client had expressed no hesitation when I'd quoted my rates during our initial telephone conversation, and she had wire-transferred a healthy retainer to my checking account the prior afternoon.

While we talked, she fingered my business card, finally noticing my full name when she glanced down. Until that moment she'd only known me as Stu Johnson. She asked about it and I told her about my conception in the backseat of my grandfather's car and my parents' subsequent shotgun wedding.

She considered my response, and then asked, "You married, Mr. Johnson?"

"I was, once," I said. "You?"

"Never." The corners of her eyes crinkled as she smiled.

I felt certain my client had a good reason for remaining single her entire life, but following that line of conversation would further delay the inevitable. I said, "Let's talk about your brother."

***

What Donna had not told me on the phone when she hired me was that her brother had been dead for forty-one years. "We thought Donnie Ray went to Canada."

I pulled my notebook from my hip pocket and flipped it open. "Why?"

"He lost the 1969 draft lottery and was scheduled for induction. Vietnam was the next stop for young men around here," she said. "Most weren't eligible for educational deferment and none had political connections."

I had missed Vietnam by a few years but remembered older friends sweating the draft. A few enlisted just to avoid the stress. Others prayed that their number would not be called but they did not protest the war, burn their draft cards, or seek refuge outside the country. "Your brother was a draft dodger?"

Donna winced. "That's what people thought when a pair of FBI agents came to town and knocked on a few doors looking for him. They said Donnie Ray failed to appear for his induction physical and there was a warrant out for his arrest. They told my mother all my brother had to do to get out from under it was to show up at the induction center."

"And he never did."

"At first my mother hoped we'd hear from Donnie Ray, that he'd call or send a letter and let us know he was somewhere in Canada and that he was okay. After several months, she stopped talking about him." My client stared over my shoulder as if looking into the past, and I let silence settle over her kitchen until she gathered her thoughts. "I made chocolate chip cookies last night," she said, "from scratch. Let me get you some."

She pushed herself from the table and bustled around the kitchen for a few minutes. She refilled our tea glasses, stacked cookies on a plate, and put paper napkins on the table. I liked the way she moved around the kitchen and appreciated the way her cotton dress stretched tight across her behind when she bent to retrieve a dropped napkin. I had always favored wide-hipped women, perhaps because the widow I had desired in my youth had been built much like my client.

When she finally settled into her chair, I asked, "How was Donnie Ray's body found?"

"The aquifer is drying up," my client explained. "If the drought continues much longer, West Texas towns like Quarryville won't have enough water to survive."

The abandoned quarry outside of town flooded soon after the mining company shut off the pumps in the mid-1950s, and by the early 1960s it had become a favorite swimming hole for teenagers willing to trespass. As the most recent drought wore on and the aquifer dried up, the water level in the quarry receded, much as water levels had receded on lakes and reservoirs throughout the state. One Sunday afternoon, a trio of boys went to the quarry for a swim and spotted a 1965 Pontiac Grand Prix resting where the water had once been too deep to see what lay at the bottom.

The three boys made a game of diving down to touch the car's roof until one of them went a little deeper and discovered human remains in the driver's seat. "The Sheriff brought in divers to examine the wreck and then brought in a crane to recover the car," Donna explained. "They matched the car's VIN and license plates to the last known owner, and that led them to me. DNA testing confirmed that the body was Donnie Ray."

My client reached into a drawer behind her, pulled out a thin file folder, and pushed it across the table. I opened the folder and found the Sheriff's incident report, the autopsy, and a handful of digital photos printed on plain paper. What she didn't offer were photos of her brother or any personal documents. When I asked why, she said she hadn't any. I read the reports and examined photos of the Grand Prix and the body inside. A .38 caliber revolver with five chambered bullets and one spent shell had been found on the floorboard. The top of the skeleton's head had an exit wound, and a spent slug embedded in the roof of the car had likely passed through Donnie Ray and through the car's headliner. From the angle of entry and exit wounds, the coroner inferred that the .38's barrel had been pressed upward against the bottom of Donnie Ray's chin when it was fired, consistent with a self-inflicted gunshot wound, and had therefore determined his death was a suicide.

When I finished reading and examining everything Donna had given me, I looked up. My client was leaning forward, her breasts resting on the tabletop and displaying cleavage deep enough to dive into.

"Do you have any reason to doubt the coroner's conclusion?"

"I have no reason to think my brother was suicidal, but what would I know?" Donna said. "I was ten when he left."

"So if I take the report at face value, and you can give me no reason why I shouldn't, what you want to know is why he killed himself."

She nodded. "And one other thing: If my brother shot himself, how did his car wind up at the bottom of the quarry?"

I had no answers for her and presented no conjecture. "I'll start nosing around tomorrow," I said, "but I'll need a place to stay tonight."

"The Quarryville Inn on the east side of town," she said. "You should have passed it on your way here."

I told her about my trouble at the motel. "Is there somewhere else?"

"There's not another motel for fifty miles in any direction," she said. "You can stay in my guest room."

"I don't want to impose."

"It's no imposition," my client explained. "It saves me the cost of a room and you won't be wasting my time and money traveling back-and-forth."

I accepted her offer and Donna gave me a quick tour of the house. There wasn't much to it—the living room and kitchen on the east side of the house, two bedrooms connected by a short hall and separated by a bathroom on the west. After I collected my overnight bag, she said, "It's getting late, and I have to be at the bank by eight."

She disappeared into the front bedroom and closed the door. I didn't hear it lock.

***

The next morning, Donna handed me a key to her house.

"You're placing a lot of trust in me."

"I have to, Mr. Johnson," she said. She wore a navy blue skirt suit over a white blouse, and I admired the way it fit her body as if it had been tailored for her. "I have no one else."

After Donna left for work at the Quarryville Bank & Trust, I finished my morning routine, reviewed my notes and thumbed through the brochures I had lifted from the motel's front counter while I drank the last cup from a pot of coffee my client had prepared. Then, with no clear guidance from her, I began work.

I made the Quarryville School my first stop and found that the two-story stone building had been turned into a museum. A woman with gray hair piled atop her head in a lopsided beehive perched on a stool behind the front counter. She had spent decades in the harsh West Texas sun and her skin had turned the color and texture of worn shoe leather.

I removed a business card from my shirt pocket and offered it to her. "I'm Stu Johnson, and I'm looking for—"

"I know who you are, Mr. Johnson." She made no effort to take the card from my outstretched hand. "We all know who you are."

I returned the card to my pocket.

"You can go on home," she continued. "We don't need you stirring up trouble. This town has seen enough heartbreak."

I asked what she meant and she told me how the closing of the quarry had left the town's young men with few employment options. Vietnam and both Iraq wars had gutted the population of young men because war gave them opportunities they would not otherwise have. "They didn't all come back."

Fifty Shades of Grey Fedora

I let my gaze wander over the displays surrounding us and felt as if I were in someone's attic, looking through faded family photos and the accumulated junk of dead relatives. "What happened to the school?"

"Closed about ten years back," she said. "There weren't enough students to keep it open, so now we bus the kids to the consolidated schools over in the county seat."

"And Donnie Ray?" I asked.

"He was a troubled young man."

I asked, "How well do you remember him?"

"I remember him well enough." She held out her hand. "It's five dollars."

I removed a five-dollar bill from my wallet, waited while she prepared a receipt, and then moseyed down the central hall. Faded black-and-white photographs with typewritten descriptions tacked beside them lined the walls, and, as I read each one, I learned the town's history. A spring that served as a watering hole for Indians later became a stop for the stagecoach line across Texas, and a small town grew up around the stagecoach stop. Growth remained stagnant until the late 1800s when the quarry opened outside of town and the railroad built a spur to serve it. The town grew up on both sides of the track—the business district and wealthier residents on one side and quarry employees on the other side.

When I finished examining the photos lining the hall, I worked my way through the six classrooms on the ground floor until I found one dedicated to the school's history. I examined the class photos hung there—the school had never had enough students to justify producing yearbooks—until I found the class of 1969 and identified the thumb-sized photo of Donnie Ray. As I wrote the names of his classmates in my notebook, I examined the photo. Donnie Ray didn't look like any draft dodger I'd ever seen—clean-shaven with a crew cut—but he also didn't look much like the other young men in his class photo. He appeared smaller and younger, as if puberty had yet to blossom within him.

***

I drove from the schoolhouse-turned-museum out Quarry Road to where it ended at a rusting and barely legible "No Trespassing" sign and a chain-link fence that had collapsed. I drove over the downed fence, followed the tracks of an untold number of vehicles, and soon found myself staring at a gigantic hole in the ground. Much like an in-ground swimming pool but on a massive scale, one end sloped down toward a bottom littered with abandoned mining equipment. The slope ended at a pool of water constrained on three sides by a sheer cliff face.

While exploring the museum, I had examined many photos of the quarry in operation, when the equipment now littering the floor of the abandoned quarry had been operating at full capacity, and the backbreaking work had kept many families fed. I tried to imagine what the quarry had looked like before the drought, when it had been full of water and cavorting teenagers. What I could not imagine is why a young man had taken his life forty-one years earlier and how he and his car had wound up in the deepest part of the quarry. I drove to the other end, found a spot downhill from where Donnie Ray's car must have gone over the edge, and stood at the lip looking at the remaining water far below.

After several minutes, I returned to my SUV and to town. I pulled into the full-service Texaco and stopped next to the pumps. At I shut off the engine, a wiry old man in an oil-stained gimme cap tapped on my window. After I eased it down, he said, "What'll you have?"

"Regular," I said. "Fill it."

"Check the oil for you?"

"No, thanks," I said. "I'm good."

He walked around my SUV, started pumping gas, and washed my windows with water not much cleaner than the dirt he was squeegeeing off. After he finished, he collected my credit card, walked inside, and returned a few minutes later to have me sign a receipt. Before he would let me go, he asked, "You that private eye from Waco everybody's talking about?"

I said I was.

"You really think it's a good idea to go nosing around in other people's business?"

"Ms. Devonshire wants to know what happened to her brother."

"Damn fool boy went and blew his brains out, that's what happened," he said. "Why's she got to know any more than that?"

***

I drove to the county seat and spoke with the pot-bellied deputy who had caught the case.

"Open and shut," he said around the end of a wet toothpick.

"So you didn't do any investigating?"

"Don't know how they do it where you come from," he said, "but 'round here we don't investigate suicides. We located the deceased's next of kin and let her claim the body when the coroner finished with it."

"She had a copy of your report." I held the thin file folder in my hand and showed him that I now had it.

"And I was glad to share," he said. "I don't know what she's looking for, but I'm damned certain the answer's not in there."

"What about the car?" I asked. "Do you think Donnie Ray shot himself and then drove into the quarry?"

"Can't say how it happened."

"Was the car in gear? Was the ignition engaged?"

He stared at me for a moment before taking the file folder from my hand. When he couldn't find the photograph he wanted, the deputy turned to his computer, opened the digital photographs and enlarged three of them so we could examine the dashboard, the steering column, and the automatic shift console between the front bucket seats. Keys hung from the ignition but it wasn't possible to determine if the ignition was engaged or not from the angle of the photo. We were able to determine that the parking brake had not been set and that the console shifter was in neutral.

"I suppose it could have rolled in after he shot himself," the deputy said.

"I was at the quarry a few hours ago," I said. "His car would have had to roll uphill. Think it could have done that? And what about the damage to the rear bumper?"

The deputy closed the images on his computer screen and turned to me. "You saying someone killed him?"

I peeled the file folder Donna had given me off the deputy's desk. "I'm not saying anything," I said. "I'm just asking questions."

"It's suicide," the deputy said. "Open-and-shut case and there's no reason to think otherwise."

Fifty Shades of Grey Fedora

***

I returned to Quarryville and located the three teenagers who had found Donnie Ray's car at the bottom of the quarry. They were sitting on the tailgate of a Ford F-150 the colors of dust and rust, drinking Lone Star, and firing chewing-tobacco-colored streams of spit at an open paint can. They were the first people I'd encountered other than my client who willingly talked with me about what had happened. Unfortunately, they couldn't tell me anything more than what I already knew about the discovery of Donnie Ray's body.

I was about to leave when one of them stopped me cold. "My daddy said things was better when everybody thought that boy run off to Canada."

"Did your father know Donnie Ray?"

"Not so much, but my uncle sure did. Him and that boy were in the same class."

"They were friends?"

"Not to hear my uncle tell it. That little fag didn't have no friends."

"He was gay?"

"Queer as a three dollar bill, my uncle said."

When I asked for his uncle's name, the boys looked at each other.

The boy I'd been speaking with looked down and mumbled, "I said too much already."

"That's okay," I told him. "I can figure out who he is without your help."

One by one the boys finished their beer or spit out their chew and hopped off the tailgate. I knew our conversation had ended, so I returned to my SUV, checked the time, and returned to my client's home.

***

I didn't need the key because Donna had already returned from the bank. I left my files on the coffee table and found her in the kitchen, her skirt suit already exchanged for a light cotton dress like the one she'd had on when I first arrived. The dress swayed with the movement of her hips as she bustled around the small kitchen preparing dinner, and her unexpected domesticity surprised me.

"I didn't know what you might like," she said as I settled onto a chair at the kitchen table, which had already been set for two, "so I'm making chicken fried steak with mashed potatoes and white gravy. Everybody likes chicken fried."

"Yes, ma'am, they do." I didn't tell her my doctor had me on a low-salt, low-fat diet to mitigate the damage caused to my cardiovascular system from years of poor dining choices.

"I heard you visited the museum," Donna said over her shoulder. I liked the way the cotton dress clung to her ample assets and I found myself mesmerized by the way it moved as she moved. I remembered years earlier sitting in the widow's kitchen, watching her much as I watched my client. I had spent many hours alone in the bathroom fantasizing about seducing the widow until several years later when I met and lost my virginity to the slender woman who became my first wife. Donna turned and caught me watching her, but she said nothing about my attention. Instead, she asked, "You learn anything from your visit?"

She was paying for my time and deserved to know what I had learned, but there wasn't much to tell and it didn't take long to tell it. I ended by recapping my conversation with the boys without mentioning the homosexual slur they used to describe Donnie Ray. "They said your brother didn't have any friends."

"He had at least one," she said. "Donnie Ray used to meet him at the quarry."

I pulled my notebook from my pocket and flipped pages until I found my original notes. "You didn't mention him earlier."

"I never knew who it was." She placed bowls of mashed potatoes, white gravy, and corn on the table. "Remember, my brother was nine years older than me and he never told me much of anything."

Donna returned to the stove, placed saucer-sized chicken fried steaks on a pair of plates, and returned to the table with them. After she filled two glasses with sweet tea, she settled onto the chair on the other side of the table.

I looked at all the food. "You didn't have to do this."

"You're a guest in my house, Mr. Johnson," she said. "My mother taught me to treat guests like family."

I glanced around. Though everything was neat and clean, the kitchen appeared original to the house, with a white-enamel four-burner stove and a refrigerator a generation removed from being an icebox. The walls were bead board painted white, and the kitchen table and wooden chairs were shabby chic, though by choice or by chance I could not tell. I said something about her house being well cared for.

"I grew up here," she explained, "and I've never lived anywhere else. The room where you're sleeping was my brother's. He was gone several months before my mother cleaned it out and allowed me to move into it. She gave away his clothes and books and other things. Then she stopped talking about him, as if he had never existed."

"You seem to have made the place yours."

"It's taken many years," she said. "My father died in an accident before I was born, my brother left when I was ten, and cancer took my mother when I was twenty. I had to live long enough that the sadness seeped out of the walls and left room for happiness to move in."

I cut into the chicken fried, forked a piece into my mouth, and let it melt in my mouth. I watched Donna as I ate—entranced by the way she took food between her lips, the way she chewed, and the look of pleasure when she swallowed. She enjoyed her meal in a way that anemic, weight-watching bone bags did not, and when she licked a bit of gravy off the corner of her mouth with the tip of her tongue, I briefly imagined what other things her tongue could do.

Because my client knew little about her brother and had no family documents or photo albums to share, I made her tell me about her life in Quarryville. She had few friends, had lost herself in books, imagining lives unlike the one she lived, and had graduated high school at the top of her class. She'd worked part-time at the Dairy Queen throughout school, and had been offered a full-time job at the Quarryville Bank & Trust the same week she graduated.

"I've been there ever since," she said, "but I've only been head teller for about four years."

"Why did you apply for a job at the bank instead of going to college?"

"I didn't," she said. "Mr. Dubchek offered me the job. College had never been an option and my mother had been diagnosed with cancer a month earlier, so I took the job. It was full-time, paid better than DQ, and offered benefits. I've done right by the bank and the bank's done right by me."

After dinner, I helped clear the table. When I realized Donna did not have a dishwasher, I volunteered for the task.

"You're not like the men around here," she said as she placed one hand on my arm. Heat from her touch spread through my entire body.

"How's that?"

"I've never known one to touch a dirty dish."

I smiled. "My mother taught me how to be a good guest."

Donna let me wash while she dried, and we stood so close I could smell the delicate vanilla and cinnamon of her perfume even though I stood above a sink full of hot, soapy dishwater. Our fingers touched each time I passed a wet dish to her, and her hip pressed against mine several times as she worked around me while putting things away. Had I reason to believe our contact was anything but incidental, I might have pulled her into my arms after the last dish was put away, pressed her against the counter, and let her feel how she had aroused me.

Instead, I accepted her thanks, dried my hands, and moved to the living room, where I had left my files. Donna sat in a chair and read while I spread my notes and the case file from the sheriff's department across the coffee table. I easily identified the uncle of the young man I'd spoken to late that afternoon and confirmed that Dubchek was one of the names I had copied from the photograph of Donnie Ray's classmates.

Every so often I interrupted my client's reading to ask her a question about something in my notes, learning that the man who hired her at the bank had been the bank's president and the father of her brother's classmate. When I asked why everyone had been so certain that her brother had fled to Canada, she told me that every other draftee had left his car behind when inducted, and that no other family had ever had a visit from the FBI.

When it grew late, Donna excused herself, disappeared into her bedroom, and reappeared a few minutes later wearing a white gown that seemed even thinner than the cotton dress she'd worn earlier, and it was evident, when she passed between the light and me on the way to the kitchen, that she wore nothing beneath it. I watched her cross the living room again on her return trip, a glass of water in hand, and she stopped in the hall to wish me a good night.

Though I should have been thinking about the case, I had lost my ability to concentrate on the information I'd gathered. I put myself to bed a few minutes later and fell asleep thinking of my client, of her touch when we washed dishes, of the way her cotton dresses stretched across her backside when she bent over, and of her silhouette seen through her gown. I had once before become involved with a client—a brief, torrid affair that destroyed my marriage and somehow strengthened hers—and I knew the risks involved in allowing my carnal desires to distract me from my job.

***

My second morning in Quarryville, my client pushed open the bathroom door without knocking and saw me standing naked before the sink, fresh from the shower, my chin covered with shaving cream and a razor in my hand. I could not control the slow swelling of my cock when I realized she was watching me shave, but I didn't stop. After a moment, she backed out of the room and pulled the door closed.

"I'm sorry," Donna said over coffee a few minutes later. She was dressed for work at the bank and I was dressed in a short-sleeve shirt, Wrangler jeans, and ropers. "I didn't mean to stare. It's just that it's been so long since—"

I reached across the table and placed my hand over hers. "It's okay."

Instead of pulling her hand away, Donna entwined her fingers with mine.

"How did you get that scar?"

She meant the pucker in my left shoulder. "Shoot-out with a drug dealer."

"You win or lose?"

"I'd call it a draw," I explained. "He's in Huntsville wearing an ostomy bag. I took early retirement."

"I'm sorry," Donna said. Her eyes searched mine. I don't know what she was looking for and I don't know what she found, but after a moment, she drew back her hand, finished her coffee, and stood. "Be back in time for dinner?"

I told her I would.

***

While sitting on my client's couch the previous evening I had made a list of people I wanted to talk to about Donnie Ray. Between the slender directory Donna kept next to her telephone and some Internet sleuthing on my iPhone, I found home and work addresses for those still in Quarryville. Two of Donnie Ray's classmates had been killed in Vietnam and were buried in the Methodist church's graveyard north of town, and many others had moved away. Four men—the Texaco's on-duty mechanic, a bartender at The Watering Hole, a handyman, and the Quarryville Bank & Trust's current president—remained in town.

I started with the handyman, uncle to the young man I had spoken with the previous day, because he lived closest to Donna. I found him loading paint cans into the bed of his truck. He was a big man gone to fat who had neither shaved nor bathed for several days.

"I ain't got time to talk to you," he said as I approached. "I'm getting a late start as it is."

"I just have a few questions."

He stopped and turned. "Well, I ain't got no answers."

"You went to school with Donnie Ray Devonshire."

"And I didn't have nothing to do with that little faggot's death." I knew then where his nephew came by his attitude. The big man stepped toward me and continued. "Why don't you get on back where you came from and leave us to hell alone?"

"Don't you want Ms. Devonshire to know why her brother died?"

"Why should I care what that uppity bitch wants?" he demanded. He stepped closer. His distended stomach threatened to press against mine, and the stench of cheap liquor reeking from his body made my eyes water. I held my ground and he continued. "Thinks she's better'n the rest of us 'cause she works at the bank. She wouldn't have that job if Dub hadn't been hot for her all these years."

"Dub?"

"Dubchek. He's president of the bank now, just like his daddy was, and just like his granddaddy was before that."

"You don't think Donna deserves closure?"

"I don't think that faggot's sister deserves nothing," he said. "My nephew and his friends shouldn't'a said nothing to nobody about that car in the quarry. Everything was fine when we all thought Donnie Ray run off to Canada 'cause he was too chicken to serve in Vietnam."

The big man glared at me for a moment and then turned away and continued loading his truck. I knew I wouldn't get any more from him so I returned to my SUV and drove to the Texaco. I parked in what little shade I could find and left my windows partway down before I walked into the service bay.

The little man in the grease-stained gimme cap was filling the tank of a blue Lincoln, and I found the mechanic on duty sitting in a plastic chair with his nose buried in a titty magazine. He wore his gray hair cut in a flat top, and thick jowls made him look like a basset hound's progeny. He looked up when he heard me approach. He said, "Figured you'd be back."

"Why's that?"

"You want to talk to the people who knew Donnie Ray." He closed the magazine and tossed it onto the workbench behind him.

"And you did?"

"We weren't friends, but we went to school together," he said as he stood, "and graduated the same year. You want a beer?"

"A little early to start drinking, isn't it?"

"Not if you want to talk."

I followed him down the block to The Watering Hole, where the day-shift bartender—the third man on my list—had opened for the day. I stepped inside to find walls covered with neon beer signs and the mounted heads of dead animals. A muted flat-screen television above the bar had been tuned to ESPN. The man behind the bar had a narrow face, as if someone had compressed his head in a vise when he was a baby, and he opened three bottles of Dos Equis and put them on the bar as we approached.

He knew why we were there and we didn't bother with introductions.

"Tell me about Donnie Ray."

"There's not a lot to tell," said the mechanic. He took a long pull from his beer before continuing. "The other guys used to pick on Donnie Ray. We never did anything about it because they would have turned on us and pushed us around the way they did Donnie Ray."

"The other boys bullied him?"

"Incessantly," the bartender said. "I'm not proud to admit it, but we did, too."

They described some of the things they and the other boys had done to Donnie Ray, things that went beyond name-calling and the usual maltreatment of a boy at the bottom of the teenage pecking order.

"His father died when he was about nine, so there was nobody to teach him to defend himself. His mother couldn't help, what with the baby and all."

I held my beer bottle in one fist but I had yet to take a drink. "You think that's what drove him to suicide?"

The mechanic shook his head. "He'd been putting up with it all his life and he was about to get away from it."

"We figure something happened that night."

"But you don't know what."

"If anybody does, it's Dub," the auto mechanic said. "I saw his pick-up the day after Donnie Ray left town. The front end was messed up pretty bad. He said he'd hit a deer and we didn't think anything about it at the time. But the other day, when we heard the back end of Donnie Ray's car was damaged—"

He let the sentence hang and let me draw my own conclusion. "So why won't anybody talk to Donnie Ray's sister about her brother, and why are y'all so eager for me to leave town?"

"Nobody wants to think bad things ever happen in Quarryville and that one homosexual's suicide forty-one years ago should be swept under the rug."

"Except we don't think Donnie Ray was gay," said the mechanic. "We just think he was... different."

***

After I finished my beer and walked alone to my SUV, I drove to the Quarryville Bank & Trust and parked on the street in front of the granite-fronted building. I didn't want to cause problems for my client at her workplace, but I had to go where the case led me. So, I made my way up the steps and into a lobby that didn't appear to have changed much since the bank first opened its doors. I told the pinch-faced woman behind the desk that I wanted to see Mr. Dubchek.

"Do you have an appointment?"

I told her I didn't.

"Your name?" The pinch tightened when I told her. "I'm afraid Mr. Dubchek isn't in."

"That's okay," I said as I glanced around and found a trio of hardback chairs lining the wall nearby. "I'll wait over there."

"I wouldn't waste my time, if I were you. Mr. Dubchek has gone for the day."

I considered spending my day sitting in the bank lobby to prove I was more stubborn than the woman before me, but I knew I would gain nothing from the effort. I placed one of my cards in front of her and said, "Tell him I was here."

Without waiting for her response, I walked out of the bank and around to the employee parking lot, where I found a blue Lincoln parked in the spot reserved for the bank president.

From the bank, I drove to Dubchek's home, a two-story antebellum mansion situated in the middle of several landscaped acres that were suffering from the drought as much as the lawns on the other side of the track, proving that money couldn't buy rain.

I returned to Main Street, the name given the state highway for the several blocks it ran parallel to the railroad track through town, and pulled into the Dairy Queen for a dip cone. I had almost finished it when my cell phone rang. I checked caller I.D. and found that the caller's number had been blocked. I answered anyhow.

A voice on the other end said, "You've been asking a lot of questions about Donnie Ray Devonshire."

I admitted that I had.

"Your questions are upsetting people." The voice did not match that of anyone I had spoken with since arriving in town.

"Maybe it isn't my questions that are upsetting," I said. "Maybe it's the answers."

"No one wants to admit that they turned their back on Donnie Ray and could have done something to save him," said the voice. "As long as we all thought he went to Canada we could live with ourselves."

"So what did happen?"

"I can tell you everything you want to know, but not on the phone."

"When?" I asked. "Where?"

He suggested the quarry at midnight. "This is your one opportunity to learn the truth," said the voice. "Take it or leave it."

I assured the man at the other end of the conversation that I would meet him. After he disconnected the call, I finished my dip cone and drove to my client's home, let myself in, and spread my notes across the coffee table, seeking the answer to a question I had failed to ask.

Donna walked in a few hours later while I was still poring over my notes. She smiled the moment she saw me sitting on her couch.

"I saw you at the bank today," she said as she placed her purse on the rocking chair. "So did everyone else. They were all talking about you asking to see Mr. Dubchek."

"He wouldn't meet with me."

"Why would he?" she asked as she unbuttoned the top few buttons of her white blouse and fanned herself with one of the flaps of cloth, providing me with an intermittent view of her ample cleavage. "If he knew anything about my brother's death, I'm certain he would have told me."

"Why?" I asked. "No one else seems willing to talk to you about it."

"Because, well—" Donna hesitated as she considered how to respond to my question. "Dub's father offered me the job at the bank, but he did it because Dub insisted."

"Someone I spoke with today said he was hot for you. Were you ever—?"

"Never." My client stepped out of her heels and pulled her blouse from the waistband of her skirt. "He's been my guardian angel, and he's done a lot for me, but he's never once asked for anything in return."

Watching Donna's slow striptease while I questioned her about her employer sent mixed signals. Though my brain was engaged in the conversation, my cock throbbed each time she revealed a bit of skin, whether it was the swell of her ample breasts or the soft pale flesh of her abdomen. When she reached down for her shoes, her skirt stretched tight across her backside, tighter than her cotton dresses ever did. She straightened, grabbed her purse, and crossed the living room. When she reached the hall, she asked, "What else did you learn today?"

I began to tell her and she stopped me.

"Not through the wall," she said. "Come in here."

I pushed myself off the couch, followed Donna into her bedroom, and sat on the side of her bed. She had placed her purse on the nightstand and she stood in front of the open closet with her back to me. As I told her about my day—without mentioning the abuse her brother had suffered and without mentioning my meeting later that night—she slipped out of her blouse, unzipped her skit, and stepped out of it. She stood before me wearing a white lace bra and white lace high-cut brief. I had once seen the widow similarly attired when she left her bedroom door open during one of my visits to her home, and I had left in a panic after ejaculating in my underwear. Several years passed before I wondered if the widow had left her door open on purpose, intending to seduce me. I wondered the same thing about Donna until she reached into her closet for a cotton print dress similar to the others she'd worn. She pulled the dress over her head, slipped her arms into place, and let it drop to her hips, where it hesitated before the hem dropped down to her knees.

Donna looked over her shoulder. "Zip me up?"

I stood and stepped to her. The zipper rested at the swell of her buttocks and I took it between my fingers. Before I could tug it upward, Donna shifted position, leaned back into me, and pressed herself against my crotch.

Into her ear I whispered, "You don't really want me to zip you up, do you?"

Without waiting for a response, I pushed aside her shoulder-length auburn hair and kissed the back of Donna's neck. She moaned and ground her hips, causing my cock to swell inside my jeans and press into the division of her ample buttocks.

"I've been imagining this ever since I found you on my porch," she whispered as I continued kissing her neck. "I haven't been sleeping well knowing you're in the next room, and this morning, when I walked in on you, I —"

I spun her around and silenced her by covering her mouth with mine. I kissed her long and deep and hard.

She moved my hands upward to her breasts. Even through the thick lace of her bra and the thin cotton of her dress, I could feel her nipples straining for my touch. I pulled her dress off her shoulders so that it slid from her. After her dress dropped to the floor, I unclasped the hooks fastening her bra. She shook it off, revealing heavy, milk-white breasts, each capped with a thick nipple and half-dollar-sized areola constricted with desire. I cupped them in my hands and thumbed her nipples.

She unbuckled my belt, unfastened my jeans, and struggled my zipper down. Then she reached under the waistband of my briefs and wrapped her soft hand around my erection.

A moment later she stepped back, hooked her thumbs in the waistband of her high-cut brief, and pulled it down her thighs until it fell the rest of the way to the floor. She stepped out of it as I sat on the side of her bed to pull off my ropers. As soon as my boots thumped to the floor, she helped me remove the rest of my clothes.

Donna touched my shoulder and let her fingers linger in the scar left by the drug dealer's bullet, an intensely personal touch. "Does it hurt?"

"It did," I said. "It doesn't now."

She kissed the pucker, drew back, and looked up at me. When I pushed her back on the bed, her heavy breasts slid toward her armpits. I took one thick nipple between my lips and caressed it back to attention. I did the same with her other nipple before kissing my way lower, past her belly button to the juncture of her thighs. I shifted position, knelt between her widespread legs, and buried my face between them. As I snaked my tongue along the length of her slit, she hooked her legs over my shoulders. Her curly, gray-flecked auburn pubic hair tickled my nose as I parted her lips with my tongue, sucked at her swollen labia, and found the tightening bud of her clit. I lapped at it as I slid my right hand beneath her buttocks and slipped my thumb into her female opening. As I pistoned my thumb in and out of her, I drew her swollen clit between my teeth and teased it with the tip of my tongue.

Donna wrapped her hands around the back of my head and ground her pelvis against my face. Her hips bucked up and down on the bed, her pubic bone introducing itself to my nose with increasing urgency. My client cried out when she came, and released a flood of sexual effluent over my thumb and fingers and down the crack of her ass. She didn't release my head until her vagina quit clenching and unclenching, and, when she did, I rose up on my knees to reveal my straining erection.

Even though the orgasm had turned her to jelly, Donna wanted more. She rolled to the side, retrieved a new three-pack of lubricated condoms from her purse, and peeled open one square foil packet. She removed the condom and slipped it over my erection.

I pulled her to the side of the bed and turned her over. Standing behind her, I lifted her hips until she was on all fours, her knees barely on the edge of the bed, and I stepped between her legs. I pressed the head of my condom-covered cock against her slickened female opening, grabbed her hips, and thrust forward. After I buried myself deep inside her, I drew back and did it again.

I moved my right hand from her hip to the small of her back and I slid my thumb between her buttocks until it pressed against the tight pucker of her sphincter. My thumb was slickened with her juices, and she opened to the pressure of it.

A moment later I pulled out of her and pressed the head of my condom-covered cock against her sphincter where my thumb had been. The pre-lubricated condom, now coated with additional lubrication from Donna's vagina, made it easy for me to push into her ass, and I buried my entire length within her as she moaned with pleasure. I drew back until the head of my cock remained captured by her sphincter muscles before pressing forward again.

I pumped into Donna's ample ass hard and fast. She reached between her thighs and stroked her clit with her two middle fingers, matching my rhythm stroke for stroke. As she neared orgasm, she stroked faster, sliding her fingers forward and back over her engorged clit. She came first and would have collapsed on the bed if I hadn't been holding her hips.

I drove into her half a dozen more times before I came. I held her tight to my hips until I caught my breath and stopped spasming within her. After I withdrew, Donna rolled onto her back and looked up at me. "There isn't a man in this town who could do that for me."

Later, after we used a second condom, my client fell asleep in my arms. I also fell asleep, but my phone's alarm woke me at eleven and I slipped out of bed without disturbing her.

***

The man sitting on the hood of the blue Lincoln waiting for me at the edge of the deep end of the quarry had aged well, having bought his way into his sixties. He didn't offer to shake my hand when I parked my SUV next to his car and climbed out.

"You have to understand that my classmates and I were among the last children born while the quarry was still prosperous," the bank president said without preamble. "By the time we reached high school, the quarry had closed. The future looked bleak for everyone, but especially for the young men who thought they would follow their fathers into the pit. Then Vietnam became a storm cloud on our horizon. Most of us were trapped between an abandoned rock pit and a hard place in the world."

I didn't have time for a history lesson. "What about Donnie Ray?"

"I'm pretty sure Donnie Ray was a hermaphrodite." Dubchek glanced at me. "I didn't learn that word until I went away to college. We all thought he was effeminate and slow to mature. There weren't a lot of options in those days and his parents apparently chose to raise him as a boy. But he wasn't a boy, not truly. As we grew older and Donnie Ray's external genitalia failed to develop, some of the guys thought he was a homosexual, though that wasn't the word they used back then. They bullied him."

"You didn't?"

Dubchek shook his head. "When the other guys got too rough with Donnie Ray I could usually get them to back off, but I could never stop them."

"How rough was too rough?"

He described some of the things the other young men did to Donnie Ray. "He had no one to turn to," he said. "His father was gone and his mother thought he was God's punishment for premarital sex. I often wondered if I could have survived similar treatment."

"You must have been his only friend."

"Maybe," he said. "I couldn't be seen with Donnie Ray, but we would meet out here at night and talk. He was afraid of what might happen when I left for college, so I got him the gun. I never expected him to use it."

"But he did."

Dubchek didn't speak for the longest time and I thought I saw something glisten in the corner of his eye. "I found him on a night like this. His car was right about there." He pointed. "Donnie Ray was scheduled to have his induction physical the next day and the physical would have revealed his under-developed genitalia. What was worse, going into the Army the way he was or coming back home because he failed the physical? I knew what he had done and why, and I knew I couldn't leave him like that for someone else to find. I knew what things would be like for his family, so I used my truck to push his car into the quarry. I wasn't thinking, though. After I put his car in neutral and released the parking brake, it rolled backward, and smashed into the front of my truck."

"You told your friends you'd hit a deer."

Dubchek nodded. "That was the first lie, and I kept right on lying. Donnie Ray had talked about going to Canada, so I made certain that's what everybody thought happened, especially after the FBI came nosing around. As long as Donnie Ray's family thought he had escaped Quarryville and Vietnam, they had hope. Not until I was older did I realize that any false hope that came from not knowing his fate may have been worse than the truth. By then it was too late to admit what I had done."

We sat in silence until Dubchek continued.

"Donnie Ray left a note." He pulled a folded square of yellowed college-ruled notebook paper from his shirt pocket and handed it to me. "This was on the dashboard. I've kept it all these years. Maybe it's time for Donna to have it."

I slipped it into my pocket.

He paused, took a deep breath, and continued. "I had graduated college and was working for my father at the bank when cancer took Donnie Ray's mother and left his sister alone. I've done what I could for Donna ever since. I guess I'm paying penance for my sin."

"You didn't kill Donnie Ray."

Dubchek turned to me. "But I didn't save him, either."

He searched my eyes for absolution, but he didn't find any.

Fifty Shades of Grey Fedora

***

When I tried to slip back into my client's bed a short time after leaving Dubchek sitting alone at the quarry, she rolled over and sleepily asked, "Where have you been?"

"With your brother's friend." Throughout my daily reports to Donna I had never mentioned the names of the townspeople with whom I had spoken, and I didn't start by naming Dubchek.

"And?"

"And I know what happened that night and how Donnie Ray wound up at the bottom of the quarry."

Donna sat up quickly, turned on the bedside lamp, and wiped the sleep from her eyes.

"Your brother may have taken his own life," I explained, "but this entire town had its finger on the trigger. The people of Quarryville failed Donnie Ray because they abused him in ways that went beyond mere bullying or they turned a blind eye to the people who did. Even your brother's best friend couldn't save him." I described some of the things the other young men had done to her brother—the cruelties that men had inflicted upon one another for generations stretching back to Cain's murder of Abel—and color drained from her face.

"But why?"

"Fear because he was different." I told her about Donnie Ray's apparent medical condition and how her parents had chosen to raise him.

Several seconds passed while Donna stared at me without speaking. "My mother never said anything about it," she finally said. "After she died I went through all of her files and found nothing about Donnie Ray, not even a copy of his birth certificate, as if she had erased him from existence."

"She wasn't the only one. This town erased your brother from its collective memory. Finding his body at the bottom of the quarry brought back all their old fears and prejudices and reminded them of their collective guilt." I let that sink in before I said, "Your brother left a note."

I removed the note from my pocket and told her I'd not read it as I handed it to her. I watched as she unfolded the yellowed square of paper and read her brother's final message. When she finished, she returned it to me and I read it.

I don't know what I am, but I don't belong here, Donnie Ray had written.

"Your brother's friend found Donnie Ray's body the night he shot himself. He thought he was protecting your family when he pushed your brother's car into the quarry, but even more, he thought he was protecting Donnie Ray."

"What more could they have done to him after he died?"

I had no answer. "Donnie Ray's account is closed and any debt this town owes your family for what it did to him was paid long ago." Though Donna didn't realize it, Dubchek had paid a greater portion of the debt than anyone else, and he would be carrying that load for the rest of his life.

"Hold me," Donna said, and I did.

Later, after she'd shed her last tear, we used the third condom, making love as the sun rose over Quarryville. After breakfast, I packed my overnight case and carried it outside. There was nothing left to do but say good-bye as we stood on the dead grass in front of her pale yellow house.

"I'll send you a final report after I return to my office," I offered, "with names, dates, additional details."

"Don't bother," Donna said. "I have to live with these people for however much longer Quarryville survives, so maybe I don't want to know everything you learned about them."

The young men who had tormented Donnie Ray, and thousands more like them, had gone to Vietnam and returned changed in ways no one could have predicted. Donna had not known them well before they left but she had to live with the people they had become, and she knew far better than I what that entailed.

I opened the SUV's door and tossed my overnight bag onto the passenger seat. "If you're ever in Waco, look me up."

"I will," my client replied, though I knew I would never see her again. I had spent three days picking at the town's scab for her, and the wound I'd uncovered required more than an adhesive bandage to conceal.

I climbed into my SUV and drove east into the morning sun, leaving Donna Devonshire to grieve for her brother while entropy continued to desiccate Quarryville, Texas.

NATURAL DEATH, INC.
by Max Allan Collins

She'd been pretty, once. She was still sexy, in a slutty way, if you'd had enough beers and it was just before closing time.

Kathleen O'Meara, who ran the dingy dive that sported her last name, would have been a well-preserved fifty, if she hadn't been forty. But I knew from the background materials I'd been provided that she was born in 1899, here in the dirt-poor Irish neighborhood of Cleveland known as the Angles, a scattering of brick and frame dwellings and businesses at the north end of 25th Street in the industrial flats.

Kathleen O'Meara's husband, Frank, had been dead barely a month now, but Katie wasn't wearing black: her blouse was white with red polka dots, a low-cut peasant affair out of which spilled well-powdered, bowling ball-size breasts. Her mouth was a heavily red-rouged chasm within which gleamed white storebought choppers; her eyes were lovely, within their pouches, long-lashed and money-green.

"What's your pleasure, handsome?" she asked, her soprano voice musical in a calliope sort of way, a hint of Irish lilt in it.

I guess I was handsome, for this crowd anyway, six feet, one-hundred-eighty pounds poured into threadbare mismatched suitcoat and pants, a wilted excuse for a fedora snugged low over my reddish brown hair, chin and cheeks stubbled with two days growth, looking back at myself in the streaked smudgy mirror behind the bar. A chilly March afternoon had driven better than a dozen men inside the shabby walls of O'Meara's, where a churning exhaust fan did little to stave off the bouquet of stale smoke and beer-soaked sawdust.

"Suds is all I can afford," I said.

"There's worse ways to die," she said, eyes sparkling.

"Ain't been reduced to canned heat yet," I admitted.

At least half of the clientele around me couldn't have made that claim; while those standing at the bar, with a foot on the rail, like me, wore the sweatstained workclothes that branded them employed, the men hunkered at tables and booths wore the tattered rags of the derelict. A skinny dark-haired dead-eyed sunken-cheeked barmaid in an off-white waitress uniform was collecting empty mugs and replacing them with foaming new ones.

The bosomy saloonkeeper set a sloshing mug before me. "Railroad worker?"

I sipped; it was warm and bitter. "Steel mill. Pretty lean in Gary; heard they was hiring at Republic."

"That was last month."

"Yeah. Found that out in a hurry."

She extended a pudgy hand. "Kathleen O'Meara, at your service."

"William O'Hara," I said. Nathan Heller, actually. The Jewish last name came from my father, but the Irish mug that was fooling the saloonkeeper was courtesy of my mother.

"Two O's, that's us," she grinned; that mouth must have have been something, once. "My pals call me Katie. Feel free."

"Well, thanks, Katie. And my pals call me Bill." Nate.

"Got a place to stay, Bill?"

"No. Thought I'd hop a freight tonight. See what's shakin' up at Flint."

"They ain't hiring up there, neither."

"Well, I dunno, then."

"I got rooms upstairs, Bill."

"Couldn't afford it, Katie."

"Another mug?"

"Couldn't afford that, either."

She winked. "Handsome, you got me wrapped around your little pinkie, ain't ya noticed?"

She fetched me a second beer, then attended to the rest of her customers at the bar. I watched her, feeling both attracted and repulsed; what is it about a beautiful woman run to fat, gone to seed, that can still summon the male in a man?

I was nursing the second beer, knowing that if I had enough of these I might do something I'd regret in the morning, when she trundled back over and leaned on the bar with both elbows.

"A room just opened up. Yours, if you want it."

"I told ya, Katie, I'm flat-busted."

"But I'm not," she said with a lecherous smile, and I couldn't be sure whether she meant money or her billowing powdered bosoms. "I could use a helpin' hand around here... I'm a widow lady, Bill, runnin' this big old place by her lonesome."

"You mean sweep up and do dishes and the like."

Her cute nose wrinkled as if a bad smell had caught its attention; a little late for that, in this joint. "My daughter does most of the drudgery." She nodded toward the barmaid, who was moving through the room like a zombie with a beer tray. "Wouldn't insult ya with woman's work, Bill... But there's things only a man can do."

She said "things" like "tings."

"What kind of things?"

Her eyes had a twinkle, like broken glass. "Things... Interested?"

"Sure, Katie."

And it was just that easy.

Three days earlier, I had been seated at a conference table in the spacious dark-wood and pebbled-glass office of the Public Safety Director in Cleveland's City Hall.

"It's going to be necessary to swear you in as a part of my staff," Eliot Ness said.

I had known Eliot since we were both teenagers at the University of Chicago. I'd dropped out, finished up at a community college and gone into law enforcement; Eliot had graduated and became a private investigator, often working for insurance companies. Somewhere along the way, we'd swapped jobs.

His dark brown hair brushed with gray at the temples, Eliot's faintly freckled, boyish good looks were going puffy on him, gray eyes pouchy and marked by crow's feet. But even in his late thirties, the former Treasury agent who had been instrumental in Al Capone's fall was the youngest Public Safety Director in the nation.

When I was on the Chicago P.D., I had been one of the few cops Eliot could trust for information; and when I opened up the one-man

A-1 Detective Agency, Eliot had returned the favor as my only trustworthy source within the law enforcement community. I had remained in Chicago and he had gone on to more government crimebusting in various corners of the midwest, winding up with this high profile job as Cleveland's "top cop"; since 1935, he had made national headlines cleaning up the police department, busting crooked labor unions and curtailing the numbers racket.

Eliot was perched on the edge of the table, a casual posture at odds with his three-piece suit and tie. "Just a formality," he explained. "I caught a little heat recently from the City Council for hiring outside investigators."

I'd been brought in on several other cases, over the past five or six years.

"It's an undercover assignment?"

He nodded. "Yes, and I'd love to tackle it myself, but I'm afraid at this point, even in the Angles, this puss of mine is too well-known."

Eliot, a boyhood Sherlock Holmes fan, was not one to stay behind his desk; even as Public Safety Director, he was known to lead raids, wielding an ax, and go undercover, in disguise.

I said, "You've never been shy about staying out of the papers."

I was one of the few people who could make a crack like that and not get a rebuke; in fact, I got a little smile out of the stone face.

"Well, I don't like what's been in the papers, lately," he admitted, brushing the stray comma of hair off his forehead, for what good it did him. "You know I've made traffic safety a priority."

"Sure. Can't jaywalk in this burg without getting a ticket."

When Eliot came into office, Cleveland was ranked the second un-safest city in America, after Los Angeles. By 1938, Cleveland was ranked the safest big city, and by 1939 the safest city, period. This reflected Eliot instituting a public safety campaign through education and "warning" tickets, and reorganizing the traffic division, putting in two-way radios in patrol cars and creating a fleet of motorcycle cops.

"Well, we're in no danger of receiving any 'safest city' honors this year," he said, dryly. He settled into the wooden chair next to mine, folded his hands prayerfully. "We've already had thirty-two traffic fatalities this year. That's more than double where we stood, this time last year."

"What's the reason for it?"

"We thought it had to do with increased industrial activity."

"You mean, companies are hiring again, and more people are driving to work."

"Right. We've had employers insert 'drive carefully' cards in pay envelopes, we've made elaborate safety presentations... There's also an increase in teenage drivers, you know, kids driving to high school."

"More parents working, more kids with cars. Follows."

"Yes. And we stepped up educational efforts, at schools, accordingly. Plus, we've cracked down on traffic violators of all stripe -- four times as many speeding arrests; traffic violations arrests up twenty-five-percent, intoxication arrests almost double."

"What sort of results are you having?"

"In these specific areas -- industrial drivers, teenage drivers -- very positive. These are efforts that went into effect around the middle of last year -- and yet this year, the statistics are far worse."

"You wouldn't be sending me undercover if you didn't have the problem pinpointed."

He nodded. "My Traffic Analysis Bureau came up with several interesting stats: seventy-two percent of our traffic fatalities this year are age 45 or older. But only twenty percent of our population falls in that category. And thirty-six percent of those fatalities are 65 or up... a category that comprises only four percent of Cleveland's population."

"So more older people are getting hit by cars than younger people," I said with a shrug. "Is that a surprise? The elderly don't have the reflexes of young bucks like us."

"Forty-five isn't 'elderly,'" Eliot said, "as we'll both find out sooner than we'd like."

The intercom on Eliot's nearby rolltop desk buzzed and he rose and responded to it. His secretary's voice informed us that Dr. Jeffers was here to see him.

"Send her in," Eliot said.

The woman who entered was small and wore a white shirt and matching trousers, baggy oversize apparel that gave little hint of any shape beneath; though her heart-shaped face was attractive, she wore no make-up and her dark hair was cut mannishly short, clunky thick-lensed tortoise-shell glasses distorting dark almond-shaped eyes.

"Alice, thank you for coming," Eliot said, rising, shaking her hand. "Nate Heller, this is Dr. Alice Jeffers, assistant county coroner."

"A pleasure, Dr. Jeffers," I said, rising, shaking her cool, dry hand, as she twitched me a smile.

Eliot pulled out a chair for her opposite me at the conference table, telling her, "I've been filling Nate in. I'm just up to your part in this investigation."

With no further prompting, Dr. Jeffers said, "I was alerted by a morgue attendant, actually. It seemed we'd had an unusual number of hit-and-skip fatalities in the last six months, particularly in January, from a certain part of the city, and a certain part of community."

"Alice is referring to a part of Cleveland called the Angles," Eliot explained, "which is just across the Detroit Bridge, opposite the factory and warehouse district."

"I've been there," I said. The Angles was a classic waterfront area, where bars and whorehouses and cheap rooming houses serviced a clientele of workingmen and longshoremen. It was also an area rife with derelicts, particularly since Eliot burned out the Hoovervilles nestling in Kingsbury Run and under various bridges.

"These hit-and-skip victims were vagrants," Dr. Jeffers said, her eyes unblinking and intelligent behind the thick lenses, "and tended to be in their fifties or sixties, though they looked much older."

"Rummies," I said.

"Yes. With Director Ness's blessing, and Coroner Gerber's permission, I conducted several autopsies, and encountered individuals in advanced stages of alcoholism. Cirrhosis of the liver, kidney disease, general debilitation. Had they not been struck by cars, they would surely have died within a matter of years or possibly months or even weeks."

"Walking dead men."

"Poetic but apt. My contact at the morgue began keeping me alerted when vagrant 'customers' came through, and I soon realized that automobile fatalities were only part of the story."

"How so?" I asked.

"We had several fatal falls-down-stairs, and a surprising number of fatalities by exposure to the cold weather, death by freezing, by pneumonia. Again, I performed autopsies where normally we would not. These victims were invariably intoxicated at the times of their deaths, and in advanced stages of acute alcoholism."

I was thoroughly confused. "What's the percentage in bumping off bums? You got another psychopath at large, Eliot? Or is the Butcher back, changing his style?"

I was referring to the so-called Mad Butcher of Kingsbury Run, who had cut up a number of indigents here in Cleveland, Jack the Ripper style; but the killings had stopped, long ago.

"This isn't the Butcher," Eliot confidently. "And it isn't psychosis... it's commerce."

"There's money in killing bums?"

"If they're insured, there is."

"Okay, okay," I said, nodding, getting it, or starting to. "But if you overinsure some worthless derelict, surely it's going to attract the attention of the adjusters for the insurance company."

"This is more subtle than that," Eliot said. "When Alice informed me of this, I contacted the State Insurance Division. Their chief investigator, Gaspar Corso -- who we'll meet with later this afternoon, Nate -- dug through our 'drunk cards' on file at the Central Police Station, some 20,000 of them. He came up with information that corroborated Alice's, and confirmed suspicions of mine."

Corso had an office in the Standard Building -- no name on the door, no listing in the building directory. Eliot, Dr. Jeffers and I met with Corso in the latter's small, spare office, wooden chairs pulled up around a wooden desk that faced the wall, so that Corso was swung around facing us.

He was small and compactly muscular -- a former high school football star, according to Eliot -- bald with calm blue eyes under black beetle eyebrows. A gold watch chain crossed the vest of his three-piece tweed.

"A majority of the drunks dying either by accident or 'natural causes,'" he said in a mellow baritone, "come from the West Side -- the Angles."

"And they were over-insured?" I asked.

"Yes, but not in the way you might expect. Do you know what industrial insurance is, Mr. Heller?"

"You mean, burial insurance?"

"That's right. Small policies designed to pay funeral expenses and the like."

"Is that what these bums are being bumped off for? Pennies?"

A tiny half smile formed on the impassive investigator's thin lips. "Hardly. Multiple policies have been taken out on these individuals, dozens in some cases... each small policy with a different insurance company."

"No wonder no alarms went off," I said. "Each company got hit for peanuts."

"Some of these policies are for two-hundred-and-fifty dollars, never higher than a thousand. But I have one victim here..." He turned to his desk, riffled through some papers. "... who I determined, by crosschecking with various companies, racked up a $24,000 payout."

"Christ. Who was the beneficiary?"

"A Kathleen O'Meara," Eliot said. "She runs a saloon in the Angles, with a rooming house upstairs."

"Her husband died last month," Dr. Jeffers said. "I performed the autopsy myself... He was intoxicated at the time of his death, and was in an advanced stage of cirrhosis of the liver. Hit by a car. But there was one difference."

"Yes?"

"He was fairly well-dressed, and was definitely not malnourished."

O'Meara's did not serve food, but a greasy spoon down the block did, and that's where Katie took me for supper, around seven, leaving the running of the saloon to her sullen skinny daughter, Maggie.

"Maggie doesn't say much," I said, over a plate of meat loaf and mashed potatoes and gray. Like Katie, it was surprisingly appetizing, particularly if you didn't look too closely and were half-bombed.

We were in a booth by a window that showed no evidence of ever having been cleaned; cold March wind rattled it and leached through.

"I spoiled her," Katie admitted. "But, to be fair, she's still grieving over her papa. She was the apple of his eye."

"You miss your old man?"

"I miss the help. He took care of the books. I got a head for business, but not for figures. Thing is, he got greedy."

"Really?"

"Yeah, caught him featherin' his own nest. Skimmin'. He had a bank account of his own he never told me about."

"You fight over that?"

"Naw. Forgive and forget, I always say." Katie was having the same thing as me, and she was shoveling meat loaf into her mouth like coal into a boiler.

"I'm, uh, pretty good with figures," I said.

Her licentious smile was part lip rouge, part gravy. "I'll just bet you are... Ever do time, Bill?"

"Some. I'm not no thief, though... I wouldn't steal a partner's money."

"What were you in for?"

"Manslaughter."

"Kill somebody, did you?"

"Sort of."

She giggled. "How do you 'sort of' kill somebody, Bill?"

"I beat a guy to death with my fists. I was drunk."

"Why?"

"I've always drunk too much."

"No, why'd you beat him to death? With your fists."

I shrugged, chewed meat loaf. "He insulted a woman I was with. I don't like a man that don't respect a woman."

She sighed. Shook her head. "You're a real gent, Bill. Here I thought chivalry was dead."

Three evenings before, I'd been in a yellow-leather booth by a blue-mirrored wall in the Vogue Room of the Hollenden Hotel. Clean-shaven and in my best brown suit, I was in the company of Eliot and his recent bride, the former Ev McMillan, a fashion illustrator who worked for Higbee's department store.

Ev, an almond-eyed slender attractive brunette, wore a simple cobalt blue evening dress with pearls; Eliot was in the three-piece suit he'd worn to work. We'd had prime rib and were enjoying after dinner drinks; Eliot was on his second, and he'd had two before dinner, as well. Martinis. Ev was only one drink behind him.

Personal chit-chat had lapsed back into talking business.

"It's goddamn ghoulish," Eliot said. He was quietly soused, as evidenced by his use of the word "goddamn" -- for a tough cop, he usually had a Boy Scout's vocabulary.

"It's coldblooded, all right," I said.

"How does the racket work?" Ev asked.

"I shouldn't have brought it up," Eliot said. "It doesn't make for pleasant after-dinner conversation..."

"No, I'm interested," she said. She was a keenly intelligent young woman. "You compared it to a lottery... how so?"

"Well," I said, "as it's been explained to me, speculators 'invest' in dozens of small insurance policies on vagrants who were already drinking themselves to imminent graves... malnourished men crushed by dope and/or drink, sleeping in parks and in doorways in all kinds of weather."

"Men likely to meet an early death by so-called natural causes," Eliot said. "That's how we came to nickname the racket 'Natural Death, Inc.'"

"Getting hit by a car isn't exactly a 'natural' death," Ev pointed out.

Eliot sipped his martini. "At first, the speculators were just helping nature along by plying their investments with free, large quantities of drink... hastening their death by alcoholism or just making them more prone to stumble in front of a car."

"Now it looks like these insured derelicts are being shoved in front of cars," I said.

"Or the drivers of the cars are purposely running them down," Eliot said. "Dear, this really is unpleasant conversation; I apologize for getting into it..."

"Nonsense," she said. "Who *are* these speculators?"

"Women, mostly," he said. "Harridans running West Side beer parlors and roominghouses. They exchange information, but they aren't exactly an organized ring or anything, which makes our work difficult. I'm siccing Nate here on the worst offender, the closest thing there is to a ringleader -- a woman we've confirmed is holding fifty policies on various 'risks.'"

Ev frowned. "How do these women get their victims to go along with them? I mean, aren't the insured's signatures required on the policies?"

"There's been some forgery going on," Eliot said. "But mostly these poor bastards are willingly trading their signatures for free booze."

Fifty Shades of Grey Fedora

Ev twitched a non-smile above the rim of her martini glass. "Life in slum areas breeds such tragedy."

The subject changed to local politics -- I'd heard rumors of Eliot running for mayor, which he unconvincingly pooh-poohed -- and, a few drinks later, Eliot spotted some reporter friends of his, Clayton Fritchey and Sam Wild, and excused himself to go over and speak to them.

"If I'm not being out of line," I said to Mrs. Ness, "Eliot's hitting the sauce pretty hard himself. Hope you don't have any extra policies out on him."

She managed a wry little smile. "I do my best to keep up with him, but it's difficult. Ironic, isn't it? The nation's most famous Prohibition agent, with a drinking problem."

"*Is* it a problem?"

"Eliot doesn't think so. He says he just has to relax. It's a stressful job."

"It is at that. But, Ev -- I've been around Eliot during 'stressful' times before... like when the entire Capone gang was gunning for him. And he never put it away like that, then."

She was studied the olive in her martini. "You were part of that case, weren't you?"

"What case? Capone?"

"No -- the Butcher."

I nodded. I'd been part of the capture of the lunatic responsible for those brutal slayings of vagrants. I was one of the handful who knew that Eliot had been forced to make a deal with his influential political backers to allow the son of a bitch -- who had a society pedigree -- to avoid arrest and instead be voluntarily committed to a madhouse.

"It bothers him, huh?" I said, and grunted a laugh. "Mr. Squeaky Clean, the 'Untouchable' Eliot Ness having to cut a deal like that."

"I think so," she admitted. "He never says. You know how quiet he can be."

"Well, I think he should grow up. For Christ sake, for somebody from Chicago, somebody who's seen every kind of crime and corruption, he can be as naive as a schoolgirl."

"An alcoholic schoolgirl," Ev said with a smirk, and a martini sip.

"... You want me to talk to him?"

"I don't know. Maybe... I think this case, these poor homeless men being victimized again, got memories stirred up."

"Of the Butcher case, you mean."

"Yes... and Nate, we've been getting postcards from that crazy man."

"What crazy man? Capone?"

"No! The Butcher... threatening postcards postmarked the town where that asylum is."

"Is there any chance Watterson can get out?"

Lloyd Watterson: the Butcher.

"Eliot says no," Ev said. "He's been assured of that."

"Well, these killings aren't the work of a madman. This is murder for profit, plain and simple. Good old-fashioned garden variety evil."

"Help him clear this up," she said, and an edge of desperation was in her voice. "I think it would... might... make a difference."

Then Eliot was back, and sat down with a fresh martini in hand.

"I hope I didn't miss anything good," he said.

My room was small but seemed larger due to the sparseness of the furnishings, metallic, institutional-gray clothes cabinet, a chair and a metal cot. A bare bulb bulged from the wall near the door, as if it had blossomed from the faded, fraying floral-print wallpaper. The wooden floor had a greasy, grimy look.

Katie was saying, "Hope it will do."

"You still haven't said what my duties are."

"I'll think of something. Now, if you need anything, I'm down the hall. Let me show you... "

I followed her to a doorway at the end of the narrow gloomy hallway. She unlocked the door with a key extracted from between her massive breasts, and ushered me into another world.

The livingroom of her apartment held a showroom-like suite of walnut furniture with carved arms, feet and base rails, the chairs and davenport sporting matching green mohair cushions, assembled on a green and blue wall-to-wall Axminster carpet. Pale yellow wallpaper with gold and pink highlights created a tapestry effect, while floral satin damask draperies dressed up the windows, venetian blinds keeping out prying eyes. Surprisingly tasteful, the room didn't look very lived in.

"Posh digs," I said, genuinely impressed.

"Came into some money recently. Spruced the joint up a little... Now, if you need me after hours, be sure to knock good and loud." She swayed over to a doorless doorway and nodded for me to come to her. "I'm a heavy sleeper."

The bedroom was similarly decked out with new furnishings -- a walnut-veener double bed, dresser and nightstand and three-mirror vanity with modern lines and zebrawood design panels -- against ladylike pink-and-white floral wallpaper. The vanity top was neatly arranged with perfumes and face powder and the like, their combined scents lending the room a feminine bouquet. Framed prints of airbrushed flowers hung here and there, a large one over the bed, where sheets and blankets were neatly folded back below lush overstuffed feather pillows, as if by a maid.

"I had this room re-done, too," she said. "My late husband, rest his soul, was a slob."

Indeed it was hard to imagine a man sharing this room with her. There was a daintiness that didn't match up with its inhabitant. The only sign that anybody lived here were the movie magazines on the bedstand in the radiance of the only light, a creamy glazed pottery-base lamp whose gold parchment shade gave the room a glow.

The only person more out of place in this tidy, feminine suite than me, in my tattered secondhand store suit, was my blowsy hostess in her polka-dot peasant blouse and flowing dark skirt. She was excited and proud, showing off her fancy living quarters, bobbing up and down like an eager kid; it was cute and a little sickening.

Or maybe that was the cheap beer. I wasn't drunk but I'd had three glasses of it.

"You okay, Bill?" she asked.

"Demon meatloaf," I said.

"Sit, sit."

And I was sitting on the edge of the bed. She stood before me, looming over me, frightening and oddly comely, with her massive bosom spilling from the blouse, her red-rouged mouth, her half-lidded long-lashed green eyes, mother/goddess/whore.

"It's been lonely, Bill," she said, "without my man."

"Suh... sorry for your loss."

"I could use a man around here, Bill."

Fifty Shades of Grey Fedora

"Try to help."

"It could be sweet for you."

She tugged the peasant blouse down over the full, round, white-powdered melons that were her bosom, and pulled my head between them. Their suffocation was pleasant, even heady, and I was wondering whether I'd lost count of those beers when I fished in my trousers for my wallet for the lambskin.

I wasn't *that* far gone.

I had never been with a woman as overweight as Kathleen O'Meara before, and I don't believe I ever was again; many a man might dismiss her as fat. But the sheer womanliness of her was overwhelming; there was so much of her, and she smelled so good, particularly for a saloonkeeper, her skin so smooth, her breasts and behind as firm as they were large and round, that the three nights I spent in her bed remain bittersweet memories. I didn't love her, obviously, nor did she me -- we were using each other, in our various nasty ways.

But it's odd, how many times, over the years, the memory of carnality in Katie's bed pops unbidden into my mind. On more than one occasion, in bed with a slender young girlish thing, the image of womanly, obscenely voluptuous Katie would taunt me, as if saying, *Now I was a* real *woman!*

Katie was also a real monster. She waited until the second night, when I lay next to her in the recently purchased bed, in her luxuriant remodeled suite of rooms in a waterfront rooming house where her pitiful clientele slept on pancake-flat piss-scented mattresses, to invite me to be her accomplice.

"Someday I'll move from here," she said in the golden glow of the parchment lamp and the volcanic sex we'd just had. She was on her back, the sheet only half-covering the globes of her bosom; she was smoking, staring at the ceiling.

I was on my back, too -- I wasn't smoking, cigarettes being one filthy habit I didn't partake of. "But, Katie -- this place is hunky-dory."

"These rooms are nice, love. But little Katie was meant for a better life than the Angles can provide."

"You got a good business, here."

She chuckled. "Better than you know."

"What do you mean?"

She leaned on one elbow and the sheet fell away from the large, lovely bosoms. "Don't you wonder why I'm so good to these stumblebums?"

"You give a lot of free beer away, I noticed."

"Why do you suppose Katie does that?"

"Cause you're a good Christian woman?"

She roared with laughter, globes shimmering like Jello. "Don't be a child! Have you heard of burial insurance, love?"

And she filled me in on the scheme -- the lottery portion of it, at least, taking out policies on men who were good bets for quick rides to potter's field. But she didn't mention anything about helping speed the insured to even quicker, surer deaths.

"You disappointed in Katie?" she asked. "That I'm not such a good Christian woman?"

I grinned at her. "I'm tickled pink to find out how smart you are, baby. Was your old man in on this?"

"He was. But he wasn't trustworthy."

"Lucky for you he croaked."

"Lucky."

"Hey... I didn't mean to be coldhearted, baby. I know you miss him."

Her plump pretty face was as blank as a bisque baby's. "He disappointed me."

"How'd he die?"

"Got drunk and stepped in front of a car."

"Sorry."

"Don't pay for a dipso to run a bar, too much helpin' himself... I notice you don't hit the sauce so hard. You don't drink too much, and you hold what you do drink."

"Thanks."

"You're just a good joe, down on his luck. Could use a break."

"Who couldn't?"

"And I can use a man. I can use a partner."

"What do I have to do?"

"Just be friendly to these rummies. Get 'em on your good side, get 'em to sign up. Usually all it takes is a friendly ear and a pint of rotgut."

"And when they finally drink themselves into a grave, we get a nice payday."

"Yup. And enough nice paydays, we can leave the Angles behind. Retire rich while we're still young and pretty."

His name was Harold Wilson. He looked at least sixty but when we filled out the application, he managed to remember he was forty-three.

He and I sat in a booth at O'Meara's and I plied him with cheap beers, which Katie's hollow-eyed daughter dutifully delivered, while Harold told me, in bits and pieces, the sad story that had brought him to the Angles.

Hunkered over the beer, he seemed small, but he'd been of stature once, physically and otherwise. In a face that was both withered and puffy, bloodshot powder-blue eyes peered from pouches, by turns rheumy and teary.

He had been a stock broker. When the Crash came, he chose to jump a freight rather than out a window, leaving behind a well-bred wife and two young daughters.

"I meant to go back," Harold said, in a baritone voice whose dignity had been sandpapered away, leaving scratchiness and quaver behind. "For years, I did menial jobs... seasonal work, janitorial work, chopping firewood, shoveling walks, mowing grass... and I'd save. But the money never grew. I'd either get jackrolled or spend it on..."

He finished the sentence by grabbing the latest foamy mug of warm beer from Maggie O'Meara and guzzling it.

I listened to Harold's sad story all afternoon and into the evening; he repeated himself a lot, and he signed three burial policies, one for $450, another for $750 and finally the jackpot, $1000. Death would probably be a merciful way out for the poor bastard, but even at this stage of his life, Harold Wilson deserved a better legacy than helping provide for Katie O'Meara's retirement.

Late in the evening, he said, "Did go back, once... to Elmhurst... Tha's Chicago."

"Yeah, I know, Harold."

"Thomas Wolfe said, 'Can't go home again.' Shouldn't go home again's more like it."

"Did you talk to them?"

"No! No. It was Chrissmuss. Sad story, huh? Looked in the

window. Didn't expect to see 'em, my family; figured they'd lose the house."

"But they didn't? How'd they manage that?"

"Mary... that's my wife... her family had some money. Must not've got hurt as bad as me in the Crash. Figure they musta bought the house for her."

"I see."

"Sure wasn't her new husband. I recognized him; fella I went to high school with. A postman."

"A mail carrier?"

"Yeah. 'Fore the Crash, Mary, she woulda looked down on a lowly civil servant like that... But in Depression times, that's a hell of a good job."

"True enough."

The eyes were distant and runny. "My girls was grown. College age. Blond and pretty, with boy friends, holdin' hands... The place hadn't changed. Same furniture. Chrissmuss tree where we always put it, in the front window... We'd move the couch out of the way and... anyway. Nothing different. Except in the middle of it, no me. A mailman took my place."

For a moment I thought he said "male man."

O'Meara's closed at two a.m. I helped Maggie clean up, even though Katie hadn't asked me to. Katie was upstairs, waiting for me in her bedroom. Frankly, I didn't feel like doing my duty tonight, pleasant though it admittedly was. On the one hand, I was using Katie, banging this broad I was undercover, and undercovers, to get the goods on, which made me a louse; and on the other hand, spending the day with her next victim, Harold Wilson, brought home what an enormous louse she was.

I was helping daughter Maggie put chairs on tables; she hadn't said a word to me yet. She had her mother's pretty green eyes and she might have been pretty herself if her scarecrow thin frame and narrow, hatchet face had a little meat on them.

The room was tidied when she said, "Nightcap?"

Surprised, I said, "Sure."

"I got a pot of coffee on, if you're sick of warm beer."

The kitchen in back was small and neat and Maggie's living

quarters were back here, as well. She and her mother did not live together; in fact, they rarely spoke, other than Katie issuing commands. I sat at a wooden table in the midst of the small cupboard-lined kitchen and sipped the coffee Maggie provided in a chipped cup. In her white waitress uniform, she looked like a wilted nurse.

"That suit you're wearing," she said.

Katie had given me clothes to wear; I was in a brown suit and a yellow-and-brown tie, nothing fancy but a step or two up from the threadbare duds "Bill O'Hara" had worn into O'Meara's.

"What about 'em?"

"Those were my father's." Maggie sipped her coffee. "You're about his size."

I'd guessed as much. "I didn't know. I don't mean to be a scavenger, Miss O'Meara, but life can do that to you. The Angles ain't high society."

"You were talking to that man all afternoon."

"Harold Wilson. Sure. Nice fella."

"Ma's signing up policies on him."

"That's right. You know about that, do you?"

"I know more than you know. If you knew what I knew, you wouldn't be so eager to sleep with that cow."

"Now, let's not be disrespectful..."

"To you or the cow?... Mr. O'Hara, you seem like a decent enough sort. Careful what you get yourself into. Remember how my papa died."

"No one ever told me," I lied. "He got run down by a car. I think he got pushed."

"Really? Who'd do a thing like that?"

The voice behind us said, "This is cozy."

She was in the doorway, Katie, in a red Kimono with yellow flowers on it; you could've rigged out a sailboat with all that cloth.

"Mr. O'Hara helped me tidy up," Maggie said coldly. No fear in her voice. "I offered him coffee."

"Just don't offer him anything else," Katie snapped. The green eyes were hard as jade.

Maggie blushed, and rose, taking her empty cup and mine and depositing them awkwardly, clatteringly, in the sink.

In bed, Katie said, "Good job today with our investment, Bill."

"Thanks."

"Know what Harold Wilson's worth, now?"

"No."

"Ten thousand... Poor sad soul. Terrible to see him suffering like that. Like it's terrible for us to have to wait and wait, before we can leave all this behind."

"What are you sayin', love?"

"I'm sayin', were somebody to put that poor man out of his misery, they'd be doin' him a favor, is all I'm sayin'."

"You're probably right, at that. Poor bastard."

"You know how cars'll come up over the hill... 25th Street, headin' for the bridge? Movin' quick through this here bad part of a town?"

"Yeah, what about 'em?"

"If someone were to shove some poor soul out in front of a car, just as it was coming up and over, there'd be no time for stoppin'."

I pretended to digest that, then said, "That'd be murder, Katie."

"Would it?"

"Still... You might be doin' the poor bastard a favor, at that."

"And make ourselves $10,000 richer."

"... You ever do this before, Katie?"

She pressed a hand to her generous bare bosom. "No! No. But I never had a man I could trust before."

Late the next morning, I met with Eliot in a back booth at Mickey's, a dimly lit hole-in-the-wall saloon a stone's throw from City Hall. He was having a late breakfast -- a bloody Mary -- and I had coffee.

"How'd you get away from Kathleen O'Meara?" he wondered. He looked businesslike in his usual three-piece suit; I was wearing a blue number from the Frank O'Meara Collection.

"She sleeps till noon. I told her daughter I was taking a walk."

"Long walk."

"The taxi'll be on my expense account. Eliot, I don't know how much more of this I can stand. She sent the forms in and paid the premiums on Harold Wilson, and she's talking murder all right, but if you want to catch her in the act, she's plannin' to wait at least a month before we give Harold a friendly push."

47

"That's a long time for you to stay undercover," Eliot admitted, stirring his bloody Mary with its celery stalk. "But it's in my budget."

I sighed. "I never knew being a city employee could be so exhausting."

"I take it you and Katie are friendly."

"She's a ride, all right. I've never been so disgusted with myself in my life."

"It's that distasteful?"

"Hell, no, I'm having a whale of time, so to speak. It's just shredding what little's left of my self-respect, and shabby little code of ethics, is all. Banging a big fat murdering bitch and liking it." I shuddered.

"This woman is an ogre, no question... and I'm not talking about her looks. Nate, if we can stop her, and expose what's she done, it'll pave the way for prosecuting the other women in the Natural Death, Inc., racket... or at the very least scaring them out of it."

That evening Katie and I were walking up the hill. No streetlights in this part of town, and no moon to light the way; lights in the frame and brick houses we passed, and the headlights of cars heading toward the bridge, threw yellow light on the cracked sidewalk we trundled up, arm in arm, Katie and me. She wore a yellow peasant blouse, always pleased to show off her treasure chest, and a full green skirt.

"Any second thoughts, handsome?"

"Just one."

She stopped; we were near the rise of the hill and the lights of cars came up and over and fell like prison searchlights seeking us out. "Which is?"

"I'm willing to do a dirty deed for a tidy dollar, don't get me wrong, love. It's just... didn't your husband die this same way?"

"He did."

"Heavily insured and pushed in front of his oncoming destiny?"

There was no shame, no denial; if anything, her expression -- chin high, eyes cool and hard -- spoke pride. "He did. And I pushed him."

"Did you, now? That gives a new accomplice pause."

"I guess it would. But I told you he cheated me. He salted money away. And he was seeing other women. I won't put up with disloyalty in a man."

"Obviously not."

"I'm the most loyal steadfast woman in the world... 'less you cross me. Frank O'Meara's loss is your gain... if you have the stomach for the work that needs doing."

A truck came rumbling up over the rise, gears shifting into low gear, and for a detective, I'm ashamed to admit I didn't know we'd been shadowed; but we had. We'd been followed, or anticipated; to this day I'm not sure whether she came from the bushes or behind us, whether fate had helped her or careful planning and knowledge of her mother's ways. Whatever the case, Maggie O'Meara came flying out of somewhere, hurling her skinny stick-like arms forward, shoving the much bigger woman into the path of the truck.

Katie had time to scream, and to look back at the wild-eyed smiling face of her daughter washed in the yellow headlights. The big rig's big tires rolled over her, her girth presenting no problem, bones popping like twigs, blood streaming like water.

The trucker was no hit-and-skip guy. He came to a squealing stop and hopped out and trotted back and looked at the squashed shapeless shape, yellow and green clothing stained crimson, limbs, legs, turned to pulp, head cracked like a melon, oozing.

I had a twinge of sorrow for Katie O'Meara, that beautiful horror, that horrible beauty; but it passed.

"She just jumped right out in front of me!" the trucker blurted. He was a small, wiry man with a mustache, and his eyes were wild.

I glanced at Maggie; she looked blankly back at me.

"I know," I said. "We saw it, her daughter and I... poor woman's been despondent."

I told the uniform cops the same story about Katie, depressed over the loss of her dear husband, leaping in front of the truck. Before long, Eliot arrived himself, topcoat flapping in the breeze as he stepped from the sedan that bore his special EN-1 license plate.

"I'm afraid I added a statistic to your fatalities," I admitted.

"What's the real story?" he asked me, getting me to one side. "None of this suicide nonsense."

I told Eliot that Katie had been demonstrating to me how she wanted me to push Harold Wilson, lost her footing and stumbled to an ironic death. He didn't believe me, of course, and I think he figured that I'd pushed her myself.

He didn't mind, because I produced such a great witness for him. Maggie O'Meara had the goods on the Natural Death racket, knew the names of every woman in her mother's ring, and in May was the star of eighty witnesses in the Grand Jury inquiry. Harold Wilson and many other of the "unwitting pawns in the death-gambling insurance racket" (as reporter Clayton Fritchey put it) were among those witnesses. So were Dr. Alice Jeffers, investigator Gaspar Corso and me.

That night, the night of Katie O'Meara's "suicide," after the police were through with us, Maggie had wept at her kitchen table while I fixed coffee for her, though her tears were not for her mother or out of guilt, but for her murdered father. Maggie never seemed to put together that her dad had been an accomplice in the insurance scheme, or anyway never allowed herself to admit it.

Finally, she asked, "Are you... are you really going to cover for me?"

That was when I told her she was going to testify.

She came out of it, fine; she inherited a lot of money from her late mother -- the various insurance companies did not contest previous pay-outs -- and I understand she sold O'Meara's and moved on, with a considerable nest egg. I have no idea what became of her, after that.

Busting the Natural Death, Inc., racket was Eliot's last major triumph in Cleveland law enforcement. The following March, after a night of dining, dancing and drinking at the Vogue Room, Eliot and Ev Ness were in an automobile accident, Eliot sliding into another driver's car. With Ev minorly hurt, Eliot -- after checking the other driver and finding him dazed but all right -- rushed her to a hospital and became a hit-and-run driver. He made some efforts to cover up and, even when he finally fessed up in a press conference, claimed he'd not been intoxicated behind that wheel; his political enemies crucified him, and a month later Eliot resigned as Public Safety Director.

During the war, Eliot headed up the government's efforts to control venereal disease on military bases; but he never held a law enforcement position again. He and Ev divorced in 1945. He married a third time, in 1946, and ran, unsuccessfully for mayor of Cleveland in '47, spending the rest of his life trying, without luck, to make it in the world of business, often playing on his reputation as a famed gangbuster.

In May, 1957, Eliot Ness collapsed in his kitchen shortly after he had arrived home from the liquor store, where he had bought a bottle of Scotch.

He died with less than a thousand dollars to his name -- I kicked in several hundred bucks on the funeral, wishing his wife had taken out some damn burial insurance on him.

AUTHOR'S NOTE: Fact, speculation and fiction are freely mixed within this story, which is based on an actual case in the career of Eliot Ness. My thanks to George Hagenauer for his research assistance. This story was originally published in 1999.

Fifty Shades of Grey Fedora

I WISH I HAD YOUR JOB
A "Tex" Texeira Story
by Ted Fitzgerald

1.

No, you don't.

It was a source of constant amazement to my suspect circle of acquaintances at the Metacomet Café that I'd landed a freelance gig with *Vertical Smile* magazine. I was the only PI in New England under contract to conduct background checks on prospective centerfolds. It came about because I met the publisher, Linda Tarpon, while doing security at a political fundraiser in Boston. We both appreciated what we saw and I invited her to stick around an extra day or two and I'd show her the city. We showed each other a thing or three and parted with warm smiles and damp underwear. I expected that to be the last of things until she called me three months later.

"Tex, say yes now so I don't need to talk too long."

Linda wasn't much for small talk. I'd carried most of the post-coital conversation, filling her in about my glory days as a high-school basketball, my hitches in the Navy and in law enforcement, my supplementing two pensions with work as a private investigator and above all, my endearing affection for the ladies, while she kneaded my sac like a ball of Play-Doh, squeezing hard whenever I mentioned another woman.

Fifty Shades of Grey Fedora

"All right, make me beg, Tex. I need an investigator. My last guy croaked over a potential Miss November. I need someone who can conduct a background investigation without having a coronary every time he sees a naked woman. Some of these gals have backgrounds as colorful and twisted as their tattoos. I don't need a centerfold who turns out to be on the run from the FBI and I sure as hell don't need any underage honey traps. The pay is good. We'll expense just about anything you need except condoms, lubricants and wedding licenses. In other words, hands off."

"What? That's cruel and unusual! I pride myself on deep investigations."

"Yeah, you know about "deep", you cute bastard. I did some back grounding of you, Tex. You're the horniest guy around but you're a good investigator and I happen to know from personal experience you prefer women to girls, so I'll take a chance on you. Now, will you say 'Yes' so I don't need to go beg some ex-boxer from Boston?"

Thus, I was hired. It was a good gig, too. I worked four or five times a year and it took me all over New England, sniffing out the bona fides of prospective peelers ranging from a private school runaway from the Connecticut Gold Coast to an ambitious donut shop server in northern Maine to a 22-year-old Brazilian heartbreaker in Framingham who changed her mind after figuring out she could make more money in real estate. Sometimes they made the cut and sometimes I saved the magazine a lot of potential grief, but it was never boring work and it was pretty easy on the eyes. And there was always a story.

So, this Tuesday, I'm sitting at my table at the Metacomet Cafe, lunching on Steak Mozambique and leafing through my mail when I spy an envelope with the familiar VS logo. I slit it open and eased out the data sheet and a pair of photos. My assignment was Dulce Nunes, Fall River, Mass., age 23. Maybe. Likes: animals, flowers, sunsets, generous people. Sorry, Dulce, this isn't *Playboy*. Turn-offs: rude people, pollution, narrow-minded assholes. Ah, Dulce, -my sweet, now you're getting interesting.

I turned to the photos. There were only two of them, unusual.

Fifty Shades of Grey Fedora

Also, they were high contrast black and white, not something off the cellphone. In the first, Dulce Nunes showed a round, almost plump face wreathed in a cascade of lush dark hair, thick pouty lips that whispered "fellatio" and an Asian hint around her eyes that suggested a granddad who served in Vietnam and brought back a wife. The eyes were a statement all of their own, staring you down, daring you to fuck with her at your peril.

She was perched atop a chair, with rounded muscular legs crimped into a pair of stilettos so tight that the bottoms of her toes seemed to ooze out of them. Judging by the perspective, she was petite, meaning that the perfectly round breasts that sat high and unsupported were proportionately large for her size --for my money, a decent handful-- rather than an embarrassment of riches. With onyx nipples that you could tape a half-dollar over and still not cover. She had one leg crossed over the other, so that most of her pubic hair was obscured. I felt disappointed. Which may have been the point. Maybe Dulce was crafty enough to know the value of holding back a bit to entice your audience.

The second photo was an over-the-shoulder come hither shot that displayed to full effect a perfectly curved ass the cheeks of which sloped off in opposite directions like soft hills. And something else. A tattoo on each cheek. On her left buttock the word "MY" was rendered in Olde English script in what I imagined would be fire engine red ink; matching it on the right buttock in every detail was the word "ASS". I looked at her eyes which had even more of a "Try it and die" fierceness. Yikes. Dulce, ma'am, you look like you could be a handful of a different sort.

It was then that a drop of spittle hit my steak. I looked up to see Slip Murphy, the cabdriver, staring down, rheumy eyes cloudy behind smudged glasses. I wondered if he could even see the picture. He could.

"Holy Jesus!" he whispered. "Praise the Lord and pass the Viagra! Those are the most beautiful things I've ever seen. I'll trade jobs with you, Tex!"

"Ol' Texy's got the job everyone wants, don't you Tex?" This was Cinch the bookmaker weighing in. "Like a license to hunt quail, huh?"

"Now, you guys never understand," I protested. "This is mostly paper work. Confirm who they say they are, make sure they have no outstanding warrants and make sure the Mann Act isn't violated if they're flown out to L.A. for a photo shoot. Dull as dishwater. Don't you believe me?"

Judging by their laughter, they didn't. But, in their place, neither would I. I told Slip to finish my lunch and headed off to do the job everyone else wished they had.

Lucky me.

Sure...

2.

I started with the paper trail, making the rounds of schools and municipal offices. Dulce had attended a Catholic girls' high school but had left at the end of her sophomore year for being a "disruptive influence". Probably meant she liked boys, which was okay in my book. Snagged an associate's degree in accounting at the local community college. She had a driver's license. And then, nothing for four years. No taxes, no voting, no arrests, no warrants. So, what had she been doing for four years besides posing nude for two photographs? Time to check with the family.

The Nunes address was a triple-decker in Fall River's Flint neighborhood. I parked across from it in the lot of a onetime curtain factory turned community center. The door was answered by an older, slightly plumper version of Dulce with the same sharp dark eyes, shiny black hair, smooth olive skin, petite size and, despite being clad in sweats, all the curves one could ask for. She was quite eye-catching and – to use a term I hear too often these days and like not at all – "age appropriate".

"Mrs. Nunes? My name is Texeira. I represent --"

"Don't even start, Wilt the Stilt," she said, glaring up at me. "Last tall, sweet talking, good-looking beanpole I let get past my door left me with a big mortgage, a bum credit rating and a wild child I can't afford."

"It's your daughter I'm here to see, Mrs. Nunes –"

"You think that's going to win you points with me, think again, LeBron."

"Mrs. Nunes, I represent *Vertical Smile* magazine. Your daughter--"

"Why'd you take so long getting to the point? Come in!" She grabbed my wrist and spun me into the hallway. While I was regaining my balance, she slammed the door, spun me around again and propelled me into the living room. I sought refuge by planting myself on an overstuffed couch. She plopped down next to me and dove right in.

"Now, basic package for a centerfold these days is fifty thousand minimum, right? That's for photo shoot, magazine appearance and one year endorsement agreement, personal appearances, web chats. Your group pays all the expenses and travel costs and, if a gal is really popular, you can extend the contract?"

"I believe that's the figure but those decision are above my pay grade. I'm just here to verify a few details about your daughter, that she's who she says she is, isn't in trouble with the law, is the age she says she is and doesn't have any communicable diseases."

"How dare you talk about my daughter that way! I'll have you know that I raised a perfectly decent hellion!"

"I'm sure you have, ma'am, but I need to see Dulce in person to verify these things and have her sign a release saying that she's agreeing to this. The publisher is very picky about this, you can imagine. So, if you can please tell me when Dulce will be home or where I can find her, we'll get things started."

She hit me with a startled look that in my younger days usually accompanied the announcement of a positive pregnancy test or the arrival of a previously unmentioned husband.

"I wish I knew. She wasn't home two weeks and she was already hanging her bum off the back of a motorcycle while holding on to some lowlife looked like he was from *Duck Dynasty*. Said she had a job doing the books for a small manufacturer but she didn't say who."

"Didn't you ask her?"

"Sure, but Dulce's strong-willed. She won't say what she doesn't want to say, but expects you to listen to whatever it is that she wants to say when she wants to say it. Make a great husband for someone, that girl. Maybe she already is. She hasn't been home for three weeks. She could be shacked up with someone or off on a long trip with a sugar daddy. Beats me."

"Any idea where she hangs out?"

"I know where the biker hangs out. Big Mamie's. Does that help?"

"Yes and no."

Yes, I knew Big Mamie's. And no, I didn't want to go there.

3.

Big Mamie's took its name from the battleship *USS Massachusetts* in whose shadow it crouched on a grungy block near Battleship Cove. It was located between an abandoned tailor shop that once specialized in First Communion suits and a check cashing service that specialized in taking the clothes off its customers' back. I wondered which one, the bar or the cashing service, charged the stiffest vigorish.

Four motorcycles were parked in front. Recently, too, judging by the ticking of their cooling engines which sounded like crickets on the summer night I convinced Sue Ellen Kosnoski to pull her blouse over her head just as her father and two brother came out of the family's corn field carrying baseball bats. It was a painful memory. I hoped that this afternoon's memories would be less so.

Big Mamie's followed the old formula of the rougher the bar, the fewer the windows. The color-sucking glow of overhead fluorescent lighting replaced the afternoon sunlight leaving me feeling like I was in purgatory. Assuming that purgatory smelled like a combination of beer suds, leather, tobacco and a backed-up toilet and sounded like daytime television, clacking billiard balls and clinking chains. The quartet that belonged to the bikes, all tall, wide and ugly, were standing around a pool table and the place was empty except for them. As I stepped up to the bar, a blond with the biggest breasts I'd ever seen came out from the back. In men's mamarial hierarchy, these were not just breasts or boobs or boulders. No, my son, these were bazooms! That's the only word that would do. With an exclamation point. Part of me stood at attention as she let them rest atop the bar.

"What are you looking for?" she asked.

"Three things: Your phone number, a cold beer and a little lead on one of your customers, in that order." I showed her a head shot of Dulce I'd had made from the first photo. "Are you Mamie?"

"Close as you'll ever get."

She lit up a cigarette and dropped the match to the floor as she eyeballed the photo. So much for any state-mandated smoking ban in Mamie's. I just hoped that the floor didn't ignite from all the motor oil it had probably absorbed over the decades from its gearhead clientele.

"Why are you looking for Dulce Nunes?" Mamie asked in a clear and distinct voice as she blew smoke in my face.

"She applied for a job and I'm doing the background check for the HR office."

"Uh, huh," She popped a shot glass on the bar and filled it with clear liquid from an unmarked bottle. "*Cachaça*. Have a belt instead of the beer."

"Moonshine? Why?"

"Because it'll be more help than beer. It'll make your insides feel so bad, you won't mind how much the rest of you will hurt."

Before I could ask for an explanation, four pairs of arms lifted me up and tossed me backwards across the room. I landed on one of the pool tables, which responded by collapsing under my weight. I slid to the floor, and promptly rolled under an adjoining table, despite the fire that was now traveling up my left arm and around my shoulder. Since there was no window to jump through, I crawled and slid under the tables and around the corner hoping to make the street before the Four Bikemen of the Apocalypse caught up with me. Who knows? Maybe there was a cop out front. Even better, a tornado that would take me to Oz or Kansas. Either one looked pretty good right about now.

I was within a couple feet of the door when my ankles were vise-gripped and I was dragged back along the floor, picked up and propped me against the bar. I heard the door lock and suddenly that summer evening with Sue Ellen's menfolk seemed to be a tender memory of better times.

"The boys don't like it when someone asks questions about one of the regulars," said Mamie. "Now, you can tell us why you're really here and, if we like the answers, you'll be spared a real beating."

I knew what that meant. "Truth won't set me free?"

"Not a chance."

"Then, could I take you up on that offer of a drink?"

They were quick and efficient. I must have been bored because I went to sleep right away.

4.

I've generally woken up to prettier faces then that of Lt. Detective Mike Santos but I wasn't holding that against him. Judging by the sound of beeps, the medicinal smells and the antiseptic aura, I was in a hospital. Which was the logical place for me to be, under the circumstances. I'd never woken up feeling like a used piñata before, either.

"Tex Texeira. How they hanging, old man?" He was smiling as he spoke. It was more smile than the situation called for. "Or did they leave you anything that could be said to hang?"

"Watch who you're calling an old man," I said. "Don't mistake experience for impotence. I could still whip you on or off the basketball court; definitely on the dance floor."

"Piece of advice, Studley Do Right. Nothing vents off all that excess testosterone like marriage. Find a nice gal, settle down and you won't be making a fool of yourself at singles dances and biker bars. It'll help you survive to a nice comfortable old age."

Mike and I had both played high school basketball. We were respectful rivals who joined the Navy together and we both made the State Police when we returned home. Mike had married his high school sweetheart and advanced through the ranks. I took an early retirement due to a bullet and a fondness for the ladies that didn't go over well in some professional circles. Mike had a nice family. I had my freedom. I liked to think that I had the advantage on him.

"So, where am I? Where did they find me?"

"You're in St. Anne's. Witnesses saw some biker types hauling what looked like a body across the Braga Bridge. Described it as a Viking funeral in the making. Apparently, they were getting ready to give you a heave-ho into the river when they heard a siren and split. You're a lucky man, Tex."

I wheezed in agreement. It hurt too much to move my head.

"Now, why would someone do something like this to a fine lad such as yourself? Were you fooling around with someone's woman? Again?"

Mike knew about my VS gig so I laid it all out for him. He grunted about halfway through it then stepped over and put his face close to my ear. He spoke in a quiet tone.

"The Anteaters – don't laugh at the name; no else does – among other pastimes, hire themselves out to Jake Sarno for drug running, bodyguarding, muscle work and debt collection. You look as if you caught them on a good day. It's not healthy for a loner like you to go around looking for people who may be connected to Jake the Snake. My advice is this: Go back up the highway to home, heal up and then ask out some divorcee for a wild weekend at one of the casinos. A biker chick who wants to show her all in a skin magazine isn't worth the pain and suffering. Blink once if you agree with me."

I blinked. It was all I could do at the moment. But a whole new line of questions had just opened up for me.

5.

I spent the next day licking my wounds – by myself unfortunately – surfing the Internet in pursuit of any info on Dulce Nunes and pondering why Mike Santos was warning me off. It could be that he was genuinely concerned about my well-being but it seemed more like he knew something I didn't and that revved my engine more than a tall redhead in a Catholic schoolgirl uniform and a pair of fuck-me pumps. It wasn't the answer as much as it was getting the answer. It sounded like The Anteaters had really intended to deep-six me but that begged the question of what was I doing that would get me dead in a hurry? Of course, if Jake Sarno, the closest thing to the godfather in what passed for organized crime in Bristol County, was involved, it could be that he just didn't like my face.

Then, I remembered something Dulce's mother had said, so I called her.

"Mrs. Nunes? I –"

"You again? You stalking me or something, Larry Bird? Do I gotta call the cops on you, Barkley? Say, did you find Dulce?"

"No, and I'm hoping you can help me on that," I spoke quickly, hoping she wouldn't hang up or, worse, keep talking.

"How so?"

"You mentioned that she had come back from somewhere. She

graduated high school five years ago. Where did she go?"

"What? You didn't know? She was in the Army. I thought it straightened her out but now I don't know."

"Do you know where she was stationed, what she did?"

"You kidding? The mother's always the last to know. She waltzed in, said 'Honorable discharge, ma. No warrants. What's for dinner? Haven't had a decent quahog in four years.' That's what I know."

"But it was the Army, correct?"

"That's what she said."

Which was the punchline to an old joke and I wasn't feeling humorous. "Mrs. Nunes. Did Dulce ever mention Jake Sarno?"

"Nah, she never mentioned that lowlife. Although he'd be a step up in class. Why do you think I want her in the skin magazine? Get her some bucks. Let her meet a better class of grifter. Somebody'll help keep Dulce's old mother in the style to which she's never been accustomed."

Do me a favor, Mrs. Nunes? Let me know if Dulce comes home and, if she does, keep her there."

"So you can darken my door again, Paul Bunyan? Sure. And call me Clothilde."

6.

I spent the rest of the afternoon pulling strings and calling in favors trying to access military databases with no luck. Nothing to substantiate that a Dulce Nunes from Fall River had served in the Army or any other service branch. Even a contact at the local Congressman's office who I'd helped out of a blackmail matter once upon a time couldn't find anything.

"Tex, my sources are empty. Either she never enlisted or they're stonewalling for some reason. Information is drier than Aunt Delia's delta. What's so important about this gal? You thinking of marrying her?"

I let that one slide and tried another approach. If official channels were useless, it was time to pump somebody who really knew what went on in Fall River. And Ginger Frechette was eminently pumpable.

Let me explain. Ginger and I had been in high school together at good old Monsignor Mather Memorial. We'd introduced each other to the pleasures of the flesh during our junior year and gotten along just fine ever since. We'd always caught each other on the rebound but that seemed to work for us. Together, we were a rich dessert rather than a steady diet. Ginger was a robust French Canadian with lots of ambition and no shame about her appetites. She'd worked a long time at City Hall and later went into real estate which, judging by the billboards on I-95, was treating her well indeed. She knew everyone and everything that went on around the South Coast and she was a lot of fun to be with. It was always a pleasure to mix both business and pleasure with her. I called her.

"Tex, you old sonovabitch! You still taking the little blue pill?"

"Ginger! The only blue pill I take is a multi-vitamin. You know that!"

"Do I? It's been a while old chum, if you know what I mean. Thought maybe you'd lost your edge and your interest and that's why I hadn't heard from you. Which was sad as I can think of at least two things you're always interested in: What's in my head and what's in my –"

"I'm one of those guys that doesn't separate a woman into parts. I like your brain as well as your –"

"I know what you like, pal. Here's what I'd like. Dinner. Providence. Fancy, expensive place. Overnight reservations at the Biltmore. Roses and candlelight. Laughs. And no business until well after pleasure. Think you can handle that, lover boy?"

"How about tomorrow night?"

"How about tonight?"

I groaned. And it wasn't the type of groan Ginger was used to hearing from me.

"Need to get in shape? Okay, tomorrow. Don't be late. And don't leave your stamina at home, Hercules."

I spent the rest of the afternoon making reservations and ordering the roses, did some speculating on a possible nexus of Dulce Nunes and Jake Sarno and some musing on the definite nexus of Tex Texeira and Ginger Frechette until I gave it up to get some much needed sleep. On the way to pick up Ginger the next night, I stopped at a Walgreens to pick up a ten pack of Trojans, burn ointment, Advil and multivitamins. I'd need them all before the crack of dawn.

7.

I often wondered if Ginger was religious. She always seemed to mention the Almighty with a Pentecostal fervor whenever we frolicked: *"Oh Jeeezuz! God! Jesus, Mary and Joseph!"* and tonight was no exception. She was as loud as a revival meeting, which was how I always responded to our couplings, praise Jesus, but I hoped that our room was soundproofed or the Biltmore house detective was on vacation. I also worried about paying for a damaged ceiling as Ginger's approach to being on top was to slide up my shaft at high speed, her head always just missing the ceiling, before she plunged down my pole like a firefighter heading to a five-alarmer. And we were generating plenty of smoke.

Finally, Ginger hit her acme and slammed down on me so hard I expected the entire bed to crash through the floor to the room below. "Goddam, that was good!" she exhaled lustily. She threw her head back and shivered. I was trying to see if I could move at all.

She shifted forward and lay her head on my chest and used one foot to flip the covers over us. It felt warm and close and not bad at all. She stroked my chest with her right hand and ran her left index finger along my jaw. I managed to tangle a couple of my fingers in her hair and we spent a few minutes basking in the afterglow and getting our breathing back to normal.

"You better grill me now, lover, before I go to sleep. I need to recover my strength before we have a second go-round."

"Ack!"

"Now, don't be difficult. You don't need your beauty sleep like I do," She gave my balls a light squeeze. "Now, what do you need to know?"

I leaned over the side of the bed and retrieved my jacket from the floor. I flipped on the nightstand lamp as I handed Ginger the head shot of Dulce.

"Recognize her?"

Ginger focused, turning the picture to different angles, moving it closer to the lamplight. I could see the concentration in her eyes. If this woman didn't know everyone in town, she wanted to and soon would. She stroked her chin with her thumbnail and lightly batted the photo against my cheek.

"She reminds me of two people. I mean, I'm sure I've seen her. If you put her hair up, put glasses on her and dressed her in a business suit, she looks like a woman I've seen at The Cove during the cocktail hour."

"Do you know her name?"

"I tried striking up a conversation with her because you never know where a lead will come from but she was standoffish. A bartender told me that she kept the book for a sausage manufacturer. There was something about her that seemed familiar though, and looking at this picture... Shave a couple of years off her and she looks a lot like a girl my youngest, Shauna, went to high school with. Well, they started together at Our Lady of Fatima but her friend was asked to leave..."

"A 'disruptive influence'?"

"That's just what Shauna said that Dulce said that the nuns said."

"Dulce Nunes?" I was stirring.

"Mmmmmm. She was a rough kid, but sharp. Type that could know as much as the teachers but spent more time being a pain in the ass. I was a little worried about Shauna hanging around with her but she helped Shauna with her science courses and SATs, so she was able to get into college. And she never cracked up a car with Shauna in it and they never got arrested, so I let things be."

"Did they keep in touch after high school?"

"For a while. Shauna said Dulce got an associate's degree from the community college and then went into the Army. That was a few years ago, but I haven't heard anything since."

"Could you check with Shauna? It could be important."

"Right about now, I think she's in Fiji with her boyfriend and nowhere near an Internet café. Say! What's this?" A big smile lit up her face and she pulled up the sheet and peeked in on my pleasantly unexpected and swiftly growing pride. "I'll say you don't need a little blue pill! This is record recovery time for you. Was it something I said?"

"Always, my angel."

"Always, my ass. It's kind of an insult when what's coming out of my mouth turns you on more than what else I can do with my mouth. So, let me get down there and punish you, Mike Hammer."

Ginger ducked under the covers and what she did next had me loudly professing my faith until the people in the next room started pounding on the wall.

8.

We woke up early the next morning, giggly, to the sound of our insomniac neighbors vacating their room. I hung a Do Not Disturb sign on the door and we feasted until 9 a.m., then checked out and ate breakfast. I dropped Ginger off and headed back to my place. I squeezed in a nap and then squeezed into my singles bar outfit, stonewashed jeans, pink silk shirt and brown leather sports coat. I also attached a holster to my belt and checked and stashed my Sig Sauer in it. I was in a cautious mood.

The Cove was an expense account restaurant/cocktail lounge perched atop a renovated office building overlooking the river. There was an attached parking garage and next to that The Louis Linguica Co., purveyors of fine Portuguese sausage sold for export only. I spent my waking hours in the afternoon checking property records and connecting dots. It appeared that all three businesses, as well as a healthy chunk of other properties in Fall River were owned wholly or in part by companies in which Jake Sarno held an interest.

The intel on Jake was that he hadn't more than a 8th grade education, and a "D" average at that, but he was street smart, conceptual and shrewd enough to hire or pressure people who knew what they were doing to help him make his money. His holdings were well enough hidden that neither the feds nor the Attorney General's office had ever been able to make a case against him. But maybe that was changing. Which was why I was on the prowl in The Cove looking to chat up a particular young lady.

It was early so there were only a few people sitting at the curved bar. My quarry was seated so she faced away from the window and toward the entrance. I made a beeline for her but found my steps slowing and my breathing becoming shallow the closer I came to her. Part of it was seeing her in person and in color: Her hair was auburn, her coloring almost copper and her lipstick candy apple red. The pinstriped, short-skirted business suit that fitted her like a sausage casing was navy blue as were her hose and her heels. I couldn't make out her eyes – she'd lowered her head and was busying herself with her phone – but I imagined that they were blazing.

The phone business was the new technology approach to the age-old response of freezing out an unwanted visitor. The seat next to her held a briefcase as if she was waiting for someone. It could be that or just an impediment for a wolf like me. That wasn't stopping me. I didn't have the time and, I feared, neither did Dulce Nunes. I rested my arm on the top of the seat that held the briefcase and leaned in close.

"Dulce Nunes," I didn't make it a question.

"You've mistaken me for someone else," she said, with a cool even tone. She didn't look up or skip a beat, just kept tapping away at her phone. "Now, beat it, or I'll have them bounce you out of here and make sure you hit all the steps on the way down."

"Dulce, your mother's worried about you. She won't say so but she's concerned that she hasn't seen you for three weeks. She thinks you went off on a long trip with a sugar daddy. What would she say if she found out you were hanging out across town in a high-end bistro, dressed to the nines and keeping books for Jake the Snake?"

She stopped tapping and looked me in the eye. Her eyes were as cold and dark and distant as a dead moon. Her voice matched them. She barely spoke above a whisper.

"I'm going to the ladies room. You wait a couple of minutes, then meet me in the parking garage, this level. I don't want to be seen with you."

I draped my hand on the briefcase.

"I'll keep an eye on this for you," I said. "We don't want you running off and leaving me."

"You'll just have to trust me," She yanked the case from my hands and strode away, just another sexy woman heading to the ladies room, studiously ignoring the fact that the eyes of every male in the place, and maybe a few females, were focused on her, their owners imagining ways of starting a conversation, of getting closer to her, of learning her secrets and having her whisper them into their ears. Me, too. Except that she wasn't just another woman, I was sure of that, and I'd already started the conversation. I wondered what she'd say.

9.

"Who the fuck are you and why are you trying to fuck me up? I want answers, now!"

Those were her first words, delivered in what seemed a millisecond after I entered the parking garage. She'd grabbed me, whirled me around, twisted both my arms behind my back and slammed me into a concrete wall.

"Did your get that move from your mother?" I asked, though it was difficult to be understood with my face plastered against the wall. She pulled me back an inch and increased the pressure on my arms.

"One chance," she said. "I can break both your arms in a heartbeat and I'm in the mood. No jokes, no jive."

"Oww! Okay. My name's Tex Texeira, I'm a private investigator. *Vertical Smile* magazine hires me to vet potential centerfolds. Ouch! Wait! I'm telling the truth. Check my wallet. It's in my right front pocket!"

She gripped me with just one hand now but the pressure didn't lessen. Having her hand fish through my pocket would have normally been a pleasant experience but not right now. If I had an erection it wasn't because of lust and I wasn't enjoying it. I was literally scared stiff.

"Where did you get this photo?" She pushed me back into the wall, held me for a few seconds, then pulled me back so I could respond.

"The magazine sent the photos to me. Now, I haven't seen you naked in the flesh but I've had a lot of experience with women's shapes and I'd say, judging by the way you fill out that outfit you're wearing, that it's you in those photos. Now, if you didn't send them into the magazine, someone sent them on your behalf. Any idea who that would be?"

She squeezed harder and my arm started going numb. Then she exhaled and said one word in that tone of voice that women reserve for just one person in their lives:

"Mom!... Goddammit!"

She released me and spun me around to face her. If she didn't beat me to death, the vertigo would do the job.

Fifty Shades of Grey Fedora

"I thought there was another set of prints but I wasn't sure. What was she thinking? Shit, shit, shit! We need to move fast. How much do you know or think you know, Texeira?"

"For sure, not much. What I know is that Dulce Nunes spent four years in the military but there's no readily available record. To me, that suggests military intelligence which in turn suggests a post-service career in law enforcement. The feds have been trying to hang something on Jake the Snake for years. What better way to gin up a RICO beef or a tax rap than get someone on the inside who has access to Jake's records? But how to get someone inside who Jake will trust, as much as he trusts anyone? How about someone from the neighborhood with an attitude and aptitude who's also a looker, assuming Jake thinks with his dick?"

"I think I need to review my low opinion of you, Tex. We manufactured a background for me that had me keeping books for a shady recycling operation in Buffalo. The story was I got out one step ahead of the EPA closing the place down and came home to Fall River to cool off. I hung out with The Anteaters to get an intro to Jake who needed a bookkeeper since his regular guy was suddenly having problems with the IRS."

"Nice timing. That doesn't explain the photos, though. Or the tattoos."

Her hair had come loose when she was bracing me. Dulce twirled a tendril with her finger and favored me with a smile.

"Right. Figured you'd get around to that. I wasn't about to sleep with a leper like Jake but I needed to show him that I wouldn't be pushed around. I told him that the pictures were for my boyfriend, a mercenary who was an Army sniper."

"Your way of saying 'no way'. Did it persuade him?"

"After I dislocated his finger when he tried to pull down my slacks for a look. The tattoos were a message that my ass is *mine*, not his, and that no screwing around was a non-negotiable condition of employment. Few things intimidate a pig more than a woman who won't put up with his bullshit, especially when he needs her, and she can hurt him."

"What do we want to do now?"

"Your asking questions has put me in a delicate spot. I was emailing my office, telling them to get the wheels in gear to grab a warrant and stage a raid on the office, when you came in. I suggest we take that briefcase and find someplace out of the way to wait until the warrant is executed."

"That would be my pleasure."

"Don't start, Tex. I was beginning to like you."

Before I could reply two Viking warriors, one for each of us, emerged from the shadows and pinned our arms. A third figure, just as tall and twice as wide, appeared. Jake Sarno had to weigh 300 pounds, with an extra 15 added for the Goodfellas toupee that crowned his head. He was Jabba the Hutt in a three piece suit, a bad visual made more disturbing by the revolver he held in one hand.

"And I was beginning to like you, sweetie," he said to Dulce.

"Assaulting a federal agent will put you away as long as tax beef, Jake," she replied.

"Only with evidence, sweetie. The books are in the sausage factory. Like you said, it takes time to get a warrant. By the time your boys are there, they'll be no records, no agent and no witness. We grind the sausage for export because the filler we add would never get past the FDA. Think of the protein you'll add for some kid in Guatemala."

"Jake, you're not that stupid," I said, hoping it was true.

"I wouldn't be calling people stupid if I were you, Tex. I'm gonna feed you to the machine first while I finish some business with the bitch here."

That did not sit well with Dulce. "In case I never said it clear enough to you, Jake, fuck you!"

With that, Jake backhanded Dulce, then grabbed the top of her blouse and pulled down, ripping it apart and taking her bra along with it.

I don't know where the strength came from but I slammed my biker back against the wall. His grip loosened, I headbutted him, he groaned, let go completely and started sliding to the floor. I roared toward Jake who stopped ogling Dulce's exposed breasts long enough to grab my arms and toss me against the wall. This time, I groaned and gave into gravity.

Dulce seemed to be doing better at first. She dug the heel of one of her stilettos into her captor's leg, then twirled around and gave him a flying kick in the nuts. He made a noise like a garbage disposal and sunk to his knees. As Dulce turned she went off balance and Jake grabbed for her hips. She raked his face with her fingernails. He gave a high-pitched wail and threw her against the wall. I hadn't learned my lesson so I took another run at him and came bouncing back, of course, landing on top of Dulce this time.

Jake brought up his gun and aimed it at us.

"Up, you two. We're getting in my car or I'll say 'fuck it' and blast you here."

Then I started using my brain. My left arm was behind me so Jake couldn't see it. I used it grab one of Dulce's hands and edge it up beneath the rear of my jacket. She pulled back.

"Say hello to my little friend," I whispered, grabbing it again.

"What? You figure you're going to die, you want a cheap feel first?" But Dulce fell silent when she felt the holster and what it contained. She wasted no time pulling out the Sig Sauer. What I didn't expect was for her to bring it up between my legs.

"First and last chance, Jake!" she shouted.

"Fuck me!" he replied.

And she did. Dulce pulled the trigger once. The bullet entered Jake's gaping mouth and exited through the back of his skull in a pinwheel of flesh and blood, brain matter and bullshit. I looked down at the smoke rising from above where my best friend in the world lived. He'd gone as far back into his cave as he could.

"I don't believe you did that!" I cried.

Dulce brought her lips up to my ear, so close that my earlobe vibrated when she spoke.

"From now on, Tex, I'm calling you Peter Gunn."

10.

A week later, I was sitting at the bar of the Metacomet Café, nursing a beer and going through my mail when Dulce Nunes sauntered in. That was the only word to describe it. She was wearing a shag sweater and tight blue jeans that accentuated the perfect circles of her breasts and buttocks and black high-heeled boots that made everything move in perfect unity. I couldn't take my eyes off her and neither could anyone else in the place. I heard two beer bottles tip over and one glass break before she perched herself on the stool next to mine. She looked different. Her hair was down but that wasn't it. She was smiling. With her eyes as well as her lips.

"Bourbon, neat." She told Dolan, the perennially grumpy bartender. "The gentleman – and I believe he is one, contrary to the evidence – is paying." Dolan placed it reverently next to her. Dulce smiled at him and damned if he wasn't beaming from ear to ear. Dulce lifted her glass. "Here's to crime!" We clicked glasses. I took a sip and she downed her shot. She waved Dolan away when he came back with the bottle. "Can't stay long but the way you're ogling me, Tex, I'd say you've regained your equilibrium."

"What's a near-death experience among friends? How are you doing, Agent Nunes?"

"Pretty well. Saved the taxpayers the cost of a trial but there was enough ancillary information in the files to warrant charges against a number of Jake's business partners and get the sausage plant shut down. It'll be a while before another Jake the Snake slithers his way up out of the river. How did your bosses react?"

"*Vertical Smile* was fine. I'm supposed to prevent problems for them and it looks like I did, although Linda Tarpon is disappointed you won't be posing for her."

"Um. She contacted me. I told her I'd consider posing after I retire. To promote my memoirs. But she did send me the photos. After a little persuading. Speaking of which..."

I slid an envelope over. "My only copies are there, along with the head shots I had made. I didn't even keep one for my memory book."

"Really, Tex?" She looked inside and did some quick counting. "I find that hard to believe."

"A photo is just a cold object. I prefer the real thing, warm and smooth and breathing. You know, this was a traumatic experience for both of us. Maybe we could take the ferry over to Nantucket for few days."

"You really do think you're God's gift to women, don't you, Tex?" The words were accusatory but her tone was flirtatious. I hoped. "You want to get a look at the tattoo, don't you? Find out if it's real? Find out if I'm the wild woman in the pictures?"

"I'm only human. Aren't you?"

"Tex, the only one in a position to know is my boyfriend, who I'm meeting shortly. You remember I mentioned him?"

"The Army sniper? I thought that was part of your cover story."

"The best cover stories contain elements of truth. You should know that from all the sweet talking you've snowed the ladies with over the decades."

"I wish you hadn't said 'decades' but at least I know how to bow out gracefully." I held out my hand. "Thanks for saving my life."

"Thanks for the help. And the laughs. By the way, I had a good talking to with my mom about the photos and a few other things. You should give her a call.

"I thought she couldn't stand me!"

"Apparently, you grew on her. Give her a call," Dulce turned so I could enjoy the full effect of her breasts in profile. "Remember, these didn't fall far from the tree."

With that she strode to the door and exited without a look back. I heard only one glass break this time and that was from behind the bar. I turned back to my beer and mused on Clothilde Nunes. I could call her and, maybe some day or night when we were frolicking in the altogether, Dulce would stop by and I'd invite her to... oh, grow up, Tex.

Dolan placed another bottle in front of me. "I don't usually go along with what these clowns in here say but, looking at her, I have to say that I wish I had your job, Tex."

The mood I was in, there was only one possible response:

"My. Ass, you do!"

Fifty Shades of Grey Fedora

THE POLICY
by Carolina Garcia-Aguilera

Miami, August 2014

Wearing a crisp white cotton shirt and a body hugging, knee length khaki pencil skirt, five inch high black leather strappy shoes, an oversized bag casually slung over her shoulders, the tall, blonde woman with an astonishingly curvaceous body who walked into my office that stiflingly hot August morning was a dead ringer for Kathleen Turner in Body Heat, my all time favorite actress in my all time favorite film. As she crossed the room, approaching me, her entire body moved smoothly as if to a tune with a rhythm that only she could hear.

"Mr. Hillstone?" She stretched out her right hand. As I took it, I could not help but notice how soft her skin was. "I'm Melodie Morningstar." I was momentarily taken aback as her husky, whiskey-and-cigarettes voice was exactly the same as that of the actress. My infatuation with the film, and with Kathleen Turner, in particular, was a well-known fact, so much so, that it had almost become a kind of a joke. Mercy Stanton, my former law partner, would often declare that she was jealous of my attraction to the actress. I could feel myself becoming aroused by Ms. Morningstar.

"Yes, hello. Welcome. I was expecting you." I greeted her, aware that my words sounded stilted. I fervently hoped that I would not embarrass myself by the obvious way I was showing my attraction to her. As I watched the woman with perfect posture standing before me, I began having flashbacks of the steamy sex scenes between Kathleen Turner and William Hurt in Body Heat. Set in Florida's Delray (aka: Dull-ray) Beach, a sleepy town an hour north of Miami, the plot of the film revolved around a sexy, sultry woman, Matty Walker, (Turner) who convinces a small town lawyer, Ned Racine, (Hurt) with whom she had been having a passionate affair, to kill her wealthy, older husband. The film, which took place during a particularly fierce heat wave- identical to the one we were having at exactly this moment in Miami- had been released thirty some years before; however, periodically, I would dream of Kathleen Turner. Granted, I did not go to the movies much, still, to me, the actress had been spectacularly memorable in the role. And now, Kathleen Turner's double was in my office. Was the heat getting to me?

"Thank you." Ms. Morningstar replied, as she disinterestedly looked around my office, giving the impression she thought she was slumming. Just as Matty Walker would have done to Ned Racine. Although it was insulting, I found her dismissive attitude exciting.

"Please take a seat." I indicated she sit in one of the slightly worn client chairs that faced my desk.

Ms. Morningstar took the chair on the right, the only one that was unoccupied. Sherlock, my ten-year old Bassett Hound was sound asleep on the other, loudly snoring away. I saw that she was looking a bit askance at Sherlock. "Sorry, is he bothering you?" I asked a bit lamely. I was so used to having Sherlock with me in the office that I seldom kept track of his whereabouts.

"No, it's fine." Ms. Morningstar replied. The way she spoke, I was not sure I believed her, but I let it go. I instinctively took a dislike to individuals that objected to Sherlock's presence, so I was pleased by her acceptance, even if it was desultory.

I took the opportunity to check my visitor out more thoroughly as she opened her purse and took out a Kleenex. She carefully and deliberately unfolded the tissue and began dabbing at invisible tears. Ms. Morningstar was certainly a looker, with her huge black eyes framed by long lashes, light complexion with a touch of suntan, full red lips, sparkling white teeth and shoulder length blonde hair with expertly applied highlights. Dressed in the provocatively way she was for our meeting, she certainly did not come across as a recent widow. Widow or not, she oozed sex. I was having trouble keeping my composure.

"I understand that you have a few questions for me, Mr. Hillstone, before your company will release the funds. " Ms. Morningstar looked straight at me as she spoke. By her calm demeanor, it would have been impossible to guess how important this interview was for her. "That's why the life insurance company asked me to meet with you today, here." She raised her right arm and vaguely waved around the room. As she moved her arm, I could see she was wearing a white lace brassiere under her sheer shirt; the dark colored nipples at the center of her significant areolas were erect, hopefully due to my presence. I could hardly tear my eyes away from them to her face.

"Yes, that's correct." I opened the folder on my desk, and began reading from it. "I appreciate your coming into my office to answer them." I looked up at her and added. "I know you're very busy these days. You being a new mother of twins and all that." Was she still breastfeeding her babies? The thought of all that milk spurting from those amazing breasts almost caused me to ejaculate.

"They do keep me busy, even though I have help." She agreed. "I know I'm fortunate that way." She smoothed her skirt, tugging at the hem to pull it down, but all she succeeded in doing was hiking it up. Was she doing that on purpose? I fervently hoped so. I told myself to concentrate on the conversation, but it was becoming increasingly difficult to do so as the distractions were just too great. "I know you wanted to meet with me earlier, and I apologize that it took a month for me to come in."

I had thought it unusual that Ms. Morningstar had delayed our meeting for a month- most claimants wanted to receive their money as soon as possible- but I understood. Still, it was unusual. "Well, you're here now."

Ms. Morningstar might have appeared composed, but we both knew that the results of the interview that morning was the only issue standing between her and five million dollars, the amount of the life insurance policy that had been taken out on her husband five years before. Forty-seven year old Eric Antonius, Ms. Morningstar's late husband, had been a very successful, highly regarded artist, who passed away four months before, reportedly as a result of complications from his many health issues. However, in spite of Mr. Antonius' numerous physical ailments, the "cause of death" on the medical examiner's report had stated the reason for his unfortunate demise was "inconclusive." I had been contacted by the American Life Insurance Policy Company to investigate the circumstances regarding Mr. Antonius' death before paying out the five million dollars to his widow.

I had worked as an investigator for the life insurance company for close to ten years, starting a year after I'd been disbarred. My former law practice partner, Mercy Stanton, had gotten me the gig, in appreciation for my having taken the fall for her actions. I had known Mercy my whole life, meeting her in the first grade at St. Rose of Lima Elementary School in Miami Lakes through to graduation from the high school there, to four years undergraduate studies at the University of Miami to the law school there. We tried to fall in love with each other, but that had not worked out, so we had settled for being friends and law partners.

The ink was barely dry on the letter that announced that we had passed the Bar exam when we opened our firm: Hillstone and Stanton. Miami being a city that attracted individuals with checkered pasts and a propensity for crime, we decided that we would specialize in criminal cases. Miami, like Monaco, had a well-deserved reputation as being a sunny place for shady people and all that.

For all her smarts as a lawyer, Mercy had a regrettable taste in men, as she demonstrated by marrying Elliot Masters the summer after graduation from law school. Elliot's, who had not worked a day in his life, claim to fame was that he impregnated Mercy five times in six years. Not surprisingly, he was a stay-at-home-dad, so it fell on Mercy to support the family. I had been aware that money was very tight, but, unbeknownst to me, she not only had begun dipping into escrow accounts- an absolute "no-no"-but, even worse, she had also been bribing two judges to make sure her clients won.

I was in my office the day that the police came to arrest Mercy. I protested so forcefully that I managed to prevent her being taken away to jail in handcuffs. After the officers left, Mercy went into my office and sobbing, told me her many and incrementally increasing troubles, from her marital problems with Elliot to her financial woes. Although I was extremely angry and disappointed in Mercy, she was first and foremost my friend- the mother of five children under the age of seven- so I knew I could not let her go to jail. I just couldn't. Maybe I really had been in love with her, who knows, but given that she was now a married woman- even if to a total loser- it was a possibility I could not pursue.

Fifty Shades of Grey Fedora

I dug around a bit and, it did not take long to discover what the story was. Apparently, the State Attorney had suspected that those two judges had been taking bribes- five other attorneys were involved- and, promisingly leniency to the jurists if they cooperated, the prosecutors had wired them up, gathering information to arrest and subsequently charge the lawyers. The evidence against Mercy was not very strong, but the prosecutors, media hounds all, were determined to claim victory in their efforts to "clean up" the system: they basically wanted the six lawyers' scalps. I figured that any six lawyers would do, so, in spite of the fact that I had absolutely nothing to do with the bribing of the judges, I took the fall for Mercy, and negotiated a plea deal that avoided jail time, but in which I would agree to be disbarred. The truth was that I'd never really enjoyed being a lawyer, and although I would not have chosen to leave the field the way I had, it had not been such a terrible thing.

It had not taken long for me to figure what to do next. While working our cases, Mercy and I had used the services of Big Bill Berman, our "in house" private investigator, a former New York City police officer who, after retirement, had moved to Miami. I'd always enjoyed discussing investigative techniques with Big Bill, and had learned quite a bit from him as a result. It seemed natural to become a private investigator, and, after earning my license, opened my own firm. Mercy, ever grateful, and forever acknowledging what an enormous favor I had done for her, continuously sent me cases.

Phyllis, who had been my secretary since the beginning at Hillstone and Stanton, had agreed to work for me in my new career. She never discussed why she had chosen to do so- it was definitely more prestigious to work at a law firm than at a private investigator's- but I suspected that at the core, her doing so had to do with the fact that she had always had a dislike and distrust of Mercy. Being a smart cookie, it had not taken her long to figure out that I had taken the fall for Mercy, confirming that her instinct had been correct all along.

In spite of having been married and divorced four times and, ever the optimist, about to succumb to holy matrimony for the fifth time, Phyllis had total confidence in her ability to judge individuals, and was quite vocal in expressing her opinions of the women who had been in my life. I was quite realistic about my appearance- although I certainly did not have movie star looks, no woman had ever vomited after having had sex with me. I was 6'2", with light blue eyes, dark brown hair that fortunately had not yet started to fall out; an acceptable body (no, I did not go to the gym, but thankfully, that did not show- no belly fat); still had all my teeth; no prostate problems; and practiced good physical hygiene. I had not been in a relationship in years, and, honestly, I was not interested.

I was a rarity, a member of an increasingly endangered species: a bachelor at forty years of age. I had no ex-wives; no serious ex- girl friends; I did not fear opening my mail on Father's Day in case I were to receive a card. My longest lasting loving relationship had been with Sherlock- the fact that he farted and snored, and mostly ate big Macs- did not bother me at all; I found those traits to be endearing. There was a McDonalds across the parking lot from the building where our office was located, and Phyllis, who was rail thin, and Sherlock, who was not, were the fast food restaurant's most faithful patrons.

In the years that I'd been a private investigator, I'd worked both civil and criminal cases- I had significant legal bills to pay as a result of my troubles so I would accept pretty much any and all cases- but, as time passed, I mostly concentrated on the criminal ones. I attributed that preference to my background as an attorney who had exclusively practiced criminal law.

I'd wanted to start my "new" life clean and sober, so, although I had never had a drinking problem, I gave up liquor altogether. I kept a bottle of Jack Daniels in the bottom drawer of my desk for emergencies or, in case one of my clients needed it. So far, thankfully, I had not had occasion to open the bottle.

Two years ago, Mercy had sent me a referral from a long time client, the American Life Insurance Policy Company, to investigate the background of an individual who the company strongly felt had falsified information in order to claim the principal of a multi million dollar policy. I'd been curious as to how a life insurance company operated, so I accepted the case. Sure enough, the individual in question had committed fraud: he had created a false identity for the purposes of defrauding the company and collecting the cash following the demise of an eighty year old lady who he had claimed to be his grandmother. It really had not been a complicated situation: all I'd had to do was to follow the individual around for a day, and, within hours, I knew who he really was. However, I did not let on how easy it had been- no point in that, right? The Company had been so pleased with my work that, one month later, had retained me again in another case, one that I'd been able to solve quickly as well. By now, I'd investigated over a dozen cases for them, saving the Company millions while fattening my bank account. Finally, I was debt free, and had even managed to save some money.

I had discovered fraud in all twelve cases that I had investigated to date, so it was not surprising that, in spite of my obvious physical attraction to her, I had approached Ms. Morningstar with suspicion. The individuals that I had checked out in those cases had tried to sway me in various ways, lying about their situations, misrepresenting facts so I would approve their claims, and four had even tried to bribe me, but I had not caved. Because of my recommendations, they had all been denied. Ms. Morningstar, by far, was the most interesting case, and not because of her startling physical resemblance to Kathleen Turner. Prior to that day's interview I had conducted background checks on both her and her husband, and had discovered some very interesting facts. I was curious to see if Ms. Morningstar's answers to my questions would be the same as to what I had uncovered during the course of my background checks.

Melodie Morningstar would be the thirteenth case I'd investigate for the Company. Thirteen had always been an unlucky number for me. Later, I would come to realize I should have paid more attention to that crucial fact; it would have saved me a shitload of grief.

"So, Ms. Morningstar, how long had you and Mr. Antonius known each other before you married?" I began. "I see you were married for ten years before he passed away this past April." I looked up at her. Thankfully, at that point, I had managed to compose myself a bit. "My condolences for your loss."

"Thank you." Ms. Morningstar dabbed again at her eyes. "Eric and I met while we were students at NYU- at a drama class." She cocked her head to the right. "Let me think, I guess we've known each other for over twenty years. After graduation, we stayed in New York for the next fifteen years, living in a loft in Tribeca. Eric went on to become an artist, a painter. As an undergraduate, I studied film at NYU- they have a terrific program there, you know- but, in the end, I'd always liked computers- my father was an engineer- and I'd done well in science, so I went to graduate school there, earning a Masters of Science in Computer Science. I took a job in the computer department of First Trust Bank, as a programmer. I used to work security there, in the department that was responsible for preventing hacking. It was a very interesting job- I learned a lot there." Ms. Morningstar smiled at the memory, the first time I had seen her soften. "Later on, I was promoted to writing code, which I loved. I can pretty much make a computer do anything." She proudly declared. "Anything."

I found it interesting that so far she had only shown her feelings while describing her own career. "You worked in computers at the bank for how long?'

"The whole time that we were in New York after finishing graduate school." She frowned slightly. "I guess that would be something like fourteen years. I was fortunate that I found a job right away- a job I really liked and, that I was good at."

I knew her work history, of course. I was asking the questions to get a feel for her, to understand her. The longer I observed Melodie Morningstar, the more she resembled Kathleen Turner in the film. It was kind of frightening, really, uncanny that her mannerisms were so similar. Suddenly, a thought occurred to me: Could she be doing that on purpose? But I dismissed that thought immediately; how would she have known of my infatuation with the role that the actress played in Body Heat? The woman and I had just met.

"Yes, that is fortunate." I agreed. "And, Mr. Antonius?'

"Eric had studied finance at NYU, even getting an MBA, but he really did not want to be a money guy: He wanted to be an artist. I wasn't really surprised by that- he had painted for years, but his family was very disappointed in his decision, and gave him a hard time." Ms. Morningstar shook her head slowly at the memory. I could tell it still rankled. "But, it worked out well. Eric was very talented, and his reputation grew quickly. He signed with a well-known gallery; the owner promoted him, and he became very successful very fast. I'm sure you would recognize his work- he painted huge canvases-he's in most of the big museums- the Met, the Pompidou Center in Paris, among others."

"And, you've been living in Miami for the past five?" I

prompted her. So far, her answers had been truthful. By that time in the interview, I had become more interested in her affect than her replies. Ms. Morningstar would know that the company had researched her and her husband's history thoroughly, so it was in her best interests to answer truthfully.

Ms. Morningstar nodded. "Yes, after being together for fifteen years, the last five married, we thought it time to start a family." She looked at me, those huge black eyes boring into me, in an attempt to get into my head. I knew perfectly well what she was doing; although I must confess it was tempting to see where that would lead, I resolved to not let it affect me. "We weren't getting any younger, you know. Ticking clock and all that." She added. "And, then there was the matter of Eric's health- the New York winters were taking a toll on him. We needed to get to a warm place." She emitted a deep sigh, a movement calculated to make me look at her perfect beasts again. The lacy brassiere that she wore under her sheer cotton shirt- her nipples more erect than before, if possible- did not leave much to the imagination. It was becoming increasingly obvious that Ms. Morningstar was trying her best to seduce me. And, so far, she was succeeding, as I was totally aroused. Still, I was a professional, and business was business. In spite of my physical discomfort- my aching balls felt as if they were about to burst- I somehow managed to continue with the interview.

Yet again, as I watched Melodie Morningstar's attempts to work me over- she was now running her hands over her breasts in an excruciatingly, exciting way- I was vividly reminded of the scenes in Body Heat where Kathleen Turner's character, Matty Walker, manipulates William Hurt's character, Ned Racine, into falling in love- or, rather, lust- so he would do her bidding. Matty had succeeded so brilliantly in making Ned totally and completely infatuated with her that she was able to control him, making him commit acts that he never would have done had he not been under her spell. And, he sure as hell paid the price for that.

"Sadly, your husband passed away a month before the twins were born, is that right?" It was difficult, but I steered the conversation back to business.

The tissue came back out. Ms. Morningstar must have been an excellent pupil in the drama class at NYU because she may have been dabbing at her eyes, but they remained cold, expressionless. My antenna- the one that kicks in when I suspect fraud- was staring to vibrate. I may have been attracted to Ms. Morningstar, but that would not get in the way of my decision. Would this be the thirteen claim that I would turn down?

"Yes, he never met them." Ms. Morningstar spoke regretfully. I almost believed her. "A real tragedy."

"That's very sad." I commiserated with her.

"We had tried for years to have children, but that did not happen. The doctors suspected it could have been because of Eric's physical problems, his health issues." Ms. Morningstar revealed. "So, we had to go the I.V.F route. " Again, she brought the tissue up to her eyes. "I got pregnant on the third try."

"Going through that must have been difficult." I looked at the file again. "So, you were eight months pregnant when your husband died?" I knew the answer to that, of course; I wanted to gage Ms. Morningstar's reaction to that question.

"That's right." She agreed, nodding. "I was so close to my due date that my ob/gyn did not want me to go to the funeral, but I went anyway.'

I noticed that Ms. Morningstar did not show any emotion whenever she spoke of her husband. From what I could see, only her work with computers elicited positive reaction. She would, however, touch her eyes with the tissue she held in her hand. Although her eyes would glisten slightly, no tears could be seen. Nothing Ms. Morningstar was saying was incriminating, but, still, my fraud antenna was going crazy, vibrating so much so that the engineers at NASA could pick up the signal. At that point in the interview, it did seem as if Ms. Morningstar would be the thirteenth denial. However, I needed concrete evidence to come to that conclusion, and not just instinct. I had to be very careful not to allow my physical attraction to her cloud my judgment.

I decided it was time to put the pressure on, to get some revealing answers. "So, Ms. Morningstar, who is Denise Pines?"

For the first time since the interview began, Ms. Morningstar lost her composure. "Denise Pines?' She repeated the name as if searching her memory. "Oh, yes, I remember her. She was an artist in New York, one of Eric's protégées. She became quite successful."

"That's right. Ms. Pines is a successful artist in New York City." I nodded. A moment later, I spoke again. "But, are you sure that's all she was to Mr. Antonius, that their relationship was limited to her only being his protégée?"

Ms. Morningstar shifted in her chair. Again, I could see the outlines of her generous breasts that were now spilling out of their lacy confines. I thought I could detect a spreading stain? Beast milk? I could barely contain myself. I could almost read her mind as it raced to decide how much I knew about the true nature of the relationship between Denise Pines and her husband. "As far as I know, yes, that's what it was."

"Okay." I began reading from the file again. "Do you know a Natalia Menendez?"

"I'm not sure." As before, Ms. Morningstar shifted in her chair. "Let me think."

"Maybe I can help you out." I looked at her. "Ms. Menendez is an artist here in Miami." I smiled at Ms. Morningstar. "Another young protégée of your husband's. Also, Miriam Maldonado. And, Stacy Lamont?"

Ms. Morningstar glared at me. "Yes, I knew about the women in Eric's life." She spat out the words. "What does this have to do with the life insurance money? I was his wife; the mother of his children! Not them!"

"That's true." I agreed. "But I'm retained by the company to investigate the claim- and yours is a significant one- over five million dollars- so I have to look at any and all facts behind such a claim." I explained, speaking in a calm tone of voice.

Melodie Morningstar and I looked at each other like two chess players, competing in a high stakes game, trying to anticipate each other's next move. We were very aware that that were both playing each other- who would prevail was the only question remaining. The more I observed her, the more she resembled Matty Walker in Body Heat. I cautioned myself not to fall into the same kind of trap that the William Hurt character, Ned Racine, had done, that of allowing his lust for the Kathleen Turner character to overcome his suspicions of her. Regardless of my increasing attraction for Ms. Morningstar, I had to continue to be aware of the fact that she may not only have had something to do with her husband's death, but that she was in the process of committing fraud to acquire the funds of his life insurance policy. And, that the results of my interview with her was the only thing standing between her and five million tax free dollars.

"What else do you need to know?' Ms. Morningstar finally spoke.

"Well, the medical examiner's report states that the cause of death was "inconclusive." I was treading on a delicate subject, so I had to be very careful in how I went about my questioning. After all, Ms. Morningstar had just lost her husband, and there really was no evidence that she had had anything to do with that. I could not browbeat her. Still, my antenna was on overdrive. "Of course, I know you are not a doctor; however, as his wife, you must have had an opinion as to the reason. It's true, your husband had a host of health issues, but, his medical records said he had improved significantly since the move to Miami five years ago." I prompted her.

"Eric was doing better in Miami." Ms. Morningstar agreed. "His health had definitely improved."

"So, what do you think happened that he died so quickly, and without any warning?" I took out the official copy of Mr. Antonius' death certificate that was in the file that the Company had given to me and handed it over the desk to his widow.

Ms. Morningstar barely gave it a look. "I know what it says."

"You really have no idea as to the cause of death of your husband?" I asked her again, this time speaking with a suspicious tone of voice.

I was starting to form an opinion as to what had happened to Mr. Antonius. Ms. Morningstar had gotten tired of her husband's numerous, extra marital relationships- it was a well-known fact that he had had a never ending parade of 'protégées'- publicly humiliating her by his actions. Ms. Morningstar had decided that the only way to get out of her situation was to kill him. She had bided her time, and, when she became pregnant, that offered her the opportunity she was looking for. She figured no one would suspect an eight-month pregnant woman of killing her husband who had been in poor health, especially as it was known that they had been trying for years to conceive- the fact that she was expecting twins was an added bonus. The five million life insurance policy would ensure that she would not have to worry about earning a living for a long, long time. It was a win-win situation. She would have the twins without the annoyance of a husband and she would be rich. And, if she was to run out of money, she could sell off his art- a dead artist's work was worth more than a live one. True, at that point, it was speculation, but my theory did make sense, I thought. I needed more information, though, to confirm it.

"No, I don't." Ms. Morningstar replied. "Eric just died- maybe all the wild and crazy things he had done in his youth had made him sick- some germs and bacteria live in the body for years, you know, Mr. Hillstone." After taking a deep breath, an action that confirmed that those were definitely milk stains coming from her breasts (how much would I have loved to lick them?) she continued speaking. "After high school, before he went to NYU, Eric took a year off and traveled through South America- mostly in Peru. He told me of all the drugs he had experimented with- could be that those stayed dormant in his body for years, and then, attacked him."

"So, that's your theory?" I was curious. "That bacteria he had contracted thirty years prior while traveling in Peru was the cause of death?"

"Maybe." She shrugged her shoulders.

"Did you tell anyone this? His doctor? The medical examiner? The EMT's that came to your house the night be died?" I knew she hadn't, but, still, I had to ask.

"No." Ms. Morningstar shook her head. "It had not occurred to me then. I only thought of that a few days ago."

"I have to tell you, Ms. Morningstar, I find your story a bit puzzling." I shook my head. "I know you thought you would have a decision today as to what will happen with your claim, but I'm afraid I'm going to have to investigate the situation further. I have concerns...."

Ms. Morningstar looked puzzled. "What is it that's troubling you? I've answered your questions the best I could- truthfully."

I could not tell her it was mostly my instinct that was making come to that conclusion. Could the fact that Ms. Morningstar reminded me so much of Matty Walker that I was hesitant to be taken as Ned Racine had been by her charms through the course of the film? If I were to be honest with myself, I had to admit that the resemblance of Ms. Morningstar to Matty Walker was at the root of my suspicions. It really wasn't fair of me to turn down Ms.

Morningstar's claim simply because I did not want to be taken in by her, just as Ned Racine had been taken in by Matty Walker. I had to investigate further.

"I'm afraid I cannot tell you that. I'll call you to set up another appointment." I stood up to indicate the interview was over. "I'm sorry but I can't give you a decision today. That will have to wait until I complete my investigation."

Ms. Morningstar looked at me with total disbelief. "You're going to deny the claim, aren't you?" She stood up. "I know you will." She picked up her purse that she had placed on the floor earlier, and started to walk towards the door. Then, just before getting there, turned to me, with hate in her eyes, and announced. "I'll change your mind. I'll make you approve my claim." Slowly, deliberately, she walked back across the room, her eyes locked on mine.

She placed her purse on the chair where she had been sitting, and, after hiking up her skirt around her waist, climbed over my desk. She sat on it, her legs open, facing me. I was still in my office chair, watching her act, not saying anything. She was not wearing panties- nor did she have any pubic hair. It was kind of shocking for me, really, to see such a gleamingly bare area. Her black eyes still fixed on mine, she slowly began unbuttoning her shirt. At that point, her breasts were barely in the lacy brassiere. And, yes, that was milk, I was able to confirm as I licked her breasts. I was already erect, and bursting to ejaculate, so there was no need for any kind of foreplay- nor did Ms. Morningstar seem to expect it.

We had crude, hungry, almost violent sex on my desk. As I entered Ms. Morningstar, and felt myself release, I realized that my most fervent fantasy had been realized: I was having sex with Matty Walker! And not just in the missionary position, but anal one, as well. By her expertise and familiarity with the different positions we performed, it was clear that this was not the first time that Ms. Morningstar had had sex in this manner- she had been to this rodeo before. The whole act could not have taken more than five minutes, but it was extraordinarily satisfying- at least for me. There was no illusion on both our parts that we were even remotely interested in each other or, that any kind of affection- real or otherwise- was involved. Amazingly, Sherlock had slept through the whole time, for which I was most thankful.

I knew the sex we had just had would not affect my decision on the claim; I would continue with my investigation as if it had not taken place. After all, although I had been a willing participant, I had neither instigated it not required it. I suspected that Ms. Morningstar might have had a difference of opinion on that very important point. By having had sex with me- an act that I clearly wanted to take place- she had delivered her part of the bargain, and now it was time for me to do the same. We had an unspoken deal, and that was it.

I cleaned myself off with some tissues as best I could, and zipped up my pants. Then, I watched as Ms. Morningstar put her clothes back on and made herself presentable. It did not take her long. "So, when can I expect to receive the funds?" She looked at me intently. "The five million?"

"Ms. Morningstar, as I told you before, I still have some investigating to do before I make a decision." I explained. "Regardless of what happened here, I have to do my job."

"What?" She looked incredulous. "You're not going to give me my money?" she raised her hand as if to strike me.

"I told you, I still have some questions." I replied. Ms. Morningstar was starting to frighten me. I needed to get her out of my office. "I have to follow protocol. I'll contact you in a few days and let you know the decision the company will make." I stood up and began walking towards her.

"I won't let you deny my claim. I'll make sure I get my money. And, you won't get in my way!" Ms. Morningstar threatened. "You watch out- I'll make sure you end up like Ned Racine! I'll be your Matty Walker! I know about you and that film! You deny the claim, and I swear I'll do a number on you that you won't survive. I can and I will!" She vowed as she picked up her purse and ran out of the building.

I could not believe what I was hearing. I was frozen behind my desk. "Matty Walker? Ned Racine?" How did Melodie Morningstar know about my love for Body Heat? I ran after her to ask her, but she had disappeared as thoroughly as if she had never been there. A cold tremor ran through my body, and I found myself shivering in spite of the heat. Did Ms. Morningstar dress and act like Matty Walker for the interview because she knew of my obsession with her? Oh, God!

Back in my office, I sat on the client chair next to where

Sherlock was snoozing and hugged him. I desperately needed the comfort he could provide. What did Ms. Morningstar mean when she threatened to turn me into Ned Racine? Was I going to end up in jail like he had? What did she have on me that would ensure that happening? Was that why she'd had sex with me? To blackmail me? I would not put it past her. The woman was toxic, capable of anything.

I gave Sherlock one last hug, walked over to my desk and took out the bottle of Jack Daniels. I opened it, and took a swig. It had been my first drink in nine years, and I welcomed the warmth as the liquid went down my throat. Not having any idea as to what Ms. Morningstar had in store for me, all I could do was wait. Not a pleasant prospect, but it was my only option.

The rest of the day crawled by. I have to admit that I was tempted to take a couple more swallows of bourbon, but I resisted. Finally, what seemed like an eternity later, it was time to go home. I closed my laptop, and woke Sherlock. Phyllis had already left, so I turned off the lights, and set the alarm.

The drive from my office on Brickell Avenue to the townhouse in Coconut Grove where Sherlock and I lived did not take very long. Once home, I looked through the rooms carefully, to see if anything had been disturbed. As I did so, I told myself I was being paranoid, that there was no way Ms. Morningstar could have broken in and set a bomb or anything. Everything seemed fine, so I began to relax. Really, there was nothing that woman could do to me, I kept repeating. We'd had consensual sex. There was something in the way she had told me I would end up like Ned Racine that kept me on edge. I still could not figure out the whole Body Heat situation: she had dressed like Matty Walker; had moved like her; had talked like her. Ms. Morningstar had gone to a lot of trouble to transform herself into Matty Walker. Why? Five million dollars was a hell of a lot of money.

It took four days for Ms. Morningstar to make good on her threat. At three o'clock in the morning, my cellphone rang. I had been in a deep sleep, so I was groggy when I answered it. "Hey, Ned, check out your computer." That unmistakable voice whispered. "Turn it on. You'll enjoy seeing my work."

Ned? What the hell? I sat straight up in bed. "Ms. Morningstar? Is that you? What do you want?"

"My five million dollars." She replied. "And, you're going to give them to me."

Just before hanging up, she laughed in that throaty way that Kathleen Turner had done in the film.

Shaking, I moved Sherlock over- he liked to sleep right next to me- and got out of bed. I walked over to the kitchen where the desktop computer was, and turned it on. On the screen appeared a scene with two people, one of whom was Ms. Morningstar, and the other, me. Ms. Morningstar was wearing the same clothes she had during the visit to my office. I, also, was attired as I had been. On the screen we were talking in an agitated manner. Then, the sex on my desk began. The film was a clear as if Steven Spielberg had directed it. I was mesmerized as I continued to watch. How the hell had she done this? I thought furiously to the scene in my office. Of course! She'd had a camera in her purse. I recall she had placed it on the client chair, where she had sat.

Suddenly, my phone rang again. "Seen enough?" Ms. Morningstar asked. "I thought it was quite clever really, the way to frame you for having sex with a claimant, especially one that will be approved to receive five million dollars."

"You're crazy!" I yelled into the phone. "No one would believe you."

"Of course they would." She replied sweetly. "Everyone knows of your infatuation with Body Heat. We could have been role playing- me in the part of Matty Walker, and you, Ned Recine. And, it's not hard to believe you would succumb to my charms, especially with the money involved." She laughed again. "And, of course, there is the matter of your background- how you were disbarred for bribing judges. It's all on your record."

My hands itched to strangle her. "You conducted a background check on me?"

"Of course, I did. That's why it took me a month to come to your office for the interview." She revealed. "I had to know with whom I would be dealing. That's why I dressed the way I did, knowing that you would immediately think of me as the Kathleen Turner character." That laughter again, jarring me. "So, I should come to your office tomorrow to get the money?"

"You are a heartless bitch." I said. "First, you kill your husband, then threaten me this way? What kind of a woman are you?" I took a deep breath. "I feel sorry for your children, having a mother like you. A woman who would kill their father before they were even born!""

"Right, I did, didn't I! Now I don't have to share them with him, nor share the money!" Ms. Morningstar laughed again. "By the way, how do you know they are Eric's children?"

"You really are something." I commented. "Heartless and shameless. And, a blackmailer, too."

"Well, Mr. Hillstone, after tomorrow, when I have my money, you won't have to deal with me anymore. You can go back to your boring life, and I'll get on to mine- mine as a rich widow."

"It's not that easy to get the funds released." I told myself to keep calm. "I have to fill out a lot of paperwork. It takes at least three days."

"Three days, really?" Ms. Morningstar repeated. "Okay- but if you cross me in any way, I'll release the video, and, then God knows what will happen to you." She threatened. I heard a click, and she was gone.

I had suspected that Ms. Morningstar would try to trap me somehow, the way Matty Walker had done to Ned Racine. She had correctly calculated I would fall for her, that she could seduce me. But as I had not known, of course, how, exactly, she would do that, I had wasted no time in making my preparations. And now, as a result of the telephone conversation with Ms. Morningstar, I had additional evidence against her. In Florida, it is against the law to tape a conversation if one instigates it. However, if another places the call, it is perfectly legal to tape it. Anticipating that the widow would call me, I had taped our conversation; as a result, I had Ms. Morningstar on tape, blackmailing me, and admitting that not only had she killed her husband, the children that she had given birth to, weren't even his! DNA tests would certainly confirm that.

Clearly, Ms. Morningstar was an expert in recording videos. I genuinely admired the video she had created to such a degree that I burned a copy for myself, so I could watch myself having sex with Kathleen Turner.

Later that morning, while at the office, I approved Ms. Morningstar's claim. I had lied to her when I had told her that it took three days for the funds to be released. The transaction only took a few hours. However, instead of the funds being transferred to her account, the one in the file, I directed the money to go to a new one that I had opened.

Three days later, just as she said she would, Ms. Morningstar appeared in my office, ready to claim her money. She may have surprised me by knowing all about my fascination with Body Heat, I had several surprises for her as well. I greeted her as if nothing untoward had taken place between us. Although it was extremely difficult to do so, I behaved in the most courteous manner possible. It was crucial she not suspect anything.

"Ms. Morningstar, please come in." I welcomed her. "Take a seat." I indicated she take the chair where she had sat on the previous visit. I did not want Sherlock to come into contact with such a vile woman, so I had left him at home. After all, he could fall asleep anywhere, and I was very protective of him. It was very important that she not suspect anything. "The paperwork is ready." I opened the file on my desk. "You have to sign quite a few documents. It's a lot of money, you understand."

"I'm ready." Ms. Morningstar announced. For this meeting, she had discarded the Matty Walker look, and was dressed informally, in a light blue cotton shirt and jeans, and espadrilles. Her light brown hair was pulled back in a ponytail, and from what I could see, she was not wearing any make up. This look suited her much better than the other- she should have stuck to it.

I handed her a pen, and watched as she signed the dozen or so forms I put in front of her. I would explain what it was she was signing as we flipped through the sheets, but she was not really interested, so she paid scant attention. Good. She was way more focused on the money. When we reached the last page, she turned to me and asked. "When do I get the cash?"

"Actually, it's not quite that easy." I announced. I turned and walked towards the front door. I opened it, and invited Mercy into the room.

"Ms. Morningstar, this is my former law partner, Mercy Stanton. I invited her here today to witness what I am about to tell you." I reached for my cellphone, and flipped through the contents until I reached the section that I had recorded the night that she had called me. I played the entire conversation, increasing the volume when it hit the part about her having admitted to not only having killed her husband, but that the twins were not his.

Ms. Morningstar looked at me with hate such as I had never seen before. "You bastard! How could you?"

"Oh, but I'm not done yet." I smiled sweetly. "You see these documents you signed?" I shuffled through the dozen or so on the desk. I held one up. "This one is where you consent to a DNA test be performed on the twins to establish paternity, if necessary. If it turns out that Mr. Antonius is not the father, then the twins cannot inherit anything, as he is not their father, so the money will revert back to the Company, and you will be charged with fraud. .Not just that, but everyone will know the truth about how you screwed around on your husband. This is an insurance policy that you will not fuck with us. "

"You are a shit!" She yelled. "I can't believe you are doing this."

Ms. Morningstar tried to grab the paper out of my hand, but I was quicker than her. "And, this other one, is where you renounce your claim to the five million dollars in favor of your children. The funds are in a separate account, one I opened two days ago. " I looked over at Mercy. I held up a third paper and declared. "This document that you just signed appoints Ms. Stanton as their trustee. You cannot take a penny out of the account without Ms. Stanton's approval."

"I hate you!" She yelled. "I hope you rot in hell! I'll get back at you. I swear I will. You motherfucker!" Ms. Morningstar was shaking with rage as she kept hurling insults and threats at me. I, for one, was very relieved that Sherlock, my boy, was not there to witness such a disturbing scene.

"Please, Ms. Morningstar, calm down." Mercy tried to hold her by the arm. "You're not helping the situation by acting this way."

"I'll get you, too!" Ms. Morningstar vowed. "I'll fuck with you, too."

"Well, I think there is nothing left to discuss." I approached Ms. Morningstar. "Although I could have, I did not have you arrested because of your twins. They lost a father, and I won't be party to their losing their mother, regardless of what a terrible person you are."

"You are not doing me any favors." Ms. Morningstar screeched. "I'll release the video. You'll be ruined!"

Mercy and I looked at each other. "No, I don't think so."

"Yeah, why?" Ms. Morningstar spat out the words. She may

have lost the battle, but it was obvious she felt she could still win the war.

"Because I'm gay." I replied. "Except for the sex I had with you on the desk the other day, when you totally seduced me, I've not been with a woman in years." I took Ms. Morningstar's arm and escorted her to the door. I opened it, and almost pushed her out into the corridor. "So, you see, you went to all that trouble for nothing." I shook my head. "All that research about me, and you did not discover that. Really sloppy job you did. In spite of the video, no one will ever believe that I had sex with you- rough or otherwise. Videos can be photo shopped, and with your background with film and computers, well, that's what I can say happened, you were that desperate for the money."

"You motherfucker!" Ms. Morningstar was so furious for a moment I thought she might have a stroke.

At that point, I was enjoying myself. "I was playing with you that first meeting, letting you think you were seducing me. As I said, I hadn't had sex in years, and you were available- so I let you seduce me. I've had fantasies about Matty Walker for thirty years- even a gay guy can fall for a straight woman- so you did me a favor, really." I was about to close the door behind her, when I announced. "Matty Walker would have known that."

I laughed as I shoved her out the door and slammed it behind her. "Good riddance."

"You're not gay, Henry." Mercy looked at me as if I was crazy. "Why did you tell her that?'

"I know I'm not gay.." I agreed. "But, I wanted to mess with her head. Now, she'll spend a lot of time berating herself for having missed that." I laughed again.

Melodie Morningstar, in spite of her best efforts, could never have turned me into Ned Racine. If anything, I had become Matty Walker. Tonight, Sherlock and I would watch Body Heat again- the real movie. Then, maybe, the video.

Thirteen had not been such a bad luck number after all.

THE NAKED AND THE DEAD
by Parnell Hall

I was cradling the naked woman with the nipple clips and the butt plug when the police burst in and arrested me. It occurred to me if the semen matted in her pubic hair tested positive for my DNA I was in a lot of trouble.

I was in a lot of trouble already. The cop in charge was Sergeant Thurman. I know Sergeant Thurman, and our relationship has not been pleasant. The first time he met me he arrested me. That was also with a naked woman, which probably established a bad precedent. I hoped he didn't remember. You never knew with Thurman. He had a selective memory, often faulty. But a naked woman might ring a bell.

It was a half hour before he got to me. During that time I'd been handcuffed to a radiator. I don't think that's entirely kosher, but it didn't seem like the time to be demanding my rights. My attorney would be bound to mention it later.

Thurman fixed me with a penetrating stare. I could tell a cogent, insightful interrogation was coming.

"Why'd you shove a cork up her ass?"

"It's a butt plug."

"Why'd you stick it up her ass?"

"I didn't."

"I'm not saying you killed her. Maybe you found her, couldn't resist trying the kinky equipment."

"I'm not into necrophilia."

"Huh?"

"Sex with dead people. I'm not into it. They're just so unresponsive."

"You making fun?"

"Heaven forbid. Come on, Thurman. Who'd you think called nine-one-one?"

"You claimin' you did?"

"I'm not claiming anything. Check the records."

"That's just like something you might do. Call the cops to divert suspicion off yourself."

"You figure I killed her, stripped the body, adorned her with sex toys, and called the cops to come see my handiwork?"

"Maybe you were having rough sex and it went a little too far."

"She wasn't fucked to death, Thurman. She was stabbed with a knife."

"How do you know that?"

"The gaping wound in her chest was a clue. At first I thought it was made by a penis, but the slicing quality of the wound seemed to rule out all but the most rapier-dicked."

He frowned. "What?"

"She was stabbed in the heart. If you don't believe me, ask the medical examiner."

"If that's so, where's the knife?"

"Well, I don't have it. If you can't find it, wouldn't that tend to indicate the murderer took it away with him?"

"No."

"Why not?"

"You're still here."

MacAullif arrived shortly after that, which was fortunate. If he disapproved of the radiator shackles, he didn't mention it. MacAullif was my friend on the force. I use the term loosely, as in lesser of two evils. I hadn't known how much less when I called him. That was before Thurman walked in.

"You were caught with the dead woman?"

"I wasn't caught. I was the one who called the cops."

"You sure about that?"

"You're a cop."

"Don't be an asshole. You called nine-one-one?"

"Yeah."

"Told 'em you were playin' sex games with a dead broad, and would they like to join the party?"

"That wasn't exactly how I phrased it."

"You're covered with blood."

"I was trying to revive her"

"How'd that work for you?"

"Not as well as I'd hoped."

"I think I'd better take a look at the crime scene."

"Right, right. You said that casually and indifferently, as if you didn't know she was naked."

"Naked, is she? You don't say."

"I don't have to. Everyone else is. Every other question. If you can think of one I haven't heard, feel free."

MacAullif stomped off in the direction of the crime scene. A frightening thought. If he came back with whips and chains, I was gonna freak.

Thurman didn't give me much chance for speculation. He popped in the door to say, "So, you chickenshit, you had to call your buddy."

"Well, I wanted someone I know on the investigation, Thurman. If I knew it was your case, I wouldn't have bothered."

"Yeah, right," Thurman said. "Because you and I are thick as thieves. You tell MacAullif you didn't do it?"

"No, I figured he knew that."

"Don't count on it. Right now every cop on the force pegs you for it."

"At least I'm consistent."

"Did you go in the leather room?"

"What leather room?"

"To get the toys. Did you get them from the leather room?"

"I didn't know there was a leather room."

"So any fingerprints we find in there won't be yours?"

"Not unless you lift 'em and mislabel the cards."

MacAullif came stomping back. "That's an ugly bit of business."

"Thank you."

"For what?"

"Not asking why I hacked her up."

"Oh, I know that. You got pissed off when the butt plug didn't fit."

"I guess I gave you too much credit."

"You found her that way?"

"Yeah."

"Tried to help her?"

"That's right."

"Why didn't you take the paraphernalia off?"

"If I got my fingerprints on it your buddy Thurman would have had me in handcuffs."

"You *are* in handcuffs."

"If she was alive I wanted to keep her that way, but I wasn't messin' with the body."

"There's a blood trail from the leather room out to where she's lying."

"Makes sense."

"You hadn't seen it?"

"I found her right there. I called the cops on my cellphone and tried to revive her."

"How'd you come to find her?"

"You wouldn't believe."

Albert Ponds was the most apologetic man I'd ever met. He came slinking into my office as if sorry for disturbing me. He sat in a folding chair, looked at his hands, looked at the floor, looked anywhere but at me. Which didn't fit his image. He was tall, handsome, young, well-dressed. He acted like a beggar off the street, expecting to be refused help and thrown back out there.

I didn't have time for such a man. I had four cases lined up for the day, two trip-and-falls, and auto accident, and a product liability. I work for a negligence lawyer, signing up the people who call in response to his TV ads.

I looked up from the cash voucher I was filling out to get reimbursed a whopping twenty three dollars and seventy five cents. "Can I help you?"

"I'm sorry. I didn't mean to interrupt."

"That's okay, but I am busy. Tell me what you need and I'll see if I can help."

He took it as a reprimand. "Oh."

I figured I'd speed things along. "Did you want to hire me?"

"I think so."

"Come back when you know."

He frowned, got to his feet. "I should go."

"No, you should stay and tell me what you want. Sit down."

He did, like a trained dog. Waited for more instructions.

"You have a problem or you wouldn't be here. Tell me your problem."

"It's my wife."

I nodded. "It usually is. You think she's seeing someone else?"

"Oh, I know she is."

"You do?"

"She does it all the time to humiliate me. She brings men back to the house."

"She flaunts them in your face?"

"Of course."

"There's no of course about it. It's unusual behavior. Why does she do that?"

"She's a dominant. Punishing me is what she does."

"And you put up with it?"

"I'm a submissive. That's my role."

"Do you like your role?"

"It's not a question of like. It's who I am."

"And what do you want with a private investigator?"

"You're right, it's silly, I should go." He popped up again.

I said, "Sit," and he did. I felt bad about it, but I had a client waiting in Queens who thought a broken leg was the ultimate indignity. "If you don't want to find out if your wife's cheating, what do you want?"

"I want to keep her safe."

"What do you mean?"

"I'm out of town a lot. On business trips. I don't know what she does while I'm gone."

"You assume she goes out?"

"Yes, but I don't know."

"What does she tell you she does?"

"She says she goes out. But she'd tell me that whether she did or didn't. She's not entirely honest."

"Why do you stay with her?"

"I love her."

Fifty Shades of Grey Fedora

I guess he did. I don't understand the whole submissive/dominant scene. If the truth be known, I don't understand women, though I've been married more years than I care to think about. That's no reflection on my wife, I'd just rather not grow old.

"I'm leaving on a business trip this afternoon. Just Philadelphia, but still. I got a ticket on a four o'clock Acela."

"So?"

"I don't like this guy she's seeing. Seems slimy to me."

"You met him?"

"No."

"Then how do you know that?"

From his guilty look, *he* could have been the one picking up guys and bringing them home. "I read his email. I'm ashamed, but I was worried. She mentioned the guy—-she likes to flaunt them in my face-—and he didn't sound right. For one thing, he didn't give a last name. Just Galahad. Galahad, for Christ's sake."

"So, he didn't give his right name. I'm sure a lot of on-line hookups don't."

"Anyway, she rubbed it in my face, told me she'd be going out, asked me what I wanted her to do."

"Wanted her to do?"

"Yeah. Oral, anal, bondage, golden shower. What kind of kinky sex she should be having while I'm gone. So I can be thinking about it while I'm in Philadelphia."

"She hates you that much?"

"She loves me. It's just how we are."

"What'd you decide on?"

He bristled. "Is that relevant?"

"Not at all. Go on."

"She claims she's not meeting anyone on line, she'll pick up someone in a bar. That's better, because at least you see their face. The way they look now. Not some Photoshopped picture from twenty years ago."

"So what do you want me to do?"

"Scope him out. See if he's the type of guy you'd want going home with your daughter."

"I haven't got a daughter."

"You know what I mean. You're a private eye. You meet a lot of people. You got a feel for 'em. You know if something's not right."

I kept a straight face, tried not to betray just how much he was overstating it. According to my wife, I couldn't tell if the guy she picked up was Jack the Ripper or Paul McCartney.

"You want me to follow your wife to a singles bar?"

"That's right."

"What makes you think she'll go there?"

"She always does."

I picked her up after work. My work, not hers. The lady was a lily of the field--she toiled not, neither did she spin. Her many activities left no time for work: lunch with the girls, none of whom seemed to work, sort of a Sex and the City scenario with women who could actually afford it; shopping at boutiques so ritzy I didn't even know they existed; and squash at the club, which was either a very long game, or more post-match drinks than could possibly be advisable, even if one were loading up for golden showers. Finally she emerged, her hair wet and slightly different, still I had no trouble picking her out from the photo hubby supplied. She hailed a cab and went home to a townhouse on East 37th Street. Which was good and bad. It was bad in that if she didn't go out I couldn't follow her, and good in that if someone came to call on her I'd know it since they owned the whole house.

With my luck, neither would happen, and I'd feel guilty billing the guy for my time, which I certainly planned to do. After all, a submissive wasn't going to refuse to pay, was he? I know, I know, Inappropriate Thought

#

738.

She was out at six forty five, looking like a million bucks in a flimsy piece of material that passed for a dress and probably cost more than my car. It would slip off in a second, assuming some caveman didn't rip it down the front.

She hailed a cab, and I was lucky enough to get one too, just like in the movies. I wonder what TV detectives do when there's no cab available. Cut to commercial? I can't do that. Standing in the street

Fifty Shades of Grey Fedora

like an asshole trying to figure out what to tell my client is my default position. Not this time. I not only had no problem getting a cab, I got a driver who spoke English and was perfectly happy to play follow-the-leader. I've been in cabs that won't make a move unless you tell them your destination.

I tailed her to a singles bar in the East Eighties, the type of place I wouldn't go to unless I won the lottery. And got divorced. And discovered the fountain of youth.

The joint was jumping. From the looks of it, most singles had already hooked up. I don't understand that scene. If I went into a singles bar, I'd be too shy to talk to anybody.

I squeezed into the bar, ordered a diet Coke on the expense account. From the price, one would have thought I'd exceeded Bloomberg's big soda policy, but the glass was actually the size of a rum and coke. I wondered what it would cost with the rum. I paid cash so as not to leave a credit card trail, a private eye technique of no consequence whatsoever in this situation. I sipped my drink, wondered whether the amount I'd paid entitled me to a free refill. Or a share of the bar.

I glanced over at my quarry to see whether she'd hooked up. She had not. She had purchased some fruffy drink or other and was bearing down on me. Good lord, was it possible? Granted, I seemed to be the only unattached male at the moment, but there was a considerable difference in our ages. Had I still got it? Did she want me? Oh, my god, I wonder what kinky sex act she and her husband agreed on!

She looked up at me and smiled. I think my heart stopped.

"Why are you following me?"

"Huh?"

"Why are you following me?"

"You're a little paranoid, aren't you?"

"Nice try. You and I both know you're following me."

"It's nice we have something in common."

"It's not funny. If you don't leave me alone, I'm going to call a cop."

"That would really put a damper on the evening."

"Please. Stop trying to be suave. You're a little too old, your suit's a little too cheap. My husband hired you, didn't he?"

"What makes you think that?"

"Ah, the usual deflection. Answering a question with a question. It ever work for you?"

"Nothing works for me. I hang out in these bars, every girl I meet thinks I'm a cop."

"You're a cop?"

"The women *think* I'm a cop. Or just an undesirable date."

"How about an undesirable cop?"

"Works for me. Buy you a drink?"

"You can if you admit you're following me."

"Fine. I'm following you. Make my life easy by having a drink. What are you drinking?"

"Relax, I got one. Let's speed through this so you don't spoil my day. My husband hired you to see if I'm going out. Which is pretty stupid. I told him I was seeing someone."

"Maybe he wants to know who."

"I tell him that too. All he has to do is ask. Hell, he doesn't even have to do that. I'll volunteer the information. So, relax, have a sandwich, my husband's paying. Don't worry, I'll let you know when I leave. You got time. He's not even here yet."

"You got a date with someone?"

"Of course. I just don't know who."

She turned and disappeared into the crowd.

I did not have a sandwich. Call me paranoid, but I couldn't shake the nagging suspicion she had it all fixed up with the bartender to detain me over the bill if she slipped him the high sign.

In less time than it takes to tell she managed to pick up a long-haired lothario with more muscles than you'd find on most wrestling teams. I wondered if she planned to dominate him.

They went outside and hailed a cab. She waited to make sure I got one too, then climbed in with a sly smile over her shoulder. I found that embarrassing. Of course, she was a dominant.

They went straight home. She flashed me another smile as they went inside.

I whipped out my cellphone and called my client. "She picked up a guy in a singles bar and took him home."

"You sure?"

"Yeah." I didn't mention the fact she'd made me in the bar.

She'd probably tell him, but that would be after he'd paid his bill. "Your suspicions are confirmed. Should I knock off and go home?"

"No. Wait till he comes out."

"Why?"

"So I'll know. Was it a quick in and out? Did he stay the night?"

"You want me to stay here all night?"

"I don't think that will happen. She'll throw him out when she's done."

She may have thrown him out, but the guy didn't look the least bit unhappy when he emerged an hour and a half later. I watched him disappear up the street and called my client.

"Okay, good work," he said. "You can knock off. I'll be in tomorrow to settle the bill."

"I won't be in the office."

"Oh?"

"I have cases. I'll be out on the road."

"I'll call you on your cell."

I don't give out my cellphone number because I don't want people to call me on the road. Even the girls in the office don't have it. They beep me, and I call in. But I figured this would be a one shot deal. I had no intention of ever working for the guy again.

I was already adding up expenses as I got off the phone. It occurred to me one more taxi ride wouldn't hurt. It was late, I was tired, and the subway seemed a depressing prospect. I stepped out in the street and flagged a cab.

The phone rang halfway home. Wouldn't you know it. I fished it out of my pocket, cursing the lapse of judgment that had induced me to give the number out.

"Yeah," I growled, in a tone of voice hostile enough to make even the most hardened submissive hang up.

He never noticed. "Oh, thank god I got you! I'm so scared, so scared! Where are you?"

"On my way home."

"You gotta go back!"

"What?"

"I can't get her on the phone!"

"Are you kidding me?"

"She always calls me. Right after. To taunt me with what she's done. She didn't, so I called her. There's no answer!"

"Maybe she went out."

"It's a cellphone! She's never without it! You gotta get down there! See what's wrong!"

"Oh, for Christ's sake!"

"You're wasting time. This is serious."

"If it's serious, call the cops."

"I can't do that. She'd never forgive me."

"She will if something's wrong."

"What if it isn't?"

"Then I don't have to go."

"Stop it. I'm going crazy. You want more money, is that it? Fine. I'll pay you double. Just get down there."

I didn't do it for the money. I did it to get him off the phone. He had my number. He could call me back. "Sorry," I told the cabbie. "We're turning around."

The cabbie drove me back to the townhouse. I went up the front steps, rang the bell. There was no answer. But the door was ajar. I didn't like it. I read too many crime novels. I pushed the door open and went in.

She was lying in the middle of the living room rug. Naked. Bleeding. Blood still flowed. I didn't know if that meant she was still alive. I rushed to her, fishing my cellphone out of my pocket even as I felt for a pulse I could not find.

Thurman worked fast. Ten-thirty the next morning I was back on the job, photographing a pothole in Brooklyn when my beeper went off. I called the office, got a message to call him.

I had a case to do first, a signup with a client who had no phone so I couldn't postpone it, and after the way Thurman had treated me at the crime scene, I wasn't dropping everything to accommodate him.

I dove out and signed up Rosie Cooper, who'd fallen on a city bus. She was impatient to see me because her boyfriend's brother who owned a car was showing up any minute to take her to her follow-up doctor's appointment, and the signup took twice as long as usual because the poor woman couldn't answer a simple question without digressing into a litany of indignities, not the least of which was my being ten minutes late.

By the time I got out of there my head was spinning and it didn't help when my beeper went off. I called the office, hoping it wasn't Sergeant Thurman again, and got a message to call MacAullif.

I got him on the phone, said, "What's up?"

"Thurman's looking for you."

"I know."

"Wants you to give him a call."

"He called you?"

"He left a message with the girls at the office and you didn't call back."

"I was busy."

"You gonna call him?"

"Hadn't planned on it."

"If you don't, he's gonna call *me* back."

"Tell him something noncommittal, like go fuck himself."

"I'm afraid you gotta do it."

"Why?"

"He wants you to look at a lineup."

The five guys who paraded into the box could not have been less alike. The guy I followed from the bar was number four.

Thurman frowned at me impatiently. He was still pissed I hadn't come when called. "Well?" he demanded.

I scanned the lineup.

"See anyone you recognize?"

"I can't say."

Thurman nearly gagged. "That's not him?"

I shrugged.

"We picked up the guy from the bar. He's exactly what you described."

"That's the problem."

"What?"

"One guy looks like that. Two are plainclothes cops, one is Asian, one's the kid from the coffee cart. How can I pick him out of a lineup if he's not in a lineup?"

"He's in a lineup."

"He's in a lineup of one. The identification's worthless."

"This is the guy. You know it's the guy. Stop being an asshole and say it's the guy."

"Threatening a witness? That's not going to look good in court."

Thurman was ready to punch me in the jaw. The only thing stopping him was how *that* would look in court. He took a deep breath.

"Get the fuck out of here."

My beeper went off before I got to my car. It was a message to call MacAullif.

He wasn't happy. "Are you out of your fucking mind?"

"The jury's still out on that. Why do you ask?"

"You blew off the lineup!"

"Thurman wanted me to pick a perp out of a lineup of girl scouts. I'm not going to be a part of that charade."

"That's a noble sentiment. I'm not sure you thought it through."

"I guess Thurman's really pissed."

"That's nothing," MacAullif said.

"What do you mean?"

"How's your client going to feel about it?"

Albert Ponds was in a tizzy. "You fool! How could you be so stupid! Don't you realize what you've done? You couldn't identify the man who killed my wife! A private detective, and you couldn't identify him! And they let him go! He killed my wife, and he's out walking around!"

"Are you sure he's the guy?"

He stared at me incredulously. "You *know* he's the guy! You described him! The police traced him to the bar!"

"How'd they do that?"

"The bartender knows him."

"Then he can ID him."

"As the guy in the bar! Not as the guy who took her home! Now he's out there somewhere, and I told the police he killed my wife because you said he killed my wife, and now you say he *didn't* kill my wife, but he thinks I think so, and now he'll be coming after me!"

"That isn't even a remote possibility."

"Easy for you to say. You didn't just lose your wife. You didn't just say a man's a murderer. And you know he did it."

"I don't know he did it. I only know what I know."

"You told the police you followed him to my house. Then you told them he wasn't him. What's that all about? Did the man pay you off? Did you take a bribe?"

I shook my head. "Nobody offered me one."

I got a message to call Thurman. I figured I'd better do it before he sent a squad car.

"I put together another lineup."

"I thought you might."

"I got five guys of the same description. Will that satisfy you?"

"It will if the guy I saw this morning's wearing a different outfit. Even then, his attorney's going to be able to argue one lineup tainted the other."

"By then we'll have a semen match. We just need enough to hold him."

"Be right there. Do me a favor, will you?"

"You expect *me* to do *you* a favor?"

"I have a feeling you won't mind."

"What?"

"Husband's pretty pissed at me for not making the ID. Why don't you have him there when I do."

I brought MacAullif. I figured Thurman would have a harder time pounding me to a pulp with MacAullif there.

Thurman brought a pair of uniformed cops. I had a feeling if I failed to make the ID, I would be promptly placed in handcuffs and led off into the deepest darkest reaches of the prison system never to be seen again.

He also brought my client. He must have thought it over and figured the potential benefits outweighed his natural abhorrence of doing what I wanted.

"All right, asshole, ready to make the ID?"

"Absolutely."

Thurman gave a signal and five men were marched in. My guy was number two, probably so I couldn't claim the police tried to tip the scale by putting him in the same spot.

"All right," Thurman said. "You recognize anyone?"

"It's hard to say. They all look alike."

Thurman turned on me. "You son of a bitch!"

I shrugged helplessly. "I mean that one looks like that one-"

"You fucking asshole! You wouldn't pick him out because they didn't look alike, now you won't pick him out because they do?"

"Give me a break, Thurman. Take a look at those guys. Can you tell 'em apart?"

"Yes, I can, and I didn't follow them around all night. What's your problem?"

Albert Ponds, who'd been who'd been looking back and forth between us in growing incredulity, suddenly exploded. "I don't believe this! Stop quibbling! Just make the ID!"

I turned to my client. "I'd like to help you but you see how hard it is."

"Hard?" he said. "Hard? You're a private eye! You followed the guy around all night and you don't recognize him! Are you an idiot? It's number two!"

"Really?" I said. "And just how do you know that, Albert?"

His eyes faltered. "Are you kidding me?" he blustered. "Look at him. He's fidgeting, nervous. The others aren't worried. They're just doing their job."

I smiled. "Nice save. But you know it's him. You were watching from the street when he came out of your house. You weren't a block away from me when I called to tell you he'd left. If your cellphone hadn't been on vibrate, I'd have heard it ring. You told me to knock off for the night. As soon as I left, you went in and killed your wife. You called me in a tizzy to say you couldn't reach her on the phone, then tore off for Philadelphia.

"You must have put a bunch of miles on someone's car, racing back and forth so you could take the train. If you rented it, you're screwed. And if you didn't, you're screwed, because I bet the cops can tell where you were when you made a cellphone call. At least whether you were in New York or Philadelphia."

Sergeant Thurman might have been skeptical, but one look at my client's face was enough to tip the scale.

"Son of a bitch," Thurman murmured.

Fifty Shades of Grey Fedora

I walked into MacAullif's office two days later. "Any progress on the Albert Ponds case?"

"Not my case. It's Thurman's."

"I have a feeling Thurman doesn't want to see me for a while."

"You solved his case for him."

"That's why."

"Hey, Thurman's not a bad cop."

"By what definition?"

"He'd rather convict a killer than an innocent man."

"That's not setting the bar very high."

"You do tend to piss people off."

"The guy confess yet?"

"No. You expect him to?"

"Actually, I don't."

"You had him pegged for this from the beginning, didn't you?"

"Yeah."

"How come?"

"He was supposed to be submissive, but he wasn't. You push him, he'd react. Dig in his heels. I noticed it the first time he came to my office. I was willing to overlook it for a fat fee. As long as it was domestic surveillance. When it turned into murder I wasn't. And the way he set it up. Good lord. It was just too pat. I'm the witness who saw the guy go home with his wife. And found her dead a half an hour later. After conveniently leaving long enough for the murderer to get in and out."

"Well, when you put it that way." MacAullif leaned back in his chair. "You blew the ID on purpose to give your client a chance to make it."

"No, just to piss him off. It never occurred to me he'd be that stupid. Not that I'm complaining."

"Why'd you do it? The whole charade?"

"I was in a tough spot, MacAullif. They guy's my client. I can't go running to the cops and say my client killed someone. It's not kosher. On the other hand, I can't let a killer go free."

"Yeah, right. Private eyes have a code."

"Private eyes in books, maybe. I chase ambulances. Our code is don't leave till they sign the retainer."

"And that's part of the code, isn't it? Never admit you *have* a code."

"Yeah, MacAullif. Like you'd let a perp walk."

"We have perp walks all the time."

"Very funny."

"So, you're saying this guy was just pretending to be a wimp, but actually he wasn't?"

I waggled my hand. "Pretending is too strong a word. She was a very attractive woman. Young, rich, attractive, owned a town house, liked kinky sex. She was a dominant, wanted a submissive. How hard would it be to fall into that role?"

"I suppose."

"But if he's not really one hundred percent submissive, it's gotta start to grate. Particularly when she's so gung ho, grind-his-nose-in-the-dirt, break out the whips and chains and full speed ahead."

"Why kill her? Why not just leave her?"

"He can't. She's dominant. He's submissive."

"You said he's not."

"Women are a mystical thing. Men tend to be what they want them to be."

"Tell me about it."

"Problems with the wife?"

He shrugged. "No more than usual."

I got up to go. "Anyway, thanks for coming to the lineup. I thought Thurman might deck me if I balked again."

"You might have let me in on it."

"If I had, would you have come?"

MacAullif grimaced. Exhaled. "Have it your own way."

"So, that's that." I smiled. "Anything else I can help you with?" I said ironically.

He considered. Held up one finger. "The butt plug."

I frowned. "What about it?"

"Shove it up your ass."

EMILY'S TEARS
by David Housewright

Emily could hear faint music as she slowly approached the mansion. Normally, it would have pleased her; Emily loved to dance. Yet the sound of it caused her stomach to clench. What if someone actually asked her to dance? It had been a long time since she had attended a social event without her husband's arm to lean on.

She didn't want to be there, but Crystal had insisted. The woman had stood in Emily's doorway just that morning and personally handed her the invitation; she made it clear she wouldn't accept no for an answer.

"You need to get out of the house," she said. "You need to start rebuilding your life. Now is as good a time to start as any."

Crystal's concern had surprised her. She had always been Jack's friend, never hers, and Emily wondered if her recent divorce from her own husband had caused her to reach out. Sisters united, something like that.

It had been a struggle to choose the right dress. Emily hadn't realized until that afternoon how little color there was in her wardrobe. Most of her outfits were black, chosen to emphasize the golden hair that cascaded over her shoulders in shiny waves - and she would not wear black.

"I'm not in mourning," she told the reflection in the floor-length mirror.

Instead, she settled on the pale blue dress with a flowing skirt that swirled around her calves. She had not worn the dress in many years and was surprised and pleased at how well it clung to her. She left her house in an ebullient mood, choosing to stroll to Crystal's place along the narrow path that wound along the shoreline and connected all of the properties on the huge lake. As Emily approached the mansion she began to have second thoughts, though, and not just because she had walked nearly a mile in two-inch heels.

"People will ask questions," she told herself. "What should I say?"

"Good evening."

Emily spun to see a young man approaching - at least he was younger than she was. He was holding a bottle of wine in his hand.

"I presume you're here for the party," he said. "If not, that's the boldest jogging outfit I've ever seen."

"What, this old thing?"

He offered his hand.

"Peter Cain," he said.

Emily hesitated before shaking the hand.

"Emily Stone," she said.

"I've never been to a house party where they had live music before." Peter glanced at the label of the bottle he carried. "I should have brought something more expensive."

"I take it this is your first time to one of Crystal's soirees."

"I met her about a month ago. You?"

"I've known Crystal for twenty, twenty-five years."

"So, you're old friends, then."

"In a manner of speaking."

"Should we sally forth?" Peter asked.

"Why not?"

Emily allowed Peter to take her arm. Together they marched toward the heavy front door of Crystal's mansion. Peter pulled the door open and the faint music became a roar. Laughter and voices speaking loudly mixed with the music. Peter felt the sudden tension in Emily's body. He turned to her.

"Are you alright?" he asked.

"Emily."

A woman pounced on her as if she had been waiting for Emily to step through the door. She bussed both of Emily's cheek.

"So good of you to come," she said.

"Crystal. Thanks for inviting me. It really is a big party, isn't it?"

"Those are the best kind. Is this dear, sweet Peter holding your arm?"

Crystal hugged the younger man as if they had been best friends since grade school. For his part, Peter hugged the woman back as if they had met her six minutes ago. The expression on his face caused Emily to smile and with the smile, the tension in her own body began to recede.

"I don't know what I would have done without him," Crystal said. "Peter saved my life. Just saved it, didn't you dear? Is this for me?"

Crystal took the bottle, glanced at the label, and set it on the table next to the door.

"Now come," she said. "This is a party and you two are to have absolute fun."

She took Peter's hand and Emily's hand and folded them together.

"I can't believe you've already met," Chrystal said. "I wanted you to meet. It must be kismet. Oh, there's someone I must speak to. You two, mingle, mingle, mingle."

She dashed deeper into the house, leaving Emily and Peter to gaze into each other's eyes.

"Kismet," Peter said.

"So, you're a hero."

"I need a drink." Peter released Emily's hand. "I'll see you later."

***

Despite her misgivings, Emily enjoyed herself. Most of the people she met for the first time were pleasant and friendly and those she already knew didn't ask questions even though she was sure they must be bursting with curiosity. As for Crystal, she was busy socializing and except for the occasional wave from across the crowded room, left her mercifully alone.

Still, she did not dance and after being asked for what seemed like the one hundredth time, Emily escaped to the deserted veranda overlooking the lake. She leaned against the stone railing and watched the moon reflecting off the calm water while she sipped a glass of Austrian Riesling. There was a gazebo between the house and the lake and in the cool quiet Emily could hear the giggling of a young woman coming from inside. She closed her eyes and for a moment she imagined that she was the young woman. It hadn't been so long ago that she could have been. When she and Jack were first married...

"Good evening, again." Emily flinched in surprise. She turned her head and watched Peter emerge from the shadows. "Was it getting too loud for you, too?"

"A little bit. Having fun?"

"A little bit."

"Only a little? That's too bad."

"I prefer small parties."

"To be honest, so do I."

He moved close enough to her to touch, yet did not touch. For reasons Emily could not explain, she felt a sudden rush of warmth inside that was both familiar and unexpected. It made her want to inch closer to the man - and run away.

From the gazebo the young woman giggled again followed by a loud "Oh, oh, oh."

"I wonder what's going on down there?" Peter said.

"If you weren't so young, I'd explain it."

"I guess I'm not much of a detective, am I?"

"You're a detective?"

"Private investigator."

"Before, when Crystal said you saved her life..."

"She was referring to something I did during her divorce."

"What was that?"

"I really can't say."

"Are you being modest?"

"Along with my services, clients also receive complete confidentiality."

Emily nodded as if she understood perfectly.

"I should get back to the party," she said. "Crystal might be wondering where I am."

"Mrs. Stone, where's your husband?"

"Excuse me?"

"You're wearing his ring, yet I don't see him around."

"I don't think that's any of your business."

"This isn't about business. I'm asking for personal reasons."

"What reasons?"

"You're the most beautiful woman I've met in a long, long time."

It was the most alarming compliment she had ever received. It made her feel warm inside - again. Yet it also chilled her skin, causing her to shiver. What could make this young man say such a thing, she wondered. Of course, he wasn't young. And she wasn't old. In any case, she was married. Even if she wasn't...

"Nonsense," she said.

"That's not quite the response I was looking for."

"I've been married for twenty-nine years."

"Wait. How old are you?"

There it is, Emily thought.

"If you must know, I'm fifty-two," she said.

"No kidding?"

"Women don't kid about things like that."

"If you told me you were forty-two I would have said you looked young for your age."

"Nonsense."

"There's that word again. Look, what difference does it make? After a certain age, we're all adults, aren't we?"

"Some of us are more adult than others."

"I'll give you that. It doesn't change what I said before, though. You are flat out gorgeous. You can be outraged by that as much as you want. It won't change the truth."

"The truth?'

"There are eighteen-year-old girls who would do anything to look as good as you do - except diet and exercise, of course."

Emily tried hard to remain stern, yet she thought the joke was funny and after pausing one beat, two beats, three beats, she started to laugh. When she finished she said, "Why are you telling me this?"

"Because I want to spend time with you. Buy you dinner; take you to a movie. People still do that, don't they?"

"I told you, Peter. I'm married."

"Which brings us back to my original question - where is your husband?"

"It's a long story."

"I'm a very good listener."

"Good night," she said.

***

Peter caught up to her at the front door. Emily was telling Crystal she needed to go home and Crystal was attempting to talk her out of it.

"Peter," Crystal said. "Help me. Emily is pooping on my party."

"Sorry. What?"

"She's being a party-pooper."

"How much have you had to drink?"

"Never mind that. Emily is leaving. She's walking home. Alone. I won't have it. Peter, you must go with her."

"I'd be happy, too."

"It isn't necessary," Emily said.

"I insist," Crystal said. "It's a bad neighborhood."

"It's one of the most expensive neighborhoods in Minnesota."

"Exactly. We're knee-deep in criminals. Tell me I'm wrong."

"Goodnight, Crystal."

***

Ten minutes later, they were standing at the mouth of the narrow path that wound around the lake.

"This is where we first met," Peter said. "Good times."

Emily turned on him. She meant to counter his attempt at humor with a withering glare, only there was a smile behind the frown and after a moment it fought its way through.

"Okay, fine," she said. "You can walk me home. But keep your hands in your pockets at all times."

He immediately thrust his hands into the pockets of his sports jacket.

"Yes, Ma'am," he said. "Thank you, Ma'am."

"Ma'am? I'm not that old."

"I never said you were old. You said you were old."

Emily started down the path. Peter followed. She kept waiting for him to say something, yet he remained quiet.

The night had grown considerably colder and Emily brought her hands up to cover her bare arms. A moment later, she felt Peter's sports jacket being draped over her shoulders.

"Thank you," she said.

His hands caressed her arms through the material for a moment. Yet Emily was sure it was the cool air that made her shiver. He stepped back without speaking, slid his hands into his pants pockets, and together they continued down the path.

Halfway to her house, Emily stopped. Peter stopped, too. She reached out and rested a hand on Peter's shoulder. Using him for balance she removed first one shoe, then the other. Her bare feet were cool against the path, yet she didn't mind.

"My husband and I are separated," she said.

"I didn't say a word."

"I know. Your silence is deafening."

They continued walking.

"One morning he got up, announced that he needed a change, and walked out," Emily said. "That was over thirteen months ago."

"You're still married? After thirteen months?"

"I told you, it's complicated."

"I told you, I'm a good listener."

"The *Reader's Digest* version, then - we married out of college. He was an engineer. I was a copywriter for an advertising agency. He wanted to own his own business. I inherited nearly a million dollars when my parents died within six months of each other. We used that as seed to start the business. Now it's worth about forty million. The problem is - we have a contract. Not a pre-nup, a contract. It was drawn up when I gave him my inheritance to make his dream come true. I might have been an English major, but I wasn't an idiot.

"The contract states that if we divorce for any reason, all of our existing assets will be divided fifty-fifty. There's a catch, though - instead of disposing of the business and splitting the proceeds, the firm will remain intact and we will split the profits. However, it falls to the Board of Directors to decide who will be allowed to actually run the company, Jack or me. Jack was - is - terrific at product development. However, he's a lousy manager. His people skills are brutal. I, on the other hand, am loveable."

"I've noticed," Peter said.

"Jack knows the board will most likely choose me over him so, we remain married until he can figure a way to gain control of the firm."

"Why don't you divorce him?"

"At first, it was because I thought he would come back to me. I thought he was suffering a mid-life crisis and when it passed, he would realize the error of his ways, and crawl back. Now, I don't know…"

"You must be awfully lonely."

"We're here."

They stopped in front of a large, white house with a spectacular view of the lake.

"Do you live alone?" Peter asked.

"Just me and the contractors. I'm having some work done and I've been taking bids."

"You know, I'm pretty handy."

Emily ignored the remark. She slipped off the sports jacket and handed it back. Peter removed his hands from his pockets to accept it.

"Thank you," Emily said.

"It's my pleasure."

"Tell me - how old are you, anyway?"

"Thirty-four."

Peter could see her doing the math in her head.

"What they say," he told her, "divide your age by two and add seven years. I just make the cut, don't I?"

"Put your hands back in your pockets."

"What?"

"Hands in your pockets."

When Peter did as he was told him, Emily moved close to him, hesitated, cupped his chin with both of her hands, and kissed him ever so gently on the lips. To Peter the kiss was as soft as a butterfly's wings.

"Kids," she said.

A moment later, she was unlocking her door and stepping inside. Peter called to her.

"You're weakening, I can tell."

***

She drifted into her bedroom while drying her long hair between the folds of a towel. Emily dropped the towel on her bed, opened the top drawer of her bureau and removed a pair of panties. She slipped them on, then opened a second drawer, and found a maroon and gold tee-shirt with the emblem of the University of Minnesota on front. She turned before putting it on and caught her reflection in the floor length mirror.

Emily regarded herself carefully, rotating this way and that, sucking in her stomach, straightening her back; lifting her hair off her neck with both hands. All she saw were the imperfections.

"What could a young man possibly see in you?" she asked.

The reflection made no reply and for the umpteenth time that day, that week, that month, that year, she felt the alone feeling wrapping its arms around her. Experience told her there was nothing for it, though, except to shrug it off and move on.

Emily found her copy of *One Hundred Years of Solitude* by Gabriel García Márquez, crawled into bed, and began to read…

Warm lips gently caressed her neck, and a hand slid down her body until it found the swell of her breast. Her nipple became hard and tingled with tiny electric shocks as her lover slowly rubbed the peak. The aching between her thighs was insistent and when the hand slipped lower she stretched languidly and spread her legs wide. Fingers delved between her thighs and began to explore the warm wetness. Emily closed her eyes and arched her back.

"Please," she murmured.

The skillful fingers used some of her wetness to lubricate her clitoris. Tension curled deep inside and her thighs began to tremble with arousal. Small sharp spasms of pleasure began to gather in her sex.

Emily could feel herself hovering on the edge as she opened her eyes and gazed upon her lover.

"Peter," she said.

The book slipped from her hand and landed with a loud thud on the floor. Emily's eyes snapped open. Her heart was racing and her breath came in soft gasps; she felt a throbbing between her legs that matched her pulse.

"Oh, crap," she said. Her cheeks flushed and a sense of guilt gripped her stomach. "This is ridiculous."

***

Fifty Shades of Grey Fedora

You might think that a person would feel less lonely in a big crowd, yet Emily discovered long ago that it wasn't true. She never felt more alone than when she went from booth to booth at the farmer's market, loading up on fresh kohlrabi, cabbage, broccoli, carrots, finger potatoes and colored peppers that she knew only she would eat.

There were four separate booths representing orchards and she visited each in turn in search of SweeTango apples. She left disappointed.

"I never heard of them," a voice said.

Emily turned to see Peter standing there, a happy grin on his handsome face - at least she thought it was handsome. His shirt was tight, and so were his jeans, and for a moment she was catapulted back into her dream and she didn't know where to look.

"What?" she said.

"SweeTango apples."

"They're a new breed from the University of Minnesota; a cross between Honey Crisp and Zestar! apples. They're my favorite, but they're really hard to come by. Peter, are you stalking me?"

"No. Actually, I was going to wait until tomorrow to call to prove that I wasn't stalking you."

Emily followed his eyes as they swept up and down her body, taking in her tight Capris and tank top. He smiled some more and she prayed her cheeks weren't as flushed as they felt.

"Since we're here…" Peter gestured toward an open area next to one of the apple booths. There was an apple press and several small tables set up. "Buy you a drink?"

Before Emily could respond, he flashed another smile and began to relieve her of her shopping bags before moving toward the tables. She followed. Her eyes caught his backside. She scolded herself for looking.

Emily ordered fresh squeezed apple juice and Peter had cider - "Because I'm rugged," he said. They sat at a table and talked. For a time, all she could think about was the memory of hands caressing her skin and lips tasting hers, yet that soon passed. Instead, she found herself listening to what he had to say. Even more surprising to her, he seemed genuinely interested in what she said to him.

"Damn he's charming," Emily told herself.

"I like you," she said aloud.

"I like you. A lot."

"Peter..."

"I know what you're going to say." He glanced at his watch. "But it's taken you nearly forty minutes to get there this time, so... I think the tide is starting to turn in my favor."

"You're incorrigible."

"I'm also cute. Ask my mom."

"Your mother and I probably went to school together."

"I dreamt about you last night."

The remark caused Emily to shudder and again she felt her face flush.

"What did you dream?" she asked.

"I dreamt that we had dinner - at a moderately priced restaurant."

"Nice try."

Peter stood and circled the table to where she sat. He hugged her shoulders and kissed the top of her head.

"I'll try again," he said.

She almost said "please do," yet somehow managed to leave the words unspoken.

Emily rested her hot cheek against her hand and watched as Peter disappeared into the crowd. Maybe menopause is kicking in, she told herself. There had to be some medical reason to explain her feelings.

***

When the doorbell rang at three PM two days later, Emily jumped in her chair, nearly spilling her cup of tea. When she opened the door she found a young man - Peter's age, she told herself - dressed as if he worked with his hands. He was carrying a notebook and pencil.

"Harrison Remodeling," he said. "You wanted a bid on redoing your downstairs bathroom?"

Emily thought she had already seen the last contractor on her schedule, but so many had come and gone in the past couple of days she was sure she had lost track.

"Yes," she said. "This way."

He followed her through the house until they reached the bathroom off the large kitchen. It was decorated with wood paneling.

"I know," Emily said. "It's hideous. I want to replace the wood with marble and slate tiles; add a corner shower stall, new toilet and sink; new medicine cabinet. I want to open up the room and make it seem bigger - without moving walls. The last two contractors wanted to move walls. And light. I need more light. I was thinking of putting in a chandelier."

The other contractors had laughed when she spoke of a chandelier in a bathroom, yet Harrison didn't even smile. Instead, he brought out a tape measure and started writing down numbers while Emily watched. Afterward, he moved to a patch of wood paneling and examined it in great detail.

"Looks like rot," he said. "You might have a leak somewhere."

"You're kidding."

She walked over to see what he was looking at.

"See those tiny holes in the wood?" Harrison said.

"No, not really."

It looked like old wood to her, filled with knots and grainy lines. He stood close behind her and she could feel his hot breath on her neck

"You're not looking closely enough," he said.

Sirens went off in Emily's head. She could feel his hands creeping around her waist; feel the heat of his body through her summer dress.

"You're a very beautiful woman," Harrison said. "I bet you're lonely in this big house all by yourself."

His hands moved up higher and she could hear his breathing growing harsher in her ear. The smell of stale sweat caused her stomach to heave; panic gripped her. She tried to pull away, but he held her firmly. His hands reached her breasts. His lips brushed her neck.

"Don't do this," she said.

"I know you want me. I saw it in your eyes the moment you opened the door."

"Let me go."

Emily struggled harder. This was not going to happen to her, she vowed.

Harrison grabbed her hair and pulled back, making her cry out. Her dress was torn across the shoulder, exposing her bra.

Emily screamed; her voice echoed in the small room. She turned. Her scalp ached in protest and she felt tears stinging her eyes.

Harrison's free hand gripped her breast, even as Emily raked his face with her nails.

He grabbed her arm.

She brought her knee up sharply between his legs.

He released her hair and fell to his knees.

She tried to run.

He took hold of her leg.

She screamed again as she tried to pull free.

A voice floated to her from another room.

"Emily, are you there?"

"Help me," Emily said. She pulled her leg free and ran from the bathroom into the kitchen. "Help me."

She found Peter's waiting arms and ran into them.

The fear in her eyes, the torn dress, Harrison sliding out of the bathroom; his eyes searching for an escape route - Peter stepped around the woman. He grabbed the man by the arm and spun him into the wall. Well-aimed body blows followed.

"It's not what you think," Harrison said.

Peter hit him again.

"It's all a misunderstanding. I thought, I thought -"

"Get out of my house," Emily said. Her voice was filled with anger, fear and pain.

"We should call the police," Peter said.

"Out, out, out."

Peter twisted Harrison's arm behind his back and pushed him through the doorway toward the front of the house. Emily sat in a chair at her kitchen table. She heard Peter shouting.

"If I see you again, I'll kill you."

Emily began to tremble. By the time Peter returned, the trembling had become uncontrollable shaking.

"I don't know what's wrong with me," she said.

Peter had a wool afghan that he had taken from the back of a living room chair and he wrapped it around her.

"It's shock," he said.

She nodded numbly and pulled the afghan tighter. It was warm in the kitchen yet she felt chilled to the bone.

"I'm so cold," she said.

There was tea in a pot on the stove. Peter filled a mug, warmed it in the microwave, and gave it to Emily.

"Here, drink this," he said.

She drank half of it and returned the mug.

"Thank you," she said.

"Probably you shouldn't eat or drink anything when you're in shock..."

Emily burst into tears.

"I'm so sorry," she said.

"No, no, no, don't cry." He took her firmly in his arms. "You've done nothing wrong. It's all on us."

"Us?"

"Men."

Emily buried her face in Peter's neck and wept. She wept for a long time. Through it all Peter made soft cooing sounds, and kept repeating "It's okay, it's okay;" he didn't lessen his grip once.

Finally, Emily pushed him away.

"I'm okay," she said.

She was aware that Peter was watching her intently.

"I must be a pretty sight," she said.

"Yes, you are. You're beautiful."

It wasn't true, Emily told herself. She was old and her dress was torn and her face was streaked with tears. He was just trying to make her feel better.

"Peter, why are you here?" she asked.

"Given everything that's happened, I don't want to leave you alone."

"No, I mean, why are you here?"

Peter hesitated before answering.

"Oh my God, I forgot the apples," he said.

"What apples?"

"The SweeTangos. I'll be right back."

Peter went to the front of the house. He returned with a wicker basket filled with apples. Emily smiled weakly and yawned. She put her hand over her mouth.

"I'm sorry," she said. "I'm so sleepy."

"It's the shock."

"I better go and change."

Emily rose unsteadily.

"What's wrong with me?" she said.

Peter swept her up in his arms.

"You need to lie down," he said.

He carried her through the kitchen and the living room to the carpeted staircase. He found the master bedroom at the top of the staircase and down a short corridor. He rested her on top of the bed. There was a quilt neatly folded at the foot and he draped it over her.

"You really are a hero," Emily said.

Minutes later she was asleep.

***

Peter opened the back door and waved his partner into the house.

"Did you need to hit me so hard?" Harrison said.

"I put a couple of drops in her tea. She should be out for at least a few hours. Put your camera in the living room facing the sofa. I'll take the bedroom."

"Are we sure about this?"

"Now's not the time, Harrison."

"We were hired to get the goods on her so the board of directors will side with Mr. Stone…"

"I remember. I was there."

"And yeah, the man has sent a lot of business our way over the years - mergers and acquisitions investigations, employee background checks, gathering intelligence on business competitors, what else?"

"We had this conversation before."

"I'm just saying - it reminds me of what Kenneth Bainbridge told Oppenheimer when they detonated the first atomic bomb."

"Oh, for chrissake."

"Now we're all sonsuvbitches."

***

Emily's eyes opened slowly. The room was gray from the gathering dusk, but there was a floor lamp burning in the corner. Peter was sitting in a chair beneath the lamp and reading her copy of

One Hundred Years of Solitude.

"What time is it?" she asked.

"Hey," Peter said. He dropped the book on the chair and crossed the room. He sat on the edge of the bed and squeezed Emily's hand between his. "How do you feel?"

"Better. Have I slept long?"

"About five hours."

"You're still here."

"I didn't want you to wake up alone."

Emily sat up in bed and wrapped her arms around him. She rested her face against his chest. Traces of aftershave tickled her nose and she inhaled deeply. She pulled back and looked into his eyes. She could see his concern.

"I'm alright," she said.

"Hungry?"

"Very."

"I'll be happy to make you dinner if you trust me alone in your kitchen."

"I don't want to impose on you - you've already done enough."

"You take a shower and change. I'll take care of the rest."

***

Twenty minutes later, Emily descended her staircase dressed in panties, tee-shirt, a long, fluffy white robe cinched at the waist and old bunny slippers - one of the slippers had lost an eye; the other a nose. She stepped silently into the kitchen and found the large basket of SweeTango apples sitting on the island. She moved to the basket and gently caressed the wicker. She had never been so happy to see apples in her life.

"Just in time," Peter said. "Have a seat."

Emily sat at the table; she was served a pan-fried pork chop, apples glazed with sugar and cinnamon, and something she had not eaten before.

"Kohlrabi fritters," Peter said. "I shred them, toss them with egg, salt and cayenne, and fry them like hash browns."

"You save damsels in distress and you cook. Tell me that you can dance, too."

He said he could and over the next hour he told other things as well, mostly stories of his life as a private eye, including his early days working under the license of a man he called Doc who, Peter explained, actually wore a trench coat and fedora. Emily couldn't remember the last time she laughed so heartily. The horror of Harrison's rape attempt receded in her mind. Yet it didn't go away completely.

"I should go," Peter said.

"No. I mean - can't you stay a little longer? I don't want to be alone."

***

Peter was stunned to learn that Emily had never seen the classic film-noir *Laura*.

"A woman your age," he said.

"Stop that."

They sat next to each other on the sofa and faced the large HDTV. There were several inches between them, yet neither attempted to close the distance until the midpoint of the film.

"She's alive?" Emily said.

"Yep."

"There's a chance for a happy ending after all."

Emily moved against Peter until her head was resting between his shoulder and chest. Peter draped his arm around her own shoulder and drew her close. They stayed that way until the closing credits.

"The detective got the girl at the end," Emily said.

"Or was it the other way around?"

Emily shifted her position until her head was resting against the back of the sofa.

"Kiss me," she said.

Peter leaned in and kissed the side of her mouth just as softly as she had kissed him.

"Again."

This time Peter put more effort into it. When he finished, Emily draped her hand around his neck and pulled him back down.

"I'll tell you when to stop," she said.

Emily had forgotten the simple pleasure of kissing and wanted more of it. She felt his body pressing against her; felt the heat of it through her clothes. She wanted more of that, too. She inhaled sharply when Peter's hand slid up her rib cage and brushed the undersides of her breasts through the robe, yet did nothing to dissuade him. He shifted his weight and Emily could feel his hard erection pressing against her thigh. It pleased her to know that she had this effect on him. And it frightened her.

She felt him fumbling with the belt of her robe. Her hands covered his and he stopped. He brought a hand up and brushed the hair away from her face.

"You okay?" he asked.

"I'm much too old for you," she said. "And I'm married. And, and..."

"Stop thinking about it so much."

Yes, Emily told herself. Stop thinking. Just this once - this one time - live for the moment. Forget everything else. To hell with Jack.

"Carry me to bed like you did before," she said.

***

Emily felt breathless. She stood in her bedroom and allowed Peter to remove her robe from behind, revealing her maroon and gold tee-shirt. God, help me, she thought as his hands circled her chest and covered her breasts, caressing her. She leaned backward until her head was against his shoulder. He dropped his hands, sliding them slowly along her body, exploring every line and every curve until they reached the hem of her shirt.

"Turn 'round," he said.

Emily hesitated, not sure if she could face him like this, with the lights burning bright. He gently took hold of her waist and spun her toward him. She stared at the floor as he grasped the hem of her shirt and pulled it up and off. She lifted her eyes until she found Peter's face. He was smiling at her.

"Why do you want me?" she asked.

"You're beautiful and I want to erase that sad look in your eyes."

Peter bent his head and touched his lips to hers. She parted her lips to give his tongue entry. Her breasts brushed his shirt. Her hands came up and she began to fumble with his buttons. The shirt opened and Emily ran her fingers up his chest, pausing when she reached his nipples. She rubbed the hard nubs and inwardly smiled when Peter groaned against her mouth. He pulled her tight against his body and she felt his hard erection straining against the fabric of his trousers. She dropped a hand and stroked his length.

All her doubts and fears were gone.

"Emily." Peter's voice sounded rough with need. He stepped back and quickly undressed while Emily watched until he stood naked before her.

"You're beautiful, too," she said.

He kissed her lightly even as he slid his hands up her body until he reached her throat. She broke his embrace and moved to the bed. She pulled down the spread and sheets and laid down. Peter joined her. He laid half on her; her body trembled at his warmth. He kissed her. Emily kissed him back. He began to stroke her flesh; she arched her back when his fingers found her nipples. She reached between them and firmly took his hardness in her hand.

Peter rolled her on top of him in one swift movement; her long hair fell against his chest. She felt him nudging her entrance and she lifted up slightly, allowing him to slide inside her wetness. For a second, Emily froze, lost in the sensation of being penetrated for the first time in over thirteen months.

She saw him watching her, his face taut. His hands gripped her hips and he began to thrust gently, rocking her body as she sat astride him. Her breasts swayed near his mouth and he captured a nipple between his lips, tugging gently.

Emily told herself she should be embarrassed at the wanton way she was behaving, yet she felt only pleasure. She rested her hands on Peter's chest and began to move her hips in a circular motion, even as he pushed deeper inside her. She leaned forward and kissed him, biting his lip as he increased the speed of his movements.

"Harder," she said.

Peter began to thrust deeper, faster. She eagerly met his movements. With a final deep thrust, he burst inside her. Emily's own orgasm came as a surprise. It seemed to explode upon her; a starburst of energy and light that blinded her for a moment as her body rippled with spasms of bliss.

She collapsed on his chest. If her weight was a burden to him, he did nothing to show it. Her body shivered with tiny aftershocks. To her surprise, Emily's felt tears flowing from the corners of her eyes.

"Hey, hey, don't cry," Peter said. He gently lifted her head and brushed the tears with his thumb. "Don't do that. Please, Emily."

She tried to smile. "I'm sorry. It's just - I don't know."

Peter held her tight.

"Shhh," he said. "I understand."

"I'm glad we did this."

"Me, too."

"Peter?"

"Hmm?"

"Can we do it again?"

***

The name on the door read Cain and Harrison Private Investigations, yet Jack Stone entered as if he owned the place.

"I received your message," Stone said. "What do you have to show me?"

Peter was sitting behind his desk at one end of the office and his partner Harrison was at his desk on the other. They both looked up when Stone arrived. Emily was sitting in front of Peter's desk and sipping coffee from a cardboard cup. She didn't look up, yet Stone recognized her immediately.

"What is that bitch doing here?" he asked.

"Hi, Jack," Emily said. "Long time, no see."

"Dammit, what's going on?"

"Here," Peter said.

He directed Jack to a chair in front of a computer screen. He glanced at his partner who rolled his eyes and grinned as if he was waiting for the punchline of a joke he already knew. Peter hit a button on the keyboard and the screen came alive with video of a man having sex with woman in her bedroom.

"That's it, right there, right there," the woman said.

"You like that, baby?" the man replied.

"What the hell?" Stone rose quickly from the chair. "That's me and Alexis."

He moved backward several feet, yet kept his eyes fixed on the computer screen. Peter hit pause and the video of Stone having sex with the woman from behind became a portrait.

"Seriously, Jack," Emily said. "*Alexis Mullin?* We went to her first birthday party. We attended the open house when she graduated from high school."

"She's young, she's beautiful, she's rich, and I'm going to marry her."

"Yes, and her father owns Mullin Industries and he's looking to groom a successor. Do you think that's going to be you?"

"If we merge with Mullin Industries, we'll go from forty million to one hundred million overnight."

"If the board goes along with you."

"Dammit, Cain. How can you side with this slut after all the business I've given you?"

Peter spoke carefully, trying to keep the anger from his voice.

"Mr. Stone," he said. "You keep calling your wife names but Emily isn't a bitch or a slut, is she? Is she?"

Stone leaned against the door, crossed his arms over his chest, and glanced down at the floor.

"No, I don't suppose she is," he said.

"Her only crime is that she's fifty-two."

"Fifty-five."

Peter turned to look at Emily.

"So, I qualify for the senior discount at Perkins," she said. "So sue me."

"What happens next?" Stone asked.

"You're going to give your wife a divorce according to the conditions that you two have already agreed upon," Peter said

"Or what? You're going to send the video to the board? You know how it works. They might demonize Em for fucking someone thirty years younger but they'll congratulate me."

"I'm only twenty years younger. Anyway, we're going to send the board a different video. If you don't do what we ask, we'll also send it to Alexis and her old man."

Peter hit a couple more keys and the first video was replaced by a second. In this one, an African-American woman was kneeling in front of Stone while he said, "Suck it, bitch. That's right, suck it."

"Where did you get this?" Stone wanted to know. "I didn't even know her until last night. The whore hit on me."

"Hey, hey, hey," Harrison said. "You're talking about a friend of ours."

"Her name is Karla," Peter said.

"You bastards. You set me up."

"Yeah, we did. Sorry about that."

"But why?"

"Harrison and I don't want to end up like Bainbridge and Oppenheimer."

"I don't know what that means."

"Well, then let's just say I can't stand to see a woman cry."

"Don't take it so hard, Jack," Emily said. "You never know. The board might side with you and your merger, after all. I know I could stand to be richer."

***

Ten minutes later, Stone was gone. Emily went to her feet and moved towards the door.

"Thank you, gentlemen," she said.

"Mrs. Stone," Harrison said. "I'm sorry for my part in all of this. I'm sorry for what I did."

Emily nodded her head almost imperceptibly. She knew now that the assault had been staged, yet that did little to alleviate the fear she had felt; that continued to ripple through her even days later. The deep scratches in Harrison's face made her feel better, though.

"Call me Emily," she said.

"Emily," Peter said.

"You can call me Mrs. Stone."

"May I take you to dinner, tonight?"

"It still bothers me that you're young enough to be my son."

"It doesn't bother me at all that you're old enough to be my mother."

Yet Emily remained unconvinced.

"Everything I said to you before is true," Peter said.

"Everything?"

"Yes."

"Time will tell. Okay, dinner, but afterward we'll have dessert at my house. As it turns out, I make a terrific apple pie."

LOVE FOR BAIL
A Nick Polo Adventure
by Jerry Kennealy

"I'm tellin' you, Nick," Ducky Puglisi said, "She was something else. An angel's face, long, golden blonde hair, legs that reached up to her shoulders, boobs that defied gravity and a mouth like a vacuum cleaner. She was the best piece of ass I've had in my entire life."

We were sitting in the private office of Ducky's Bail Bonds, which was conveniently located just across the street from the San Francisco Hall of Justice.

It was a cramped, l-shaped room, filled with opened cardboard boxes that contained liquor bottles, stationary supplies, and computer parts. The walls were slathered with San Francisco Giants and 49ers memorabilia.

Ducky was what I called one of my "desperate" clients; he only called me when all else had failed.

He was in his fifties, just a shade over five feet tall, with a round face, slick gray hair and a stomach bay-windowed from a lifetime of abundant food and booze. He had picked up the "Ducky" name when he was a kid, thanks to his way of waddling when he walked.

Ducky flopped down into the high back leather chair behind his desk. "You gotta help me on this one, Nick."

"Give me all of the gory details."

"She came in to post bail on her husband, at least she claimed he was her husband. Roger LaRue." He slid a brick-red manila folder across the desk. "All the info is in the file. LaRue had been busted for drunk driving. He ran into the back of a SUV driven by some soccer mom."

"Was anyone injured?"

"Not LaRue; he was too drunk to get hurt. The other driver is claiming whiplash, a bad back and all that other bullshit. There was very little damage to either car. LaRue was driving a red 2003 Ford Mustang that he'd inherited from his father. His wife said he loves the car more than he does her."

"How much was the bail?"

"A hundred K."

"A hundred thousand dollars is a high bail on a drunk driving charge, Ducky."

"It was his second offense, he had no insurance, and there was an unlicensed gun, an old Colt .45, in the car. LaRue claimed that the gun must have been his father's, that he knew nothing about it."

"So Mrs. LaRue came to see you, coughed up ten thousand dollars and you posted the bond."

He ran a hand across his jaw and grimaced. "Yeah, kinda. Trouble was, she didn't have the ten thou. She had five hundred in cash, and gave me a check for forty-five hundred bucks. Said she'd deliver the rest, in cash, to me in two days."

And you believed her?"

Ducky sighed, pulled out the bottom drawer of the desk and took out a bottle of Jack Daniels and two shot glasses.

"We had a few drinks, Nick," he said as he poured the whiskey. "One thing led to another and we ended up in the back room. Roger LaRue missed his court date. I had sixty days to find him or I have to swallow the hundred thousand dollar bond. This is now day fifty-seven."

"What's Mrs. LaRue's first name?"

"Lorna, she said," He handed me a filled-to-the-brim shot glass, and then patted the manila folder. "The checking account had been closed four months ago; the address she gave me was for an apartment on Taraval Street. They'd moved out right after the accident, owing two months' rent. I ran them both through all the data bases, but here was no record of a marriage in California, no records under her name at all. There's a mug shot of Roger LaRue in the file."

"But none of Mrs. LaRue."

"No pictures, but I've got something better than that," he said with a wide smile. He clicked away on his desk top computer for a minute or so, then swiveled the screen in my direction.

The top of the screen showed the address of the Porn-Are-Us website. There was a tall, beautiful blonde in her early twenties wearing the usual uniform: garter-belt, black nylons and high-heel shoes. She also had a black harness around her waist that held a strap-on dildo the size of my forearm, and a small leather flogging whip in her right hand. Her co-star was a young white guy with a shaved head and a body awash in tattoos. He had a bright red ball gag in his mouth and was wearing handcuffs; nothing else.

"That's Mrs. LaRue, also known as Lorna Licksit," Ducky said, as he got to his feet and came around to look over my shoulder.

"How did you pull that name?"

"Before I called you, I worked my ass off trying to find LaRue. His last job was tending bar at the Hang Five, a surfer's bar out by the beach. He was fired a week before the accident for tapping the till. I asked about his wife; no one had heard about her, but quite a few knew about his girlfriend, Lorna. She'd give blowjobs for a hundred bucks, right in the parking lot. One guy knew all about her porno films."

Ducky tapped the monitor with his forefinger. "Look at that; is she limber or what?"

I'd seen enough. I swiveled the monitor around.

"Can you help me, Nick?"

"Ducky, the two of them are out of town by now, probably in Reno or Vegas."

"I don't think so. Lorna called me three days ago with a big sob story of how Roger had beaten her up. She says she can turn him over to me; for twenty-five thousand bucks. I think they're both here in town or somewhere close."

I had to smile. "Sweet girl. What are you going to do?"

Ducky drained his shot glass in one gulp, wiped his lips and said, "Twenty-five is a lot less than a hundred. She called me again this morning; said she could only keep Roger around for another day, so I had to make up my mind."

"Are you going to pay her off?"

"No, you are, Nick. She says she won't deal directly with me."

"It's another scam, Ducky. She'll take the money and you'll never see LaRue."

"There's five grand in it for you, Nick. Ten grand if you get LaRue and don't have to give her the money."

When I hesitated, Ducky said, "A thousand up front."

I took Ducky's file on LaRue home with me to my flat on Green Street and went through it carefully. LaRue's mug shot showed him to be a good-looking guy in his thirties, with spiky dark hair, an off-center nose, low-set ears, and a Zapata mustache that curled around his lips and reached down to his jawline. He was listed as 6'1", two-hundred and fourteen pounds.

Ducky was good at tracking down missing clients and he had done his homework; checked all the right data bases: Social Security, criminal records, property records, and DMV.

The request date on the DMV data base that he'd used was dated two weeks ago, which meant that LaRue had had fourteen days to get into some vehicular mischief. Since he hadn't paid his rent or his car insurance, I didn't think he'd be the type to pay for parking tickets

I drove down at the Hall of Justice, and carried a Starbuck's pumpkin latte to the Police Personnel Only window of the traffic records clerks' room.

Nancy Cramer, a sweet-faced woman in her fifties with a mop of sandy-gray hair smiled when she saw me. She had been clerking at the Homicide Detail, years ago when I was in the department.

"For me, Nick?" she said reaching for the coffee cup.

"Who else?"

"Whatcha need?"

I gave her a slip of paper with the Mustang's license plate number. "I'm curious if this car has picked up any parking tickets lately."

"And you expect to bribe me with just a cup of coffee?"

"It's a Vente, Nancy."

The city's squadrons of meter maids issued 12,000 parking tags a month, and that information didn't show up on any of the data bases Ducky had used.

I was in luck. LaRue's Mustang had been ticketed nine times; six of them over the last three months at addresses in the Sunset District where he'd lived and worked. There were three tags for red zone and expired meter violations issued in the last two days in the rough-and-tumble Tenderloin District of the city.

The Tenderloin was located at the bottom of Nob Hill and had more than its share of drug dealers, street dopers, hookers of every sex and persuasion, sex club and a few surprisingly good restaurants. What it didn't have was many parking places.

I drove to the area and within twenty minutes found LaRue's red Mustang coupe parked on Eddy Street.

The damage from the accident was visible - a dented right fender, the headlight patched with duct tape. There were fast food wrappers, crumbled cardboard coffee cups and a man's leather jacket strewn around the flooring and backseats.

There were dozens apartment houses and old hotels in the area, where LaRue could have been holed up.

So I did what private eyes do, parked in a red zone with a view of the Mustang and waited.

It was a long wait, almost three hours. A tall brunette wearing tight white shorts, a yellow halter top and black patent leather high heels made her way over to the Mustang. She had a bright red purse the size of a paperback book dangling over one shoulder. She popped the Mustang's trunk and took out a carry-on size black leather suitcase. Her dark hair was cut short, a pixie-cut, but the rest of her fit the description Ducky had given me of Lorna Licksit, and the girl I'd seen in the porn flick: beautiful face, long legs, and jiggling breasts that seemed to defy gravity. Mrs. Roger LaRue in the flesh.

The fact that Roger LaRue had a gun in his car at the time of the accident made me a little nervous. He'd had more than enough time to pick up another weapon.

Guns are heavy, cumbersome, and uncomfortable, no matter what kind of holster you use, which is why I seldom carry one. But I do keep one close by; in the hollowed out headrest of my car's passenger seat. I retrieved .38 S&W snub nose and slipped it into my sport coat pocket.

Lorna drew a lot of admiring glances from the passing pedestrians as she sauntered down Eddy Street.

I followed her to the entrance of a rundown apartment building with a faded neon sign that said The Excelsior hanging alongside the fire escape. She paced back and forth, swinging the suitcase. I moved in close, hoping that it was Roger LaRue that she was waiting for.

She stopped her pacing when a balding, middle-aged man wearing a pinstriped suit approached her.

She was all smiles and giggles. He looked nervous as hell.

Lorna handed him the suitcase and then slipped her hand between his arm, chatting away merrily as they climbed the steps up to the Excelsior's front door.

I hurried over and timed it so that I was right behind them when Lorna opened the door with a key.

The Excelsior wasn't the kind of place that attracted jewel thieves. Social welfare cases, hanging-by-a-thread seniors, burned out druggies, poor bastards just hoping to make it to the next day, and hookers filled the rooms, which were rented by the day or week.

The linoleum floor was heel-chipped and the wall paint cracked like an eggshell

As Lorna and her new boyfriend sauntered over to the elevator, I took the stairs, and stopped at the second landing, waiting for the elevator to kick into gear.

The ragged tweed stair-runner was worn down to bare wood in spots, and the air smelled of years of cigarette and cigar smoke, spilled beer, old socks, and things I didn't want to think about.

I had no problem keeping up with the elevator as it chugged and chortled up to the fifth floor. I squatted down and peered through the stairway spindles as Lorna and Pinstripe played grab-ass until she opened the door to unit 506. The door slammed with a bang.

I edged up and put my ear to the door. Footsteps, giggles, then a radio came on – The Gypsy Kings, doing "Bomboleo."

I retreated back to the stairwell. I had Lorna; but she was no good to me or Ducky, without Roger LaRue.

While I was debating my next move, the elevator started chugging again. Down to the first floor, then onward and upward. All the way to the fifth floor.

The lone passenger was tall, over six feet, clean shaven, with dark hair worn in a longish crewcut style. He was wearing a strawberry colored Tommy Bahama Hawaiian shirt and knee-length khaki shorts. His flip-flops made faint kissing sounds on the linoleum. He had an off-center nose, and low-set ears. Roger LaRue, all cleaned up, mustache gone, but his attempt at a disguise wasn't much better than Lorna's.

He stopped in front of the door to room 506, checked his wristwatch, then took an iPhone from his pants pocket and used his index finger to scroll the screen. After a few minutes, he checked his watch again, shook his head and went back to scrolling.

Finally the door opened and a long lovely arm reached out and dragged him into the room.

I padded over and put my ear to the door again. No music, no voices.

I tried the door handle. Locked, but the doorframe was old and warped. Credit cards are what you do not want to use to slip a lock; they often break in half and leave your ID in the door. I took a fireman's shove-knife from my jacket pocket – a piece of semi-rigid 10 gauge steel the size of a pocket comb with an indented end that first-responders use to open doors in an emergency.

It's popular with firefighters, cops, private eyes, and burglars. You can pick one up on Amazon and EBay for a few bucks.

The lock clicked open. I took a deep breath and peaked inside. A dingy room with a beaten-up maroon couch, a pair of wooden folding chairs, a countertop with a 2- ring electric stove top and a small TV set that had been bolted to the counter.

The sounds of laughter, giggling, and what sounded like muffled screams was coming from an adjoining room near the couch. The door was open just an inch or so, but that was enough for me to get a look at Lorna, back in her porno outfit - the garter belt, the high heels, the big rubber dildo, and a flogging whip in her right hand.

Roger was laughing as he took photos of the man on the bed with his iPhone.

Poor Mr. Pinstripe was naked, a red ball-gag in his mouth; his hands and feet handcuffed to the iron bed frame. His milky white skin was scored by red marks from the whip, and his stub of a penis was hidden in a bird's nest of gray pubic hair.

Lorna trailed the whip-ends down the length of his body while she said, "Your wife is going to love these pictures, honey."

I shoved the door open and said, "Is this a private party, or can anyone join in?"

Lorna wheeled around, raised the whip over her head, and said, "Who the fuck are you?"

"Ducky sent me."

Roger dropped the iPhone to the floor and started moving toward me. He stopped when he saw my gun.

The gun didn't seem to bother Lorna. She screamed at the top of her lungs and came at me with the whip.

I fired one round into the mattress, between Mr. Pinstripe's shackled legs, and she came to an abrupt halt. She dropped the whip, flopped onto the bed and turned on the tears.

"Why didn't Ducky wait?" she blubbered. "Why?"

"I can think of twenty-five thousand reasons, Lorna. She was going to sell you to the bail bondsman for twenty-five thousand dollars," I explained to Roger LaRue, who was standing statue still, his face screwed up into a mask of rage and confusion.

I patted LaRue down – no gun. I pocketed his iPhone then had him undo Mr. Pinstripe's handcuffs.

The cuffs came in handy. I cuffed Roger to the bed and Lorna to a radiator at the far end of the room. They were shouting obscenities at each other so loudly, that I had to move into the other room to call Ducky and gave him the good news.

Mr. Pinstripe turned out to be a mortgage broker, with; he assured me, a wife and four wonderful children. He was more than relieved when I told him to scram before the police showed up.

"The...the pic-pic pictures," he stuttered. "That the man took. I'll pay you --"

"Not necessary. I'll delete the pictures."

He didn't seem to know whether to believe me or just take off. He took off, moving awkwardly; perhaps because he'd been in such a hurry he hadn't put on his socks or tied his shoes.

The two lovebirds were still going at it when Ducky arrived with a pair of NFL linemen-sized Samoans he used to handle "difficult clients."

Roger LaRue didn't put up any resistance; he had that "ridden hard, put away wet" look that people get when they know they're going straight to jail.

Lorna was another story. She claimed that everything was Roger's fault; that he'd beaten her, forced her into a life of crime. She threatened Ducky with sexual harassment, sexual assault, and me with assault and battery for cuffing her to the radiator.

Actually, there was nothing that she could be charged with. Mr. Pinstripe was long gone. There were photos of six other dumb clucks handcuffed to a bed on Roger's iPhone, but there was no way to identify them.

So in the end, Lorna walked, or jiggled away, in her white shorts, yellow top, the suitcase with the handcuffs, dildo, whips, and the keys to Roger's beloved Mustang.

Before she left she gave me the finger and a dirty look, then moved in close to Ducky and whispered something into his ear.

Ducky closed his eyes tight as he listened; his head moving slightly from side to side. She kept whispering and finally Ducky nodded affirmatively, his chin dropping to his chest. When he opened his eyes, Lorna was gone.

"Don't ask, Nick. Just don't ask."

I didn't ask, because I didn't want to know. Ducky, like Mr. Pinstripe, was a sharp, successful, tough-minded businessman; but the Lorna Larues of the world had no trouble in turning them into chumps. As a wise man once said, experience is the best teacher, but the tuition is damned expensive.

Fifty Shades of Grey Fedora

THE FEDORA
by Terrell Lee Lankford

I didn't get into this job for romantic reasons. I never watched the old detective movies. I didn't even really know who Humphrey Bogart and Alan Ladd were. I never liked old movies. Especially ones that were in black and white. I became a private investigator because my uncle had a business and he said I could make some dough running down insurance scams and tracking down debtors on the dodge. He didn't usually handle divorce cases because no one cared why anyone got divorced any more. And he knew if someone wanted a romantic partner followed it was because they wanted to find out if that partner was cheating on them. And if they did find out and the offended party went bonkers and killed the cheater or cheaters then my uncle could get sued and his insurance would go through the roof. So he specialized in insurance fraud and debt collection. There was more than enough of that to go around.

All that changed when my uncle's pal Milo asked us to keep an eye on his wife, Deloris. Milo was going out of the country for six months to work on an oil rig in Dubai and he couldn't take his wife with him. He wanted to make sure he was the only one in the family who would be working the drills during that time, if you know what I mean (and I think you do). So my uncle made him a sweet deal and told him that I would keep an eye on Deloris while he was away. I'd do it in my spare time, checking in whenever I could, so it wouldn't break Milo's bank while I was at it. Milo said it would be easy to keep track of Deloris when she went out at night because she always wore a fedora. I didn't even know what a fedora was. I had to look it up on Wikipedia. It's a hat. A guy's hat at that. But guys don't wear hats any more, so I didn't understand why a woman would.

But then I saw her in it.

It was the very first night I was watching her house after Milo had left for his rig. She came out at precisely 9:14 pm, wearing her fedora and a raincoat. It wasn't raining out. It wasn't going to rain. As a matter of fact it wasn't even cold. Even though it was December, it was warm out. We were in L.A. for Christssake. Why would anyone wear a raincoat when it's not raining? Despite the fact that she was wearing a raincoat and a hat, she looked sexy as hell as she walked to her car in the driveway. I could tell she had a figure and she was using it, swaying with every step. I knew this lady was up to no good. Something about being so covered up made her look extra naughty. What was she hiding?

I followed her out of Santa Monica all the way up into the Valley to a little jazz club on Ventura Boulevard. Along with black and white movies, I never acquired a taste for jazz. Rock and roll was more my style. Bob Seger. Tom Petty. Skynrd! But I liked the music that was playing in the joint. A sexy asian girl named Grace Kelly was playing with a four piece band. She played the sax and sang too. She was really good.

Deloris took a seat at a table off to the side in the club and watched the band through both sets. I thought she was waiting for someone, but if she was they never showed. A couple guys approached her at different times and asked if they could buy her drinks. She refused politely and they left her alone. She was being a good girl.

But I still didn't trust her.

She never took off the hat and the place was pretty dark, but I saw her face a few times by the light of the little candle on her table and I could tell she was beautiful. I just couldn't tell exactly *how* beautiful. Milo was nuts to have a job where he had to leave her for six months at a time. Any time you don't spend with your woman, someone else will.

She had only the required two drinks while she was there. No more. And no food. She seemed to just be there for the music. During the break between sets she read a paperback book. Not one of those electric devices everyone reads on nowadays, but an old fashioned paperback book. Like my dad used to read. I couldn't see what the title was, but it must have been good, because she never looked up once from it until the band returned to the stage.

Fifty Shades of Grey Fedora

When the show was over she got up and left. I followed her home. As far as I could tell, she never noticed me. Not in the club and not on the road. She didn't seem interested in anything except listening to music and reading her book.

So this is how it started. We'd repeat this same exact experience every night for the next few weeks. Sure, she'd go to a different little jazz club in the city and she'd see a different little jazz group. But nothing else would change. She would always just watch them quietly. Always just have her two drinks. Always read her paperback book during intermission. (Although it seemed to change every other day or so. Once in a while I could spot a title: The Deadly Yellow Rain, The Smiling Dog, The Long Goodbye. I wrote down any title I could read from a distance, but I didn't know crap about books.) And she always left without anyone in tow and drove back to her house in Santa Monica. I had found a great spot to watch her place from a block away. A large oak tree gave me cover and I could lean forward and check on the place from time to time, then lean back without her ever being able to see me from her house or her yard. I had a clear view of the street so if anyone showed up to visit, I'd know it. Her back yard butted up to a neighbor's back yard. Unless she was having an affair with a 72 year old woman named Gloria Carthem who was good at scaling fences, that was not an angle I needed to cover. If she was having an affair with anyone, the guy must have been using a tunnel to get into the place. I checked up on her during the day whenever I could. But she never seemed to go out in daylight. I think she was sleeping most of the time, because when she would come home at night I could always see the light from her TV flickering in her bedroom until daybreak. She either watched TV all night or she went to sleep with it on. Occasionally her drapes would be open a little and I could see a piece of the TV. It was always one of those black and white movies I had no interest in. This lady was a freak. But not the kind I thought I'd be following. I don't know why Milo was worried about her. She seemed to have no interest in any man who approached her in the clubs and she certainly wasn't entertaining anyone at the house – at least not on my watch. But every now and then I would see her shadow moving on the other side of those drapes and I got why Milo was worried. A body like hers needed guarding. No matter what her head was up to.

Fifty Shades of Grey Fedora

I found myself being distracted by thoughts of her during my day work. I was becoming less and less interested in the various insurance cheats I was following and photographing and more and more interested in keeping Delores distant company at night. She was mysterious and despite the fact that I said I didn't get into this business for romantic reasons, every man likes a mystery. Especially a hot mystery.

I had been on her tail for almost a month before the trouble began. She was in a joint called The Baked Potato in Studio City watching a group called The Open Hands when the tall guy approached her table. He bent over and said something to her. She shook her head no, but he sat down anyway. He leaned into her ear and said something else. It went on for more than a minute. She just sat there, listening. The brim of her hat created a shadow under the stage lights so I couldn't get a read on her expression. She was just sitting rock still. After he was done she spoke into his ear for about thirty seconds. He smiled. Shook his head, got up and walked out of the club. She went back to watching the group. I have to admit they were good. I was starting to like this jazz stuff. You listen to anything long enough and you are bound to find something about it to like, right?

She seemed fidgety for the next ten minutes. Like she wanted to leave. I had a feeling she was going to split, maybe to rendezvous with the tall guy. It looked like her hubby was right. But who could blame her? She'd been without a man for a month. Some women can't handle that. She took one last sip of her drink, left the rest and a tip on the table, gathered her stuff and walked out. I gave her a thirty second head start, then followed after her.

When I came around the corner and looked into the parking lot I assumed my suspicions had been correct. She was standing at her car, lighting a cigarette. The tall man was walking towards her, a big smile on his face. I couldn't tell if this was an old relationship or a new one starting to blossom, but in a moment I realized my entire theory was wrong. The tall man put his hand on Delores' shoulder and leaned down to say something. What neither he nor I had noticed was that Delores had her right hand in her purse. He didn't see it happen, but I did – she brought her hand out of the purse and deftly shot him in the face with pepper spray.

He stumbled backwards and started yelling, "What the fuck!

You bitch! You fucking bitch!" and variations on that theme. She'd been a cool character when she sprayed him, but now she looked a little nervous. He charged forward, but he was blind, so she sidestepped him easily and he crashed into her car. She jumped away as he swung toward her, but he caught the shoulder of her rain coat in his hand. I crossed the distance between us in the parking lot without thinking. He was yanking her towards him and had raised his free hand in the air to slap her. But I went low and headbutted him in the stomach, slamming him back against her car again. He was shocked by the unexpected attack, but brought his knee up in reflex, catching me in the jaw. I saw some stars, then went to work on his lower body with some quick jabs, then an uppercut to his nuts that ended the squabble. He lifted into the air and landed on the hood of her car, trying to grab his nuts with one hand and his eyes with the other. He slowly rolled off the car onto the asphalt, moaning. There was a big ass dent where he had landed in the center of the hood.

I stood up fully and looked at Delores. My head was still swimming from the knee shot, but I could see that she had lost her hat in the ruckus and she was standing in the light of club's large marquee. It was the first time I really got a good look at her and boy was she gorgeous. She had long dark hair that had fallen loose during the struggle, full pouty lips, and sparkling green eyes (or were they blue? I couldn't be sure in that mixed light). She had high cheekbones and a soft round chin that kept her out of supermodel status but made her look human enough to approach.

She looked at me and said, "Thanks."

I wasn't sure how to react. I had blown my cover, but maybe I could salvage things and save my job.

"No problem," I said. "Is he your boyfriend?"

"Don't be ridiculous. I've never seen that guy in my life." She had a low, husky voice. I couldn't tell if it was an act of if she was born that way.

"What happened?"

"He approached me in the club. Made some inappropriate comments. I told him to scram. I thought he had, but he had messed up my vibe so I decided to go home. I didn't know he was out here waiting for me. But when I saw him coming toward me I decided I'd had enough of his nonsense."

"What did he say to you in the club?"

"I'd rather not repeat it."

"It was dirty stuff?"

"Filthy."

I walked to the front of the car where the guy was still laying and moaning. I put a knee on his chest and slapped his face a couple times to get his attention.

"You're a dirty little scumbag, aren't you? You like to attack women? She's half your size!"

"I didn't attack her! She attacked me!" He screamed it like a three year old would.

I looked up at her. She was watching us, a small grin on her face.

"You want to call the cops and have this guy arrested?" I asked.

"No. I just want to go home. I've had enough excitement for the night."

I stood up and looked at her car. "He dented the hell out of your hood. He's should pay for it."

"He already did. In humiliation. Besides, I have insurance."

"What about your deductible?"

"You have a point."

I kneeled down beside the guy's face. He was rubbing his eyes with both hands now, trying to clear them. His head was resting in a puddle of tears.

"The lady said she is willing to not have you arrested. But you need to cover the deductible on the insurance."

"Fuck you. Fuck you both!"

I grabbed his hair and slapped him on the side of the face again – twice – to help him clear his eyes. "I'd take her up on the offer. Otherwise I'll stay here with you and file my own report with the cops. I've got nothing better to do. You'll definitely end up in a cell tonight."

He started to reach under his jacket. I put a hand on his arm and controlled it as he brought out his wallet, just in case he had something else waiting under there. He dropped the wallet on the ground. I picked it up and opened it. The guy was loaded. He had twelve hundreds and a bunch of smaller bills.

"What's your deductible?"

"I think it's five hundred."

"You sure? It's usually more like a grand."

"Might be. I'd have to look."

"Forget about it. It's a grand."

I reached into the wallet, pulled out the bills, counted out ten of the hundreds, then dropped the wallet and the rest of the money on the guy's face.

"You're covered. Jerk. But I see you around this place any more and I'm going to take it personal."

I got up and the guy turned over onto his belly. He was still hurting all over.

Delores was standing by her car door now. She had picked her hat up off the ground and was putting it back on. I handed her the grand.

"I should give you at least half for your services."

"This was no heist. I'm just trying to make things right."

"You've done a fine job of it. Thank you."

"Are you okay to drive?"

"What?"

"Aren't you rattled? You were just attacked."

"No. I'm fine. But you can follow me home if you want - to make sure I drive properly."

"Why would I do that? I'm not a cop."

"Well, you've been following me ever since my husband left town. Why would you stop now?"

My face turned red. I couldn't help it. I was so busted. I was worried I had blown my cover, but there had been no cover to blow. She had been on to me from the start. Some private investigator I was.

"Okay. I'll follow you. Just to make sure you get home safely."

"Right."

We got in our cars and drove out of the parking lot, leaving the tall guy to consider the error of his ways underneath a BMW, where he had decided to rest. As I followed her my mind went to places that it shouldn't have. She knew she had been being followed from the start. And she didn't mind. If anything, she seemed to like it. She had a real twinkle in her eye when she exposed me. I was definitely feeling some chemistry there. And now she *wanted* me to follow her home. That sounded like an invitation. But what was her game? Had she been playing the good girl all along because she knew I was following her? Or had her husband told her I would be on the job from the start so she would behave? I was beginning to feel played. I just wasn't sure which one of them was playing me.

By the time I pulled up in front of her house her car was already parked in the driveway and she was opening her front door. She went in without even looking back at me. Any fantasies I might have had of being asked in for a drink immediately faded away. I watched the house for the next hour. Same routine as always. Dark windows as she got ready for bed, then blueish and gray shadows in her bedroom as she watched TV. Annoyed with the situation, I went home early. But I didn't sleep well.

I decided not to show up at her house for the next few days. I didn't know whether to discuss what had happened with my uncle or not, so I put that conversation on hold until I could get a read on what the scam might be. If there was one.

But I kept thinking about her. She had gotten into my head.

Finally I couldn't take it anymore. I went down to her house but her car was not in the driveway. I parked right across the street this time, not even trying to be subtle. It started to rain and I fell asleep. When I woke up her car was in the driveway. I checked my phone. It was after 3am. I'd been out for hours. The TV was on in her bedroom but I could see no movement behind the drapes. The rain was still coming down. We were having a rare series of storms, the Pineapple Express is what they called it, but no matter how much rain came down, a few days later they would still be telling us we were in a drought. You could flood this place and it would never drink enough to be well. It was a desert! Why did they think they could plant 12 million thirsty people on it?

The rain made me drowsy again and soon I drifted off to sleep. I was awakened by rapping on my window. I jumped like a bunny, thinking the cops were rousting me. But it was her. She was standing in the rain, an umbrella keeping her from getting soaked. I turned on my car and considered speeding away, but instead I lowered my window.

"Why are you being stupid?" she said to me.

"Huh?"

"Why are you sitting out here in the rain?"

"It's my job."

"Why don't you come in? I'll make you some tea. Or coffee. Whatever."

"I don't think that's a good idea."

"Sure it is. And don't tell me you haven't been wanting to come inside for a long time now. I saw how you looked at me in that parking lot."

Damn. She had me figured. She was ahead of me every step of the way. I gave up. Turned the car off and followed her inside.

"Take off your shoes," she said after we were on the other side of the door.

We both took off our wet shoes. She was wearing that raincoat of hers. It had finally rained! She kept it on and led me into the kitchen.

"Coffee or tea?"

"Coffee."

"Mind if it's reheated? I still have half a pot from this afternoon."

"No problem."

She nuked us both cups of coffee and we sat in the kitchen, drinking them black.

"Don't you want to take off your raincoat?"

"It's not just a raincoat. It's a trench coat. Feel it."

She stuck out her arm and I felt the grey material. It was soft.

"Raincoats are made out of waterproof material. This was made for warmth and comfort. It's a trench coat. There's a difference."

"Okay. Don't you want to take off your trench coat?"

"Can't. Got nothing on under it."

"Oh." I took a sip of coffee. Tried not to spill it.

"I like your voice," she said. "It sounds like you've been up all night drinking whisky and smoking cigarettes."

"I don't smoke. That's for suckers."

She smiled. "I smoke."

"I know."

"So you're a private eye? A real private eye?"

"I'm a private investigator."

"That's what the "eye" stands for."

"Oh. But we don't call ourselves that. That for old movies."

"I like old movies."

"I know."

"Have you been peeping into my window at night?"

"No. But I can see the light from your TV. It's almost never in color."

"You have no idea how much this whole thing excites me. A private eye following me at night. It's like a girl's dream come true."

"That would make you a pretty strange girl."

"I'm old fashioned. I like the old things. I'm not much interested in the way things are today. All this technology. There's no more romance any more."

"I follow your thinking there."

"I wish I was born in the twenties. I would have loved to be young in the forties."

"You'd be pretty old now. Or you'd be dead."

"But I would have lived. *Really* lived. How great would it have been to live through the forties and the fifties and the sixties? Those were exciting times. Face it. We were born in lame times."

"I don't know. I think life is what you make of it."

"That's because you're an animal. You'd be fine no matter when you were born. You'd have been fine as a gladiator."

I smiled. "Yeah. That would have been fun."

She finished her cup of coffee, then took mine while I was in mid sip, put them both in the sink, then took me by the hand and said, "Let's go."

She led me into the bedroom. It was dark in there except for the TV, which was on mute. One of those old gangster movies was playing. Bunch of guys in suits shooting it out.

She turned to me and opened the trench coat. She was right. She wasn't wearing anything underneath. Hell, she was right about everything. I'd never seen anything so right in my life.

She dropped the coat on the floor and stood there, waiting for me to make the next move. The blue light of the TV played over the curves of her body. She wasn't one of those skinny girls I'd been dating lately who looked like they only ate one meal a day. But nobody would mistake her for an aerobics instructor either. She was full bodied. Firm, but not lean. Not muscular. She had a body as old fashioned as her taste in movies, music and books. Big breasts, big hips. A natural beauty, not a calculated one.

I took her in my arms and kissed her. She gasped and I felt a jolt go through her body, like she was being attacked. I stopped and looked at her.

"I thought..."

"It's okay. I just haven't been touched by anyone in a long time. Not even by my husband. I forgot what it felt like."

"You and Milo?"

"Not for over a year."

"His mistake."

I kissed her again. This time she met me halfway. Soon we were off our feet and into the sky. We did everything we could think of and then a little bit more. She was the hungriest woman I had ever met. And that made me hungry too. I know there are chemicals that run our bodies and brains and they make us feel things like "love" and "passion," so a person should always take that kind of thing with a grain of salt. That stuff wears off after awhile and if you take it too serious it just makes things complicated. I was fully aware of the tricks that were running the show, but it didn't make a difference. Whatever those chemicals were in both of us they combined and turned into dynamite that first night. We were just one long explosion for the next few hours, wrapped so tightly around and inside each other we had no idea where I ended and she began. It was *intense*.

By the time we came up for air, the sun was on the rise. We lay still on the bed for a long time before she spoke.

"Do you like what you do?" she asked.

"Sometimes. It's fun to catch cheaters in the act."

"What about us? We're cheaters now, too."

"I look at this as a moral failure. I blame my parents. They didn't raise me right."

She laughed.

"I knew you were a bad pony the moment I set eyes on you."

She stopped laughing and looked serious.

"I'm not bad. Not usually. I've never done this before."

"Really?"

"Really."

"Then why did Milo want you followed?"

"I have no idea. I don't think he ever did that before. If so I never knew about it."

"I must be pretty bad at my job if you spotted me right away."

"You stand out in a jazz club."

"How's that?"

"You spent more time watching me than watching the players."

I looked at her beautiful body glistening with sweat in the dawning light. "You're a lot more interesting to look at."

And then it began again. It was noon by the time we stopped. I was tired. But it was the *gooood* kind of tired.

***

We began a bit of a routine, if you can call it that. We kept playing our parts, in public. It excited her. I would follow her to a club at night. We would never talk to each other there. I would follow her home. I would wait in my car for an undetermined period of time, then I would slip into the house and we would make love like horny teenagers. We would never know exactly when it would happen. The suspense drove us both wild. She loved being followed. She said it made her feel like she was in one of those old movies she watched all the time. I started watching them too, when we would rest. They were pretty good. Those people definitely had style back then. And it was usually pretty easy to tell the good guys from the bad guys. It was as simple as, well, black and white. I could see what she liked about them.

We only talked about her husband once more. She said he was a very jealous man. His work took him to far off places for long periods of time so his paranoia had been growing as the years went on. And his paranoia had begun to manifest into hostility towards her. One that extended into the bedroom. He wasn't sure if he was mad at her or bored with her, but he no longer made sexual advances. He didn't want her, but he didn't want anyone else to have her either. She had considered leaving him, but never had the guts. And she couldn't imagine starting over again. Even with me. She said she'd rather play out the string. Live out her days in a world of fantasy, because nothing, even what we had going, could live up to the world she had built for herself in her mind. I wasn't sure I understood everything she said, but I knew she lived in a lonely place. Even when I was with her.

I usually tried to leave before daybreak so the neighbors wouldn't notice. One morning around five a.m. I went out to my car, only to find my uncle leaning against it.

"Kind of following a little close, don't you think?" he said, shaking his head.

"What the hell are you doing here?"

"Your reports started sounding like bullshit, so I thought I should check up on you."

"That's fucked up."

"Really? You're going to play the injured party? You know we take money from her husband, who happens to be a friend of mine, while you are in there banging her, right? That's what's fucked up."

"Okay. I admit it. It's a bad situation."

"Yeah? Well, it's about to get worse. Milo is coming back to town."

I stared at him as he walked toward his car. He turned and looked at me as he opened his door. "End this shit. Now. Or don't come back to the office. Ever."

***

I didn't sleep the rest of the day. I was between insurance investigations. I had not been given a case in two weeks and now I knew why. My uncle knew I had compromised the company and he was deciding my fate. He didn't want to get me tied up on anything if he was going to fire me. How long had he known? But I had the feeling the visit was more about warning me that Milo was going to return than scolding me for my indiscretion. After all, we were family. Milo was just his friend.

I was sitting on my deck, watching the sun set over L.A. when she called me.

"He's home."

"I heard."

"Even worse. He says they've offered him a permanent position in Dubai. We're moving there."

"When?"

"Immediately."

"What?"

"We're leaving in two days. He just came back here to get some of his things and tell me to pack a couple bags. The movers will be shipping the rest. He's selling the house!"

"Where are you?"

"I'm at home."

"Where is he?"

"In the shower. Wait... He just finished. I've got to go."

"Hold on... " But she had hung up.

Later that night I drove by the house. The lights were all off, but her car was in the driveway. He had two vintage rides in the garage, a '67 Mustang and a '70 Challenger, so she could never park in there. I wondered if he was going to ship those cars to Dubai along with my lover. I returned later that night and sat across the street for awhile, hoping to get some hint of what was going on inside. But there was nothing. Not even light from the TV.

I spent the next two days freaking out. I had never let a woman get to me like this one had. Not since I was a kid at least. I didn't want to lose her now. But she wasn't mine, was she? *I* was the interloper. The intruder. I thought she would call but she didn't. Either she couldn't or she didn't want to. I had no way of knowing.

I tried to think of a course of action that would bring us happiness without creating chaos. I couldn't come up with a thing. So I decided to charge forward and let the chaos begin. I would find her. I would tell her to leave him. I would take her from him and she would be mine. And if Milo tried to stop us I would break him in half.

I went to her house. Her car was not in the driveway. I stayed in front of the place all day and through the night into the next morning, but the car never returned. I tried her number, but it was disconnected. She was gone.

***

As the months rolled on the intense feelings I had for her slowly faded and things returned to normal. Our time together began to seem like some kind of mysterious dream. My uncle forgave me – or at least he said he did. But I knew our trust had been broken. I worked, but not as often as I used to. He gave me only the simplest of jobs. And they never involved beautiful women. Even ones who had "slipped and fallen" in the grocery store.

I found I had developed a taste for jazz and old movies though. I started watching Turner Classics late at night and downloaded a bunch of jazz to listen to while on observation. I even dropped into the clubs once in awhile to see one of the acts. And maybe hope to find her there one night as well, sitting in the dark in her trench coat and fedora, sipping a cocktail, tapping her foot to the beat.

One day, about six months after she left, I found a package next to my front door. A medium sized box covered with international stickers. It took me a moment to realize that it was from Dubai. I opened it without even going into the house. In it I found a fedora, just like hers. I smiled. She hadn't forgotten me. She had sent me a gift. I took it into the house, dropped the box on the floor and put on the hat. I looked at myself in the living room mirror and realized it was too small for me. I looked ridiculous in it. But then I thought about it and began to get nervous.

I picked the box up and looked inside. There was a note there that I had missed. It read: "Thought you might want this hat as a trophy. Delores won't be needing it anymore."

I took off the fedora and looked at it more closely. It wasn't a gift she had bought for me. It was *her* fedora. And Milo had sent it to me. He *knew*. I saw a dried, crusty substance on the back of the fedora. I wet my fingers and drew some of it from the lining of the hat. As I rubbed it between my fingers they turned dark red.

I looked at myself in the mirror again, standing there, holding the fedora. And a fool looked back.

Fifty Shades of Grey Fedora

ON THE JOB
by Dick Lochte

Officer Angie O'Connell got her first good look at the man known as Reynolds Fowler when he left the Windsor Court Hotel at approximately eight pm that night. Tall, sandy colored hair, moved well. Handsome? She supposed you'd have to say handsome. Not exactly Brad Pitt, but a strong, intelligent face with an easy smile that he wasted on the uniformed doorman. She watched him carefully as he waved away a cab and began walking across Canal Street, heading toward the French Quarter.

"How you wanna work it?" Eddie Mac asked, starting up the unmarked vehicle. He was born and bred in Bootee, Louisiana, and had a Cajun accent you couldn't cut with a Bowie knife. His full name was Officer Edward Jamie Macaluso, but he liked to be called Eddie Mac. Not Eddie or Mac. Eddie Mac.

"He leads, we follow," Angie said.

Eddie Mac's jaws stopped working on a wad of Big Red for a moment while he asked, "You sure you up for this?"

"I'm sure," she lied.

Commander Harlan Keresan, the chief of their Investigations Division, had given them the guy's photograph, his name and a little, damn little, of his history. Just that he was "an out-of-state Fed come to Nola on some big fucking secret investigation, one we're certain involves the NOPD." Angie, backed up by Eddie Mac, was supposed to, as the commander ordered, "get close" to the Fed to find out what she could and then "do whatever necessary to, ah, get him in a position that will discredit him. Then he'll be our boy." Eddie Mac was given a camera. And several foil packets of heroin from the evidence locker, "to put the icing on the cake."

Fowler moved past the other tourists and nighttime strollers at a fast clip, then paused at the corner of Canal and Royal. He turned down Royal, checking out the action. He cruised past an oyster bar, an antiques shop with windows crusted with street grime, a vacant storefront, a tinny Dixieland dive where, only a few months ago, Angie and her original partner, Joe Charbonnet, had collared a vicious pimp with the colorful name of Vermillion Cabriolet.

The Fed paused by a strip joint run by Remy Ragusa, the acting head of Louisiana's first family of crime, the Benedettos. He spent a minute or so grinning at the nearly naked blonde positioned just past the front door as a lure.

"The *federale*'s got his horns up," Eddie Mac said. "This gonna be a snap, cher'."

"Isn't it always?" Angie said, watching Fowler stroll into the heart of the French Quarter.

Eddie Mac followed him to the sawhorses that limited Royal to foot traffic, uttered a little grunt of annoyance and worked the car into a semi legal parking spot on Bienville. He was about to get out when Angie said, "Sit tight. He's perched."

She told him she'd seen Fowler enter a club on Royal. Satchmo's Joint.

"Wal' now, Miz Angela," Eddie Mac said, trying to remember why he'd once arrested the young, incredibly skinny barker in front of Satchmo's, "what you want me to do, eh?"

"Lose that gum you're chewing. The smell of it makes me want to puke."

Eddie chuckled. "Nervous, huh, cher'?"

She didn't answer. Nervous? Hell, yes, nervous. Less than six months on Vice, and now, with the whole department under investigation, she finally gets her first major assignment and it's this weird, sleazy deal.

"We could switch places, cher'," Eddie Mac told her. "On'y I doan suppose he be mah type."

Asshole, she thought, but kept it to herself. She didn't want to piss him off. After Joe Charbonnet died, Eddie Mac had been the only one willing to team up with her. A few of the others had blamed her for Joe's death. It didn't matter the bastard had been off duty, shacked up with some bimbo in a Bucktown motel when he got shot. They figured Angie should have been there to cover his ass from the still-unknown shooter. Her other brothers in blue simply had no use for women in uniform. She suspected the only reason Eddie Mac had agreed to the partnership was that he wanted to get into her pants. But he was too much of a romantic to make a heavy move. Compared to the other guys in Vice, Eddie Mac was a regular white knight.

"You goin' in, or what?" he asked.

"Give him time to get settled, order a drink," she said.

"Give'm too much time, he gonna fine hisself another playmate." Eddie looked at her and grinned again. "Second thought, it don't matter if he do. One look at you, cher', an' she's gone, gone, gone like the gypsy."

"Thanks," she said, successfully keeping the sarcasm out of her voice.

"You gonna do okay, Angela," he said, letting his hand drop casually to her knee. "Not on'y one fine lookin' woman, you know how to handle yo'self on the job."

"You ever get an assignment like this before?" she asked, fighting the revulsion she was feeling from the intimacy of his hand, pretending her knee was made of wood.

"Naw. Closest I come was bein' ordered to get some totally innocent nigra gen'man to confess to peddlin' drugs, jus' to pad the arrest sheet." His hand began to rub her knee, friendly like. "The one thing you gotta remember, cher', long as you obey orders, ever'thing's copacetic."

She shifted away from him and grabbed the door handle. "Magic time," she said.

"I be close by," he said. "But I surely do wish you was wearin' a wire, 'stead a that little gran'ma recorder."

She stared at him and instead of saying anything just shook her head. They'd gone over the subject several times. A wire didn't make much sense in a situation where she would probably be removing her clothes. That was the reason she'd given. But, in fact, she could have wired up her purse. But she chose to use a recorder. That way she'd be in control. With a wire, there was no telling who might be out there in the electronic universe listening in or, more to the point, what use they'd make of what they heard. The recorder gave her more flexibility. She could turn it on or off. She could erase any or all of its contents.

"How will I know when to come in?" he asked.

"I'll draw the blinds," she said.

"You carryin', right?"

"I'm gonna be in a hotel room with this unknown. What do you think?"

She got out of the car, smoothed down her short dress over her thighs and then squeezed her purse to reassure herself that the gun was there. Along with three packets of heroin.

Here goes nothing, she told herself.

She'd been in Satchmo's once before, back when she was a rookie, dragged there by a big blonde girl named Lou Anne who was happy to have another sistuh in blue to commiserate with. Lou Anne was now pregnant and about to lose her desk job at First Division on Rampart Street. The club's walls were still decorated with blow up snapshots of the city's own Louis Armstrong — singing with Crosby, singing with Sinatra, shaking hands with the Queen of England, singing with Ella and singing by himself, eyes closed in seeming rapture, his fist clasping both trumpet and white handkerchief.

The furniture looked the same — chrome and leather and polished wood. But the clientele had changed. It was still a meat market operation, only the meat was a bit more on the premium side. The post college guys, like that Tulane med school student she'd met—¬what the hell was his name? what the hell did it matter? — had been replaced by businessmen wearing Boss and Armani. Like Fowler. The post college girls had given way to expensively dressed, handsome women who were there working. Like her.

From the loudspeakers, Armstrong's great gravelly voice was making the musical suggestion that the crowd do it, like the birds and the bees and the educated fleas. Judging by the look of things, the customers didn't need much encouragement. Fowler was sitting at the center of the bar, chatting with a redhead. She was attractive enough, Angie thought, if you overlooked the ersatz mahogany color of her hair, the crow's feet hidden under a mound of makeup and the football sized breasts that would drop to her lap when she unstrapped.

There was an empty stool on the other side of the redhead and Angie slipped onto it. A bright eyed bartender who wore a diamond in his nose drifted over to her and cocked his head as if he were listening to distant silver bells. Angie wanted a beer, but ordered a Sapphire martini. The bartender nodded as if he approved. She assumed he would have given her the same nod if she'd asked for Scotch and Pepsi.

Even before the martini arrived, she was approached by an overweight man flaunting a diamond ring on his pinkie. She dismissed him with, "Actually, I'm waiting for a guy with only one chin."

Two more followed. The one who smelled of some musky cologne she asked if he'd mind standing somewhere else, "preferably downwind?" The third, who rather reminded her of the med student, she got rid of by saying she didn't like men. At the moment, it was the truth. Of course, she didn't like women either.

Louis was now singing a soft rendition of "Willow Weep For Me," allowing her to eavesdrop as the redhead told Fowler about her last trip to Acapulco, during which she'd decided that Mexico was for peasants, really. She didn't hear Fowler's reply, but the redhead did a little backpedaling with, "Well, o'course 'at's true. An' theah's quite a lot about th' cultcha an' the people that is praiseworthy. I imagine a lot of mah unhappiness had to do with the fact that I was not egg'zackly compatible with mah travelin' companion." The redhead chuckled. "He was all talk an' no ack-shun."

Angie rolled her eyes. She didn't hear what Fowler replied, but it prompted the redhead to say, "Well, y' know what they say about us gals with red haih. Flame on top an' fire down below."

Jesus, Angie thought, she's going to be copping his joint in a minute. Where the hell was Eddie Mac?

Then she saw him, strolling through the room in his rumpled sports coat and baggy trousers, as full of himself as if he was parading down a runway at Saks.' Angie waited while the Cajun cop flirted with a table full of Ninth Ward princesses who were responding in kind. When, finally, he looked in her general direction, he saw the redhead and his narrow face broke into a grin.

He elbowed his way through the crowd near the bar and stopped behind the redhead's chair. She'd been extolling her expertise as a masseuse and was in the middle of a yarn involving her special warm love oil when she spotted Eddie Mac's reflection in the mirror behind the bar. She tensed and forgot the point she was making about the love oil.

"Hi, Ruby," Eddie Mac said to the redhead. "Sorry I be so late, but I got stuck at the office."

He leaned down to kiss the redhead's left cheek. Angie heard him whisper, "Let's us get outta heah, right now."

"Aw, c'mon, Eddie Mac. Ah like it heah."

He lowered his voice so that even Angie couldn't hear and whatever he said got the redhead's full attention. She made a fast pivot on her stool toward Fowler and patted his hand. "Sorry, honey, but my... brutha reminded me ah'm supposed to be at a family dinnah ta-night."

Fowler took the news like a champ. Eddie Mac rubbed it in a little, giving him a patronizing pat on the shoulder and thanking him for taking care of his "big sis."

The Cajun cop hustled Ruby out of the club, leaving Angie with the task of gracefully breaking the ice with Fowler. She wasn't very good at small talk and was working on an opener when he said, "I met him once, when I was about your age."

He was staring past her to a far corner of the room. "I'm sorry," she said. "Are you talking to me?"

He shifted his eyes and looked at her. "I've been wanting to since you walked in," he said. "Hope you don't mind."

"I don't. But I didn't get what you were saying."

"Oh. Of course not." She couldn't tell in the dim light if his eyes were green or blue. "I was talking about the guy with Louie Armstrong in that poster." He pointed to the photo of Louie and Frank Sinatra. "I met him when I was still in my twenties."

"Are you in show business?" she asked.

He smiled wistfully. "Sad to say, no."

"But you met Sinatra."

"Yep. I was —" He was interrupted by a dark woman with aqua eye shadow who moved between them claiming the stool vacated by the redhead.

"Would you mind if we switched?" Fowler asked her. "The lady and I were talking."

The dark woman gave Angie a cursory appraisal, shrugged, and exchanged stools with Fowler, who instructed the bartender to put the woman's drink on his tab.

"Would you like a fresh one of those?" he asked, pointing to Angie's half empty martini glass.

She knew that the answer should have been no, but she said, "Only if you promise to tell me the story about you and Sinatra."

"I shouldn't have made such a big deal of it," he said. "I was at this party in D.C. He was walking across this huge ballroom and I interrupted him and introduced myself and started asking him question after question about his movies and his years recording with Nelson Riddle. We talked for a couple of minutes and then he said, 'Excuse me, pally, I'll love to stand here reminiscing with you, but I'm not as young as I once was and if I don't hit the *liquorino* in about sixty seconds I'll be pissing all over the both of us.'

"And that's my Frank Sinatra story."

She smiled. "That's some brush with fame," she said.

"I guess it would be better if he'd pissed on me."

She took a sip of her martini and asked, "Are you from D.C.?"

"No. I worked there for a while and may be going back." It amused her to realize that it might be up to her whether he went back or not. "What about you?" he asked. "I don't hear much of a New Orleans accent."

"It's there," she said. "I think it's gone, but after a martini or two, it comes back full force. Born and bred in Nola."

The waiter arrived with another round and Fowler watched her finish her first drink. "My name's Reynolds, by the way," he said. "Reynolds Fowler."

"Reynolds seems a little formal for the occasion," she said.

"My friends call me Ren. What do your friends call you?"

"Angie," she said. No reason to lie about that.

"Well, Angie, this is a very interesting city you have here."

"You wouldn't be with a convention, would you, Ren?"

"Nope. Just a little business trip."

"What do you do?" she asked.

He hesitated. "It's not the most popular of professions," he said.

"You're a lawyer."

He grinned. "Actually, I am. But I don't practice. And what I do is a little lower on the scale than even a lawyer."

"Car salesman, garbage man, club D.J.? Am I getting warm?"

"I, ah, work for the government," he said, his remarkably expressive face resembling a little boy's who'd been caught eating candy before supper. She was so intrigued by the ease with which he shifted his appearance that she forgot to reply.

"Well, hell," he said, responding to her silence. "Another beautiful friendship bites the dust. It's a lousy job, I know, but somebody's got to do it."

"I'm sorry," she said, vowing not to touch the martini in front of her. "I just sort of drifted off."

"It's the effect I have on some people."

"What sort of government work?"

"Smoothing out the rough edges."

"Now you're being mysterious."

"Not at all. I'm kind of a behind the scenes guy. Get stuff done."

"Give me an example."

He grinned. "Later, maybe. We'll see."

So we will, she thought, and wished that he'd lie to her just a little or do something that would make her feel better about her assignment. Before she realized it, she was sipping from her drink.

She turned and saw that he was looking at her intently, forehead furrowed in a strangely familiar way. It was as if her late partner Joe Charbonnet were seated beside her. But only for a heartbeat. She shook her head, chasing the image away.

"What?" Ren Fowler asked, relaxing.

"You reminded me of someone."

"Somebody worth remembering or somebody you'd rather forget."

"Both, I guess." The smile on her face felt forced. She reached for her martini and was surprised to see that the glass was empty.

Ren signaled to the bartender, but she shook her head. "No, no more, thank you."

"Then what about dinner, Angie? I hear this place Emeril's is pretty good."

"I'd love that," she replied. Too eagerly?

Ren didn't seem to think so. He began settling with the bartender. Armstrong and Ella Fitzgerald were singing "A Fine Romance."

Admiring the clean line of Ren's profile, she realized she was losing control of the situation. She could count on the fingers of one hand the times she'd wanted to forget everything else and just fuck a guy's brains out. More to the point, let him fuck her brains out. But this would not happen when she was on the job.

She'd get it together.

As they crossed Canal Street, she took a quick glance back and saw Eddie Mac in the traffic jumble behind them. She wasn't sure if she felt relieved or annoyed.

In the restaurant, famous for its home grown menu, they ordered. Later, she couldn't remember exactly what they'd talked about through most of dinner. But, as he poured the last of the white wine into her glass, she brought up the subject of his marital status. It was something she was supposed to have asked, anyway, but it had taken on a personal importance.

"I'm married," he said. "But neither of us works at it."

"Meaning?"

"From time to time, I enjoy the company of other ladies. My wife Emily has her male friends."

"Very modern." Her purse was beside her on the chair and she could feel the vibration of the minicorder against her thigh. "And no... problems?"

He thought about it. "No jealousy, if that's what you mean," he said. "We don't discuss our private affairs. And we don't flaunt them. Discretion is key."

Angie waved her hand through the air. "Having dinner in one of New Orleans' busiest restaurants, this is your idea of discrete?"

His face broke into a gentle smile. "There's no reason for discretion. Unless... you're suggesting we're about to have an affair."

Damnit. He'd nailed her. She felt like a fool. She wondered if her stupid comment would be evidence of entrapment. She'd erase the tape, even though there was no chance Ren could get his hands on it. At least it hadn't gone out over a wire.

"What about you, Angie?" Ren asked. "A husband? Boyfriends?"

She shook her head.

"Hard to believe, a woman as lovely as you with no men in her life."

No men? Maybe he'd like to hear about her father, the beloved Sergeant Matthew O'Donnell, the pride of the NOPD, who'd come home after her mother was sound asleep and slip into her little girl's bed to let her play with his nightstick. Or she could tell Ren about Joe Charbonnet and the promises he made when they were screwing at the Mardi Gras Motel which is where, she found out later, he took all his dumb little punchboards. "Hard to believe," she said. "But true."

The waiter arrived with a silver pot of steaming coffee and two small demitasse cups. The demitasse, or half cup of pungent black coffee, was supposed to provide a sobering finish to a meal. But New Orleans has its own spin on that tradition and the waiter's tray also contained two shot glasses brim filled with bourbon that he proceeded to pour into their little cups, filling the remaining inch or so with coffee.

Angie knew the power of alcohol. Saw the effect it had had on her father, transforming him into a child molester and wife beater. "Curse of the Irish," her mother had proclaimed. Judging by her own experiences, it was indeed a curse. But, thanks to gin and wine, she was already on the downward side of that slippery slope. And she shot her demitasse in a single gulp.

"Well, Angie," Ren asked as she put down the cup. "What shall we do now?"

Making it her choice. More taped evidence of entrapment. The hell with entrapment. And the hell with the goddamn department and its swinging dick mentality. The hell with everything but the warm tingle in her loins and the look of need on Ren Fowler's handsome face. She kept her eyes locked on his as she sneaked her hand into her purse and clicked off the recorder. "Here's how it is, Ren," she said. "Unless we leave right now, I might jus' do somethin' that's about as far from discrete as you can get."

As they walked down Carondelet, looking for a cab, she grabbed his hand and clutched it to her chest, rubbing his knuckles against her right breast. He turned slightly and drew her body to his. He was aroused and he let her know it, pressing into her while working his tongue into her mouth.

That familiar warmth spread through her body. It had been a while. A long while. She heard her daddy moaning, "Oh, my baby, yes." Heard Joe Charbonnet growling, "Work it, you little bitch." Heard the med student – she suddenly recalled his name was Roger – heard him weeping, then cursing her after she'd told him it wouldn't be happening again.

Ren Fowler's voice drowned out the others as he whispered all the things he wanted to do with her. Feeling about to burst with passion she opened her eyes and saw, past Ren's lowered shoulder, Eddie Mac parked across the street.

She pulled back from Ren and tried to regain some control of her body. Ren smiled at her and waved to a passing cab.

On the short drive to his hotel, she tried to think, tried to figure out what the hell she was doing. Was there some way this would work out? Wasn't this precisely what the bastards wanted to have happen? But what about afterwards? She saw Ren leaning back against the seat, blessing her with that lovely hungry look. She fell upon him, her hands reaching under his coat, almost shaking as they outlined his trim body while her tongue explored the inside of his mouth.

"Sorry to interrupt, but we is here, folks," the cab driver said. "Winza Coart."

He reached back and opened the door for Ren who shoved several bills into his hand.

As Angie let Ren help her from the cab, she saw Eddie Mac park down the block. She turned to Ren and said, "I can't go in with you right now."

He looked confused and maybe a shade angry. "Why not?" he asked.

"Something I have to do first."

"Don't worry," he answered, "I have everything we'll need."

"It's not that. Gimme half an hour. I'll be theah. I sweah ta Gawd." She was annoyed with herself for reverting to the Irish Channel accent she'd grown up with. A sure sign she was drunk or out of control. Both, actually.

"I'll come with you."

"No. Please. Just a half hour. Then we'll have all the time we need."

His look of apprehension melted away. He took her hand and brought it to his lips, kissed it lightly. "I'll be waiting," he said. "Suite 1104."

He watched her walk from the hotel's courtyard, then turn down Gravier. She made it to the end of the block before Eddie Mac pulled in to the curb beside her. "Wha's goin' on, Angie?" he asked as she got in.

"Nothin' goin' on," she replied. "He wasn't in the market. Drop me off at my car."

"Sure as hell looked like he was not only in the market, he was buyin' the place out. He was lickin' yo' tonsils, cher'." He stared at her. "You not doin' somethin' get us both fucked up?"

"What're you talkin' about?"

"You know this guy is here to mess with the department. It be him or us. You unnerstan,' right?"

"No," she said sarcastically, "Ah'm jus' a dumb little girl from Magazine Street."

"You drunk, cher'? You startin' to sound like mah sistuh."

"Fuck you, Eddie Mac."

"No reason gettin' riled, Angie."

"It's a shitty assignment," she said.

He nodded. 'It's like they say 'bout livin' by the sword. This Fowler guy, he makes his bread by puttin' people in the soup. So we puttin' him in the soup."

"It stinks."

"Hell, yeah. Stinks like sewer gas and you jus' has to hole yo' nose 'til you past it." He turned his head from the road. "You get anythin' on yo' tape machine?"

"Nothing worth tapin'."

He frowned but said nothing.

He saw her red Mustang, which she'd left not far from City Hall, under the Broad Street overpass. He parked right behind the Mustang. The thrumming of the nighttime traffic overhead was so loud she almost didn't hear him say, "Know what I think?"

She had the car door open. "No. And I don't care."

"I think if I go back to that hotel in about an hour, let myself in with this key they give us to room 1104, I'm gonna get myself a fine clear snapshot of you and Fowler makin' like bunnies. Just like the doctor ordered."

Angie stared at him for a few moments, then sat down again beside him. "Don't do that," she said.

"Bullshit, girl. You know what we gotta do."

"Just this once. Just this goddamn once, Eddie Mac, forget the job. Go home, have a pizza and a brew and tomorrow we can hash this whole thing out. Like partners."

"Not gonna happen, Angie," he said with as much seriousness as he'd ever spoken. "Eddie Mac does egg-zakly what he is told to do.

You go back theah and when I enter that room in about an hour, you bettah have his dick in yoah hand or yoah mouth – your choice -- an' heroin in plain view somewhere in the frame."

She glanced up and down the deserted street. She opened her purse. "Maybe you better listen to the tape first."

When her hand came out of the purse, her police special was in it, aimed at him.

"Shit!" Eddie Mac said, gawking at the gun. "Honey, you doan wanna use that thing on Eddie Mac."

"No. Not this thing." She dropped the purse and, keeping her gun on him, bent and reached under the seat for the throwdown piece he kept there. He was a few seconds slow to react when she raised the throwdown. As he leaned forward to grab it, she shot him in the face. Then, when he'd been blown back against his door, looking like the mystery guest in a splatter flick, she shot him twice more in the chest.

She used her skirt to wipe her prints from the throwdown and tossed the weapon onto Eddie Mac's bloody chest. The overpass traffic would have muffed the gunshots and the area had remained unpopulated. Without hesitation, she reached into her purse and took out the little heroin packets. She unwrapped one and placed it open on her dead partner's chest.

She exchanged her gun for her cell phone and snapped several photos of the heroin and Eddie Mac looking very much like a cop who'd been on the bad end of a drug deal gone south. Should the commander clean things up, trying to tag her for the crime, she'd send the photos to the media.

She gathered the phone and the purse and moved gingerly to her car. She was certain she was still alone in the area, but she rushed to get away. She didn't want to be late for Ren.

She could blame some of the shooting on drink, she told herself as she drove to the hotel. She still wasn't what you'd call sober. But when she'd pulled the trigger, she knew what she was doing. She'd had that uncomfortable, itchy feeling that had pushed her the other times. The first had been the night after her mother's funeral, when she got up from her father's bed to clean herself and to make him a special cocktail, his last, which she made of Jack Daniels and all the pills mom had no more use for. The second time was the night she followed Joe Charbonnet to the Mardi Gras Motel.

A chill coursed through her body — a rabbit jumping over her grave. She shook it off. None of that mattered. Ren Fowler was waiting for her. Everything was... fine.

Still, as she stood at the door to suite 1104, she was afraid to push the button, afraid that she'd created some boozy fantasy that would turn to shit as soon as the door opened.

Then Ren opened it. He stood there with a grin on his strong, handsome face. He'd taken off his coat, tie and his shoes. He looked perfect. Relaxed and yet turned-on.

"I was about to come looking for you," he said. "Your thirty minutes are up."

She rushed into his arms. They kissed. He lifted her and carried her across the carpeted room, placed her gently on the down bed. Her purse slipped from her fingers and rolled off the bed onto the floor with a clunk. They both looked down. It hadn't opened. He reached over her to pick up the purse, but she wrapped her arms around him and pulled him close.

He kissed her hard. But when she began, with shaking hands, to fumble with the buttons on his shirt, he drew back. "Slowly," he said. "We'll do this slowly."

"Could we turn off the light?" she asked.

"No," he said. "I want to see every beautiful inch of you." He unhooked her dress, slid it down, then undid the bra. He kissed her exposed breasts, nibbled at their hardening tips. She groaned and tore at his shirt, then fumbled at his belt and zipper.

"Slowly," he repeated, moving off of her. He slid away her dress, then her frilly bikini briefs. He began kissing her stomach. His right hand moved up her inner thigh, but she stopped him.

"Lie back," she demanded in a voice hoarse with emotion.

When he did, she helped him shed his pants and shorts. She studied his extended penis, caressed it, then trailed her fingertips over his body.

"Let me get a con –" he began. She silenced him with her hand pressing against his lips.

"We don't need that," she said, and moved atop him, licking at his face, his eyelids, finally plunging her tongue into his mouth.

To her delight, she discovered he was not a passive lover. While he held the kiss, his hands began their work, feeling the right places on her body, fondling, pressing here and there until he found a spot that caused her to shutter in pleasure, then concentrated on that spot. When she reached the point where she might scream from wanting him, she straddled him and took him inside her.

She preferred the on top position. The relatively few men she'd slept with hadn't seemed to mind. They'd lay back and let her do most of the work. She liked being in control. It had been her experience that the male, once he'd come, would lose most of his enthusiasm, not to mention his erection. She enjoyed bringing them close, then slipping away, keeping them active as long as she could without risking a slap or a punch.

Ren wasn't like that at all. Far from just lying there, he was meeting her more than half-way. Her father had given her a comic book when she was thirteen, a science fiction story about a sexy space girl who kept getting laid on other planets. On Mars, a crazy Martian professor forced her to fuck a robot he's programmed for that purpose and she fell in love. Ren was her robot, always in motion, making all the right moves, bucking, shifting positions, finding the sweet spot and pushing it, over and over.

She had no idea how long they'd made love, nor how many times she'd come, just that each time had been like going from ground zero into somewhere in outer space. She knew it had been good for him, too. Hopefully good enough for him to want more. Wherever he lived or was sent by the bureau, she'd follow. But she had to be as honest with him as he'd been with her. Had to warn him.

They were lying side-by-side in the softly-lit room, the air conditioner tickling their drying skin. She said, "Ren... there's something I have to tell you."

He was silent, staring at her, waiting.

"We didn't just happen to meet tonight," she began. She told him about the plan to disgrace him, maybe even to send him to prison unless he cooperated with Commander Keresan.

When she'd finished, he said, "That was an interesting idea. The bureau wouldn't do much to help an agent dumb enough to wind up in a photo like that. Except the photo wasn't taken, right? I mean, I was a little distracted."

"No," she said. "It didn't happen. That's why I needed the half hour. I had to tell Ed —my partner that it didn't work out between us, that you weren't interested."

"So as far as he knows, you both did everything you were ordered to."

It was an odd question, but she nodded.

"Lucky partner," he said and slipped from the bed.

"I don't understand," she said.

"What part do you find confusing?" he asked as he stepped into his boxers.

"What's happening? Why are you behaving like this?"

"Fun's fun," he said. "And you are absolutely the finest fuck I've had in years, but it's time for me to go."

She stared at him, totally puzzled.

He buttoned his shirt and then pulled up his trousers. "You lost, lambchop. Your partner may be stupid enough to think a guy like Ren Fowler would turn down something as tasty as you, but he did the job he was ordered to do. You, on the other hand, are definitely not a team player."

She stared at him, suddenly as cold as ice but unable to gather the covers to her naked body. "I don't... I just saved your fucking job."

He grinned. "I'm not a Fibbie," he said. "Just a private investigator from Chicago. The Bannerman Agency. Your commander hired a bunch of us to fly in and find out the weak links in his team. He was particularly concerned about you broads-in-blue with your natural inability to keep your mouths shut. Especially after a little hot sack action. The FBI really is planning an investigation of the NOPD. And all it takes is one stupid bitch to start spewing secrets –"

"This was all a test?"

"You bet your sweet ass," he said. "And it is sweet. Talk about your added perks."

He walked back to the bed and as he bent over her she thought, god help her she even hoped, it was to kiss her and tell her it was all a joke. But he was only reaching behind the headboard to remove a microwave bug.

He slipped it into his pocket. Then he went to an antique high boy against the wall and withdrew a small video camera. "The way you look and the way you fuck, baby, you sure gave the boys down in the van something to talk about." He looked into the camera and asked, "Right, boys?"

He started for the door.

She leaned out of the bed and picked up her purse. "Ren?" she called out sweetly.

He turned, grinning. "A kiss before I go?"

The smug grin froze on his handsome face when he saw the gun.

"Let's give the *boys* down in the van a real show," she said, her finger tightening on the trigger.

PROFESSOR ORYFYS AND THE CASE FOR CLIMAX CHANGE
by John Lutz

What did he care? He had tenure.

A glossy black SUV's horn blared. An angry female voice yelled, "Keep outta the way, you air-headed dingus!"

Unperturbed, Professor Jay Opus Oryfys smiled, waved, and teetered on. He wasn't sure what he was or sometimes even where he was but he was sure what he wasn't and what he wasn't was an air-headed dingus. That was clear.

He took only a few steps when he saw that the SUV driver had done him an unintentional favor by startling some pigeons near a bench and the statue of Edgar Allan Poe. As if chastised or frightened, the birds took noisy flapping flight.

Without changing pace, the professor shuffled over to where the birds had been foraging.

He bent down gingerly so he could pick up a large gray and white feather. This was certainly a good omen. He carefully removed his gray fedora and stuck the feather in its black band so it was raked slightly forward in a jaunty fashion, as if the professor were cheerfully disdaining headwinds. He was one of those always affable people who seemed to have been born wearing a fixed but genuine smile. Much about him suggested a kind of distracted innocence

He plodded on thoughtfully, a diminutive figure in his snappy fedora, gray corduroy jacket, grayer corduroy pants, even grayer leather shoes. His graying hair was thick and combed back and over his ears. He found no point in engaging in conversation with the black SUV's impolite driver.

He watched her park in a no parking zone, leaving the engine running. She was a slender girl with long raven black hair, possibly still in her twenties. All of Professor Oryfys's students were of legal age, for reasons that will become obvious later. As she exited the SUV and dashed up steps into the administration building through one of its tall oak doors, he saw that her legs were muscular and marvelously graceful, like a ballet dancer's, her breasts firm and ample.

Elegant as a swan.

A light breeze sprang up, bending the branches of the willow trees. Crisp autumn leaves made a scratching sound on the blacktop as the corduroy clad figure continued making its way across the Candildo College campus toward the ivy smothered brick administration building. Candildo was a Center for Women's Advanced Knowledge school, or CWAK. (Pronounced "Quack.")

Professor Oryfys maintained his measured pace, looking neither right nor left, but toward his destination. He didn't like being late for anything, but he often was. He forgot things.

As he trudged on toward the administration building, he saw that the young woman with the raven hair was back behind the steering wheel. She jockeyed her bulky SUV around the curve of the blacktop drive. She didn't so much as glance at Professor Oryfys as the vehicle kicked up gravel and roared across the lot toward a roundabout. Perhaps an intentional snub.

What did the professor think of that? Nothing. He had tenure and was easy in his mind.

Professor Oryfys was here for an appointment with a long time friend who would verify for the Federal Government that he (Oryfys) was indeed using his grant money for its intended purpose -- valuable research on climax control.

Tires squealed on blacktop as the woman in the SUV went too fast around the roundabout. She noticed the professor, tapped the horn, and made an improper gesture.

"Hey!" she said. "Up yours!" Laughing, she pointedly ignored him as she drove past. Still laughing. Middle finger still extended.

He smiled and waved to her. The students called what she'd done flipping him the bird. He thought that was ironic.

***

Joy Pakanum, assistant to the dean of admissions, stuck her head out of her office like a pert and curious bird and smiled a greeting. "He's waiting in the student lounge, Professor Oryfys."

"Thank you, Joy."

For the past ten years the professor's request for federal grant money had been simply a matter of automatic officialdom. His government contact had always been Luther Long, a seriously balding young man – well, middle aged now – who worked as a private detective, sometimes contracting out to one or more of those government agencies identified only as ominous faceless acronyms. (OFA) This was a change. Professor Oryfys didn't like change. Didn't trust it. Luther Long, being a shamus, would know what was going on and tell the professor. After all, they were friends.

Over a decade ago, when applying for a grant almost as a joke, Professor Oryfys had filled out a questionnaire and for some reason had carelessly written *climax change* as something of a joke. He had assumed he was too young, and not yet sufficiently comfortable in his corduroy, to actually obtain a government research grant, so why not play games?

It didn't take the professor long to forget about the impetuous, impossible grant application.

To his immense surprise, a government check arrived for him, double the hundred thousand dollar grant he'd whimsically applied for, and with its purpose printed beneath some kind of seal on the stub, stating that the payment was a grant for furthering the general study and knowledge of the imminent and inevitable danger of climax change.

A windfall, with the likelihood of more money in the future. Candildo College's regents were not the sort to look a gift horse in the mouth or anyplace else. Besides, if they lost their grant money for research, they might lose their tax free endowments plan. They met, voted, and just like that, Professor Oryfys had tenure.

At about the same time, his regular meetings with Luther Long had begun. The professor had, in fact, offered Luther as a reference while filling out the grant application.

With the usual sort of regularity, the grant checks began to arrive.

The professor never pushed himself or anyone else to learn just who Luther Long actually was. The private eye business seemed likely to be only rumor. Luther seemed not to lecture or hold classes. He was simply here and there, now and then. Professor Oryfys assumed that Luther must have something like tenure, though when he raised the point in conversation, Luther always changed the subject to baseball.

This was all okay with the professor, who was if nothing else a live and let live sort of person.

As soon as his grant money became a reality, Professor Oryfys got busy. Realizing he knew less about climax change than he'd assumed. He haunted the Internet and found it immensely informative.

He began doing actual research, using student volunteers. Sometimes they would return and volunteer even after graduation. Until one day an angry father of one of the students appeared on campus and exhibited violent and abusive, even threatening, behavior. Professor Oryfys, who had tenure, was not for one second afraid.

Once it was established that the student in question was almost thirty and that everything Professor Oryfys did was in the service of science, the man quieted down. When he discovered that student volunteers in the professor's research program received stipends, he redirected his anger so that it became money.

Luther Long handled those negotiations, and his value to Candildo College, and to the professor, was obvious. Both men became campus fixtures.

Luther continued his mysterious shamus ways.

The professor could often be found on a bench, tossing bread crumbs to the pigeons. His students, and even some of the faculty, flocked to his weekly lectures and demonstrations.

Both men were content.

#

There came a time when Professor Oryfys went for a walk on campus, near where willow trees grew along the banks of a winding creek. He heard some crows cawing in one of the trees. As the professor drew nearer, the crows cawed louder. Obviously this was a warning. Dozens of the jet black birds rose from the nearest tree and headed out over the creek. On the ground beneath the willow tree where the birds had roosted, Professor Oryfys found feathers that were somewhat larger than the pigeon feathers his previous research had provided. He collected a few and stuck them in the band of his grey fedora so they wouldn't be damaged.

The eleventh year of his grant somewhat frightened Professor Oryfys. There was trouble in Washington D.C., as well as in the state legislature. The major political parties were at war, each in a contest to cut unnecessary spending. Then of course there was the constant discord between the Hawks and Doves about possibly going to war. Some of the more militant students, including the entire Lacrosse team, even formed a Calling All Women (CAW) protest organization.

"What do you think?" Professor Oryfys asked Luther Long, as the two of them sat sipping coffee made from beans grown high in the Andes. They were in one of several faculty lounges. The one with the most comfortable chairs.

Luther sipped. Said, "Think about what? The war? The lacrosse team?"

"Improper touching."

"Whom do you want me to touch?"

"I'm speaking generally," Professor Oryfys said.

Luther looked thoughtful. "I suppose I'm for it. But I wouldn't touch just *anyone* generally. For instance, they would have to be clean."

"No, no," Professor Oryfys said. "Among the students."

Luther looked bored. "Oh, my. Has that subject come up again?"

Oryfys chewed thoughtfully on the stem of his briar pipe. He never actually lit the pipe, but it soothed him to have it clenched between his teeth.

"She might be an employee," he said, "but I see nothing in our rules and regulations that says we can't touch Joy Pakunum as part of our research. After all, we have tenure."

"So might she," Luther said. "Or something like it." He raised his eyebrows, looking surprised. "But surely you don't plan on moving along to the physical science phase of your study without assistance."

"That could be Joy Pakunum."

Luther caressed his chin with a forefinger, considering. "What precisely is the current nature of your studies and experiments?" he asked Professor Oryfys.

"I'm advancing the theories and techniques that make it possible for most women to achieve multiple orgasms without the involvement of a man – or men. And without so called marital aids." The professor took an imaginary puff on his pipe. He stared at where smoke would be if the thing were lit.

Luther Long thought long and hard. "How many orgasms?"

"As many as they choose."

"Do you really believe in that theory?"

"It doesn't seem to make any difference," Professor Oryfys said.

***

The professor had no problem again doubling the size of his grant. The money arrived in the mail fast, as if someone feared the government might regain its sanity. But, along with the checks this year came a letter from the newly created Federal Bureau of Grant Inspections (FBGI). It informed the professor that an FBGI inspector would interview him to determine what progress had been made with the local studies and applications in re the effects of tides on Climax Change.

"Don't worry about it," Luther Long said to the professor. "Just report that as of now there is little meaningful alteration to be observed in Climax Change in re tides, but there certainly might be."

Over time, Professor Oryfys had learned a lot about various agencies tasking various other agencies to examine and report on research. Long term studies were always informative but not too much so and worked well with various research agencies.

The professor didn't want someone noticing little niceties in Climax Change, like the fact that the research team hadn't come up with any sort of report. That was because there was no research team; there were no studies; and there was nothing to report other than that CC had shown no measurable advancement, and no reduction. It could also be reported that no harm had been done, but there might have been. That was a relief to some, and wasn't completely disregarded by the media.

Science marched ahead, because Professor Oryfys knew what was needed. Research, studies, instrumentation, various kinds of graphs, scientific speculation. Oryfys partnered with Luther Long, and they decided to go large into a study about multiple orgasms and their effect on sleep. To have a study, CC needed subjects.

Ads in the local papers, on public bulletin boards, and on line, attracted scores of applicants. One of the respondents was a slender young woman with long, raven black hair. She looked familiar.

***

Her name was Sasha Smith, but she told Professor Oryfys that she preferred simply Sassy. That was what her friends and enemies called her.

She displayed little modesty when required to undress before the professor. In fact, there was something in her attitude that suggested she was being challenged, and she refused to be embarrassed. Oryfys had encountered that attitude before and rather liked it.

One afternoon in the faculty lounge, Luther Long surprised Professor Oryfys by saying, "Rumor has it that your research volunteer is a private detective hired by the college at the government's request."

"Rumors are simply people parroting each other," the professor said. "Grist for the gullible."

In truth Professor Oryfys was taken aback. It was Luther Long whom most people – students and staff – suspected was the mysterious shamus. He was, after all, a professional P.I. Not like Sassy Smith who was, let's face it – prettier than she was smart.

"What would she be detecting?" the professor asked Luther.

"You, I'm afraid. That grant thing about Climate Change."

Professor Oryfys sat up straight. "Did you say Cli*mate*?"

Luther nodded.

"Not Cli*max?*"

Luther nodded again. "I'm beginning to see the problem, old friend." He tapped a long forefinger rapidly on the arm of his chair. "I'll do some detecting myself, and find out the source of these rumors. You *did* mention that you have tenure."

"Yes," the professor said in a thin yet hopeful tone. It was as if someone on the *Titanic* had just tossed him water wings.

"There's only one thing to do," Luther said. "Ask for more money."

***

Luther's suggestion worked with amazing ease. If there weren't experiments, long range studies, tuition payments, supporting statistics, there would be no need for grants -- and there *were* grants.

Professor Oryfys's grant was expanded in order to purchase a small, brick and stone cottage on a plot of ground not far from the college. It was also possible to lure Joy Pakunum away from student admissions so she could work as an assistant to the professor.

Luther Long began haunting the student's lounge, attending student functions, asking and eavesdropping as he followed the circuitous routes to rumors.

At the cottage, Professor Oryfys happily experimented, developing material that would later become fodder for lectures. Multiple orgasms, when you really got into them, were a fascinating subject. The cottage was too small for whole class assembly, so Joy Pakunum was assigned to record and post results of demonstrations and experiments. Much of what the professor and his subject did was preserved on video, and in other media.

One day, when Sassy lay nude on one of those doctors' vinyl recliners that were always cold, Professor Oryfys asked if she recalled their little dust up in the administration building parking lot.

Now she did blush. "That was rather rude, I confess," she said. "But its one of the reasons I volunteered for your classes."

Oryfys absently fastened Velcro cuffs on her ankles so she couldn't rise from the recliner without risking a fall.

"I'm sorry, Professor. I'd like to make it up to you."

"But what other reasons do you have for attending my classes?"

"I feel that I need to be punished." She couldn't meet his eyes. "Not badly hurt," she said. "Just ...straightened out."

The professor wondered, was this how most private eyes worked? Maybe. What better way for a shamus to get inside the mind of a suspect?

"We don't do pain here," the professor said.

It was early evening, and they were in the cottage. He fastened

Velcro straps about Sassy's wrists so that her arms were stretched above her head. "These are, in their manner, clinical trials." He tested the straps. "This position can be rather a strain on the back. Are you comfortable, dear?"

"Comfortable enough." There was the slightest hint of a moan in her breath.

Oryfys looked at Joy Pakunum, who was paid overtime when she aided Professor Oryfys in his research in the cottage. "Is the video camera recording?" he asked.

Joy nodded. "As of a few minutes ago."

Gently, he adjusted Sassy's head so her lovely face was turned toward the camera. "Did you do as instructed before you came here this evening?" he asked with seemingly mild interest.

"Yes."

"How many orgasms did you manage?"

"Three. The second and third with my rubber duck vibrator."

Oryfys made a note of this. "We'll soon wean you away from Mr. Duck," he said. He opened a door to a disk player and put in a CD of Ralph Vaughan Williams' *The Lark Ascending* at soft volume.

Sassy looked uncomfortable yet pleased. A delicate balance had been achieved. If any place was perfect, her facial expression said, this was it.

"And that was...?" Professor Oryfys asked.

"Six o'clock, six-thirty, and seven-oh-five," she said. "Then I drove directly here as instructed."

He made a note of the times. As did his assistant Joy. Then he spread Sassy's smooth and muscular dancer's legs, fastening the ankle cuffs to stirrups on the sides of the recliner. He raised his head so he was looking at the camera, making sure light and angle were correct. The camera could be controlled by Joy, zooming in and out for close ups, adjusting with the slightest movement of the subject. All carefully requested and observed by Professor Oryfys.

He placed on his head his gray fedora. Protruding from the hat's black band, like bullets in a cartridge belt, were half a dozen various feathers. Joy, using a computer mouse, zoomed in with the video camera.

"A common pigeon feather," the professor said, holding up the feather so it could be seen. He moved closer to Sassy, bending over her while standing to the side, so the camera could record his techniques.

It began raining harder, pattering on the cottage's slate roof, running down its windows and softening the inside light.

The lark continued to ascend.

This was, Sassy thought, the only place in the world where she could be happy and fulfilled. Where she could be lifted to a place where she would sing the mindless, magic music of a nightingale.

Indeed there were times when the professor had to remind himself that this was serious research and not cheep trills.

"We will begin with the commonly known, but little understood, applications of the feather," the professor said, while Joy made sure image, voice, and volume were at perfect pitch. As he spoke, the professor moved the tip of the feather slowly, in a counter clockwise circular motion, about the aureole of Sassy's right nipple. Barely touching, touching...

"Gentle is the concept we must keep in mind," he said, as Sassy began to moan and move about.

The professor began repeating beneath his breath, like a mantra, "Gentle...gentle...gentle..."

Sassy moaned, twisted, banged her heels.

He began a deft flicking motion with the feather in the area of the clitoris. "Gentle, gentle..." His favorite word, Sassy decided, and liked it. Worshipped it! "Are you all right, dear?" he asked.

Sassy tried to answer but her throat was so dry she could only swallow. Finally she was able to whisper, "Oh, yes, Professor!"

Oryfys laid the feather aside. He looked up at the camera and removed from his hat band a larger, black feather. "An ordinary crow feather,"

he announced for the recording DVD, holding the feather high for edification. "Marginally larger and more resilient than the pigeon feather."

Sassy moaned and thrashed about as Professor Oryfys skillfully applied the feather to her now jutting nipples. Then he replaced the crow feather in his hat band and withdrew a fresh pigeon feather. "We will apply this to areas not commonly thought of as erogenous zones," he said to the camera.

He held up the feather so Joy could zoom in on it, then he began playing it along the backs of Sassy's calves, then up the soft, tender flesh of her inner thighs. "Observe the reaction to the sensitive, but not often enough visited, area behind the knees," he said in a clinical tone, flicking expertly with the feather. "Gently, gently…"

Sassy began to shiver as if she were cold.

But she wasn't.

Joy zoomed in with the camera. Sassy looked at her as if suffering and pleading. Now the professor began a subtle circular motion with the feather. "Gentle, gentle…" There was so much to technique.

Back to her nipples. Then her clitoris, erect at attention and glistening.

Then her ears became the center of his interest. Behind her ears. So deftly, so softly. She had always been sensitive about having her ears touched, but she hadn't regarded them as erogenous zones. This fluttering, light, light touch caused her to tremble and moan with each breath. The vinyl recliner she was bound to began an almost musical vibration. Joy adjusted for volume.

Sassy's breath was ragged and rasping. Professor Oryfys set the feather aside, then deftly drew another from his hat band.

Nodding for Joy to elevate the camera for a bird's eye view, he used this latest feather to ever so gently caress the tip of Sassy's nose…then along the sensitive area at the slender curvature of her neck.

Sassy's buttocks flexed powerfully over and over, bouncing uncontrollably against the crinkled white butcher's paper covering the recliner.

She groaned as the professor suddenly withdrew the sleek black feather, holding it up for the camera to record. It had barely touched Sassy, yet it had touched her deeply.

"Remember you can never be denied this nirvana, Sassy. And from now on, never can it be denied you. Never!'

"Oh, never more, Professor! Never more!'

He leaned closer, and she could smell mint on his breath. In the gentlest of voices he whispered, "Now what's this business about a private eye?"

"Luther Long," she said hoarsely and without hesitation. Then she began to sing like a canary.

Professor Oryfys was astounded. "Luther? We've been friends for years. Why would he investigate me? All my students are of legal age and sound minds. Why would he report me to FBGI?"

"He wouldn't," said Sassy. "He didn't realize at first that *he* was the source of the rumors he'd heard and then passed on to you. The rumor mongering was actually about *him*." She gave the professor a tremulous smile. "Luther is finished investigating himself. Now no one is investigating you."

For the first time in a long while, Professor Oryfys breathed fresh air not containing danger.

***

The professor continued teaching about Climax Change to growing numbers of students. Usually he used Sassy to help illustrate. She was a more than willing subject.

"An ordinary feather," he would say, "adroitly applied to the body of a woman who only recently evoked for herself three powerful (all more than six on the orgasmometer) orgasms. These were in large measure brought about by foreplay concentrated on highly sensitive areas, some of which are not necessarily thought of as erogenous."

He began to flick lightly with the feather, while the tips of the fingers on his other hand described slow and unpredictable patterns on Sassy's delicate flesh.

He knew precisely where to touch. Where not to touch. *How to touch.* And when.

Sassy suddenly reclaimed her voice. "Oh, Joy!" she cried to the professor's assistant. "Oh, please! Oh, God! Oh, Professor. I'm so glad you have tenure!"

Professor Oryfys stepped back.

'"Please, please, Professor!" she implored. "More, more!"

Professor Oryfys smiled and shrugged, as if he'd somehow overlooked her and she was an old penny desperate to be picked up and spent.

"Sorry," he said. "I almost forgot you."

He picked up two feathers and went to work on Sassy with his left and right hands simultaneously. Almost as if he were gently, gently playing a soundless piano. Joy, assisting, had to use her hand to stifle some of Sassy's throaty screams of ecstasy. Sassy was thinking this might be too much of a wonderful thing.

Her body tensed, arched, tensed, then slumped into completely relaxed repose. Her eyelids fluttered in satisfied exhaustion.

The professor looked squarely into the camera. "I believe that's four," he said.

Then he moved closer and took on a more serious mien. "As we discussed, the purpose of these demonstrations is to increase awareness among women. With a little practice, determination, and adroitness, women can be made aware of the intense solitary pleasure they might be missing." He moved even closer to the camera for a close up. His smile was kind. Knowing. Earnest. As he spoke, he absently played the tip of a feather over the taut flesh of Sassy's bare ribs "It is through experimentation that we broaden our internal roles, our self-knowledge, and our sexual selves."

He widened his beatific smile. "Remember, ladies. Gentle, gentle… We can have pleasure without pain." It seemed to Sassy that he was speaking directly to her. "Where there's a quill there's a way."

Yes, yes! Sassy thought, wholly embracing that point of view. She decided that tomorrow she'd engineer some sort of meeting with Professor Oryfys. She knew where he could usually be found while on his lunch hour, his feather- adorned gray fedora cocked nattily on his head, reaching into a white paper sack and tossing out bread crumbs. Feeding his pigeons.

Her heart was on the wing.

Fifty Shades of Grey Fedora

JUST TELL ME WHAT YOU WANT
by Christine Matthews

"This is hard for me...I don't mean hard...you know...in that way. Difficult. This is difficult. I've never done anything like this before. It's just that my wife left me and I send all my money to her. Good thing we never had kids. The bitch would use them to hurt me more than she has. She's always been so...so...what's the word?"

It took first timers awhile to get warmed up. If he wanted to tell her his life history, all about the first time he got laid, how his bitch wife took him for everything he had, so what? The clock didn't care what went down. Tick, tick, pity money spent as good as fuck money.

She held a hand out to check her nails. Tenacious Ruby—great color. Not too flashy. When he finally ran out of steam she said, "It don't matter how you meant it, baby, it's all good. Now relax, this is supposed to be fun."

"I know...I know. And I'm trying--really. Let me take a leak first. Hold on."

She stared out the window. A big orange moon hung in the black sky. She'd been at work for hours, her ass hurt from sitting so long, she was hungry and just wanted the night to be over.

"Okay, that's better." He sounded out of breath.

"Good. Now just tell me what you want."

"I'm not sure. Jesus, I shouldn't have called. This is stupid. What ever made me think this would work? "

"Feeling good is never stupid, honey. No worries. I'll start."

When she'd signed up with the service they'd given her a script. Just some key words and scenarios to help the customer feel comfortable. But after a few calls she threw that crap away and let the slut in her take over.

"Close your eyes, baby. Imagine this: You're sitting on the edge of the bed, naked. Your dick is throbbing and you rub it. Slowly. Don't grab it, now, wait for me."

"Okay. And I'm naked."

"I walk into your bedroom. I'm so horny. My nipples are hard. I'm wearing a tight leather skirt. It fits like skin and short enough you can see my pussy. Can you see me?"

He hesitated so long she thought he'd hung up. But then he said, in a whisper, "Yeah, I see. You got on a black lace corset thing on top. Two of the hooks are open in front."

"You reach out and put your finger deep in me. Make me wet. Push two fingers up in there. Come on, baby. I'm getting so hot, it burns."

"Oh yeah, you like that. Slow and steady."

"Don't stop, baby, it feels so good."

"Your cunt's so juicy. Touch my dick. Touch it. You want to suck it. Get on your knees and suck it."

She inhaled a quick breath. "Such a nice big cock. I pull my skirt up and you rip off my top."

"Your big fat tities fall out."

"Bite my nipples. Bite 'em hard."

"I'll bite so hard you'll scream." His sounds reminded her of a baby sucking and licking at a bottle.

"I'm on my knees in front of you now. God, you're hung like a bull."

"You want to suck it, don't you, bitch? You want to eat it up."

The shy ones only needed a little coaxing. But once they got into it--they really got into it.

"Oooh, you taste so good," she moaned. "I run my tongue up and down. Over your balls. I lick up…"

"And I rub your tits, squeeze 'em. You like that, don't you? Tell me how much you love it."

"I'm so wet, baby." She licked at the phone while he groaned on the other end. After a few moments she said, "Shove that dick up inside me. Make me come."

"I pull you up on the bed, and on top of me. You like it rough, don't you? Wanna feel it real good and deep. It's only good if it hurts a little."

Fifty Shades of Grey Fedora

"Make me hurt. Fuck me until I can't take it and then fuck me some more."

"Your breasts dangle over me and I bite until you scream. I grab your ass, drive up inside. You squirm, but I know you don't want me to stop."

"Never stop…never. Oooh, I'm so wet. Your dick slides in and out of me, hot, filling me up and I love it."

"I flip you over, onto your back and go down on you." She could hear him thrashing around.

"Eat me. Lick my pussy, suck it, make me come, baby."

"Not yet, bitch. Beg for it."

"Please. Don't make me wait. Don't be so mean to me. I gotta have it."

"I'm gonna make you come so hard…"

He was jerking off now. Springs squealed as his hips slapped the mattress in a monotonous rhythm.

"That's right. Rub my clit. Harder."

He grunted with each stroke.

"Do me up the ass. Come on, it's what you really want."

It's what they all wanted.

"Yeah, I want that. Roll over."

"When you see Gigi's ass you're gonna blow your wad right there."

"Bet me. I can go all night, bitch…"

BANG!

The bullet entered her right ear, gathered some brains along the way and exited her left temple.

"Hey! You still there? Gigi? Hello? What the fuck…"

***

For two days he wondered if he should call a manager at 1-800-SEX-TALK. There had to be someone in charge. It was a business, after all. And he'd willingly given them his credit card number to pay for their services. But did he really have the balls to complain? Tell a stranger that he hadn't finished whacking off when the call abruptly ended? All this trouble because he'd been too tired and lazy to hit the bars that night. Just forget it, he told himself.

On day three, two cops showed up at his door and that marked the moment he'd never be able to forget Gigi.

"Mr. Linner? Are you Jed Linner?"

"Yes."

"I'm Detective Raleigh and this is my partner, Detective Scott." They held badges out for his inspection.

It had turned cold earlier and the men stood in his doorway wrapped in overcoats. Snow dusted their hair then immediately melted, dripping onto their collars. They were letting the heat out so he invited them in.

All he could think about was the porn he'd been watching on his laptop. Everybody did it; they couldn't be here for that. And the magazines in his bedroom were regular—not that sick shit. "Is something wrong?"

Raleigh took the lead. "Don't worry, you're not in any trouble. We just wanted to ask a few questions about an acquaintance of yours. Calley Green? You were talking to her on the night of the twelfth from eight thirteen to eight forty-one."

"Sorry," he said. "I don't have a clue who you're talking about."

"Then why was your number in her phone?" Raleigh asked.

"How would I know?" He could feel the sweat behind his ears.

"Look, Mr. Linner," Scott said, "why deny it? Apparently, she was talking to you when she got...shot. Did we mention she's dead?"

So that was the bang he heard. "Can I sit down?" His legs were giving out.

"Good idea," Raleigh said. "Let's all get comfortable."

The living room was small, but neat. Jed lowered himself onto the sofa and closed his laptop. The detectives didn't seem to notice as each settled into a chair.

"Now, Mr. Linner, we traced the last number on her phone to you, at this address."

He gulped down his anxiety, rubbed at the burning in his chest. "I was on the phone, that's true. But I was talking to Gigi. She said her name was Gigi, I swear. And I'd never met her actually. We weren't friends—nothing like that."

"Why would a stranger have your number?" Scott said. "And why would you talk to this stranger for twenty-eight minutes?"

"There was this ad on TV. You know...with sexy girls. Just to talk, that's all. Lots of guys do it. There's nothing wrong with wanting a little…"

"You were horny. I get it, Mr. Linner. When I was your age, I had a boner twenty-four seven." Raleigh smirked.

Jed nodded.

"What was the number?" Scott asked.

"One-eight-hundred-Sex-Talk."

"Those are the ads that run after midnight, right?" Raleigh took notes as he talked. "Those chicks are hot. Can't say I blame you."

"But no way are you actually talking to any of them. You're aware of that, aren't you, Mr.Linner? Those girls are hired just to make the commercial. They probably don't even talk to—"

"--So you call the number and get Gigi," Raleigh interrupted his partner. "Is that how it worked?"

"No. I got an operator first and she took my credit card number, explained the pricing and how the charge would appear on my account."

Scott nodded. "Real important to most guys that the old lady doesn't see anything out of the norm on the Visa bill, ya know? But you, Mr. Linner, you're single, right?"

"Yeah. So what?"

"So why would you care what's on your bill?"

"I don't. She said it was their policy, that I had to be informed. So I listened."

"Then what happened?" Raleigh asked.

"She said to stay near the phone and someone would call me right back."

Raleigh spoke before Scott had a chance. "And that someone was Gigi?"

"Yep. But why don't you already know all this stuff," Jed asked them. "If she got shot at work wouldn't you know the set up there? Must have been a real mess. And the other girls would have seen who killed her. Right?"

"That scenario sure would have made our jobs a whole lot easier," Scott said. "If only she had…"

"Ms. Green was in her car, parked in a real upscale area when she was shot," Raleigh told him. "One time, right to the head. The nine-one-one call came in the next morning. A gardener thought the car had been abandoned and went to have a look. Poor guy got quite a shock, seeing her like that."

Scott finished the story. "After the body was removed, the M.E. spotted her cell under the front seat. And there you were—the last person she spoke to."

The offices of 1-800-Sex-Talk were located in the basement of Samantha Ramsey's deluxe condo in Tampa, Florida—five states away from where Calley Green had been murdered. When Raleigh returned to his office, he called the number.

A sensual voice answered. "This is Sammi. Just tell me what you want, honey"

"Sammi, this is Detective Raleigh. Can I speak to your boss?"

"That would be me, detective."

"I believe you have a Miss Calley Green on your payroll. She uses the name, Gigi when she's working."

"I see you're calling from out of state. Am I correct in believing I'm not under any obligation to talk to you? Something about jurisdiction?"

He ignored her question. "Miss Green was murdered last week."

"Jesus Christ! Not Gigi."

"She was talking to Mr. Jed Linner, who I assume you set her up with, when she was shot."

"This is like something straight out of a friggin' movie, detective."

He sipped his coffee. "I'd really appreciate it if you could tell me what you have on her. There must be a file or something?"

"Sure, I can do that. Anything to help. She was a sweetheart. Real reliable. But I have to warn you, girls come and go so fast around here. It's like that in this business. So when they give me their numbers, I'm not sure if they're for real. But let's see what I can find."

"I'll wait." He could hear the clicking of her keyboard and wondered how many females were in those files.

"There she is--Calley Green. Poor girl. She's only been with us for five months. Started on May tenth."

"Do you recruit these girls?" he asked. "How do you find them?"

She laughed. Then coughed a deep, rough smoker's cough. "Oh, honey, they find us. Sex talk is good money. Not as good as strippin'. Especially if a girl's willing to go downtown, if you know what I mean? Now that woman can keep her bank account plumper than Kardashien ass. But talkin' dirty keeps a girl clean, even taps into her creative side. It's all pretend, you know. How they look, what they're wearing, even their names."

"So Miss Green came to you?"

"Says here she was referred by a friend, Barbara Samuelson. Barb's been with us for years. Does this full time. She's got a real knack."

"Do you have an address or phone number for Barbara?" he asked.

"Can't do that, detective. Barb's still alive and kickin'. I gave you Calley's info because she's…well…no longer an employee."

"I understand, Sammi. And I certainly wouldn't want you to do anything wrong. I'll just call the Tampa police department and have them pay you a visit, take a look at your operation. Maybe they can—"

"She lives up in your neck of the woods. It would be silly to bother the authorities down here. They have their hands full hunting down serial killers."

"You play golf, Scott?" Raleigh asked as they drove around the golf course and up toward the guard house.

"Used to go to the driving range with my dad. But actually play a real game? Lug around a bag of clubs and keep score? Nope."

"Me neither."

Squashed inside the small guard house was a middle aged man. He wore an official looking dark blue uniform. "Can I help you gentlemen?"

Raleigh waved his badge. "We're here to see Ms. Samuelson. Number three-thirty-five."

"Hold on a minute." The man picked up a phone and after a minute or two of nodding, hung up. "Drive straight ahead and turn right near the lake. Then follow the road around. She's the second house from the end."

"Thanks."

The gate went up and they drove into Sunset Hills.

A short, gray-haired woman opened the front door of the large house. She wore a heavy sweater and sweat pants, hugging herself to keep warm. The wind blew her hair into a wild mess.

"Is this about Calley?" she asked as they climbed the five steps to the house. "Sammi said you're detectives? My husband gets home from work in a few hours. Is this going to take long?"

Raleigh smiled. "Can we come in, Mrs. Samuelseon? It's freezing out here."

"Oh sure. It's just that I've never talked to the police before--ever."

She walked ahead and held the door open onto a room that looked as if it had been designed for formal occasions. "Let's go to the family room; it's more comfortable."

The lower level was worn-in beige. Video games, comic books and magazines filled cheap shelves. Two large televisions, one hooked up to a game system, seemed to take up two walls. A refrigerator hummed in the corner.

"My husband thinks this is his man cave. Every guy has to have a man cave now, right? But with three kids, who's he kidding? We all end up down here." She sat, then jumped up. "Let me take your coats."

"Thanks," Scott said.

"I'm good." Raleigh told her when she reached for his overcoat.

She shrugged and tossed Scott's jacket over a chair.

"Like I said, my husband will be home soon. He didn't know Calley...or any of my sex friends," she said when they were all seated. "This won't take long, I hope. I want to help, of course. Calley was a good friend but--."

"Hold up a sec, Mrs. Samuelson. Yes, we want to ask you about Ms. Green. And it shouldn't take too long. Just relax. Okay?" Scott told her.

She folded both hands in her lap, breathed in deeply and straightened her shoulders. "Okay."

"I talked with Sammi at the sex talk line," Raleigh said. "She told me you work there under the name," he checked his notes, "Mona." He stopped, waiting for a reaction from the woman. But there was none.

"True."

"She also told me you recruited Calley. How did that go down?"

"We were in a yoga class together about two years ago. We got to talking, went to lunch a few times. That led to movies and shopping, you know, just stuff. I really liked her. She was funny and always working. She had some of the craziest jobs…"

Scott smiled. "Like what?"

"Oh, she was a perfume girl at Macy's. You know, they come up and spritz you with a sample?" When neither men reacted, she continued. "Then she worked at McDonalds, waitressed for awhile at a coffee shop downtown. She was real good with old people and took care of a lady who had Alzheimer's. A few years ago she did some skip tracing for a finance company. But she never seemed to have enough money."

"Drugs? Booze? Was she addicted to anything?" Raleigh asked.

"God, no. No addictions. Well, she did like to shop, but not in a crazy way. She was a decent, kind person. Calley just wasn't good with money, that's all."

"So to help your friend out, you told her about the sex line," Scott said.

Barbara nodded. "It's easy money. No danger involved. You never see a client—face to face. Innocent fun. The day after I told her, she called Sammi."

"Did she ever complaint to you about a strange client? Someone that frightened her or made her uncomfortable?" Raleigh wanted to know."

The woman started to bite the nail on her thumb. "There's a lot of freaks out there. But the great thing is we can just hang up. All our calls come through the eight-hundred number. And the company sends us a box of cheap phones. After a week we toss the old one and use a new one. That way clients never know our personal info."

Raleigh flipped his notepad closed. "Guess that's all for now. Thanks a lot, Mrs. Samuelson." He stood up.

"I'm curious," Scott said to the woman as he put his jacket on. "What was the last job Calley had—before the sex line?"

"She'd just got her PI license and was she ever proud. But without money for an office or a website, she couldn't get the business up and running. After a year of trying, she only had one client."

"Things are tough all over," Scott said.

"Could you give me a call when you find something out?" she asked. "Calley's folks are old. She was an only child—their baby girl. I promised to keep in touch—let them know what's happening."

"Sure thing," Scott said.

Raleigh hesitated a moment. "By the way, Mrs. Samuelson, do you happen to know the name of her lone client?"

"Wait a minute, let me think. It was the same as an old time actor." She stopped short of the front door, looking down to help her concentration. "Swashbuckler, handsome guy... silent movies..."

"Douglas Fairbanks?" Raleigh asked.

"That's it! But his first name was...William...yeah she called him Bill. Bill Fairbanks."

Between interviewing anyone connected to Calley Green's sex talk job, the detectives knocked on doors in the Millstone neighborhood where her body had been found. But no one had seen anything or knew of the woman either as Gigi or Calley. They had searched her one bedroom apartment weeks before, disappointed at finding nothing even resembling an office. No desk, no computer, just a cardboard shoebox on the kitchen counter labeled: PI STUFF. Inside were three months worth of bank statements for a business account. Only one deposit had been made in all that time.

"I still don't understand why she would do her sex job from her car," Scott said. "Miles away from her home, nowhere near where her client lived. Why was she parked there at all?"

"You're new at this, Scott, but you'll get it. All the pieces come together eventually. It just takes a bullheaded, hard-ass like you to hunt and gather those damn pieces."

"Geez, Raleigh, I never know if you're complimenting or insulting me."

"Take it any damn way you want. But while you're analyzing your feelings, I've been thinking we should run William Fairbanks through the system and see what we come up with. Hopefully he'll have a record."

"No such luck," Scott said after a few minutes. "But this is interesting."

Raleigh stood behind Scott, looking over his shoulder at the computer screen and read aloud. "Married six years, no children, never been in jail, two parking tickets, good credit, owns his home. Upstanding member of the community. All around good Amereican, rah rah. So what's interesting about this guy?"

Scott pointed. "His address look familiar?"

His partner leaned in to get a better look. "Sure does." He thought a moment then said, "Get your coat."

"People around here sure take their politics seriously," Raleigh observed.

"Yeah, must be dozens of those election signs on this block."

"Big fish in little ponds. Everybody wants to be important. And the way they do it, Scott, is to hold an office—be official. County Clerk, Sheriff, Dog Catcher, it doesn't matter as long as the job comes with a title."

Scott nodded in agreement. "It's all about power, I guess." After parking the car on the street he pointed to the open garage door. "No vehicle anywhere."

The men walked toward the house. On the porch, Raleigh reached out to ring the bell. Under his breath he told his partner, "Look, someone's inside."

They stood and waited, but got no response.

Scott stepped up and knocked. "Mr. Fairbanks, we're here to ask you about your neighbor, Ms. Green," he said through the door.

A red Mini Cooper screeched down the street and swerved into the driveway. A woman slammed the car door and rushed up to them. "Can I help you, gentlemen?"

Scott tried not to stare while Raleigh introduced himself and his partner then explained the reason for their visit. But it was difficult. Somewhere he'd read that only two percent of the country's population was attractive. Mrs. Fairbanks was obviously a charter member of that elite group. Without question, she was the most beautiful woman he had ever seen—in real life. Her hair shined, her skin glowed, her smile dazzled and her eyes sparkled. She was perfection and he basked in her presence.

"When I heard the news I was shocked," she told Raleigh. "Of course I'll do anything I can to help. Calley was so nice, so sweet… Oh, what am I doing? It's freezing out here, come inside."

As he entered, Raleigh looked around the room. "Is your husband at home?"

"I'm not sure." She called out but got no answer. "Guess not. We've had a lot of excitement around here. Yesterday Bill was elected Mayor."

"Congratulations," Scott said. "I guess that makes you kind of a first lady or something?"

"All I know is he can take it from here. We've been campaigning, kissing screaming babies and gagging down way too many tasteless dinners. I have—or had-- a life of my own until all this started. Tomorrow I'm gonna have to do double time at the gym."

She kicked off her boots and hung her coat up in the small hall closet. Then she ran her hands slowly, along her hips. "These jeans never fit this tight before. You can see every crevice and bump."

"You look great," Scott said, immediately regretting his comment.

She smiled, obviously pleased. "You're sweet, Detective. Come and sit." She patted the cushion next to her on the suede couch.

Raleigh took a seat across from them and the atmosphere in the room went from friendly to serious when he flipped his notepad out. "Were you aware that your husband hired Ms. Green to do a job for him?"

"My husband is not into porn, if that's what you're insinuating, Detective Raleigh."

"So you knew about her working on the sex line?" Scott asked.

"Sure. I thought it was funny. So did Calley. We'd have coffee and write out little stories for her to read to her…Johns."

"Callers," Raleigh told her. "Let's refer to them as callers."

The woman shrugged. "Whatever. But she most certainly did not provide those services for my husband. No way—no how."

"According to what we've learned," Raleigh began, "your husband hired Ms. Green as a private investigator."

"But…Calley wasn't…she didn't know how to…I'm confused."

"She just recently got her license," Scott told her. "And so far, only had one client."

Still looking bewildered, she asked. "My husband?"

The men nodded in unison.

"But why in the world would he need a P.I.? That's just ridiculous."

"We've looked through her files, what there were, and found that he had written her a check for a thousand dollars," Raleigh said.

"Oh, that could have been for anything. Calley came over and house-sit when we traveled. She'd water the plants, bring in mail, check that windows and doors were locked, you know, things like that. Sometimes she'd help cater a party for us."

Raleigh checked his notes. "This check was deposited to Green Investigations."

"Well, I give up." She sat back. "Guess you'll have to talk to my husband then, cause I don't know a thing about it."

"Do you know when he'll be home?" Scott asked.

"He could be gone for hours," she said, irritated. "He was home all day. But when he saw you guys, he ducked out and called me. I suppose you knew that already."

Scott nodded. "And why would he do that?"

"Do you have any idea how it's been around here?" She pounded her knees with her fists. "At first people came by for support, crowding inside to strategize. Planning and plotting, so self-important. Traipsing all over our carpet, messing things up. But once the election was over, it calmed down. And I thought, finally! Then Calley got…you know…and reporters showed up. Neighbors wanting to talk about her, busy bodies driving up and down the street, gawking at where the murdered girl lived. All I want is a one good night of sleep. Look at these circles under my eyes." She turned to Scott and pointed at her face.

"But your husband's the mayor now," Raleigh told her. "He's going to have to learn how to deal with this kind of thing."

"He doesn't take office for weeks. Right now we're just ordinary citizens. There's nothing he can do for anyone. When he tells them he doesn't know anything, they don't believe it."

"Whatever his reasons, we can't leave until we've interviewed him," Scott said.

"Fine." She shot them both a disgusted look and excused herself. The detectives strained to listen as she screamed into her phone from another room.

It took and hour and fifteen minutes for the man to return. During that time, his wife smoked three cigarettes, offered and served coffee to the two men and drank several glasses of chardonnay. When Fairbanks finally arrived he was all teeth. Shaking their hands he smiled wide, apologizing over and over for any inconvenience he'd caused. Raleigh wondered if the man knew how insincere he came off.

"Funny, isn't it?" he asked after settling in next to his wife and putting an arm around her. "I was on my way out when you two rang the bell. It's been so chaotic around here, with the election and then…Calley. I thought you were reporters so I ran out the back."

"Strange that we didn't see you or hear a car," Scott said.

"Oh, I walked. City Hall's only a block over. Have to clean up some old business. Things over there are in bad shape." He rolled his eyes, giving the impression that he was the only person capable of handling the situation.

"Let's cut the crap, Mr. Fairbanks," Raleigh blurted out. "Who was Calley Green investigating for you? Don't tell me you didn't know she was a P.I. We've already gotten the run around from your wife. Whoever it was, I bet they lived in Millstone."

Mrs. Fairbanks jerked away from her husband. "Millstone? You son-of-a-bitch! "

All three men straightened in their seats, startled.

Then she jumped up, waving her arms as she shouted. "You promised to leave Chuck alone. You promised! You said as long as I was discreet…you said you didn't care…"

His smile never changed, as if permanently affixed to his lips. Fairbanks stood up and reached out to grab her hands. "Calm down, darlin'. We have company."

"I won't calm down and I won't be quiet." She slapped his hands away. "'Smile and be nice until the election is over.' That's what you said. 'Play the charming wife.' You said that's all you wanted me to do'"

Fairbanks turned away from the hysterical woman and faced the detectives. "We've had a very stressful six months. And my wife has always suffered from panic attacks—"

"Liar!" She pounded his back. "You said you'd leave us alone."

Scott came up behind the woman and pinned her arms down tight to her side. Raleigh stood and gripped Fairbanks' shoulder. "Stop it! Both of you! Now sit back down."

Fifty Shades of Grey Fedora

But the man jerked away from the detective and started to run for the door.

Raleigh drew his gun. "I don't know what's happening here but you're not leaving this house until I find out. Plant your ass over there and start talking. Or we can wait for a squad car. I'm sure you'd love all the attention that would create. And I'll tell them to make a real scene—sirens, lights—the works."

Fairbanks froze. "No, that won't be necessary, Detective."

"Call them!" Mrs. Fairbanks ordered. "I'm sure my husband would appreciate seeing his tax dollars at work. Call 'em."

"Shut up!" Fairbanks shouted to her.

Raleigh put his gun away and motioned for Scott to release the woman. "Over there," he told Fairbanks and pointed to the couch.

She slumped into a chair. "Whatever you've done, Bill, people are going to believe the worst. If you talk now or at the police station or get a lawyer--it's over. Your precious name is crap. Even a hint of scandal and no one will have anything to do with you. All for nothing…darlin' All your bullshit speeches and endless ass kissing…for nothing."

His shoulders and head drooped forward and finally, that big smile was gone. "You never loved me, did you? I told you from the start that I wanted to get into politics. From that first day we met. I told you my plan—"

"You told me a lot of things, Bill. But all I knew was that the man I married was the CEO of his own company, successful and well off. Everything was so perfect back then. Why would I believe you'd give it all up? Do I look stupid?" She stared at him, waiting for an answer.

"I've told you a million times. I had to sell the business. We had to down-size. A Mayor's salary is—"

"Shit. All this is shit," she said, making a sweeping motion with both hands. "You're weak and stupid. Your only talent, my love, is being likable. And that was my first mistake. I liked you. Oh, and you were good in bed…at the beginning."

"I loved you at first sight," he said weakly.

"Oh boo-hoo. Bring out the violins. Take a good look in the mirror sometime, will you? Why would a woman like me, be with someone like you? Did you ever ask yourself that? Money, baby.

You're like a Gucci bag. I toted you around for the status. And now you've probably fucked that up."

"You two can finish this little therapy session some other time." Raleigh glared at the couple. "But now, Mr. Fairbanks, you're going to answer my questions. Got it?"

The man nodded, defeated.

"You hired Calley to find out if your wife was cheating with some guy named Chuck? Is that what happened?"

"Chuck Nash. She followed him for a few nights. Watched them meeting at restaurants, motels, you know. When she found out his address and name, I told her to get some hard core evidence--pictures, video--anything I could use to blackmail him." Then he turned toward his wife. "Did you know he's married, sweetheart? His wife's loaded. I knew he wouldn't want that situation messed up."

"You're a real dirt bag," his wife said. "God, I hate you."

Raleigh continued. "So Ms. Green was on a stake out. Sitting in her car..."

"...moonlighting at her sex job while she did it," Scott finished his partner's thought.

"We spoke earlier that night. Calley was out front when I got there but never saw me park across the street," Fairbanks said. "My wife was inside with that asshole and all I wanted to do was hurt them. Hurt both of them so bad. I had my gun with me and I started to load it. My hands were shaking; I dropped a couple bullets. By the time I found them, I'd cooled off. Got to thinking about my career. And I wasn't going to let this bitch here and her boyfriend ruin things for me. I worked too hard for too long. So I walked over to Calley to tell her to go home, to just keep the money. As far as I was concerned, her job was done."

"What did she say?" Raleigh asked.

"Nothing. When I got closer I could see she was on the phone. So I walked away. I didn't want whoever was on the other end to hear me. I started to get back in my car but then I thought maybe she's telling someone--a girlfriend maybe or a boyfriend--telling them about what she's doing."

Mrs. Fairbanks laughed. "You're a first class idiot, Bill. Hiring Calley to do confidential work, handing over our intimate secrets, not even sure if you can trust her? How stupid is that?"

"I did trust her…at first. But then I trusted you and look what happened. All you bitches are the same. Lying, cheating, promising things. Guess it's always about money with women, isn't it? And that night, as I watched, I knew she was talking about me, laughing at the man who couldn't satisfy his own wife. She was whispering my dirty secret to someone and I couldn't let her do that. There were four people who knew what was going on and three of us weren't talking. So I had to make sure Calley wouldn't tell anyone."

"And the only way to do that was to kill her?" Scott asked.

"She could have ruined everything…all my plans."

Raleigh closed his notepad and slipped it in his breast pocket. "Looks like you did that yourself," he told the man.

Mrs. Fairbanks sat silently, witnessing her husband's paranoia, unable to look away from the sad scene. By the time he was being escorted outside she was crying.

DIGGER REDUX
by Warren Murphy

The only deep thought my mother ever confided to me was "God closes a door, then He opens a door."

"Hey, Ma, some of us are running out of doors. I've got no money and I drink too much and I'm living with you. For Christ's sake."

"God's got doors; He got lots of doors. You think God got no doors?"

All right, all right, all right. Later on, she passed through her exit door; she's gone now, no use arguing with even her memory.

Anyway, today I get a look through a new, very special door of my own as my death sentence is pronounced. This verdict is made rather cheerily by my pulmonologist who, when I ask him about my long term prospects, replied, "You don't have any. If I were you, I would not buy any tickets on myself in the office longevity pool."

"You take this matter of my impending death in rather cavalier fashion, don't you, sawbones? Do you do this with all your patients who are heading into the void?"

"No, most of them don't have your education or your sense of humor. Anyway, nothing I can do about it. I'm not the one who blew up my lungs by smoking a half a million cigarettes and drinking like a school of kissing gourami. Learn to live with it."

"In the fleeting few moments I have left?"

"Not so bad as that. It might be a year or two. They might invent something. An artificial lung that you strap to your back. You'll look like Lloyd Bridges in a Seahunt rerun but, what the hell, Archie, you might live forever. You might even swim the English channel."

For the record, my name is not Archie. It is Julian Burroughs, which honors both Catholics and Jews, each of which I once happened to be -- thanks to the lunacy of my parents -- and that should tell you all you need to know about why I am nuts to this very day. Back in the days when I was forced to work for a living, people called me Digger, not because I was a grave ghoul but because I was a very good private detective, inordinately skilled at digging up secrets people didn't want excavated. I worked in all the big cities, managed to support myself and along the way I drank more than I should, smoked vastly more than I should and now I'm dying more than I should.

Ahhh, to hell with it. The door of life was irretrievably closed. Now it's God's turn now to open one. All right, Ma, get Him on the job. I don't have forever, you know.

And, damn, like clockwork, here cometh Humphrey Chimpden Earwicker, otherwise known as God. The idiot who does the interminable Virginia weather report on the local news channel had finally stopped telling us what it was going to be like next Tuesday afternoon in Wyoming and read the winning lottery numbers and I find to my merriment that I have just won six million dollars in one of these crooked games that the commonwealth runs to keep poor people enslaved. Six million. Six million dollars. I am now a goddamn capitalist. Just imagine that, and I used to find it hard to make the $500 monthly rent on the hovel that I shared with my late sainted mother, she who opened doors. Thanks, Ma, for keeping God on the job.

What would you do if you found out that you had just won six million dollars?

Well, to each his own, but the first thing I did was to buy a bottle of very good vodka. I won't tell you the brand because now that I'm on the path to being rich and famous, there might be a law against such blatant product promotion... or at the very least I ought to get a cut for the free plug just like all those can't-act phoneys in Hollywood manage to do.

(Nicolas Cage, are you listening?)

All I will tell you is that this vodka comes from Finland. If I've broken the law, let the feds figure it out. They've got no shortage of geniuses living on my dime and I'm sure several will be investigating me by noon tomorrow.

So I moved aside the newspapers on the kitchen table, sat down and drank half the bottle and got out my checkbook from its hiding spot behind the breadbox. Now that I was going to be rich, the sky was the limit so I wrote a $5,000 check to Jews for Jesus; another 5 grand to Muslims for Sanity and Suicide; and $5,000 more to Christians Who Mind Their Own Business. I'll have to get a secretary to find out all their addresses.

Anybody else?

I did a job in Hollywood once and Clint Eastwood confided in me that his only political belief was that everybody should leave everybody else alone, but I couldn't think of any political organization that espoused such a dangerous principle. Maybe I'd start one. Maybe I'd send Clint a couple of bucks; I bet he could figure out where to send it. Aaaah, that's long term thinking. That's for next week as I settle comfortably into my life of wealth and privilege.

Important stuff first, but then my ballpoint pen ran dry so I took paper and an old crayon--what the hell was a crayon doing on my kitchen table?--and figured out that since I now had an estate, I should decide who to leave it to. It would be a real bitch if I died in the next two hours and hadn't decided whom I was going to leave behind to wallow in my filthy lucre.

I guess my ex-wife, Bruno, was one leading candidate. So were my two kids, what's-his-name and the girl.

Naaah, that wasn't going to work. The ex-wife hadn't communicated with me in in 20 years. The kids never failed on Father's Day to send me a card that was one of those ghastly things the American Legion sends out as fund-raisers and whose message was, basically, "Everybody else in the war has died. Arlington Cemetery is waiting for you."

No. I can do better than that.

Maybe the Pope. Phooey, forget him too. This guy wasn't John Paul who'd use money to get rid of communism. This guy'd spend it on ne'er-do-wells who wouldn't work and on public relations men to make himself loved by American liberals, who hated God, Jews, the Church and all popes up to him. Nope, no good, not a dime for the Pope, not on the money that I have worked so hard to accumulate over my lifetime.

I put the crayon away. I'd think about it tomorrow. So far the leading candidate was still Clint Eastwood.

Fifty Shades of Grey Fedora

I fell asleep on the couch thinking just get rich and suddenly the weight of the world is on your shoulders.

The next day I took my winning lottery ticket and my checkbook out of the crisper drawer in my empty refrigerator where I had put it to protect it all from forest fire and tore up the 14 checks I had written to Clint Eastwood while finishing the bottle of vodka. Then I called a lawyer I didn't owe any money to and, sans inspection, immediately bought a private little house on a private little lake, close to KMart and less than a mile from the local Applebee's where I generally hung out with a bunch of ex-Navy swindlers and bandits who cheated at everything, most particularly football pools which they ran constantly and which no one, except some wildly-complaining Turkish woman, ever seemed to win any money from. I also gave the lawyer my lottery ticket for safekeeping and made him lend me a thousand dollars 'cause I was short on ready cash. I further warned him, he being a lawyer, that if he stole my lottery ticket I would seek him out and kill him, my gun-carrying permit still being in full force. If I could only remember where I kept the ammunition.

My lawyer had a very beautiful and voluptuous secretary whom I had been coveting for years--I think her name was "Snarl"--and she liked to wear low cut blouses that showed enough cleavage to suffocate me. In all the years I had been dealing with her shyster boss, this babe had never once smiled at me, and now all of a sudden she was loading me down with cups of fresh coffee and brushing lint off the crotch of my pants and asking very earnest questions about the interesting life I must have been leading and maybe I could tell her about it one day.

Yeah, sure, babe. Now that I'm one of the moneyed few, we'll see how long that lasts. But who knows. File Snarl away for future reference.

And then I went home and the phone rang. Jeez, I hate that. This is how it always started back in the days when I was a working stiff, before I became one of the idle rich. I yelled at the phone: *"Dolce far niente."*

Stupid phone didn't speak Italian and kept ringing.

Okay, the guy on the phone was one of the few people in the world I regard as a friend. Big Tom Fallon. He had been a Virginia state cop and after a couple of wars, when I used to do a lot of work around here, I'd run into him a lot. He always seemed to be too straight for the job, too worried about right and wrong and guilty and innocent, and he didn't drink enough to make him really reliable, but for all of that we got along. Besides, we had a history.

Then for a long time I was working on the other side of the country for an insurance company, trying to make sure that no policy holders ever collected any money and finally I quit and came back to old Virginny to take care of my mother and eventually I found out that Big Tom had left the police force.

Well, that was all right. I'd always figured he'd quit some day but then somebody told me he went off to do something religious... maybe even become a priest... and I wasn't ready for that so I just chalked him off as another friend gone wrong.

It turned out that Tom Fallon had just gotten tired of being the enforcer of the law. He thought there was more to be gained for his immortal soul by being a believer in the law, a lover of the law, and a teacher and man of God.

I always knew there was something wrong with him.

He had been a little long in the tooth to become a priest, unlike previous wartimes when most people who signed up for the priesthood were just young draft dodgers still working on their Merle Travis-style guitar picking. Tom Fallon had already been to war and that may be why he signed up to do something for peace. War actually was where we met. He had saved my life in one of those far-away police actions and he quite neatly killed the people who were trying to kill me.

But that's something we never talked about. And we wouldn't talk about it today either. Death and the dodging thereof is nobody's business but your own.

And now here he is, pestering me on my telephone.

"Digger?"

"Yeah."

"This is Tom Fallon."

"I know. I recognize your voice. I'm not giving you any money. You'll just waste it."

"What are you talking about?"

"You went off and joined some gang of holy rollers, didn't you?"

"I joined the Catholic church, you meathead." He sighed. "Five years, not talking to you and now it's just as frustrating as it used to be. Let's get lunch. I need your help."

"Okay, but no money for the pope."

We met for lunch at Mercer's Buffalo Pub, a place near the Atlantic oceanfront where cops used to congregate and so I was there quite a bit because my work used to involve dealing with cops. Actually I was in most saloons quite a bit because that's what I did.

Tom Fallon was a big guy, even bigger than me, and he had a blond crew cut and was all decked out in a black suit and a clerical collar and looked like some refugee from a World Wide Wrestling production. .

I said "You had to wear that collar, didn't you? To make me feel uncomfortable drinking."

"It'd take more than a collar to stop you. Drink whatever you want."

The waitress approached us and Tom said "Diet coke, please." She nodded and glanced at me and I said, "vodka, rocks, piece of lime, house vodka's fine. Make it a double."

"Double?" she asked.

"Yes. I'm drinking for two."

The waitress was clearly simple because she started giggling, "Tee hee hee, drinking for two. Tee hee hee." Eventually she wandered off and I asked Tom, "So what's new and exciting?" I asked.

"We've just started having bingo on Tuesday nights," he said.

"You scare me, dear friend. Next you'll be trying to sell me chances on a new car," I told him.

"Don't worry. No proselytizing by me."

"You don't think I'm good material?"

"I know you too well, Digger. You're a piece of cake. You make believe you're different but you've always believed in that truth and justice and American way stuff, just like me. Add God and it's a perfect menu. If I wanted, I'd have you taking altar boy lessons before the day was up."

"Did you come here to recruit me?" I asked. "You get a bounty on agnostics?"

"No, this is serious stuff. I need help and you can give it. Did you ever hear of Anisette Guruji?"

Fifty Shades of Grey Fedora

"Not ever. How much does a fifth cost?"

"You've really got to get out more," Tom said. "Anisette Guruji is the crown princess of rapedom. You really never heard of her?"

"Not my field of interest, Tom. So what is she to me? Or you for that matter?"

"Remember that college soccer team down south and the phony rape charge?"

"Yeah. They got off, right?"

"Yeah, millions of dollars later; their lives messed up; wearing rapist badges for the rest of their

lives. That was the work of Anisette Guruji."

"Why her? What's she have to do with it?"

"She went to that town and she worked up everybody. It's what she does. She got all the press involved. All the morons in the prosecutor's office. All the students. The dimwit faculty who hate their schools, their students, their country and themselves."

"Easy, easy," I said. He was getting worked up.

"And the ringmaster is Anisette Guruji."

"Why her? How does she get herself involved in it? Is she a professor? Faculty? News creep? What?"

It was warm in the restaurant and Tom slid up the sleeves of his jacket. On his wrists and forearms I could see the ropy scars of old wounds. I knew where they came from. They came from saving me.

Tom saw me looking and wordlessly pushed his sleeves back down. There were some things we would never deal with. Mean are like that.

"There has been a whole bunch of make believe rapes all across the east. This state, our state, was a particular target for some reason. College fraternities get closed. Kid's lives are disrupted by phoney charges, lots of headlines and then nothing happens except some kids have their reputations and probably their lives ruined. Some even committed suicide. Books get written, TV shows, movies about crimes that never happened. Naming as criminals people who were never there. Digger, there's a whole cottage industry out there of people who are pushing the rape button all the time and the whole damned country hears the bell. They've taken on the colleges of America. Crazies are running loose. Did you see the idiot who said that one out of five sexual encounters on campus are rape. One out of five... 20 percent. You know what the real statistic is? Six out of a thousand. That stat's from the stupid justice department which is no friend of any college fraternity. That's less than one percent. But the agitators just keep lying away and the useless press just keeps printing that crap."

"Yeah, okay. Tom, enough. I've read some of that stuff. I don't pay much attention to it. Which brings up... why am I here?"

"Well, every time one of these happens, this babe Anisette Guruji shows up, and stirs the soup, and makes everybody nuts, and... well, now, now, they're coming right here to our fair city and my school and that means real trouble."

I started to answer and the tee-hee-hee waitress showed up to see if we wanted another drink. She asked Tom, "What do I call you, sir? Father? Reverend."

"Call him imam. That's what I do," I said.

"Okay. Imam it is." We ordered another drink and she went away.

"Okay. So tell me about this Anisette Guruji. That's the stupidest name I ever heard."

"She's a nothing. A cipher. She's got no degrees I can find, no teaching credentials, but she knows how to worm her way into every meeting, and take it over and she sounds like she knows what she's saying. She gets herself invited by looney students and then she takes over. I heard the last time she was at a college in West Virginia and the idiots tried to hire her for the faculty, without even knowing who she was."

"You know a lot about her."

"Hey, pal, I used to be a cop too, remember? I can find out what I need to find out. It takes me longer now but I can still do it."

"Trouble now is you can't do anything about it?"

"That's true," Tom Fallon said. "I can learn but I can't act."

"She's supposed to be coming here?"

"Next week. She'll tear this school apart. My kids in this school won't be able to deal with this. They're all church-bound. They're the next generation of priests and nuns. I've got my life staked on them. And she'll ruin their lives and I can't do anything."

"Well, count yourself blessed, Imam. I can."

Fifty Shades of Grey Fedora

***

So here I am, I've got a credit line for six million bucks –- (less taxes of course) –- burning a hole in my pocket, so I could easily afford getting a hit man to dispose of the pest, Anisette Guruji. But as soon as her naked crab-eaten body floated ashore at Rudee's Inlet, Tom Fallon would know I was behind it.

That simply would not do. Besides, if I thought that murder was any kind of a solution to anything, I never would have gotten divorced. No, it was time for me to trot out my well-worn... ahh, be honest, rusted... detecting skills and get on Anisette's trail.

The city library was my first stop. A very helpful assistant showed me how to use the computer and bring up all the stories and news items about Anisette.

I don't know what I expected. It's been my experience that most of the time, you get into rape stories and the women who are always claiming they've been assaulted, usually have faces like footprints, and you can look at them and think, it's rape or nothing.

But Anisette was something else. There were only a couple of pictures of her but they would have done justice to the winner of the pole-dancing championship at the local titty bar. She wasn't really beautiful but she wore the shortest skirts I ever saw on a female above the age of six and had the knockers of a milk maiden, She also had long hair that looked like it had been transplanted from Secretariat, red, luxurious. It wasn't quite perfect, but it wasn't bad either. Ditto the face.

I don't know what I expected. But I guess somebody who's out peddling sex stories ought to look like she's read a couple or lived a couple in her life. She qualified. Sort of. She kind of had the look of someone who's not as pretty as she really wanted to be but wasn't about to give up.

The library's computer files gave no background though on where she came from, nationality, age, all the things you'd expect would be dredged up for some media favorite. It did talk a lot about book contracts and movie deals, but no hard facts, just rumor mill stuff. Maybe the rules of press coverage were changing. Maybe the press didn't care about yesterdays anymore. Who was that stupid minister from News York, was it Al Dullard, whose deceitful, lying, thieving behavior in the past was swept under the rug so he could become a "news analyst" on some god-forsaken make believe TV channel? Nobody cared about real information anymore.

I asked the librarian on duty if I could get copies of all the clippings but she said it would have to wait until Monday when the tech worker was due in.

So I was stuck with my notes and there wasn't much factual data about Anisette Guruji but the computer had given me her schedule. Tomorrow night she was talking to a student group at a small college just across the border in North Carolina.

Tom Fallon couldn't deal with this.

But I would be there.

One of the many differences between me and Tom Fallon was that he was a cop, always firmly on that side of the law, and fair enough, good for him. But I had made my living, working in that gray land between crime and law and while I knew a lot of good cops like Tom Fallon, I used to know a lot of somewhat not-so-perfect people who worked the other side of the street.

I now went to go find me one and as luck would have it the Timbuktu Bar still had the same name in the same location where it had been years before. And it was just as black as it had been back in the long ago. I was the only white face in the place and you could almost hear people bristle when I walked in and I just glanced around, didn't see the face I was looking for, and turned back toward the door.

And then suddenly there was a scream:

"Digger! Digger!"

I turned around and had fall into my arms an incredibly beautiful young black woman, dressed in jeans and a sequined tee shirt. She reached up and kissed me on the cheek and hugged me tightly, and Jesus, god almightly, I could feel her nipples rubbing against my chest.

"What are you doing here in the heart of the Congo?"

She wasn't the only one wondering. The eight other black guys sitting around the bar were staring too.

"Just came to see Ex. I might need a favor."

"He'll be here in a couple. And anything for you."

She let go of me, turned around, and said loudly, "Listen, you mopes. This is Digger. He's Ex's friend and mine. Don't forget it."

The bartender who had been hanging back, seemingly ready to bolt into the kitchen, came up slowly and said, "You're Digger?"

I nodded.

"Welcome to Timbuktu," he said.

"He drinks vodka. He never changes," my sudden best friend said. She took my arm and pulled me down to the far end of the bar. And as soon as I sat down, she lifted the phone which was on the cord around her neck and took a picture of me.

Her name was Chili. She didn't look a day older than the last time I had seen her, which meant she might have been anything, but she looked 18 and what you'd think looking at her would have gotten you put in jail. She was the main squeeze of my old friend Shim-Sham. She was also, it turned out, a maniacal photo buff and soon I had posed for photos with all the thugs in the bar, not too many of whom were delighted about being seen in my company.

Shim-Sham, whose name in the neighborhood was Ex – that was not for Muslim; that was for Executioner and people knew not to mess with him. It was not because he was a killer. It was just that he could put such a hurting on you in so many ways that you'd wish you were dead.

I had met him years before when I had a P.I. office not far from here. One day his mother showed up and asked me to help her "little boy." He had been arrested for carrying a weapon in the neighborhood of a drugstore that had been held up earlier.

His mother was an elegant old lady and she said, "In the neighborhood, they say that you're a good man, Mister Digger, and I swear to God this was all a mistake. Lemuel (-- that was Shim-Sham's given name --) found the gun on the street and was looking for a policeman to give it to."

I don't know. You hear that stuff on the street a thousand times, but something about that lady rang true and I tracked down the real owner of the gun and got Shim-Sham off the hook, and since then I owned him.

Don't get the wrong idea. He wasn't a criminal. He was pleased to refer to himself as an entrepreneur and I absolutely know that's true. He owned part of a bakery, and a bar, maybe even this one I was in right now, and a restaurant and a carwash and maybe he had his hands in every pot in town. And did he do some stuff on the shady side? Probably but it didn't matter to me.

Most important, he kept up to date on the comings and goings of the bad folk. Fact is if I wanted somebody killed, I could call Shim-Sham. He'd find me one. If I needed a car boosted, I could call him. And if I needed somebody to teach a Sunday School class, Shim-Sham could come and do it himself.

And as smart as he was, his girlfriend Chili was every bit as smart. And they were both beautiful. It was like they belonged to some alien race that had been dropped down on earth when we weren't looking. And then one of Chili's sisters got into deep grief once with the cops and I got her out too. How do I get involved with these folks?

So I was just finishing my drink with Chili and our old-times chat when Shim-Sham showed up. He was wearing a polished tan silk suit that in my entire life I have never been able to afford and he clapped me on the back and said, "Digger, after all these years? Who do I have to hit this time?"

I said, "Go away, you fairy. If I needed somebody hit, I'd talk to Chili... the deadlier of the species."

"You're right about that one. But what do you need?" I started to tell them about the antics of Anisette Guruji, but it turned out that Chili was an inveterate news reader and watcher and knew more about the woman agitator than I did.

"So? So what? Some woman with a big mouth is out there raising hell. Nothing new there," Shim-Sham said.

"Yeah, but she's planning to come to town and talk to a church school and I don't want her to."

"You taking the vows?"

"Somebody I owe," I said.

He answered, "My lady here, and I, we both owe you. It's time we paid back too. So let's do it. Besides it would be nice to spend a day with you and anyway, I've got nothing on the schedule that won't wait."

So we all drove to the small North Carolina campus town in Shim-Sham's car which to my surprise was a rather ordinary-looking dark blue Ford sedan.

Shim-Sham and I mostly grunted at each other, pretending it was small talk, while Chili sat in back, reading clippings which she had been able to get from the library, the same ones that they had refused to make available to me. Beautiful women always get, a pass, don't they?

Once in a while, I hard a click from the back which turned out to be her taking pictures of local scenery with her cell-phone camera.

I settled back into the seat. "Nice wheels" I said.

"I keep my good one home in the garage. This is for scut work. Cops never stop you in a blue Ford. Especially driving around white guys. Have you figured out what you're going to do?"

"I thought we'd come up with something."

Chili said, "Oh, dear, lock up the children. He got a plan."

"All quiet in the cheap seats," I said. "I thought first I'd take a look at her. I'm a bear of very little brain. I've got to figure she's in this for the money somehow..."

"Naaah," Shim-Sham said. "She's in it for the glory. She wants to be famous."

"And that makes her worse," Chili said.

"If it was money, I thought we could bribe her."

Shim-Sham said, "Sometimes bribery works. But what always works is fear."

"Damn right," Chili said.

"I don't know," I said.

"You don't have to. We do," answered Shim-Sham.

***

We drove into the small North Carolina town following signs all the way pointing out the route to the state community college. Along the way, I larned that Shim-Sham and Chili had already rented a hotel room..."just in case we need it." They seemed to be in charge of everything, so as they turned onto Main Street, I said, "Stop here."

"Here?" Shim-Sham asked.

"Right here. Go get a cup of coffee or something. I'll only be a few minutes."

As I got out of the car, I thought once more that maybe it would have been smarter to bring a cop with me, instead of Shim-Sham and

Chili. Maybe that was a rule of life. If you're going to do crazy shit, have a cop with you. But it also might help more if you first had some idea what you're going to do.

I went into a small print shop on the deserted-looking central street of town and was met by an old man with thick eyeglasses and a ratty looking navy blue sweater. He was wrapping a red scarf around his neck.

"I need some business cards."

"Just getting ready to close. Maybe you come back Monday?"

"I only need a couple of cards. Very simple. Five minutes is all it would take."

"It'll only take five minutes on Monday too."

"But on Monday I won't pay fifty dollars for a half dozen cards. Today I will."

"What do you want on them?" the man said. He reached behind the counter and took an old green plastic eyeshade and put it on.

I printed it out on a piece of scrap paper.

BLOCKO-CONGLOM BOOKS & FILMS
Making tomorrow's hits today.
Beverly Hill, CA
Bradford Diggleby, Director of Productions

"You want a phone number on there, Mr. Diggleby?" the printer asked. He had used tweezers to pick out the loose pieces of type and set them into a wooden form.

"No, no phone number. You know, us big Hollywood types, we give out our number and every peasant starts pestering us."

After a few minutes the printer handed me a small pile of business cards, plain black ink on a dark thick beige paper. "Don't smear them. Give them a few minutes to dry."

"Gotcha," I said and handed the man a $50 bill. "Nice work."

Sitting in the front seat of the car, I neatly printed on one of the cards: "Let's talk. Leaving town soon but have a million dollar contract for a book called 'I Speak for the Victims.'"

Chili looked at it. "Perfect," she said.

The rally was called "When No Means No," and it was held in a student union building just near the front of the campus. I did not know what to expect, college rallies hardly being my regular cup of tea, but Anisette Gurunji clearly knew how to draw a crowd because every seat was filled and it was only because of Chili's astounding beauty that three jocks got up and gave us their seats. I was surprised that almost half the audience were males and mentioned it to Shim-Sham., who answered, "They're just trying to get laid."

There was a lot of yelling and shouting and a bunch of people getting up and bearing witness to how they had been sexually assaulted and their lives weren't worth spit since then and to my jaded ear and sensibility, they all sounded like well-rehearsed pieces of political theater.

But Anisette herself seemed to know what she was doing. It was like the performance of a professional minister who's given the sermon a hundred, a thousand times before and can do it in his sleep. She was nowhere near as good looking as she was in the clips that I had seen in the library; she was trim enough but I could see that she had been a fat girl who managed somehow to lose a lot of weight, but hadn't yet built up the muscle to replace the old suet, so she kind of looked a little pasty and soft.

"Tub of lard," Chili sniffed and whispered in my ear. "And she likes to look like a slut. That tells you something. She ought to get clothes that fit instead of waving her big ass around."

Still Anisette led the audience, told stories of colleges where rapes had occurred and said if this school hadn't reported any yet, "Don't kid yourself. You think they haven't happened. Yes, they have. You've heard them here tonight. Right here. Right among your classmates but until tonight, they're too frightened and too embarrassed to say anything. But we're going to change that. We're going to bring these evil deeds out into the open and the transgressors will be punished."

"I want you all to know that I and all the people supporting me – and there are hundreds, thousands across the country, they will be here for the victims when it happens and they're not afraid anymore. And trust me, it will happen. One out of five sexual encounters is a rape and one out of five of you young ladies will be victims. Maybe even more."

She stopped, took a deep breath, and then walked back and forth across the stage.

"My staff has not finished its investigations yet, but I can tell you that we have discovered more than five cases of rape on this campus which were never reported and which were never acted upon by the administration."

There was a buzz in the audience but Anisette Guruji waved her hands to silence the crowd. "It will be soon," she said. "And those guilty of these crimes will finally face justice.

"And now, fellow combatants in the war against sexual slaughter, good night. You will see me again." She started to move to the side of the stage.

Chili leaned over to me and said, "Give me that business car, the one you signed."

She grabbed it from me and as beautiful women were always able to make their way through crowds, she ran up to the stage, over to the wings and followed Anisette Guruji out into the side of the theater.

I sat with Shim-Sham as the crowd moved around us.

"What is she up to?"

"Whatever it is, it's smarter than anything you or me could figure out," Shim-Sham said.

Except for small clusters of students, the auditorium had mostly emptied when Chili came back to join us. She ignored me and took Shim-Sham off to a side where they did a lot of heavy-duty whispering

I waited as long as I, then finally butted in. "What's going on?" he asked.

Chili looked up at me and once again, I thought that her features were so incredibly beautiful that it was hard to believe that she was speaking to me, a mere mortal.

"Mister Digger, my friend," she said. "You don't want this woman talking in our town next week, right?"

"Right."

"She won't. Why don't we all go over to the hotel and get a drink? We rented a room in the name of Sherman."

"You can't do stuff like this," I said. "I'm the detective here."

She put her arm around me and gave him her smile for the ages. "You're absolutely right and we will let you know how it all works out. But there are things, it's better, Mister Digger, that you don't know."

The hotel was only two blocks away so we drove over and they left me waiting at the bar while they vanished for a while.

I don't dilly-dally around when I'm drinking but I only had chance to down two before Chili and Shim-Sham came back in.

"Time to go," Chili told me.

"We haven't done our business."

"Yes, we have. Time to go."

She still had her camera hanging around her neck and I asked her if we should take a picture for our scrapbook.

She and Shim-Sham laughed, and he said, "We have all the pictures we need." And Shim-Sham said again, "let's get out of here." I took my wallet out to get a credit card, but Shim-Sham said, "Not this time. This is a cash trip. No paper trail."

And Chili handed me the wrinkled business card for BLOCKO-CONGLOM BOOKS AND FILMS. "You won't be needing this any more."

We were well out of town when I finally asked, "Okay. Isn't it about time that you told me what laws we broke tonight?"

Shim-Sham laughed and said, "I'm shocked. Absolutely shocked."

"Madame Anisette won't be coming to our town," Chili said.

"You didn't kill her, did you?"

"Nope. Strictly non-violent persuasion. We owed you. We didn't want you to get into any trouble," Shim-Sham said.

Remind me not ever to get on the wrong side of this pair. As it turned out, what they did was take Anisette Gurunji to the pre-rented hotel room where they drugged her up. Then while she was passed out, they posed her in a lot of definitely non-rape positions with Shim-Sham. And then they left her copies of some of the pictures and a note that warned her basically to "Stay out of Dodge or the world gets the photos."

Chili said, "I left the tramp twenty bucks on the mantle."

"Classy," I said, kind of dumfounded by it all.

"Perfect," Chili said. "The great protector of womankind from rape turns out to be a horny little whore doing her part for twenty bucks."

"And we have done our part," Shim-Sham said

I said, "Chili, one of these days, I just may lay a million dollars on you."

Chili said, "Thrilled, I'm sure. Any special reason?"

"Because it is so rare to meet a lady of your impeccable character and your resourcefulness in the twilight of my years. And a do-gooder to boot."

Chili said, "Sounds right to me."

Shim-Sham said, "Anything we can do to speed up the arrival of this glorious day?"

"Not if I see you coming."

They left me off back at my apartment, which I would soon be leaving for the house I'd just bought. We made many promises about getting together often which somehow none of us would keep. Except maybe the threat of a million dollars would focus our minds. Then I went into the kitchen, made a disgusting pot of instant coffee, thought about the evening's festivities, and decided maybe it was time to call my lawyer's secretary, Miss Snarl. She might be able to use a million dollars too.

But I fell asleep first.

There was always tomorrow. Million, millions everywhere.

Fifty Shades of Grey Fedora

A CONCRETE GARTER BELT
by M. Ruth Myers

I'd spent an unexpected bonus from a client on a tire for my DeSoto, slugs for my Smith & Wesson and a blue silk garter belt. I'd never owned fancy undies before, and I was at my desk feeling like a Vanderbilt. Then a woman with fading brown hair walked in and guilt elbowed me over my extravagance.

She was in her mid-thirties but too much hard work and too little kindness had made her look older. Her dress had been washed so often you could read the headlines through it.

"Maggie Sullivan?" Her eyes held the uncomprehending misery of an animal hit by a car. "Izzy at the five and dime, says you're a real good detective. If you don't help me, I don't know what I'll do!"

I pushed aside the afternoon paper, which told me Dayton had finished installing two-way radios in all its police cars in preparation for a visit by FDR. The woman didn't seem to notice. She didn't notice as she came to sit in the chair in front of my desk, either. She just kept talking, scared I'd stop her before she'd said her piece.

"It's my sis. My kid sis. The police — they say since she's eighteen, they can't help unless I show there was — that she didn't leave on her own. But she wouldn't! She wouldn't go off without telling me!"

Tears started to spill down her face. I took out the bottle of gin that lent my office a homey touch and poured us both some.

"Your sister's disappeared?" I splashed in tonic and nudged one glass toward her.

She'd fished out a handkerchief as tired as her dress and was dabbing futilely at her eyes. She nodded.

"Why don't you tell me your name? We'll start there."

"Walsh. Norma Walsh. My sister's Annie. See? This is her. You've got to give this back, though." Tenderly she unwrapped a ragged towel to reveal a framed photograph. It showed an exquisitely pretty girl, her face sweet and fresh. "I raised her since she was a baby, three years old. We're all we've got, the two of us. That's why I know she'd never—"

Threatened by tears again, she took a small sip of gin.

My fancy garter belt started to pinch. Or maybe it was my conscience. I'd probably spent more on my bit of blue silk than the woman in front of me earned in a week. She'd earned it hard, too, scrubbing floors or clothes from the looks of her roughened hands. I knew she couldn't pay, but I had a little pad in my bank account just now. Regular clients that just about paid my bills. Maybe talking to her would turn up some possibility she'd overlooked.

"How long's Annie been missing?"

"A week yesterday. When she went off to work. Annie's got a good job." Norma frowned. "She was happy and humming and saying where should we go for my birthday, 'cause we save so we can take the trolley to one of the parks to walk on our birthdays. But she missed — she'd never miss my birthday! That's how I know—"

Pressing her sodden hanky to lips that threatened to crumple, she struggled to hold herself together. I swiveled my chair and looked out my open window to give her some privacy. A freight train clattered by on the nearby tracks. The scent of tomatoes that had lain in the sun all day drifted up from carts in the produce market.

What had made Norma frown when she mentioned Annie's swell job? I waited to ask until I'd learned other things: Annie worked at a secretarial service. She didn't have a boyfriend. The girls she'd gone to high school with were mostly married and she hadn't been where she worked long enough to be close to anyone there, so as far as Norma knew, she didn't have any friends.

"When you started to tell me about Annie's job, you stopped and frowned," I said. "Was she worried? Having some sort of problem?"

Norma looked down and twisted her handkerchief.

"No... Just... a couple weeks back she came home upset. Wouldn't say why at first, but then she said someone at work had gotten fresh."

"Did she tell you who?"

She shook her head. Life had returned to her eyes.

Fifty Shades of Grey Fedora

"You're going to look for her, aren't you? I went to a man detective, and at first he listened, but then he turned nasty. Told me to get and called me a deadbeat. I don't expect you to work for nothing, though, see?"

Taking a dollar bill from her pocket, she smoothed it reverently.

"It's all I've got now, but I'll pay every week—"

"Wait till I learn something."

"No. I want you to take it."

Paying mattered to her. I nodded.

"You're going to find Annie. I know it." She rose with more energy than she'd had coming in.

It was almost six o'clock on a Friday.

"I can't do anything until Monday," I said.

"Can I stop by then? After I get off work? Maybe you'll know something."

"Sure. I guess."

But Monday two paragraphs on an inside page of the morning paper told me they'd fished the body of a woman named Norma Walsh out of the river.

***

"The woman's lungs were full of water. She drowned herself."

Tipped back in his chair, the head of homicide, a grizzled guy named Freeze, squinted up at me through smoke from one of the cigarettes he smoked constantly. I stood with my fist planted on my hip to keep from popping his jellybean nose.

"Look, Freeze---"

"Yeah, I know. She gave you her last two bucks. She was coming to see you today. You already told me six times."

We were in Market House, the ornate white building where detectives and police bigwigs were headquartered. Men at nearby desks pretended to work while their ears stretched, hoping for fireworks. Freeze was a decent cop, but he didn't like ideas that weren't his own. Mine had been right enough times that he resented it.

"Look, Miss Sullivan, if you've got some kind of evidence, I'll listen. Woman's intuition or a leprechaun whispering in your ear doesn't count."

Snickers issued from several men in the squad room. Freeze let his chair down on all four legs and ground out a stub of cigarette that would fit in a thimble.

"Kid sister she dotes on is gone. Behind in her rent. Boss at the laundry she worked at had threatened to fire her because she'd been walking around like a sleepwalker. Why wouldn't the dame drown herself?"

Because she'd expected me to move mountains. Because she'd been sure I'd have something to tell her today.

Two seconds more with Freeze and I'd wind up in jail for punching him. Instead I decided to listen to the leprechaun urging me to earn Norma Walsh's retainer.

***

My client was dead, and I wasn't inclined to believe it was suicide. The sister she'd hired me to find was still missing and I was in a lousy mood. To top it off, one of the metal supporters on my pretty garter belt was twisted and driving me crazy. All in all, it seemed like a good time to hunt a new job.

Annie Walsh had worked at a second-rate secretarial service called Duncan's Dependables. It was west of Wayne Ave. Through a front window I could see at least two dozen women, all of them young, typing away at desks that were lined up like eggs in a carton. Besides the typists, two men and a couple of girls plied telephones, providing answering service. In an open-front booth a man was trying to pace while a girl took dictation.

At twenty-six I was nearly a decade older than most of them, but department store security work before I hung out my shingle had taught me some tricks about dressing. Walking back to my car, I buttoned my blouse all the way to the top and changed my hat for a perkier number. By the time I entered the secretarial service, I'd shaved off enough years to look wide-eyed in my little gray suit.

"May I help?" A man with a mustache decorating his flat face came to the side-by-side desks that served as a counter.

"Oh, I hope so," I piped. "My friend Anne Walsh said this was a nice place to work, so I've come to apply."

"We're not hiring."

"Gee, could I just have a word with Annie, then? She mentioned another place too, but I can't remember the name." I peered around as if hunting Annie. His face tightened.

At one of the typewriters closest to us, a plump girl with a pink birthmark covering half her jaw looked up with interest. Her eyes dropped to her work again when she saw I'd noticed.

"Any problem here, Mr. Brown?" A man appeared in the doorway of a small office to one side of the girl. He was neat albeit rotund. His brown hair was salted with silver and mostly still on his head.

"No, sir. Anne Walsh apparently gave her the impression we were hiring. I told her we weren't."

"Walsh... Wasn't that the girl who left a week or two back?"

"Yes, sir."

The girl with the birthmark cocked her head ever so slightly.

The boss man was eyeing my gams. He gave me a smile from small, moist lips.

"Well, now, it seems to me every young woman deserves a chance. Don't you think, my dear?" His hand eased onto my shoulder and patted. The innocent, kindly uncle.

"Oh yes, Mr.—?"

"Duncan. I'm ringmaster here." He chuckled affably. "The least we can do is let you take a typing test. I'll show her back," he added to the flat-faced man.

"Oh, thanks!" I said as Duncan's hand slipped to the small of my back to guide me gallantly around the front desk and between the rows. I had a feeling I knew who'd gotten fresh with Annie. "Gee, this does look like a nice place. Where'd Annie go?"

"I think someone told me she found a better position. Happens to us all the time," He chuckled again.

Did I imagine one of the girls shrank back as Duncan passed? Maybe not. Another, a pretty brunette with rosy cheeks, swallowed nervously and hit a wrong key as he neared. She cranked out the page she'd been working on and reached for a fresh carbon set. Duncan leaned down, covering her trembling hand with his.

"Don't worry, dear. As long as she keeps her head, a smart girl like you's not going to get fired over a spoiled page or two. In fact a little bird told me you're going to start seeing something extra in your pay envelope."

She didn't respond.

At the back of the room he told a woman whose larger desk and appurtenances identified her as a supervisor to give me a typing test and let me fill out an application. That woman didn't seem to like him much either. She gave a curt nod without looking up from her work until he'd left. When she did, her eyes flashed active loathing.

I took my time settling in at a vacant machine to take my test. The supervisor attributed it to nervousness and murmured answers. One of the young fellows answering phones noticed me and gave me a wink and a thumb up before resuming his work.

I didn't pass my typing test, but by the time I left I'd learned two things: Several women there didn't think much of affable Mr. Duncan, maybe even were wary of him. And the story of Annie getting a better job was bunk. She wouldn't have run out on the sister who'd raised her.

If Annie Walsh wasn't already dead, she was in serious trouble.

***

I spent the rest of the morning doing background checks on applicants for a job in a bank. The worn out two dollar bill from Norma Walsh held in place by the edge of my telephone reproached me silently. She'd hired me to find her sister, and if Annie was still alive, I was going to.

That afternoon a man came in wanting to hire me to find a girlfriend who'd walked out on him six months before. I looked at Norma's payment and said I couldn't.

Half an hour before quitting time, I put on a drab little Princess Eugenie hat. At a drugstore across from the secretarial service, I paged through magazines and watched the girls who'd typed all day bubble out to join other home bound workers hustling toward trolleys.

When I spotted the girl with the birthmark, I went out and fell into step a few yards behind her. I checked in windows I passed to make sure neither Duncan nor the fellow with the flat face had appeared. A pair of girls from the secretarial service trotted past me, giggling and spoke to her. I saw her shoulders slump as they hurried on. She crossed the street and walked a block to catch another line. No one spoke to her at the stop where she waited, and no one seemed to notice her. Dawdling behind her, I got on when she did and squeezed into the empty seat next to her ahead of hefty man who'd paused to mop his brow.

A frown appeared on the girl's forehead as she tried to place me. Suddenly her eyes widened.

"Yeah. I'm the one who came in asking about Annie Walsh. Her sister hired me to find her."

I gave her one of my cards.

"Oh! I don't know where she went, honest! Please! I don't want to lose my job."

She looked around in a panic, fearful of being spotted with me.

"Is that how Duncan gets away with putting his hands all over the girls? Because they're afraid of losing their jobs?" FDR's New Deal was improving things, but jobs were still too hard to find to risk losing one.

I heard her gasp.

"How did you—? Yes. But that's all I know!"

"You were curious what they'd say when I asked about Annie. It's clear you're smarter than most of the girls you work with. I'll bet you've picked up things you don't even realize." I paused. "I was hoping if you had time for me to buy you a sandwich, you could tell me what Annie was like at least. That would help some."

The way her face lighted, I knew she hadn't had many compliments. Or invitations. I didn't always like myself for the things I did to get information.

After looking around again, the girl said she guessed she had time if it would help. Her name was Irene. We got off near where she lived and she pointed out a mom and pop café. A bigger place across the way advertised booze as well as food. I asked if she'd mind going there. Her eyes got big, but she said she guessed it was okay.

They didn't have dark beer so I got a gin and tonic. She had ginger ale. I let her get comfortable first. We discussed the menu and I asked how long she'd worked at Duncan's place.

"I liked Annie," she said, broaching the subject first. "We ate lunch together sometimes. The other girls... I guess they feel uncomfortable around me. Because of... " She indicated her disfigurement. "Annie usually just had an apple or boiled egg, though. She was saving to buy a birthday gift for her sister. I guess she must be real worried, huh?"

I'd told her Norma had hired me, but not the part about her being dead.

"Tell me about Annie's last day at work. Everything you remember."

The rest of her face grew as red as the birthmark. She picked at her sandwich.

"That afternoon I went to the washroom. The supply room's back there too, and I heard a shriek. And a... like someone getting smacked. A few seconds later, Annie came in crying. One side of her blouse was pulled out. I didn't know what to do, she was so upset. So I said something stupid, like 'hey, you're going to make your eyes red if you keep crying'. And I - I left. I was at my desk typing when Mr. Duncan stomped into his office and slammed the door. He had a red streak on his cheek."

"Like someone had scratched him?"

"No. More like slapped."

"What then?"

"A little later one of Mr. Duncan's friends came in. They walked through the office and out back. I don't know why. On the way, Mr. Duncan stopped at Annie's desk and gave her shoulder one of those nasty little rubs he likes to give. I thought poor Annie was going to be sick at her stomach. Mr. Duncan came back in alone. He said something to Mrs. French — that's our supervisor — and not long after, she told Annie to take the rest of day off, that she looked peaked. That's what the girl sitting next to Annie said anyway."

Irene traced patterns in the crumbs of her sandwich while I considered the merits of another gin and tonic. I asked if the girl who'd sat next to Annie might tell me anything. Irene didn't think so. The supervisor? She had a kid and a sick husband who needed expensive medicine every month.

"What about Duncan's friend," I said. "Do you know his name?"

She thought a minute. "Charlie something. Mr. Duncan calls him Charlie."

"Do you know his last name? Where he lives? What he does?"

She started to shake her head. Then her whole face brightened.

"But we all think Mr. Duncan cats around when his wife goes to visit his sister. He comes in late and acts like he has a headache." She leaned over her elbows, her earlier fear forgotten. "He took Mrs.

Duncan down to the station this afternoon. Maybe you could follow him tomorrow like you did me — see if he goes out with Charlie."

Or maybe I could just pay Duncan a visit.

***

The phone book back at my office told me Duncan's address. I took the Smith & Wesson from its pocket under my chair. I doubted I'd need it with Duncan, but I might later. Five years of being in the business I was, and a woman, had taught me not to take chances.

Duncan lived north of the river in a section where streets were named for colleges and houses were several rungs nicer than average. Bullying young working women paid nicely, apparently.

His house was a two-story Tudors somewhat smaller than its neighbors. I hadn't expected anyone to be home. My plan was to peek in the garage in back, and if it was empty to wait. The sight of a light in a downstairs room suggested I might have to alter that plan. I parked the DeSoto and watched for ten minutes. There were no signs of life.

As quietly as possible I eased the car door closed and crossed the street. Cloud fingers tickled the moon as I went up the walk. At the door I stopped and listened. No voices. No sounds from a radio, which a household as prosperous as this would probably have. Only silence answered when I rang the bell, so I moved around to the side.

Enough light leaked out from the neighboring house for me to make out a car in Duncan's garage. Hugging the shadows, I slipped back and looked and found nothing interesting. As I turned back, I noticed a light in an upstairs room. It hadn't been visible from the street.

Someone was home and not answering the door. I wondered why. When I went around and tried the front door, it was unlocked. Stepping in softly, I moved through the downstairs rooms. No sign of life. A door with a sturdy lock led from the kitchen into a cellar. I couldn't see Duncan stashing Annie, alive or dead, where his missus might go down for a jar of peach preserves and happen upon her. In any case, I'd better find out who was upstairs before taking a look.

Before starting up, I removed the .38 from my purse. The stairs were in good repair, nary a squeak. The rooms I checked in passing were empty. From the lighted one at the rear I caught scraps of a woman's voice now, and indistinct grunts. As I moved toward the sounds, I had a not-quite-accurate hunch what I'd find. I eased the door open.

There, in what I hoped wasn't his marital bed, Duncan was hammering a bleached blonde. His naked haunches looked like lumps of biscuit dough jiggling on top of the woman, who methodically moaned 'Oh, yes, honey!' while chewing gum and examining her nails. Between her yelps and his bouncing, I was impressed she didn't swallow the gum.

When she noticed me standing there with the gun in my hand, she screamed. Duncan probably thought it was ecstasy. Crossing the room in two swift strides, I smacked one pasty buttock as hard as I could.

Duncan howled and collapsed. Apparently his playmates didn't get rough.

"Where's Annie?"

He squirmed to his side, looking dazed. Recognition came slowly. As it did, his mouth opened.

"Yeah. It's me," I said. "I flunked my typing test, but I excel at getting information." I waggled the Smith & Wesson to make my point.

The blonde had drawn herself up to the head of the bed and was watching in terror. She didn't have the look of a girlfriend. She had the look of by-the-hour at bargain rates. With my free hand I fished two dollars out of my purse and extended them. She grinned, grabbed them and her clothes and took off.

"Annie," I repeated, looking Duncan full in the eyes.

His feet were treading the tangled sheets. He tried to cover himself. I jerked the sheet from him hand.

"I don't know where she is! She's not here! You can look."

I grabbed his pinkie and bent it back, not far enough to break. He shrieked.

"Next, I shoot off one of your toes. Where is she?"

"She – she went off with a man. That's all I know!"

"Or maybe something you'd miss more than a toe."

I aimed the gun. He shrieked again. The part that led him got smaller than it already was.

"Charlie has her! Charlie has her locked up! He likes – he likes girls like her. Girls who – who struggle."

My stomach turned over.

"Charlie runs a cathouse?"

"No! It's just him and the girls."

Girls. Plural. Was pal Charlie drugging them? How else could he keep them in line? The only good part of what I was hearing was that Annie must be alive.

"Charlie's rich. He gives them everything," Duncan was babbling. "It's harmless, what he makes them do. Just a – a different kind of pleasure."

I raised the gun to his face. He shut up.

"Charlie's last name and address. Or we can go down to your study and look through your address book. If we have to do that, you'll leave bloody footprints."

He whimpered and told me. I let him put his shirt on, but not his pants. We went downstairs. Together we checked his address book so I could make sure the weasel hadn't lied.

"What are you going to do to me?" he asked when I was satisfied.

I sat in his desk chair, enjoying myself.

"Depends on whether you go on pawing girls who work for you. If you do, I might just hear about it."

He moaned.

"Why'd you kill Annie's sister?"

"I didn't! She went to see a detective. He'd done some work for me so he called me and told me this woman had come in with crazy ideas. I thought I should tell Charlie — warn him. But I didn't know he'd – he'd—"

"Dry up."

I marched him down the cellar stairs, which he didn't like much. I made him unscrew the light bulb and hand it to me, which he liked even less. Then I went back up and locked the door while he pounded the other side, pleading.

"You can't leave me down here! I'll starve!"

"Your wife will be home in a couple of days. She'll let you out."

I shoved the kitchen table in front of the door for extra resistance. The basement steps were too narrow to give him the foothold he'd need to shove hard, and anyone halfway bright who came into the kitchen would wonder why it was there.

It was almost nine now, too late for a social call, but I wasn't feeling sociable. I sat in the DeSoto with my hands wrapped around the steering wheel and waited for rage to subside. Until my knuckles no longer were white. Then I headed down Main. I contemplated calling the cops, but I still didn't have any evidence. Just the word of a man I'd locked in his cellar without his trousers.

Charlie Long's place was on the west edge of Oakwood, not as mammoth as some of its neighbors, but three stories of stone with enough lawn around it to guarantee privacy. Lights were on. People were still up.

I parked my car behind some bushes where it wouldn't be seen when the front door opened. I walked up the drive, my purse swung easily from my shoulder. The top was unsnapped. I rang the doorbell. After a bit the door opened on the ugliest redhead I'd ever seen.

"Hello," I chirped. "Is Charlie Long in? Mr. Duncan sent me to talk to him."

The redhead's hair was clipped so short it looked like fuzz. He topped six feet, and one of his earlobes was missing a piece. He was dressed like a gentleman's gentleman, but he had muscles under his nice jacket, and a shape suggesting a gun. He blinked at me in disbelief.

"Oh, come on, I took a taxi all the way out here, and it wasn't cheap. Mr. Duncan was sure Mr. Long would here tonight and he'd be real interested in me. Just let me see him for five minutes."

The redhead stared at me another minute.

"Who shall I say is calling?"

"Maggie Quinn." More than a few crooks recognized my real name, as did plenty of reputable people.

"Wait here." He disappeared down a corridor to my left.

I took quick inventory of my surroundings. The hall with its oversized paintings and polished benches would have been at home in the Art Institute. Not far from me, on a pedestal, was a marble statue which I was pretty sure depicted Leda being raped by the swan. A cage the size of an icebox held live birds I couldn't identify.

After an interval, the red haired valet returned.

"Follow the poodle," he said, and stepped aside.

A yard or so behind him, a little white dog in a fussy top like a medieval herald stood on his hind legs. Feeling like a fool, I took a step. The mutt turned and picked its way carefully toward a double door as I followed. Beside the door, a man in a green smoking jacket observed our progress. He was trimmer than Duncan, with a hedge of silvery hair surrounding the dome of his head.

"Down," he ordered when the poodle reached him. A whimper of relief escaped the dog as it dropped to a natural position. An unpleasant taste filled my mouth as I watched the pitiful creature creep off without so much as a pat or a word of approval.

"Amusing, isn't he? All it takes is the right kind of training." The undersized eyes of the man I took to be Charlie Long catalogued me rather than saw me. "Come in."

As I moved past him into an ornate study, I realized the redhead had followed at a distance. He turned back now. The heavy double doors of the room closed behind me. Charlie Long made a half circle around me and picked up a glass of brandy he'd been enjoying. A book with its place marked lay in a nearby chair. He didn't invite me to sit.

"Am I to understand Herbert sent you?" He was everything Duncan wasn't: Smooth, controlled, intelligent.

"If you mean Mr. Duncan, then yes."

"At this hour?"

"I said I thought it was awfully late, but Mr. Duncan said you were good friends. He, um, wanted to make it up to me for getting a little bit out line --- he said I could tell you that. He said you'd find me just the sort of job I deserved."

"Did he now?" Hands clasped behind him, Long began to circle me, assessing me so closely I was glad I hadn't risked wearing the Smith & Wesson under my jacket; gladder still for its reassuring weight in my purse.

"And how did he get out of line?" Long tightened the circle.

"Gee, I don't like to say---"

"You want a job, don't you?"

"Well, okay, but I know he wouldn't have done it if he hadn't been drinking---"

"Done what?"

There was a gleam in his eye. He tightened the circle again, testing to see if his closeness could make me nervous. I accommodated, twisting to look at him as he moved.

"He said I had nice legs and – and he put his hand up my skirt. But soon as I smacked him, he apologized."

Long was so close now I could feel his breath on my hair. I stepped back suddenly.

"Hey. You're making me dizzy. "

He stopped, his thin lips forming a smile.

"My, we'll have to work on helping you learn more ladylike behavior."

Tired of playing his game, I eased the .38 from my purse.

"Let's work on taking me to Annie Walsh instead."

A second passed. Fury turned his face crimson.

"Hands by your ears," I said grimly. "Forget about calling your valet, or whatever he is. I promise I'll shoot you before he can blink. Turn around. Spread your legs. Now bend over and put your hands on the edge of that fancy table."

He would have killed me if he'd been able. He wasn't, so he obeyed. I patted him down.

"Where is she?"

"I have no idea what you're talking about. Who are you?"

"A private detective. That make you feel more cooperative? No? You like women you can scare, don't you? Let's have a look around."

It would be folly to keep a prisoner on this floor when he had alternatives. I'd try upstairs first. I made my gun cozy against his ribs. The valet/bodyguard wasn't in sight. I hoped he was listening to the radio I heard playing at the rear of the house. The prospect of facing two of them wasn't a nice one, and the calm that Long was displaying now made me nervous. We climbed marble stairs.

"I can see why you and Duncan are chums," I said when we'd been through various rooms on the second floor. I'd seen a lifetime's worth of nude paintings, including one of a dwarf in cowboy attire riding a naked woman who wore a bridle.

Long flashed an expression of pure hate. "Art takes many forms. I collect examples which more mundane tastes fail to recognize. Herbert, despite his crudeness, is willing to expand his horizons."

He was watching for any opportunity to overpower me. A cage of sad-looking monkeys watched without making a peep as we climbed the stairs.

The top floor held bathrooms and two large bedrooms whose

décor matched the rest of the house. And next to a telephone stand with a curved velvet seat, one more door, which was locked.

"Open it," I said.

Long locked gazes with me, waiting for me to look away first. I didn't. Reeking of confidence, he lifted the lamp on the telephone table and picked up a key.

We went through the door together.

In the light from the hall, I saw only shapes. Keeping Long in front of me, I felt for a light switch. I flipped it and drew in a breath.

They were in a cage. Three young women, clad in flimsy see-through corsets and chained to the bars of the cage by velvet collars. One looked Asian. One had skin the color of milky tea. The third, exquisitely pretty if you didn't count a black eye and split, swollen lip, was Annie Walsh.

"Put the gun down or I shoot one."

Long's words hit me like hot coals. My seconds of disbelief had cost me dearly. He'd produced a small automatic from some hidey hole, just as he had the key. His eyes burned with pleasure.

I bent and complied, keeping my eye on him now as he started circling again.

"Not so clever after all, are you?" he asked. "As much as I'd enjoy the challenge of putting you in with the others, I fear you'd prove more trouble than you're worth. You'll have to be disposed of like her pest of a sister."

I heard a heartbroken sob. Maybe Annie hadn't known.

"The cops know Norma talked to me about finding Annie." I looked for something to use as a weapon. Some way to get the upper hand.

"Is that the best you can do? Try to bluff your way out? Red disposed of the sister without leaving tracks. He'll dispose of you." He wound around me, enjoying my helplessness. "First, though, I think I deserve recompense for the way you've spoiled my evening. Perhaps... let's see, what would you hate? A little striptease? Yes, that seems perfect."

He halted abruptly. His voice grew harsh.

"Start with your blouse." He trained his gun on the girls in the cage.

One started to moan and covered her head with her arms. Annie rattled the bars.

"If you do a nice job, I might reconsider and keep you." Long laughed at the lie.

He liked to control and humiliate. I'd deny him both. Shaking my hair out and keeping my eyes level with his, I started to twirl and strut like a burlesque queen. Startled, he let both attention and gun creep toward me as he snapped orders.

Skirt. Slip. Stockings. The bra was the hardest indignity to ignore.

Inch by inch, my movements turned him away from the girls in the cage. If I got a chance to lunge, at least I could keep them out of the line of fire.

Finally only my panties and a strip of blue silk remained. Long's eyes were bright with a twisted enjoyment that came not from lechery, but from power.

"And now the garter belt."

If I didn't act now, the next one I wore would be concrete.

"How about some applause?" I said.

His face tightened at the defiance.

Spinning, I turned my backside to him. And moved half a step closer. I unfastened some of the hooks that held the blue silk encircling me. Spinning, and moving closer again, I completed the job. I swept the garter belt to one side with abandon, then slung it around my head once... twice... gathering momentum. Six dangling metal supporters slashed into Long's eyes as I brought it down.

Long screamed in pain and animal fury. I heard him shoot. While he was temporarily blinded, I drove my foot into his chest, toppling him backward. I fell on top of him, grappling for the gun he held.

The girls in the cage were screaming, a blur of sound. I fought for myself... for Annie... for all the girls he'd mistreated.

The door to the hellish room flew open. The redhead pointed a gun. I twisted Long's automatic free and shot his valet in the midsection. As the redhead crumpled, clutching his belly, I placed a more accurate shot in his arm. Then I slammed the butt of the automatic against the side of Long's head. A couple of times. It felt good.

Coughing and gasping for air, I got to my feet. Red was on his side, holding his injured arm to his bleeding midsection and trying to inch to the weapon he'd dropped. I kicked it aside. Looking around, I found my Smith & Wesson and picked it up.

"Turn over."

He obeyed, expecting a shot in the back of the head. Instead, I gave him a knock with the butt of the gun, hard enough that he'd nap for a while. Long was still dazed enough for me to turn him face down. He deserved a stronger sleeping pill than I'd given his valet, and I saw he got it.

I looked at the women. They were no worse than when I'd found them. I, on the other hand, was stark naked except for my panties. My left arm appeared to be bleeding.

I went into the hall and sank down on the fancy telephone bench and called the cops.

"The guy who owns the place has three girls chained in a cage," I said when I'd given my name and the address. "One of them's hurt pretty bad."

I made my way back to the room where Long and his lackey were enjoying better dreams than they deserved. I was cold and lightheaded. I pulled on my skirt and my blouse and sat down with my gun in my lap to wait for the cops.

It felt good earning what Norma Walsh paid me, even though my bank account would be out quite a bit more. Including the price of a new garter belt.

A plain one.

A FAMILY AFFAIR
by Sara Paretsky

I

"He was waiting outside my office when I arrived that morning, a tall lean man with a hint of sandalwood aftershave about him. It was the smile that got to me, though, that lazy, lurking smile that says, 'we both know this is a game, but it's fun to play it.'"

"Knock it off, Warshawski," Murray Ryerson said. "I want to know how you got involved with the Teichels."

"He had legs that wouldn't stop," I said, "and those soft bronze curls—"

"That tell us your client was a giraffe," Sal Barthele interjected. "Are you writing a zipper ripper or giving Murray deep background on the case?"

I was at her bar, the Golden Glow, with Murray, recovering from an exhausting day. I didn't feel like talking about the Teichels, but I had promised Murray an exclusive.

"It started with sex, or with me misinterpreting a question about sex," I said. "And knowing Murray, or his corporate masters, I figured men whose glinting good looks make bishops kick holes in stained glass windows—"

"Philip Marlowe said that about a blond. A woman," Murray objected.

"I've known a number of blond men," I said. "My ex-husband for starters. Igor Palanyuk for another."

"Begin at the beginning," Murray said. "And I'd like another beer."

"You're buying, remember?" I said. But I began at the beginning, a Tuesday afternoon in Minna Simms High School, where I was taking part in a career day fair.

II

"Have you ever, like, slept with a suspect to get information?"

A titter ran through the room and the kid turned crimson. The guidance counselor on the stage with me stiffened and glared at the youth, but I answered gravely.

"It's important to stay alert, even on dull assignments. Booze, drugs, sex, anything that might make you sleep, especially with a suspect, should always be avoided."

A snicker and some catcalls arose from the back of the room on the right. "Maybe that's how losers get a sex life, Cory," one guy yelled. "That makes this a good career for you."

"Suspect has to be trying to get in his pants, dude, what self-respecting girl would want to be there?" another clever guy chimed in.

I'd misjudged the question and the questioner. Cory turned red; he blundered along the row of kids, heading for the exit.

"Cory, I'm sorry," I said into the mike. "I assumed you were with the feral group in the back there. Please don't leave."

It was too little, too late. He stumbled up the aisle and out the auditorium door.

I was taking part in a career fair at Minna Simms High School on Chicago's northwest side, describing life as a private investigator. I'd explained to the room full of slouching adolescents that solo ops were a rare breed; most investigators work for giant firms like Tintrey, which require a background in law enforcement or an advanced degree in law or criminal justice. I'd finished covering old-fashioned tailing—how to blend in with your surroundings—when Cory had stood to ask his question.

"That's a good example of the wrong way to conduct an investigation," I said to the now-silent room. "Jumping to conclusions about where a conversation is going. The more you can exhibit empathy with a witness, the more easily they'll talk to you. When you make fun of someone instead of listening to them, you lose the chance to gain information."

At the end of my hour, when students had asked about guns and data mining, and how to protect your own privacy if you were the target of an investigation yourself, I asked the guidance counselor how to find Cory.

Fifty Shades of Grey Fedora

Cory Teichel should have been in third-semester calculus, but he'd left the high school campus without saying anything to anyone. The guidance counselor who'd been chaperoning me said it was against school policy to give out an address or phone number. I left a note for Cory with her and went back to my office.

Impulse control. I should have told the kids impulse control was a good quality in an investigator. Follow hunches, take quick decisive action, but don't let the chip on your shoulder fly into your eye and blind you. In other words, I was annoyed with myself, but I had a heavy workload and by the end of the afternoon I'd put Cory Teichel and my gaffe out of my mind.

I was forced to think about him again the next afternoon. As I was getting ready to shut down for the day, someone rang the bell to the outer door. I looked at my security camera feed and saw a young woman in leggings and a layer of tank tops and shirts, carrying a backpack almost as big as she was. Her hair was thick and fell over her eyes and cheeks, so that it wasn't possible to make out her expression.

I buzzed her in and went down the hall to meet her.

"You're the detective?" Her voice was unexpectedly deep.

I nodded.

"You're the one who made fun of Cory yesterday?"

I nodded again. "Were you at the career fair?"

"I went to the session on architecture. But I heard about you from someone at your session. It was very unfair of you to say what you did."

"You're right, at least up to a point," I agreed, "the point being that the question was pretty snarky. Did you come here to chew me out?"

She bit her lip. "Cory disappeared. No one knows where he went."

I didn't say anything.

"You need to find him."

I cocked an eyebrow at her. "Who are you, and what's your relationship to him?"

She flushed. "I'm just a friend."

"Well, friend, here's the scoop. I don't know who you are, I don't know if Cory Teichel is missing, and if he is, I don't know if you have a legitimate interest in having him found."

Her flush deepened. "I see exactly how you behaved to Cory. That's why he ran away. If this is how you treat everyone who wants help, I'm surprised you stay in business."

"Do you always leap to conclusions like a young chamois in the Caucasus?" I was exasperated. "You come in demanding that I find Cory Teichel, but for all I know, this is a scam you and he have put together to embarrass *me* for having embarrassed him. I go looking for him and he's sitting in your basement playing video games."

"Oh." She deflated. "I hadn't thought of that. If I tell you my name, will you keep it secret?"

"Keep it confidential, you mean. Yes, unless you've committed a felony."

She came into my office, scuffing her toes like a six-year-old going to the doctor. When I showed her to the alcove where I see clients, she dumped her backpack on the floor, kicked off her boots, and sat cross-legged on the couch. Under the cascade of dark hair, she still had the soft round face of childhood, but the expression in her eyes was fierce and intelligent.

After another demand that I not tell anyone she'd come to see me, she told me her name: Erica Leahardt. She and Cory had known each other since middle school because they only lived five blocks apart. They usually rode the Peterson Avenue bus together in the mornings, but Cory hadn't been on the bus and he hadn't been in any of the classes they had together.

"And you know he's not home sick?" I asked.

"He's not answering his phone and then I went to his place but no one was home."

I suggested different possibilities—a family emergency had taken him out of town, for instance, or he was brooding with his earbuds in and didn't hear the bell.

"It's just Cory and his father. His mother took off when he was little, he doesn't even remember her, and he doesn't have any other family."

"Why don't you ask Mr. Teichel where Cory is?"

She made a horrified face. "I couldn't, it would be too weird."

"You don't think it would be extremely weird if I asked him? I don't work for the school, I don't have a legitimate reason to call him out of the blue to ask him about his son."

"You couldn't, like, hack into Cory's cellphone to find out where he is?"

"That's extremely illegal, Ms. Leahardt, even if I knew how, which I don't. It wouldn't be weird for you to call your friend's father to say you need to talk to Cory about—anything. Your calculus assignment, your upcoming camping trip, whatever it is the two of you do together. You don't have to say you think he's missing, just ask the question. He'll tell you where Cory is."

"You don't know why that would be really hard for me."

I invited her to tell me, but she clammed up mulishly and finally left, with a sullen comment about my incompetence.

I took a moment to look up the two families. Mike Teichel—original name Dmitri Teichel—had come to this country from Ukraine as a teenager before the fall of the Soviet Union. If he'd married Cory's mother, there wasn't a record of it. If his own parents were still alive, I couldn't find them. He was a freelance designer of computer games who rented office space near Northwestern University's Evanston campus—he apparently taught a seminar in their computer engineering department every winter.

Erica's parents were divorced. She lived with her mother, a systems analyst at Metargon, the big electronics firm in Northbrook. Her father was in Seattle running an art gallery.

Single dad a game designer, single mom at a big electronics firm. I thought back to Cory's question about sleeping with a suspect. Had Cory Teichel been worried that Erica's mother slept with his father to wangle gaming secrets from him? Maybe he suspected Erica was sleeping with his father. Or, à la Dustin Hoffman, was Cory sleeping with Erica's mother?

I shrugged. Not my problem.

III

Not my problem, but I called Candace Mehr at Simms high school the next morning. She was the guidance counselor who'd shepherded me through the career fair two days ago.

"Candace, V I Warshawski. I've been feeling bad about the kid I embarrassed on Tuesday. Any chance I could meet with him in person, apologize, find out what was on his mind when he asked his question?"

She said she'd check with him, get back to me, but when she called an hour later, it was to say that Cory hadn't been in school for two days. "In fact, his father was just in the principal's office, trying to find out where Cory is. He hasn't been home, either. I gave him your name."

Mike Teichel called almost as soon as I'd hung up: he needed to see me at once to discuss his son.

"At once" when you have to cover four miles during Chicago's morning rush means three quarters of an hour. I had time to finish a report and reorganize my morning meetings before Teichel showed up.

He was belligerent. Like Erica Leahardt yesterday afternoon, he blamed me for Cory's disappearance. He'd heard from Candace Mehr how I'm embarrassed his son in front of the school; it was my job to find him.

"Have you talked to the police?"

"Absolutely not. If I wanted to go to the police, I wouldn't be coming to you!"

I sat back in my chair. "Mr. Teichel, your son asked an absurd, and on the surface, insulting question in front of the school. There's a myth about the world of private eyes, that they're hard-bitten lonely men who have sex with glamorous and dangerous women. When Cory asked if I ever slept with a suspect, I thought he was trying to draw a laugh from his classmates by playing into that myth. He obviously had something else on his mind. You're his father—you tell me what that was."

Teichel breathed hard through his nose, a kind of bull in the ring sound. "Cory's seventeen. That's not an age where someone confides in his father," he said at last.

"Who would he confide in? His mother?"

The bull-ring snort grew more pronounced.

"Friends?" I finally asked, when it was clear the mother wasn't going to be talked about.

"He's a loner. I don't think he has friends."

"Erica Leahardt?"

"That lying little bitch"?" he shouted. "Are you a friend of hers, or that mother of hers?"

"Let's see where we are so far, Mr. Teichel: you say your son is missing. You claim I'm responsible. You won't go to the police. You won't discuss his mother. You don't know who his friends are. Is Cory really missing?"

Teichel's lips were pressed in a thin angry line. "He is really missing. Now tell me how you know the Leahardt females."

I shook my head. "You don't get to ask me any questions. And unless you want to hire me to find your son, and to answer some questions yourself, there's no reason for us to continue speaking."

I pulled out my phone and started returning emails, or at least pretended to. Teichel got up, walked to the door, hesitated, walked back again.

"Very well. I wish to hire you to find Cory. But only if you are not playing some game with those Leahardt females."

"I met Erica once, briefly: she was worried about your son's disappearance. I told her to talk to you."

His nostrils flared again, cornered bull. "Yes, she wouldn't do that. Not since the day I found her snooping in my files."

I raised my brows.

"Her mother works for Metargon. They are notorious thieves of other people's work. She claimed she was looking for a document that Cory had created—she had come over on the pretext of a study date with my son. That was the last time she was allowed in our home."

"How did Cory feel about that?"

"He didn't say anything about it. He probably realized she was using him, but it didn't seem to bother him."

"Maybe it did him terrible damage for you to exclude his friend," I suggested. "She seems to like him—she came all the way down here on the bus to ask me to find him."

That didn't set well with Teichel, but he wasn't stupid, only angry and confused. After railing at me for a moment, he stopped, thought, grudgingly said she could be both interested in his son and want to spy on Teichel himself.

After that rough start, we moved to the basics—when had Teichel realized his son was missing? He hadn't become seriously concerned until this morning—he'd been in San Francisco Tuesday, meeting with a corporate client, got home late yesterday. "I thought maybe he'd gone to bed early—I didn't land until eleven last night; his room was dark, I didn't try to wake him up. Then this morning, I saw the message from the school that he hadn't been to his classes yesterday. He wasn't in his room, he wasn't at school. I drove there at once, of course, and they told me about you. Your humiliating him."

"Yes, we've covered that," I said. "You're sure he wouldn't be with his mother?"

He pressed his lips together, a reflexive action—now that he'd decided to talk to me, he was going to tell me what he could. "Cory's mother disappeared from our lives before Cory's third birthday. We do not know where she is. She has never written, she has never been in touch."

We went back to the question of friends. Teichel finally dredged up the names of two kids who Cory sometimes went with to nature preserves. "He likes that kind of thing, wetlands, birds, the ecosystem. He goes some weekends as a volunteer in a prairie restoration project."

I asked if Teichel monitored his son's whereabouts. After another round of defensive hostility, he admitted that he'd put stealth software into Cory's Android, but that he hadn't been able to track him past yesterday afternoon.

"He went to the Sulzer regional library yesterday morning and he spent the day there. And he left his phone there. I picked it up this morning on my way to the school."

"Do you have it? Did you he see who he was calling or texting?"

"No one since Tuesday afternoon." He stopped, then added reluctantly. "He texted Erica: *'The PI totally bricked me. Hope the architect was better.'* I still think she was trying to use Cory to steal my secrets. Took a computer gaming class to make sense of what she saw in my office."

Bricked, as in dropped a ton of bricks on him, I supposed. "Maybe she likes gaming—there are more women than men in the gaming universe, after all."

"Maybe she likes gaming and is also a spy for her mother," Teichel snapped.

"What's been on Cory's mind lately?" I asked. "He came to my session for a reason. He wanted to know if it was okay to have sex with someone in order to get information from them. Who would he have been wanting information from?"

Teichel said he couldn't possibly know, but he only spoke after a pause and his tone was uneasy.

"You know something. You need to tell me."

"I know—that I don't know my son. Always a hard thing for a parent to admit," he said harshly. "Give me whatever paperwork you need. I need to know what's happened to my son."

"You would be much better off with the police," I said.

"Absolutely no police," Teichel hissed.

"Or a big firm. Tintrey, Balladine, they can put a lot of resources into a search. I can't. Especially not with so little to go on."

Teichel didn't want a big firm--who knew who owned whom when you were with a multi-national? He wanted someone loyal to him and his son. We finally signed a contract, me reluctantly, and demanding a $2500 deposit, more than I usually required, but I didn't like the set-up. Teichel also texted me a couple of somewhat recent photos of his son. And, very reluctantly, let me borrow Cory's Android.

When he left, I checked my police and hospital sources. No unidentified white male teens had been found in the last several days. It didn't mean Cory was still alive, but I could use it as a working assumption.

I started at the Sulzer Regional library, since that was Cory's last known location. The reference librarian was helpful; she remembered Cory, mostly because he was using the payphone, unlike every other teen glued into their handhelds. She'd been on the late shift on Tuesday; she hadn't noticed him leaving, because a second wave of heavy users starts pouring in around seven, after supper. She'd been swamped until almost closing, but he was definitely gone before then. She sent me to the security staff, who didn't remember him, but said there hadn't been any rough business in the library that day.

"Every now and then we have kids who think the library is an extension of the schoolyard or their gang turf and start mixing it up, but nothing like that happened Tuesday," the head of the detail said, after consulting his logs.

As for where the Android had been discovered, Mike Teichel had found it with his locator app: Cory had stuffed it behind the payphone he'd been using.

I sent Teichel a text, saying that the cops could get a warrant to find out what numbers Cory had calling from the payphone, but I couldn't. *NO POLICE* came back in all caps, followed by a dozen exclamation points.

I looked at Cory's Android, at the texts he'd exchanged with Erica. His last outgoing text, about being bricked, had been in response to a query from Erica. She had sent him several dozen messages from Tuesday evening through last night. None this morning.

As I looked at the log, I saw she initiated ninety percent of their contacts. Maybe more. She was chasing him, poor puppy, and he was indifferent. Unless Mike Teichel was right and she using Cory as a way to get into his dad's study and steal code.

Cory's initiating texts were messages to the guys he went hiking with, or to members of a school photography club he belonged to. His Facebook page showed seventeen friends. Despite the photography club, he had almost no pictures on the phone—a few dozen of the prairie and the wetlands, a few selfies taken there, a few with his buddies. None of Erica, nor of any other girls. Maybe he was gay. Whether gay or straight, he had the kind of thin, interesting face that attracts a lot of people, male or female. The lack of pictures was odd, very un-teenlike.

When I called Mike Teichel, he couldn't tell me his son's sexual orientation. "I've never seen signs he was interested in anyone, boy or girl, not even Erica. If he's seeing anyone it's very secretly."

I mentioned the puzzling lack of photos on the Android. Most teens like pictures of themselves and their friends, especially pictures of themselves and their lovers.

Teichel snorted. "I hope I raised Cory to be better than that; my family made it out of Ukraine with the clothes on our backs, not with Androids and selfies and all that self-indulgent crap."

"I'm sure it's a help to his confidence to know that," I said drily. "He belongs to the school photography club. I'd at least expect photos for the club."

Cory was a serious photographer, his father told me; he had two cameras, a pocket digital and a 1975 Nikon that he'd found at a flea market. As to whether he had a photo cache online, Mike couldn't say. If he did, he'd probably hidden it deeply, to avoid charges of immaturity and self-indulgence, but I kept that wry thought to myself, saying instead that I was on my way over to Teichel's to look myself.

Mike Teichel tried to argue me out of it: looking for a teen's art shots was a waste of time when I should be out beating the bushes for him.

"The way to find a needle in a haystack, or in the bushes, is to use a magnet," I said. "I need to find someone Cory felt able to confide in."

"It won't be in a roomful of negatives," Teichel snapped. After a pause, he grudgingly allowed that Cory might have talked to advisor to the school photography club. Teichel didn't know his first name; Cory only referred to him as "Mr. Spiro."

IV

Of course, if the needle is made out of plastic, a magnet won't work and you're doomed, I realized. I was waiting in the principal's office for Mr. Spiro, who also taught chemistry; when I showed the staff the contract that Mike Teichel had signed for me to find his son, they were eager to help in any way they could.

While I waited for Spiro, I texted the seventeen people in Cory's message list, telling them Cory was missing and asking them to tell me the last time they'd seen or heard from him. I wanted to talk to Erica face-to-face; the assistant principal said she'd organize that for me once I was through seeing Spiro.

Mr. Spiro—Antony Spiro, he told me as he briskly shook hands—was a wiry man in his late thirties who smelled of carbolic. He had the friendly inquisitive face of a terrier, even the same high wide cheekbones; I could see that adolescents might confide in him.

He was distressed to hear that Cory was missing. "That explains why he hasn't been in class or the club. I thought he might have gone ill."

I told Spiro the same thing I'd said to Mike Teichel, about Cory's question in my presentation. "I think now it was a cry for help—that he'd had sex with someone to get information, or maybe his father was having sex with someone inappropriate, and what should he do about it."

Spiro slowly shook his head. "He didn't confide in me, at least not directly, but there's a photo in a recent batch he took—he seemed to be trying to draw my attention to it, but I thought it was about the setting, not the people in it."

He looked at the wall clock. "I have another class in ten minutes, but I think I can find it pretty quickly."

He set off down the hallway at a fast clip, greeting students by name. I trotted behind him along the long corridors favored by early Twentieth Century school designers. Partway down the third hallway, Spiro pulled out his keys and unlocked the door to a small room. The sour smell of developing chemicals hit us. When Spiro flipped on the lights, the walls were so full of pictures that I shrank back; they seemed to make the space too small to breathe in.

Spiro didn't pay attention to me or to the pictures, but unlocked a cupboard in the far corner and pulled out an artist's portfolio with Cory's name on it. Spiro riffled through a set of black-and-white shots until he found the print he was looking for. I leaned over his shoulder as he laid it on a light table. Two men were embracing in a parking lot at night. Their stance was ambiguous. Were they lovers? Combatants? The faces were hard to make out in the poor light, but I thought the man on the right was Mike Teichel.

I bent over it, trying to get one clue to where the picture had been taken. A tan brick wall with cracks was in the left of the photo, a dumpster in the background with some slats sticking out of the top, but nothing that would help me identify the building.

"I thought he wanted advice on the focus and the lighting, but from what you're saying, I'm wondering if it was the two men."

I nodded, pointed at Cory's father. "Can you make me a j-peg of this so I can email it?"

Spiro looked at his watch and the clock on the wall, called the principal to say he'd be a few minutes late for his one-fifty class. He found the negative in Cory's folder and made a fresh print, getting as sharp a contrast as he could, then scanned and emailed it to me.

He hustled me out of the room, pointing me toward the principal's office. He took off in the other direction for his waiting chemistry class.

As I walked, I texted the photo to Mike Teichel—this made me blend in with the students, who were almost all focused on their devices, yet seemed able to hurry down the hall towards lockers or classrooms without bumping into anyone.

Cory took this shot. Does this explain his running away? Who were you with?

Teichel called me before I reached the principal's office. He was furious, he told me to stop my search and to mind my own damned business.

"If I'd known you would take that contract as a license to invade my privacy I'd never have come to you. Send me back my retainer and stop at once."

"It's not that simple, Mr. Teichel," I said. "Seeing you with this man apparently upset Cory. If you want to find him—"

"I'll find him on my own. You stop *now!*" He broke the connection.

V

"Cory is really missing?" Erica asked.

We were alone in the assistant principal's office. The assistant had been reluctant to leave us alone, but I wasn't a cop, nothing Erica said to me could be taken down and used in evidence, and Erica had insisted she wanted to speak to me privately.

"Really missing," I said. "His father won't call the cops, which makes me wonder what Mr. Teichel is afraid of. He says you were snooping in his home office. What was that about?"

Erica was mortified, she didn't want to talk about it, but I reminded her Cory's life might be on the line; I needed to know everything, and she was the only person who might know something vital.

It came in small whispered pieces. Yes, she had a crush on him, he didn't know she was alive, well, of course, they rode the bus together, they did homework together, but—*you know.*

I gave a wry smile: I knew. The adored object did not return the love.

"I thought if I got his dad all wound up, maybe Cory would say something or do something, notice me as more than a homework buddy. It was pretty pathetic. All it did was make Mr. Teichel say I couldn't come to the house—he was sure I was trying to steal something my mom could use at Metargon."

"Does he work on something she would be interested in?"

Erica flung her hands wide. "I don't think so, but I don't know. My mom doesn't work on anything secret. She's not an engineer, she does flow charts for smart home appliances. Mr. Teichel, he's like a game theory person. The software I saw was for some company in California with a weird name. Knee Ice, Ice Knee, something like that. I asked if he was making portable ice for sports injuries, because I wrecked my knee pretty good last summer and I can't play soccer now, and he acted like he was going to murder me. Like he couldn't take a joke," she added resentfully.

Knee Ice, Ice Knee. "I-C-E-N-I?" I spelled.

"Yeah, that's it."

"Iceni is one of the country's biggest defense contractors. No wonder he got so bent out of shape when he saw you looking at the file. You didn't actually take any of the code?"

"It didn't mean anything to me!" she cried. "And afterward, Cory, he—he wouldn't talk to me about it, and then he started acting all weird, not coming home after school, going off with his camera."

"Where did he go?"

She turned scarlet; how would she know.

"If you followed him, it would be great for me to know, and believe me, I won't rat you out."

She had tracked Cory to a motel on the city's tattered west side, where she'd watched him watching the parking lot. It had gotten dark, her mother was texting her, demanding to know what she was doing; of course her mother could see where she was with that ubiquitous find your friends app.

"She knew I wasn't with Melanie and Caitlin, which is what I told her, and I was leaving, because she was threatening to call the cops, and then, Mr. Teichel drove up. Cory didn't do anything, I mean, he didn't, like, run over and talk to his dad, he just started photographing him, which seemed totally weird, but I had to leave, so I don't know what they did."

I showed her the picture I'd gotten from Spiro.

"That's, like, the place, at least, I think it is. It was this old building with that kind of funny hinge for the fire escape. That's Mr. Teichel, but I didn't see the other man, I left before he showed up."

Her soft round face looked gaunt and haunted. "Is that Mr. Teichel's lover? Is that why Cory ran away?"

I shook my head; I didn't know.

Erica didn't remember the name of the hotel where she'd tracked Cory, but she could tell me the location: Pulaski Street, just north of the Lake Street L stop.

I squeezed her hand with a reassurance I didn't feel, told her to leave it all to me, but not to talk to anyone else about Cory. "And don't follow me. I may be moving fast around the city and I don't want to leave you in a place where you wouldn't be safe."

VI

The Ditchley Park Plaza on Pulaski had seen more affluent days. It had a pseudo-Byzantine façade underneath its layers of dirt and the lobby was a large high-ceilinged space, where half-dead palm trees sat in dusty tubs next to armchairs in front of an unused fireplace.

The check-in counter had a high grille across it to protect staff from wandering junkies. I pressed an old metal bell. Five minutes went by while I watched a spider move lethargically along a frond on one of the palm trees. I dinged the bell again and a woman appeared, slowly, from the back. She was thin, with deep disapproval lines gouged along her nose.

"I heard you. You need to learn some patience. You want a room?"

"I'm a detective. I'm looking for—"

"Detective? You have a warrant?"

"I'm private. No one issues warrants for me."

"Then you need to go some place else to look."

She twitched and scratched her arms while she spoke. Liver damage, probably, especially when I saw how yellow her eyes were. I'd made copies of my key photos, Cory and Mike Teichel's faces and the shot Cory had taken of his father embracing another man. I slipped these under the grille with a twenty. The clerk pocketed the twenty but didn't look at the pictures. I sighed and put another twenty on the counter.

She stabbed a finger on the man with Mike Teichel. "He came last week. This one showed up Tuesday night—she stabbed Cory's face—waited in the lobby until the older guy showed, followed him into the elevator. Haven't seen the kid since Tuesday night, but the older one comes down periodically to get a bottle or a pizza."

She jerked her head across the street where a couple of fast-food joints and a liquor store were flashing their lights. A clutch of men were lounging near the liquor store doorway. Panhandling, maybe, or dealing, or both.

"Kid hasn't shown?" I asked.

"I just said, I haven't seen him. Course I'm only here two till midnight. Could be Major's seen him. You come back at midnight, you can ask him."

"Room number?" I asked.

"People come here to be private," she said. "I don't tell their business, I leave them alone."

I had one twenty left. It wasn't enough to buy me the room number, but the clerk slipped into her flat chest anyway. And then told me I couldn't wait in the lobby: people who stayed at the Ditchley valued their privacy.

I went outside and moved my car down the street, where I could still see the front of the Ditchley but not be watching in an obvious way. I wasn't there ten minutes when the clerk emerged, heading for the liquor store. I got out of the car for a better view. She was showing one of the loungers two of my twenties. He took them and hustled her out of sight, around to the back of the building.

I pulled my picks out of the glove compartment and ran back to the Ditchley. A prim notice, back in 5 minutes, sat in front of the bell I'd rung for service. I went past the counter, around the side and found the door to the office and front desk. The lock was modern but not difficult.

The office was just big enough for a desk with two computers and a phone. One of the computers was hooked to security cameras that covered the lobby, a back door and the front exit. The other held data. It was password protected, but someone had written down the password on a Post-it and stuck it to the keyboard tray.

I logged in and searched the guest list. More people were staying there than I had thought, especially since I hadn't seen anyone coming or going. I didn't know the name of the man in the picture, but only two people had been there longer than two nights, Gene Nielsen in 227 and John Smith in 631. I voted for John, but just in case, I made keys for both rooms—the instructions were helpfully taped to the keyboard tray next to the log-in code and the combination for the wall safe.

I just had time to get out of the office, skirt the lobby's security camera, and slide into a chair behind one of the dying palms when the clerk returned. My money had bought her a certain degree of calm: she moved languorously across the lobby without looking around.

The chair gave me a good view of the elevator in the far wall and a sort of view of the parking lot, but not of the front desk. I guessed from the noises that the clerk had reinstalled herself in the office, and I didn't hear any shrieks that showed I'd left some trace behind.

I put my phone on silent and leaned back in the armchair to minimize my visibility. The chair was upholstered in a frayed and faded fabric steeped in so many decades of dust that I kept having to choke back sneezes.

A trucker pulled his rig into the parking lot and came in to get a room for the night. The clerk was floating in some kind of happy place and only appeared when the trucker had shouted her name several times. Florence. He was a regular, a long-haul driver on his way Phoenix from Bangor. When he'd gone upstairs, a young woman booked a room. The phone rang twice. And then the elevator doors wheezed open and the man in Cory's photo emerged.

He walked toward me and I braced myself, but he was merely going to a window behind me to squint at the street. He looked to be in his forties, with thick bronze curls and arms that held enough muscle to pack a serious blow if he tried to hit anyone.

He lowered the blind and went out. I went to the window myself, lifted an edge of the blinds, and saw him cross the street, heading for a pizza place on the far side of the liquor store.

I glanced at the registration counter, but didn't see Florence. The elevator stood open. I hurried over and slipped inside just as the doors started wheezing shut. Florence appeared, shouting at me in a high querulous voice: "You, PI, get out of there!"

I swore under my breath: I'd forgotten the security cameras.

I didn't know what Florence's next move would be but mine involved the agony of a ride in an elevator that had read the tortoise and the hare way too many times. When I finally reached the sixth floor, I saw a pile of discarded pizza boxes in the hall and stuffed those between the doors to keep the elevator from moving. As I knocked hard on the door to room 631, the elevator alarm began jangling.

"Housekeeping," I called, although I wasn't sure there was such a thing at the Ditchley. "We have your clean towels."

I didn't hear any movement inside the room. Knocked again, then used the card-key. The lock clicked open. I moved quickly, shoulder against door, pushing my way into the room.

Cory Teichel sat on the bed, wearing his jockeys and a t-shirt. He pulled the sheet over his legs when he saw me, his thin young face registering fear, not relief.

"I'm V I Warshawski," I said. "The detective who was stupid when you asked about sex at my presentation on Tuesday. Do you want to be here, or do you want to leave?"

He blinked, didn't move—my appearance, my sharp questions, he was having trouble following me.

"Can you get dressed?" I asked.

"He took my clothes," Cory muttered.

"Okay, we'll take his."

The man hadn't brought a suitcase, but a gym bag on a card table in the corner held a pair of sweat pants and some t-shirts. I tossed the sweats to Cory. They'd be big on him, but they'd get him out of the hotel.

The guy's passport was in the bag, too: Russian. Igor Palanyuk, written in Cyrillic and Roman. Inside was folded the photograph of a woman of about thirty-five or forty.

"He said if I leave, he'll call the FBI and they'll arrest my dad and then kill my mom. That's my mom, that picture."

"He's not going to call the FBI," I said. "Whoever Igor Palanyuk is, he kidnapped you."

Cory looked up from fumbling with the sweatpants' waist-string—his skinny adolescent body would have fit into one leg. "I came here. He didn't kidnap me. I wanted to find how to get my mom out of Russia."

"You want to stay with him?"

"No, but—"

"There's no but. He's keeping you against your will. We'll figure out your mother when we're safe and have room to act."

We both heard the tread outside the door. Cory froze. I put the chainbolt into place and ran to the room's only window, above the bed. I wrestled with the lock, but it had been painted into place. Igor began banging the door methodically to and fro against the chain. I picked up a chair and shattered the window. I half-carried Cory to the broken window, wrapped a sheet around him, thrust him outside onto the fire escape.

"Get down that ladder. When you get to the ground, stay out of sight, do not show yourself for anyone except me."

He stood on the platform, eyes big with fear.

"Move!" I screamed.

He skittered down the escape just as Palanyuk forced the bolt screws out of the door frame. The door flew open. Palanyuk's ferocious forward momentum made him stumble. When I flung the chair at him, he tripped and fell heavily.

I scrambled through the broken glass on the bed and went down the fire escape. I found Cory at the lowest escape platform, a full story above the ground, huddled against the wall. I grabbed his hand, led him to the edge of the platform, climbed onto the first step of the ladder and felt the mechanism slowly release. He followed me to the sidewalk.

City cops were massed at the Ditchley's main entrance. If Florence had called them, it would be a long night trying to explain who I was, who Cory was, and why we had a right to be running away. Holding Cory close to me, close enough to look like a lover who'd jumped out of bed in his bare feet, I led him to my car and drove away.

VII

"And that was it?" Murray said.

"'That' was far from 'it,' but once we got to Teichel's place, the whole story unspooled pretty easily. Palanyuk was with the Ukrainian Mob; he—"

"You said his passport was Russian."

"Pay attention to geo-politics, Murray. He's from Simferopol, Crimea, now part of Russia, but he's ethnic Ukrainian. Mike Teichel's wife, Irena, was Crimean. Palanyuk pretended she wanted to escape Crimea, to return to Cory and Mike—she abandoned them to return to Simferopol when Cory was three.

"As it turned out, she doesn't want to leave Russia, she doesn't care about Cory, she's remarried and has two kids over there, but that's another story. The main story is that the Russians want the software for some of the games Mike Teichel is designing for Iceni Defense Systems. They made up tales of Irena's suffering—she was in prison, Mike could get her out, get her to America, but the price was Iceni's flash drive with Teichel's software on it.

"Mike was behaving so oddly that Cory started following him, and saw him embracing Palanyuk outside the Ditchley Park Plaza. That was the first night Palanyuk arrived, when Teichel believed the sob story about Irena. At first, he embraced Palanyuk out of joy—until he found out what the price of her safety was."

"Why did Cory ask if you ever slept with a suspect?" Sal put in.

"When he first followed his dad to the Ditchley Park hotel, he thought Mike and Palanyuk were lovers. He thought maybe he could seduce Palanyuk and find out what his hold was on his dad. That ploy didn't work well—Palanyuk wasn't interested, but he realized with Cory, he had a more potent pawn to play with Mike Teichel than a long-absent wife."

"So why did Teichel hire you?" Murray demanded.

"He'd been in San Francisco when Cory took off. He didn't connect his son's disappearance with his own troubles, not until I texted him the picture Cory had taken of him with Palanyuk outside the Ditchley. I'll take another Oban, Sal," I said.

"Why do you have to drink single malt on my tab?" Murray grumbled.

"Which one of them would have made you kick a hole in a stained-glass window?" Sal poured my drink, cocking an eyebrow seductively.

"Must have been Cory—I did kick a hole in a window for him."

BULLETVILLE
by Gary Phillips

El Rancho Condor sits at the end of a moss-enshrouded road that twists through spooky ass Wildwood Swamp. A steady dribble of straight 40 weight refined crude escaped through the hole in the oil pan of my '59 Plymouth Sport Fury as I bounced over ruts and rivulets in the road. Heathen that I am, I prayed the engine wouldn't seize up until I reached my destination. Not that I couldn't huff it on foot, but my passenger was in no condition for a hike.

"Hang on, Cut," I said to the dying man beside me on the bench seat. His mouth was doing something like what a carp does gasping for air on a boat deck and his blood was starting to decorate the seat again. The material was cloth not vinyl so I knew the red stuff would never bleach out. Restoring the luster of my retro sled was the least of my problems. For barreling behind me through the light mist was one of Ma Grundy's Caddy's.

"Shit," I growled and shoved down so hard on the accelerator, I thought my foot would go through the floorboard. Guns barked from the pursuing vehicle, the back window got blown out by several hot slugs. While no fan of this swamp, I knew it well given when I was a teen, this is where I'd lose the cops chasing me and Frankie. A bullet blasted out one of the brake lights in the Fury's left rear fin, and surely their next rounds would take out a tire. But as I'd remembered, there was the stand of old oaks dead ahead to the right of the road.

Viciously cranking the wheel, I aimed the Fury toward those trees. If you were unfamiliar with this area, you'd assume I was going to ensnare the car in soggy earth. But those in the know understood there was a sliver of side road that stretched away from the oaks deeper into the swamp before petering out. Supposedly that was to have been a turn-off to a proposed resort but her highness El Reina had put the squash on that. Didn't always got what she wanted.

Yet the ribbon of asphalt still existed, as the funds to jackhammer it out had been re-allocated to El Condor -- naturally. Off the main road my tires crunched over wet leaves and roots but had purchase. I was on the side strip. Calmly I counted in my head even as bullets whizzed past it. At the right moment I turned the car again, the tires smoking under-carriage rattling. The side road made another turn but the driver in the Caddy didn't know that. The Fleetwood shot forward, straight behind me and right over the edge of the hidden road. It was instantly mired in the muck, the rear tires spinning impotently as it spewed ick into the air but got no traction.

I tumbled out of my car, crouching low, my .45 heavy in my sweaty hand. It was daytime but clouds had been rolling in that afternoon and a gray light filtered through the leafy canopy. I used the trunks of the oak for cover and came right up beside one of the goons who gotten out of the Caddy. The shanks of his slacks were covered in mud and he hefted a heavy Sig-Sauer revolver. There was no way I was gonna let him bark that dog.

"Nice gun, dipshit," I whispered up close.

He turned gaping, ready to shoot but I was quicker. The business end of my gun jammed against his forehead, I blew bone and brains across the dark wood with one squeeze of the trigger. Wiping at the backsplash on my face, I was already moving as his body crumpled to the ground like a deflated clown balloon. How many others had been in that damn car?

I crept around a wide oak and felt more than saw a shape loom up at the corner of my eye. He let loose with a stream of buckshot from a semi-auto. I was diving but part of the blast caught me in the upper shoulder and turned my body in mid-air. Blood sprayed from the wound and I landed on my back. The .45 had dropped from my hand. The shooter stepped closer.

"Big shot, now you're big dead," he sneered.

I watched him bring that bad boy up ready to turn my head into gooey grapefruit. He leaned down, smiling. I had one chance and I damn sure took it. I jabbed the pointed branch of an oak tree I'd landed on into his eye socket. He wheezed and reared back swearing, his other eye bulged like he had proptosis. He staggered about pulling the branch free with a groan of pain. Back on my feet, he brought the shotgun around but I had my .45 back in my fist and made sushi of his intestines. He fell away dead.

"They call you Stag, don't they peeper?"

She was good, this third one from the Caddy -- hadn't heard her sneak up on me in the slightest. The muzzle of her gun was cold against my warm neck. "Now and then," I answered. The family name on pop's side was Stahgorski and on mom's Rivas. First name was Carlos, but it was a no brainer to see why I'd gotten that crazy nickname.

"Turn around,' she ordered.

I complied. She was a gorgeous woman whose curves were barely contained in a pencil skirt and silky blouse getting taut over her stiffening nipples. She was dark-skinned, of uncertain ethnicity, like me. Her body, face, and gun had me captivated. I could imagine worse ways to go out than killed by a beautiful woman. Most be something off in me to think that, but there you go.

"Come with me," she said, walking backward but keeping that silver plated Smith & Wesson handgun of hers on me. She leaned against the Fury and beckoned me closer by gesturing with the gun. "I want to see if what they say about you is true."

I gulped and came forward. I was right up on her and she reached down and eased my zipper open. I was thankful she didn't catch a hair in it as she did so. She reached in and took my member in her hand.

"Hmmmm," she murmured, the gun unwaveringly aimed at my heart.

She worked her hand back and forth on my rod and despite the fear of immediate death by babe, I started to respond.

"My, that's quite a fire hose you got there, Stag."

"Yes, ma'am." I always agree with a woman handling a gun. I was getting as hard as doing Tibetan arithmetic in the dark.

"Push my skirt up," she commanded me.

I did as ordered, exposing tawny muscled thighs I'd slap the taste out of my mama's mouth to have wrapped around my head.

Gun in one hand, with her other she started to finger the moist mound encased in her purple panties. She moaned some and despite the notion that death was just a squeeze away, I was getting light headed.

"Get to work, Stag," she said and I did.

She'd propped one of her high heeled feet on a gnarly tangle of tree roots that snaked from the earth. After unbuckling my pants, I eased aside the material of her underwear and entered her as she leaned back against the side of the car.

"Give it to me, baby," she whispered in my ear, tickling it with the barrel of her weapon and even licking its steel hammer with her tongue. This had me so worked I was woozy with lust. She slapped a hand on my butt and plunged a finger between my cheeks. I yelped with pleasure.

"Do me deep," she enthused, her hand on my butt alternately pushing or kneading the flesh roughly like she was making sourdough bread. She murmured a string of dirty words as I used the only weapon at my disposal, my johnson, to satisfy my captor.

We'd started slow but soon our bodies intuited the rhythm of each others and we were bucking and thrusting and grappling and biting so much I just knew we'd cave in the side of the Fury.

"Yeah," she said hoarsely as I put my back into it, "I'm going to come... oh shit, Stag."

The muscles in her vagina clenched as she got those thighs around my middle. I too saw stars exploding behind my eyes and we both yelped and gasped as we climaxed together.

"Not bad, slick," she said breathlessly.

I was about to make a play for her gat when the squish of others approaching had me looking past her and over the Fury's roof. Three men dressed in suits and the colorful masks of the Lucador, Mexican wrestlers, came into view. These were some of the Queen's men.

"Damn, Brinna, couldn't wait, huh" The one who said that carried an assault rifle slung over his shoulder. A cigarette dangled from his mouth.

"Gotta make sure he's up to it, Walt" the woman said, smiling and taking a step away from me. She'd smoothed down her skirt but in her hand was her panties. She smiled and stuffed them in the pocket of my light jacket.

Zipping up I inquired, "You two know each other?"

The woman said, "Queen Ida situated me undercover in Ma's gang a few weeks ago. Still, it took you to shake loose where they had Fenner hidden."

I nodded as the other two men got Cut Fenner out of the Fury and onto a stretcher I hadn't noticed before.

Walt, the one who'd talked to Brinna said, "We got a doc up at the house." Chuckling he added, flicking his lit cigarette at a croaking frog. "His session is just about over and he'll be in a good mood."

He gazed at me, his dark eyes lit behind a jaguar mask studded with rhinestones. "Come along, Stag, your work isn't over yet."

We walked the rest of the way and soon were at the gates of El Rancho Condor. The main feature of the ranch was the imposing four-story structure that mansion seemed too small a word to describe. The whole of it was made of stone, wood and concrete with sloping, gabled roofs, and carved images of real and imagined bestiary. The style was a cross between feudal Japan and Aztec yet it somehow worked.

Inside they carried Fenner away. In the bar area to my left, I spotted a few familiar faces including a judge and congresswoman -- El Condor catered to the vices of both sexes.

"She's waiting for you," the woman called Brinna told me. She gave me a tender kiss on the cheek and sauntered away

I headed up the carpeted stairs, wide as what you'd see outside a courthouse. On the second level was a casino and two of the lucha libre-masked guards were speaking in Spanish, walking a loud drunk away from the blackjack table. I went down a side hallway and came to a set of double doors. There was no guard present but I knew there were several nanny cams tracking my every move. If I was unwanted, there were various death traps that would engage at a touch of a button. The doors opened automatically and I entered the Queen's inner chamber.

Queen Ida, born Edna Martz in a cold water walk-up, was a small woman with heavy glasses. That she could be taken for a librarian or DMV clerk, was understandable. She regarded me, her plain but pleasant face impassive as she sat behind her massive maple wood desk. The thing was handmade and hand carved with various erotic and mystical representations.

"Cut was able to talk some before he passed out," she said.

She'd hired me to find him a week ago. Cut was Kingdom City's premiere bookie and there'd been a payout of millions due to the big betters on the recently held World's Finest Poker Game held at the

Fountainhead Casino and Resort in town. Queenie was the biggest of the big betters and her rival Ma Grundy had kidnapped Fenner to sweat him and rip off the bank. Or so I'd been told. I knew something else was up but what it was would surface — that kind of mishegoss always does.

I said, "You want to finish it with Ma."

She nodded curtly. "I'll ad a bonus to your fee if you see it through. You have a particular skill set, Stag." An elfin light came and went behind her eyes

Okay, I'll admit it, me and Queenie had gotten it on a few times. You wouldn't think it to look at her, but behind closed doors, she was gifted when it came to handling a whip, ball cock, nipple binders, silk rope and the like. I managed to pull myself away from my heated recollections and refocused.

"The Sin and Salvation parade is tonight," Queen Ida was saying. "Ma Grundy is delivering my cash to her Macao partners during the festivities."

"That's why she nabbed Cut. How sweet it would be to use your money to further her ends."

"Exactly," she concurred.

"Ma's crew will be on alert."

"Yes and no," she said coolly. "I've already had Brinna through her contacts advance the rumor that all perished here in the swamp. Grundy will of course be wary but still, there will be some element of surprise to be taken advantage of, I'd hazard."

I needed a drink and a cigarette, and another round with the lovely Brinna. Instead, I was going to get a gun and a road map to Bullitville. Well, you couldn't get everything you wanted. What fun would that be? Not an hour later I was heading back to town with the beautiful Brinna at the wheel and two of Queen Ida's best brutes, Walt and some other cat, their masks intact. Me I was rockin' a Day of the Dead painted on skull face look in bold white and black.

"That look suits you." Brinna smiled at me and I grinned back as we bounced over a rut and made it onto the asphalt of the highway. She was looking swell as Nawlins voodoo queen Marie Laveau.

The Sin and Salvation parade began as a religious invocation decades ago. It was originally held in honor of the Spanish Jesuits who'd survived the Indians, mosquitoes, gators, and Yellow Fever of Wildwood Swamp. Grateful to the higher power, they'd founded the town and laid that heavy duty name on it. But as the years progressed, evidence was unearthed confirming the long-held rumors the surviving padres had that one bad winter feasted on the arms and legs of their less hardy fellows who'd perished – and maybe a few who were helped along to the afterlife to be sliced and roasted. The knowledge that cannibalism had happened along with the influx of Santeria, Vodun, Catholicism, and some Aztec mumbo-jumbo eventually transformed the celebration into what it was today, where it wasn't unusual to see a beefy dude clad only in a codpiece dancing in the streets with a ballerina in a aluminum tutu.

Of course driving into the part of town where the parade was going on was impossible. So we parked on the outskirts and took the elevated in along with the other partiers. As we descended the station's steps amidst a grouping of several men and women dressed as steampunk pirates, the big guy, Walt, spoke.

"We supposed to look for some Chinese humps hanging out together?"

Brinna reminded him of the city's sizeable Asian population.

"Then how do we scope out Ma's connects?" he asked irritated.

All around us swirled humanity in various costumes, regalia of the wondrous. A tall bosomy woman marched past with a three foot penis strap-on, whose head glowed neon purple. Many wore masks or sported painted faces.

"We ain't never gonna find 'em in time in al this," groused the other masked henchman.

Brinna said, "You getting any brilliant flashes, hawkshaw?"

For some reason at that moment replaying in my head was the fight I'd had earlier today. This was after tracking down Cut Fenner to the duplex Ma Grundy's boys had been holding him prisoner -- torturing him to make him talk. At that time, there were only two on duty and I'd gotten the drop on the first one, knocking him upside the head with a busted off chair leg. The second one and I tangoed.

"The lunch trucks," I murmured, walking away from the other three. They stared quizzically at me.

When me and the second bruiser tussled, we stumbled through a closed door. In that room there were several cleaned and pressed white chef-like shirts on wire hangers on a rack. There'd had been a logo on the shoulder of those uniforms. At the time, me and my ersatz sparring partner were punching the shit out of each other yet that logo's design was buried somewhere in my mind. The house was not far from where we were now.

"What's up, Stag?" Brinna asked, catching up with me.

"Hold on, it's coming back to me."

At that house, wouldn't you know it but the goon had a backup piece, a sissified derringer. He'd managed to get it loose but I'd grabbed his wrist. His shot went wild, unfortunately striking Fenner. I got the gun away from him and using the derringer's stubby grip, pistol whipped lumps the size of golf balls all over his square head. Then I hustled Fenner out of there and to the Queen, calling ahead. There was no way to keep him safe in the local hospital with Ma Grundy on a tear.

For cover, I moved us behind a conga line of revelers done up in sexed-up religious regalia – the priests were muscled shirtless boy toys with white collars around their veined necks and the nuns wore habits with leather mini-skirts, garter belts and nylons below the hemlines and platform shoes.

Nearby I also noticed a phalanx of big woman of various races and color range, all over six feet, carrying three cardboard coffins covered in fancy papier-mâché designs on their broad shoulders as they chanted in what I thought was a French patois. The woman were dressed in various stylistic interpretations of Baron Samedi, aka Baron Saturday, complete with chalked faces, tuxedo jackets, and black top hats with plumes of bright feathers. Samedi was a kind of vodou deity, the loa, spirti, of the dead.

"See the truck with the toothy chicken" I said to Brinna. I made for the vehicle before she could answer. The other three followed me. At the truck were several customers. The crew of the truck were dressed in their white chef's gear. The logo of the anthropomorphic Smiling Chicken plastered on the side of the truck matched the patches over their breasts. That was the one I'd seen during my fight earlier. Away but not far from the line of people at the truck were two men on point, their arms folded, their bullet head on swivel as they scanned and categorized civilian or potential problem. Brinna and the luchadors spotted them too.

"We got them," Walt whispered as he and his buddy circled around to the two guards.

Fifty Shades of Grey Fedora

"Look," I said to Brinna, nodding toward the truck. At the window was a tall, slender man in dark glasses. Through the order window he was being passed several wrapped bundles that could be chicken burritos. He was stuffing them in a metal attaché case.

"That's how they're transferring the money," Brinna said.

"Yep."

Walt and his shadow vamped on the two guards. The first target went down silently. But his pal got off a yelp and the truck's crew were alerted. From our right flank, the lids of the coffins popped open and out sprang three, to use the PC term, Little People -- two men and one woman. They were dressed in black suits, white shirts and black ties. But these were no singing Munchkins in their Sunday best. The song they were about to render was that of destruction. Two had handguns and one of the men brandished an aqua-colored AK.

"Shit fire," Brinna said. Odd, but this was the first time I'd heard the Texas in her voice.

Fortunately the women carrying the shooters didn't seem to be in on the bit and collectively looking aghast, dropped their cargo. People were yelling and panicking and this helped as we ran toward the truck for cover. The three shooters were pros, they didn't mow down innocents just to get a shot at us.

But AK knew what to do and advanced, spraying lead in the air to scatter the crowd. We hadn't yet gained the side of the truck and a burst of fire sizzled the air next to my head. I was bringing my gun up and saw that Brinna had taken a knee, and using both hands to steady her shot, she fired her weapon at the municipal trash receptacle Mr. AK had hunkered behind.

Turns out she was packing explosive shells and blew the receptacle apart. Mr. AK staggered backward, shards of metal sticking out of his head and face, his blood flowing freely. He dropped his assault rifle, as his brain activity ceased. As he keeled over, a new gunshot reminded us the other two were still frisky.

"Ugggh," I heard at my elbow. Brinna went down.

I also went down, flat on my stomach and let off two rounds at the women who'd clipped my voodoo girl. She'd stationed herself against a palm tree but that was no protection from a .45's bullets. They went through the trunk forcing her into the open. I dropped her with one centered in her forehead. Now where was that third gunner?

"Bri?" I dared.

"I'm still breathing," she wheezed.

Had to get this over with now. Coming up beside me was Walt and the other one, who was also leaking red.

"Bastard had a knife up his sleeve," Walt illuminated, kneeling beside Brinna, gazing at her tenderly.

"There's a third --" I began but didn't finish. For in a blink, the Queen's man with the knife wound was now on fire.

"Motherfucker," he exclaimed, his smoldering head issuing blue and yellow sparks that exploded like fireworks.

Walt and I gaped at him then realized the third shooter had traded in his handgun for a flame thrower. It was attached to the propane tanks at the rear of the grinning fowl lunch truck. The shooter rode on the wide shoulders of Ma Grundy, a cross-dresser done up in a black cocktail dress, heels, pearls and a white floor length mink coat.

Gleefully she cackled, "Die, die."

The man on fire had the presence of mind to drop and roll, his flesh and clothes all of a charred texture and color. Walt grabbed up Brinna and I moved as another burst of flame licked at us. I had a stunt in mind and would have only one chance to pull it off or be walking carne asada. Some revelers had been carrying a giant ankh and had dropped it in the chaos. It was shiny and made of gold wrapped tin.

I propped it up, the symbol of life in ancient Egypt was more than eight feet tall.

"What do you think of my handiwork, Ma?"

We locked eyes across the expanse. For the briefest of moments, the man that was Ma Grundy, my old running buddy Frankie Stewart, looked back at me. Then he was gone. A gust of fire shot from the nozzle again at the big target I'd offered. But I wasn't trying to hide behind the thing. The gold foil paper covering the ankh burned, causing the object to glow as if from within, I'd rolled beside it and came up blasting.

One of my rounds pierced a propane tank and the Smiling Chicken truck, its occupants and the gunner went up in a noisy, fiery explosion that singed my face and knocked me and big Karl over. When I got up, Ma Grundy was ash.

Fifty Shades of Grey Fedora

***

Later, after she got out of the hospital, Brinna and I had a session with Queen Ida. As I'd mentioned, she knew her way around a cat-o-nine-tales and several devilishly designed sex toys. The three of us got to experience that knowledge quite intimately.

And that's all I'll say about that.

Fifty Shades of Grey Fedora

LAST TANGO IN FLATBUSH
by Robert J. Randisi

1

Val O'Farrell looked down at the body of April Morehouse. It was hard not to look. Even in death she was a stunner. She was lying on her back with her robe wide open, and naked underneath. Her full breasts had large brown nipples, made for chewing on; she had wide hips, pale, freckled skin and a fiery bush between her legs that matched the red hair on her head. He looked up. It had rained, but the balcony above hers had kept her from getting too wet, rivulets of water were seeping over to her from the edges of the balcony.

He turned his attention to Detective Sam McKeever, who was chomping on a dead cigar.

"What am I doing in Brooklyn, Sam?" he asked. "For that matter, what are you doing here?"

"This homicide matches one I had in Manhattan a few weeks ago. You remember it? It was in the papers? Gloria Romaine."

"The actress," O'Farrell said. "Also beautiful."

"Beautiful, my ass," McKeever growled. "She was a goddess. See the tits on this broad? Nothin' compared to the hangers on Gloria Romaine."

"What makes this case so much like that one?"

"Come inside."

O'Farrell took a quick look over the balcony and down at Flatbush Avenue before following McKeever into the apartment.

"Look there," McKeever said.

He was pointing to a small table that sat next to an overstuffed armchair. On the table was a large glass ash tray with the remnants of a big, thick cigar in it—plenty of ashes and a large plug.

"That doesn't look like one of your nickel stogies," O'Farrell said.

McKeever took his cigar from his mouth, glared at it, then jammed it back in so hard O'Farrell was surprised he didn't choke on it. Around them boys in blue were scurrying about, trying to look busy. Some of them were stealing a glance whenever they could at the naked body.

"Cover that body up until the M.E. gets here!" McKeever shouted.

"Sure, boss," somebody said. A sheet appeared, and the woman was covered.

"Whataya see?" McKeever asked.

"The remains of a really good cigar."

"Look closer."

O'Farrell stepped closer to the table. Also in the ashtray was a cigar band.

"You know what that is?" McKeeveer asked.

"A cigar band?"

"The cigar band, the ashes," McKeever said, "what's left of that cigar? It's a *figurados.*"

"Sorry," O'Farrell said, "I'm not up on my Spanish."

"Figurados are oddly shaped cigars," McKeever said. "This one was a Perfecto—narrow at each end, and bulging in the middle."

"I'll take your word for it."

"We also found one of these at the scene of the Romaine murder," McKeever said. "You know who smokes these?"

"A lot of people?"

"How about Ricky Labretto?"

"The Black Hand Ricky Labretto?"

"The same."

"So you think Ricky Labretto killed these two women?" O'Farrell asked.

"He was seen with the Romaine broad," McKeever said, "and the remnants of the same kind of cigar were found in her penthouse."

"That's real circumstantial. Was he seen with this woman? Or here?"

"I know it's circumstantial," McKeever said. "We're waiting to talk to the night doorman."

"How were they killed?" O'Farrell asked. "I don't see much blood."

"A long, thin blade in the back of the neck."

"Both of them?"

"Yeah."

O'Farrell frowned.

"Okay, that's a little less circumstantial. But why am I here?"

McKeever looked around, then pulled O'Farrell over to a corner.

"I don't know who the hell I can trust in the department, Val," he said.

"Aw Sam..." O'Farrell said, shaking his head.

"Yeah, yeah, I know," McKeever said. "You're private. I tell you what. I'll hire you. Pay you outta my own pocket."

"I'm not going to take your money, Sam."

"Then do it as a favor," McKeever said. "And do it before he kills another gorgeous broad."

"What if it's a set-up?" O'Farrell asked. "Somebody planting the cigars, knowing that Frankie was seen with Gloria Romaine?"

"Then prove that," McKeever said. "Find me the right killer. I don't want crazy beautiful dames droppin' all over town, Val. Do you?"

Considering his own liking for "crazy beautiful dames," O'Farrell said, "No Sam, I don't."

2

O'Farrell didn't tell McKeever, but he knew Ricky Labretto. He and the Black Hand gangster had been dancing a sort of tango for years, never falling out of step to the point where they'd have to settle things. So he figured the best way to find out if Ricky had killed those women was to ask him.

He left the apartment, went down to Flatbush Avenue and got into his new 1922 Pierce Arrow.

Ricky was more likely to have killed this woman, since he lived in Brooklyn. Gloria Romaine lived in Manhattan, never left the island, but according to McKeever, she'd been seen with Labretto.

He drove to Ricky's house in Red Hook, parked his car out front. It was a red brick two story house, with two men on the porch. O'Farrell recognized one of them.

"Hey, Willie," he said.

"Mr. O'Farrell," Willie Benedict said. "What brings you here?"

"Just wanted to talk to Ricky for a few minutes," O'Farrell said.

"That so? About what?"

"Murder."

"You ain't a cop no more, Mr. O'Farrell," Willie said.

"I know that, Willie," O'Farrell said. "I just want to talk."

Willie looked at the other man. "Danny, go and tell Ricky Mr. O'Farrell's here."

Danny, who was much younger than Willie, asked, "Why?"

"Well," Willie said, "right now it's because I'm tellin' you to."

"But what for? Who's this guy—"

"Just do what I tell ya Danny," Willie said. "And do it now!"

Reluctantly, Danny opened the front door and went inside.

"That's what passes for good help these days, Mr. O'Farrell," Willie said. "Sad state of affairs."

"It sure is, Willie."

"That's quite a car you got there."

"I like it."

"New, ain't it?"

"Brand new."

"You must be doin' okay since you left the cops."

"I'm doing all right, Willie," O'Farrell said.

"Yeah, that's what I hear," Willie said. "Val O'Farrell's the go to guy in this town, you need somethin' done. On the right side of the law, that is."

"That's safe to say," O'Farrell said.

"Sure was sad about your friend Bat Masterson passin' that way," Willie said. "I mean, sittin' at his typewriter and all. Man like that ought to die from a bullet."

"Naw," O'Farrell said, "in the end Bat was a newspaperman and a writer. He died just the way he would have wanted."

"If you say so."

The front door opened and Danny stepped out.

"Ricky says to send him in."

"Then get out of his way," Willie said.

"Ain't we gonna search him? And walk him in?" Danny asked.

"Search him for what?"

"Well, he might have a gun."

"He does have a gun," Willie said, "but he ain't gonna use it. Now get out of his way, damn it."

Danny shook his head, but stepped aside so O'Farrell could enter.

O'Farrell had been to Ricky's house before, and had a good idea which room the man would be in.

Ricky had a special room in the house he called his solarium. In point of fact, he didn't know, when he had a room constructed with so many windows, that it was a "solarium," until Val O'Farrell told him.

When O'Farrell entered the room he was not surprised by the degree of excess he saw. Ricky Labretto saw himself as a modern day Caligula. There was a table covered with meats, cheeses and fruit, and urns of wine. And as you'd expect in such a scene, there were naked women. And in the center of it all, Ricky Labretto.

"Val," Ricky said, "my friend, come in, come in." He opened his mouth and the naked blonde sitting next to him dropped a grape into it. "Have a drink." He clapped his hands together. "Wine for my friend."

Ricky was wearing a pair of grey slack, a silk short open at the neck, with the long sleeves rolled up, and his feet were bare. The blonde with the grapes was on his right, and a brunette with wine was on his left. Both were naked, both were Ricky's type—big breasted, broad hips, pale-skinned, and young. Their nipples were large and had been rouged to make them stand out even more.

"Ricky," O'Farrell said, "we need to talk."

"So talk, my friend."

"I can't talk in here," O'Farrell said. "There are too many distractions."

As if on cue two more women appeared, one on either side of him. They were almost naked, bare-breasted, but with wisps of fabric across their hips. They leaned on him and one of them ran the back of her hand across the front of his pants, felt the bulge there.

"He's distracted, all right," she said.

"Ricky," O'Farrell said, "these girls are going to give me a heart attack."

"All right, all right," Ricky said, bounding out of his chair, "ladies, I'm going to go out and talk to my friend. Just be ready for me when I get back."

Ricky walked toward O'Farrell, shooing the girls away from him. O'Farrell noticed that they were all under twenty-five, while Ricky himself was thirty-two or three.

"Come on, my friend," Ricky said, putting his arm around O'Farrell's shoulders and leading him to another door. Beyond it they were in a more normal office setting, with a broad desk, chairs and file cabinets.

"Have a seat, Val," Ricky said, sitting behind the desk. "Tell me what's on your mind."

O'Farrell sat across from Ricky, whose entire demeanor changed. He was still wearing a silk shirt open at the throat, but he was all business.

"Gloria Romaine," O'Farrell said.

"I knew her."

"So you know she's dead."

"Of course I know," Ricky said. "The cops were all over me for that one. But they couldn't hang it on me, Black Hand or no Black Hand. I had no reason to kill Gloria. That bitch was amazing in bed."

"What about April Morehouse."

"April... what house?"

"Morehouse."

"I don't know her."

"Well, she has something in common with Gloria Romaine."

"And what's that?"

"She's dead."

Ricky sat back, reached out, and took a cigar from a humidor on the desk. As O'Farrell watched he set fire to the end of what O'Farrell now knew was a *figurados*.

"I don't know April Morehouse."

"A pity," O'Farrell said. "She's your type."

"Then it's a shame she's dead."

"Gloria and April had one more thing in common."

"What's that?"

"Something found at the scene of both deaths."

"And what was that?"

O'Farrell pointed and said, "That."

Ricky looked at his cigar.

"A cigar?"

"That cigar," O'Farrell said. "A perfecto."

Ricky looked at the cigar again, then put it down in an ash tray.

"That explains why they came after me for Gloria," he said.

"Well," O'Farrell said, "there's also the fact that she'd been seen with you."

Ricky suddenly turned very serious.

"Val," he said, "the cops are gonna try to hang this on me."

"I know it, Ricky," O'Farrell said. "McKeever already offered to pay me out of his own pocket."

"To frame me?"

"To prove it, one way or another."

"Well, I'll pay you to prove I didn't do it."

"There's only one problem with that."

"What?"

"I'd have to be convinced you didn't do it."

"So ask me," Ricky said. "Ask me and I'll tell you the truth, Val."

"Did you kill April Morehouse?"

"No."

"Did you kill Gloria Romaine?"

"No." He frowned. "Where was this April killed?"

"Here in Brooklyn."

Ricky sat up. "In my borough?"

O'Farrell nodded.

"Look Val," Ricky said, "I wanna work with you on this. First of all somebody's killin' in my borough, and second, they're tryin' to frame me by leaving Perfectos at the scene."

O'Farrell's first instinct was to say no, but if he believed Ricky that he didn't kill the two women, it could only help him to have the man along on his investigation. Ricky intimidated people.

"Okay, Ricky," O'Farrell said, "but you've got to leave the naked girls home."

Ricky smiled. "Don't worry, Val. There are plenty of naked girls out there."

3

O'Farrell waited out front with Willie and Danny. They all three had a cigarette, but while Willie passed the time with him, Danny just glared.

"How'd you get the boss to leave the house?" Willie asked. "He's got him four girls in there."

"Made him an offer he couldn't refuse, Willie," O'Farrell said. "Maybe you'll have to go in there and take care of those girls."

"I'd do that in a minute, Val," Willie said. "'cept the boss would cut off my peter if I touched any of his girls."

The door opened at that moment and Ricky stepped out. He was wearing a dark suit with a white cotton shirt. He looked more like a normal businessman, except that O'Farrell could see the bulge beneath his arm where he wore a gun.

"Ready, Val?"

"I'm ready, Ricky."

"Where to first?"

"We've got one murder in Manhattan and one in Brooklyn," O'Farrell said. "I've got eyes and ear on the streets in the city, while you have eyes and ears on the streets here in Brooklyn. Why don't we see what those eyes and ears have seen and heard?'

"Okay," Ricky said, "but I don't want us splittin' up."

"Why not?"

"If another woman is murdered, I wanna be able to say that I was with you." He tapped O'Farrell on the chest when he said "You."

"Good thinkin', Ricky."

Since they were already in Brooklyn, and the second murder took place in Brooklyn, that's where they started.

"Who's this guy?" O'Farrell asked, as they approached a building on the ass end of Flatbush Avenue.

"He runs girls in Brooklyn," Labretto said. "If somebody's killin' girls here, he'd want to know. He should know."

O'Farrell looked up at the building. It appeared to be a 4 story warehouse, with all the windows boarded up.

Labretto approached the large metal door and pounded his fist on it. It echoed inside the building.

"Again?" O'Farrell asked.

"Wait."

They waited a few minutes, in fact, and then the sound of a lock being turned preceded the opening of the door. A large man with a rifle stared at them.

"Ricky Labretto for Mongo."

"Come in."

They both entered.

"Wait."

They waited while the man relocked the door.

"Who's he?" the man asked, indicating O'Farrell.

"Val O'Farrell."

"Cop?"

"Ex," Labretto said. "Private now."

"You vouch for him?"

"I do."

The man shrugged.

"Follow me."

He led them up 4 flights of metal stairs that O'Farrell was not entirely confident would hold their combined weight.

When they got to the top floor of the empty warehouse the entire ambiance changed. The upper level was like a huge loft, with hardwood floors and brick walls, 25 foot ceilings with electric lights. At the far end a man sat at a desk. Several girls were seated around on plush sofas or cushions that were simply sitting on the floor. They eyed the three men as they went by.

"Hello, ladies," Labretto said.

"Hello, Ricky," one of them said, waving.

When they reached the man at the desk he looked up at them. He did not look the way O'Farrell imagined a man named "Mongo" would look. He wore wire-framed glasses, squinted through them, looked for all the world like a bank teller.

"Ricky," he said, "what are you doing here? Did we have an appointment?"

"No," Labretto said. "Mongo, this is—"

"Val O'Farrell," the man said. "I know. What can I do for you gents. What brings you here?"

"Murder," O'Farrell said.

"Of who?" Mongo asked.

"Women," Labretto said.

"Which women?"

"Gloria Romaine, for one," Labretto said.

"And last night, a woman named April Morehouse."

"What?" Mongo asked.

One of the girls—the one seated closest to the desk—came up off her cushion and asked, "What did he say? Did he say April's... dead?"

O'Farrell looked at the girl, a pretty blonde, and then back at Mongo.

"Lee," Mongo said to the man with the rifle, "take the girls out."

"For how long?"

"About half an hour," Mongo said. "Buy them some ice cream."

Lee hesitated, looked at the blonde and asked, "What about Rebecca."

"I'm stayin'," the woman said.

"Let her stay," Mongo said.

"Right."

Lee herded the other girls together and took them down the stairs. Mongo sat back in his chair and no one spoke until their footsteps had faded.

"Yes," Mongo said, "April was one of my girls."

"She was my friend," Rebecca said. "What happened to her?"

'Same thing that happened to Gloria Romaine," O'Farrell said. "Somebody killed her."

"Where?" Mongo asked. He looked at Rebecca. "Did she have a customer last night?"

"No," Rebecca said, "she was home."

"That's where she was killed," Labretto said. "At home."

"In her apartment?" Rebecca asked. She looked at Mongo. "She never takes anyone there."

"Well, somebody was there," O'Farrell said.

Mongo looked at Labretto. "Nobody kills one of my girls, Ricky. Who did thus?"

"I don't know."

"Who do the police think did it?" Mongo asked O'Farrell said.

"Actually," O'Farrell said, pointing at LaBretto, "They think he might have done it."

"Ricky? That's crazy."

"Why?" O'Farrell asked.

"Well, for one thing, Ricky doesn't use my girls," Mongo said. "And two, he wouldn't be that stupid. Ricky and I don't cross each other."

"It's true," LaBretto said. "We have an agreement."

"Then who else would want to harm one of your girls?" O'Farrell asked.

"It could have been a coincidence," Mongo said. "After all, the Romaine woman wasn't one of mine."

"That's true," O'Farrell said.

"So this doesn't have to be personal," Mongo said.

"It was personal for April," Rebecca said.

O'Farrell looked at her. He noticed she seemed older than the other girls, though not yet thirty. Pale skin, green eyes, ash blonde hair. She was tall and slender, wearing a silk top that clearly outlined her large nipples. He couldn't stop looking at them. It was sexier than if she'd been naked.

"What's your next move?" Mongo asked, sitting back in his chair and regarding both Labretto and O'Farrell. "Are you fellas gonna solve this together?"

"We thought we might," O'Farrell said.

"Well," Mongo said, "I wish you luck. Can you find your way out?"

"I know the way," Labretto said.

"Send Lee and the other girls back up, will you?"

"Sure, Mongo. Thanks for seein' us."

Mongo waved, and turned his attention to Rebecca.

O'Farrell followed Labretto down to the main level, where they found Lee and the girls, all smoking.

"Mongo wants you back," Labretto said.

Lee nodded, and shooed the girls back. They all dropped their cigarettes on the ground.

Outside the building O'Farrell put his hand on Labretto's arm to stop him.

"What?"

"Why did we come here?" the detective asked.

"To see what Mongo knew."

"We didn't ask him anything," O'Farrell said.

"We found out that April was one of his girls."

"Do you and he really have some sort of... treaty?"

"I thought we did."

"And now?"

Labretto turned to look up at the building.

"Why'd you bring me here, Ricky?"

Labretto looked at O'Farrell.

"It's too much of a coincidence that April was one of Mongo's girls, and you just happened to bring me here."

"Keep talkin'."

"Either you recognized her name as one of his girls," O'Farrell said, "or you know way more than you're telling me."

Labretto looked at O'Farrell and said, "Let's go get a drink."

4

Labretto took O'Farrell to a little saloon a few blocks away called McGinty's Tavern. It had an ambiance befitting the ass end of Flatbush—bare, worn wood floors and a bar dulled and stained by years of sweaty forearms.

They took two seats at the bar, and the other men in the place gave them room, obviously recognizing Ricky Labretto.

"Two beers," Labretto told the bartender.

"Yes, sir."

He brought the beers and scurried away to the other end of the bar, where his other customers had gathered.

"They're afraid of you," O'Farrell said.

"Nonsense," Labretto said. "They respect the Black Hand."

"If you say so," O'Farrell said. He drank down half his beer, set the mug back down on the bar. "Do you have something to tell me?"

Labretto drank some beer and said, "I think Mongo's tryin' to set me up."

"So you think Mongo's the killer?"

"Not on his own," Labretto said. "I think he had somebody do it for him."

"And he's trying to frame you."

"Yes."

"But you guys have an agreement," O'Farrell said, "A truce."

"And we're not even in the same business," Labretto said. "I don't run girls. That's Mongo's niche, not mine. My girls are my girls."

"What about Gloria Romaine?"

"We met at a party," he said. "She threw herself at me and I couldn't resist. But she's not my type."

"Too old?"

"Exactly."

"And April Morehouse?"

"Don't know her."

"You've never been with her?"

"Never."

"Why would Mongo choose to kill one of his own girls?"

"My guess is he wanted to get rid of her, anyway," Labretto said. "He's killin' two birds with one stone."

O'Farrell drank the rest of his beer, thought about their visit to Mongo.

"That girl Rebecca," he said.

"Yeah?"

"She seems to be the most upset about April," O'Farrell said.

"Then maybe she's the one you have to talk to."

"Me?"

"She wouldn't talk to me," Labretto said. "And you said McKeever hired you."

"Do you know where she lives?"

"Not a clue," Labretto said.

"Is there a chance she lives there?"

"No," Labretto said, "Mongo doesn't let any of his girls live there. I know that much."

"And what about his bodyguard."

"Lee? Yeah, he lives there."

"Does he escort the girls home?"

"No."

"Does anyone?"

"No," Labretto said. "Mongo's ego won't allow him to believe that anyone would approach any of his girls."

O'Farrell thought it was ironic that Labretto—the biggest egomaniac he knew—was talking about Mongo's ego.

"Okay, then."

"Another beer?" Labretto asked.

"Nope," O'Farrell said. "I've got to sit and wait for Rebecca to go home."

"And then?"

He shrugged. "Maybe she'll need a lift."

5

He stopped his Pierce Arrow alongside the girl.

"Need a lift?" he asked.

"O'Farrell, right?" she asked. "The detective?"

"Right."

She shrugged. "Sure, why not?"

She got into the car and it immediately filled with her scent.

"Where to?"

"Just keep going on Flatbush," she said.

He drove on.

'So what do you want to know?"

"What makes you think I want to know anything?"

"There are only two reasons you'd pick me up," she said. "You want to know something..."

"Or?"

"... sex."

He looked at her. She was staring straight ahead, presenting him with an exquisite profile. Would sex be such a bad idea?

"How far are we going?" O'Farrell asked.

She gave him her address. He frowned. If he was right, that was right across the street from April Morehouse's apartment building.

They chatted along the way about his car, his old job with the police, what she did before she went to work for Mongo.

"What made you go to work for Mongo?"

"Every time I had a date with a man," she said, "he'd buy me dinner, or take me to a show—or both—and then expected me to sleep with him. It occurred to me that I was being treated like a whore. Since I like sex, I figured if I was going to act like a whore, I might as well make good money for it."

"How did you get to Mongo?"

She shrugged and said, "The word on the street." That was all she offered. He figured there was more to it than that, but let it go for the moment.

When he pulled up in front of her building he saw that he was right. It was literally right across the street from April's.

"Would you like to come up?" she asked, making no move to get out. Her jacket was open and he could see the outline of her nipples beneath her silk top.

"Sure. I might as well make sure you get to your door safely, right?"

"Yes, Detective."

They got out of the car and walked to the front door of her building. She unlocked the door with her key, but he opened it for her. She brushed against him as she entered, enveloping him in the scent of her.

"Second floor," she said.

"Fine."

He walked up the stairs behind her, watching her hips and butt sway in front of him. There were four apartments on the floor, with A, B, C and D on the doors. Roughly the same layout as April Morehouse's building. She used her key to unlock her door, then turned to face him.

"Well," he said, "home, safe and sound."

He started to back away, but she stopped him by grabbing his tie. With her other hand she reached behind her and opened the door.

"Come inside," she said.

"I shouldn't—"

"I'm nervous," she told him, "after what happened to April."

"Well," he said, "in that case."

She backed into the apartment, pulling him along by his necktie.

"Turn on the light," she said. "Would you like a drink?"

"I could use one."

"The liquor is over there," she said, pointing. "I'm going to change."

He wanted to tell her to keep on the silk blouse, but kept silent. Instead he turned the light on and went to the side bar she'd indicated.

He poured two glasses of red wine, turned when he heard something behind him. She changed very quickly into a long robe that covered her from head to toe, but it was also silk, so it outlined everything underneath perfectly. He could even see how full the bush between her legs was.

"Thank you," she said, taking a glass from him. "Come, sit."

He followed her to a sofa and they sat side-by-side and drank their wine.

"Have you ever used a whore, O'Farrell?" she asked.

"In my younger days," he admitted, "but not lately."

"No," she said, "I don't supposed a man like you would have to." She ran one hand down over the silk that covered her breasts. He couldn't help but watch to see if her fingers were actually going to touch a nipple. "I'll bet you get all the women you want."

"Rebecca—"

"You can call me Becca," she said.

"Okay, Becca," he said, "you can call me Val."

"Val," she said, licking her lips. It was as if she was tasting his name. "I like that."

"Becca... do you know something that can help me?"

"Val," she said, licking the edge of her glass as she looked at him over it, "I know a lot of things that can help you."

6

"I mean—"

"I know what you mean," she said, putting her glass down. "But I think you need to relax." She took his glass and also put it down. "Now!"

He opened his mouth to object but before he could say word her mouth was on his, and her body was pressed up against him. Wine and sex mixed with the natural taste of her to form a heady cocktail. And he thought he could feel her nipples through her silk robe, and his clothes.

She kissed him deeply and he had no choice but to kiss her back. When she started to grind her crotch into his, his erection was complete and painful.

"Wait," he said, into her mouth. "Wait—"

"Wait for what?" she asked.

"My pants..."

"What about your pants?"

"They're going to burst."

She seemed delighted by that news.

"Well then, let's take then off."

She leaned back, undid his belt, and his trousers and slipped them off. Next, she grabbed his shorts and yanked them down. When his rigid penis came into view she said, "Oh my. Looks at him, all red and angry."

"Not angry," he said, reaching for her, "pleased."

She came into his arms and they kissed. He ran his hands over her silk covered body, while she reached between them to grasp him and stroke him.

"Mmm," she moaned, and slid down to take him into her mouth. As she began to suck, he lifted his butt off the sofa and began to fuck her mouth. She moaned appreciatively and slid her hands beneath his buttocks. At one point she slid a finger along the cleft between his ass cheeks, and then inserted the finger into his anus. He almost came right then and there, but although he shouted he was able to hold back.

She released him from her mouth, started to take the silk robe off.

"No," he said, "leave it on." He touched her shoulders. "I like the silk."

"Kinky," she said, with a smile.

She left the robe on, but hiked it up over her hips, slid into his lap and onto his cock. She was impossibly wet, warm and slick and he slid in so easily. Then she began to ride him up and down, slowly at first, moaning each time she came down on him, her eyes closed, her head thrown back. He leaned forward to kiss her neck, slid the robe off her shoulders just enough to kiss them. He touched her nipples through the silk, then pushed the robe aside so he could take them into his mouth. He never realized before how much he liked silk...

While she bounced up and down on his cock she tore at his jacket and shirt—he dropped his shoulder holster behind the sofa--so that now he was totally naked, and she was partially sheathed in her silk robe, shoulders, nipples and butt bare. He slid his hands beneath her, felt the warm stickiness of her juices.

"Wait, wait, wait..." she said, suddenly jumped up off of him.

"Wha—"

She turned around, made sure the robe stayed hiked up around her waist, and presented him with her smooth ass,

"This way," she said. "Come on, put it in. I'm slick enough."

He suddenly realized he was with a whore. Was she doing what a whore does, or what Becca liked? Was he going to be charged for this, or... ah, fuck it.

He got on his knees behind her, spread her cheeks and pressed the spongy head of his cock to her anus. His cock was still slick from her, and she was right, she was juicy enough so that he slid in fairly easily.

"Ooh, God, yeah," she said.

He began to fuck her that way, holding her by the hips. As he drove in and out of her, she rocked back and forth, matching his rhythm. She began to moan loudly, which struck him odd, since most of her noise had been low, up to this point. Of course, he was in her ass, but why choose this moment to get so loud...

He sensed more than heard or felt someone behind him. He turned and saw the blade, threw himself off the sofa, and out of Becca.

"Get him! Get him!" Becca shouted.

It was a man, he knew that much as he rolled away from both of them. Becca grabbed at him, and the man stepped toward him. Two killers, he thought, working together, not one.

Everything started to move very fast. There was screaming from Becca, and yelling from the man. O'Farrell kept moving, knowing that his gun was behind the sofa, which now was across the room.

"Get him, damn it!" Becca was shouting,

The look of hatred on her face totally transformed her into someone he'd never seen before. She was actually on the floor, crawling toward him, still in her silk robe. He did the only thing he could. He kicked out at her, caught her right in the head. She stopped cold. That left him and the man.

Luckily, the man seemed to only be armed with the knife, no gun. Although naked and unarmed, O'Farrell didn't feel the situation was hopeless.

There are a lot of weapon in any apartment. All you have to do is reach out and grab. As he reached out his hand encountered an expensive wooden chair, old and restored. He didn't have time to worry about its value, though. He got to his feet and held the chair out in front of him.

"Easy, Lee," he said, to Mongo's henchman.

"You hurt Becca," Lee said. "You was gonna die quick, but now I'm gonna kill you slow."

O'Farrell looked down at Becca, who was face down and still not moving. Her robe was still down over her shoulders and up over her butt. Even in that position she still stirred him.

"She didn't do a very good job of keeping me occupied, did she, Lee?" he asked. "You were supposed to slip up behind me and slide that blade in, like you did with Gloria and April.

"They had to die."

"Why?"

"For different reasons than you," Lee said, waving the knife.

It was a long blade, certainly the murder weapon Sam McKeever had been talking about. It was not a fighting knife. Lee was not in the position of advantage he thought he was.

O'Farrell put the chair down.

"That's dumb," Lee said, and lunged.

O'Farrell grabbed the vase from a nearby table and tossed it at Lee. The man flinched as the water from the vase reached him first, then the vase.

O'Farrell moved quickly past the man to the sofa, and over it. He found his gun, pulled it from the holster, then stood up. Lee was just turning to face him, holding the knife out.

"Drop it, Lee."

"Not a chance."

"I don't have any problem with killing you," O'Farrell said. "The cops want the killer, dead or alive. It's up to you."

"Fuck you," Lee said, and charged.

O'Farrell fired.

7

"Hey, Val," Willie said.

"Willie," O'Farrell said. "Hello, Danny."

Danny glared at him.

"Boss in?"

"He is," Willie said, "but it's kind of early."

"Well, I had a big night," O'Farrell said. "I think Ricky would want to hear about it."

Willie thought it over, then said, "Wait here." He started in, then said, "Danny, keep your mouth shut while I'm gone."

Danny did keep his mouth shut, but he kept staring at O'Farrell in a way meant to intimidate him. Instead, it amused the detective.

Willie reappeared and said, "Okay, go ahead. You know the way."

"Thanks."

When O'Farrell entered Ricky Labretto's inner sanctum the man was receiving oral sex from one of his girls. He was leaning back in his chair—which was very throne like—his legs splayed, his hand on the back of the girl's blonde head as it bobbed up and down on him. His eyes were closed, but when he heard O'Farrell enter he opened them.

"You want some of this, Val?"

Thinking of how his last promise of sex had almost gotten him killed O'Farrell said, "No, thanks."

"You sure?" Labretto asked, indicating the other girls in the room, who were watching, and touching themselves.

"I'm fine, Ricky."

"What brings you here, then?" he asked. "No, Sweetheart, don't stop. Mr. O'Farrell's not going to be here long."

The girl continued to gobble Labretto's cock, with a slurping sound tossed in for good measure here and there.

"I thought you should know that Mongo had nothing to do with killing those women."

"Is that right?" Labretto asked. "You caught the killer?"

"Killers," O'Farrell said. "Mongo's man Lee, and his girl Rebecca, were working together. It was the girl's idea to try and frame you for the murders."

"What did I ever do to her?"

"Nothing," O'Farrell said. "She just hates men."

"Then why not kill men?"

"She was killing women who don't hate men, and getting Lee to help her. I don't understand the psychology of it all, but I turned her over to McKeever. Let him figure it out.'

"And Lee?"

"I put a bullet in him."

Labretto put both hands behind his head and regarded O'Farrell happily while the girl continued her work.

"It's all over, then."

"Except for one thing."

"What's that?"

"You made a target out of me," O'Farrell said. "That was the point of taking me to see Mongo. You thought he was the killer, so you figured you'd let him know I was investigating the killings. He'd come after me, one of us would end up dead."

"I figured it'd be him," Labretto said, "but what hell, it all worked out, right, Val? Come on, relax. Pick a girl."

He looked at the sleek, small breasted redhead who was digging her fingers into her own rusty-colored bush, and the big-breasted brunette who was pinching her own nipples.

"No thanks, Ricky. I just want you to know, you've gotten on my wrong side. First chance I get, I'm going to take you down."

Labretto waved a hand and said, "Get out, Val. You're ruining a perfectly good blow job."

"Just remember," O'Farrell said, "you and me, we've had our last tango." He executed a slight bow, said, "Ladies," and left.

Fifty Shades of Grey Fedora

TAKE OFF YOUR CLOTHES
A "Ben Abbott" story
by Justin Scott

A curly-haired knockout parked a red GTI in front of my Benjamin Abbott Realty sign. She walked up the driveway and into my office, the glassed-in porch on my white clapboard Georgian colonial. Her low, resonant voice was rich as a cello.

"I'm Nina Russell." She shrugged out of her coat, one of those ankle-length wool French jobs with the long slit down the back.

Tall and shapely, she had a lively face, as interesting as it was beautiful, and a warm smile on full lips. She could have been one of those sweet L.L. Bean catalogue-models, but there was a kind of wink and grin about her that promised fires more forest-like than campground under the wholesome veneer.

Her eyes were huge, a blue-purple shade of late blooming asters. They roamed my windows' mullion-checked view of snowy lawns and bare-limbed trees and settled briefly on Newbury's flagpole, the tallest in Connecticut, that stands smack in the middle of Main Street. Oliver Moody, our resident Connecticut State Trooper, was ticketing the driver of a U-Haul moving van that had just sideswiped the pole while attempting to turn down Church Hill Road. Ollie had made him get out of the van. Deeply suntanned, and shivering in tropical short sleeves, the poor devil was probably wondering what had possessed him to leave Florida in the winter.

Nina's eyes lighted on the tomcat that claimed my clients' chair. "Do you mind if I sit down?" she asked him.

Tom, who had outrun the well-meaning ladies of Newbury's Spay & Neuter Association, repeatedly, surrendered his chair without even pausing to stretch, and she sat, crossing her legs with a flash of heat lightning at midnight.

I took a steadying breath, calling on years of Palates training to lower my heartbeat. Tom settled very close to her laced half boots that just covered her ankles. Nina loosened the top buttons of her sweater.

"I am so excited about meeting you, Mr. Abbott. I've been beside myself since I saw your picture on the *Newbury Clarion* website." She mimed fanning the flush I had brought to her cheeks. It looked to me more like a touch of sunburn, but who doesn't accept a compliment from a beautiful woman?

Proper, well-mannered eye contact accompanied her kind remark, but then those baby-blues locked on for an excess nanosecond. It was as compelling as if a polite cheek kiss was suddenly migrating lipward. Like those sexy boots and the custom tailored slit up the side of her otherwise L.L. Beanie skirt, it was more than enough to make even a good man reconsider his domestic arrangements.

I suggested that the newspaper's proprietor photographed purchasers of advertising space in the best light. She insisted with a believable smile that I was not a disappointment in person. By now she had my full attention. Sex aside, if such a thing could ever be, she looked like she could afford to buy a house from the upper end of my listings—a Greek Revival came to mind, as did the handsome Angell place lingering on the market—and I found myself speculating on the prospect of settling her into a new home within arms reach.

"Did you like any of my listings in the *Clarion*?"

"I'm not in the market for a house. I need a private detective."

I lied automatically and without hesitation. "I don't do much PI, anymore."

I've been a private investigator long enough to steer clear of femme fatales. They're fine in the real estate business; they make showing master bedrooms and mirrored saunas sheer delight. But not in the PI business, thank you very much, where you do not want to turn your back on one.

"I checked with the state," she said. "Your PI license is up to date."

"So's my real estate license, since I spend the vast majority of my time attempting to sell houses."

I love filling gracious old homes with graceful people—a tough gig when well-heeled customers prefer brand new McMansions, mega-mansions, and Hummer houses. But everybody's got to make a living somehow, so I pay the bills by hiring out as a private investigator. I'm qualified, having served my country in Naval Intelligence, served Mammon on Wall Street, and served time in federal prison accused of making free enterprise too free. My clients trust me to ask questions that they would rather not ask the police. While being born a half-breed—father from Main Street, mother a swamp Yankee—opens more doors to me than most New Englanders.

"You look way too young to retire," Nina said, casting a come-home-with-me smile. "And too ripped," she added, reaching across my desk to graze the hairs of my forearm with pearly fingernails.

Credit a merino polo shirt shrunken in the laundry. But why was she coming on like late night at a bar when almost anything looked better than walking to the parking lot alone? It made no sense. Her smile could empty a tavern sixty seconds before happy hour.

She wet her lips with a shapely tongue. "I see For Sale signs all over town. It looks like Newbury never got the tweet that the housing crisis is over."

She had said "see," not "saw," so I asked, "Do you live in Newbury?" I doubted she did. In such a small town, it doesn't take a real estate agent, or even a private detective, to recognize a newcomer.

"I'm house sitting the Bell place."

The Bells were visiting Singapore or Bangkok or Saigon.

"I doubt you're all that busy closing deals when so many houses are for sale, while I need, desperately, a local private investigator." Another flicker of tongue, pink and inquiring, quick as a cobra's, but infinitely warmer. "I have no one else to turn to. I hope you won't disappoint me."

"I'm very expensive," I lied.

Her smile would accelerate global warming. "I will pay anything to have you."

I doubled my usual rate. She whipped out a check book and handed me an enormous retainer.

"How can I help you, Ms. Russell?"

"Call me Nina."

Fifty Shades of Grey Fedora

"Nina, what can I do for you?"

"Find Scupper McKay."

I sat up straight. I stared. Neither a hard stare, nor a poker-faced stare, but a genuinely puzzled stare. I was already working a missing-person case—pounding shoe leather, keyboard, and keypads twenty-four-seven.

I doubted there were two missing Scupper McKays.

Vaguely reliable witnesses reported they might have seen Scupper fishing for trout in the Housatonic River. Poaching months ahead of the season fit Scupper's profile. Waders were found floating by New Milford, but Scupper was not in them. It was not an unusual story. You do not kick off chest high rubber wading boots like bedroom slippers. If you stumble into a hole and the river gets inside your waders and fills them with water and the current takes you, you're gone. Wedged in some rapids-pounded rocks somewhere between Newbury and New Milford was a body, people assumed. Bones at low water next summer. Scupper's? Who knew?

"Why are you looking for him?" I asked her.

Scupper was an antiques guy—a brilliant antiques guy. He had never held a real job, nor maintained a home other than a rented storage barn with a rollout bed in his office, but if you wanted to know a coming trend in American antiques before they got expensive, Scupper McKay was your man.

"He has something of mine."

"What?"

"Mr. Abbott." The aster color in her eyes shifted toward the chilly, gray-blue that beat a killing frost. "Ben. I can't tell you what he has of mine. That doesn't mean that I don't want you to work for me. It doesn't mean I won't pay you well." She warmed, again. "It doesn't mean that we can't enjoy whatever time we have together in whatever position we happen to end up in."

I switched my Positions browser to Sleep mode. "Did Scupper steal it from you?"

"That's a strange question to ask."

"Not at all. I've known Scupper since I was a kid. Did he steal it from you?"

"That depends whether you call taking, stealing."

"Which would be more accurate?"

"Let's just say he kept it."

Here's what it sounded like to me: Nina had commissioned him to buy an antique she wanted; Scupper found it; then Scupper found someone else who would pay more for it and had not delivered. Would Scupper do such an unethical thing? That depended.

"Are you a dealer?" I asked.

"Just a collector who loses all control when her hormones start raging and she falls in love."

Maybe I guessed wrong. Scupper would take great pleasure in screwing a rival dealer. But he regarded customers like Nina as innocents put on earth to be gently fleeced, according to their means, but not ripped off, so as to be gently fleeced, repeatedly. So Scupper wouldn't have found it and kept it—unless he had a very compelling reason.

"What period do you collect?"

"There was a time when I could be had for early American Empire." She made her face even lovelier with a fresh come-home-with-me smile. "But these days, there is nothing I wouldn't do for a piece of Eighteenth Century Connecticut. Have you lived here, long, Ben?"

"What pieces?"

"Beds," she answered, cello in full throat.

I put major effort into recalling my obligation to the client who was already paying me. I thought back on the hard-earned common sense that said never dip your pen in the company ink. I recollected the damage wreaked by beautiful, sophisticated female clients on private eyes as sharp as Sam Spade and Philip Marlow. I envisaged the suffering in store for a part-time, small-town PI who couldn't keep his mind off a femme fatale's shapely tongue, flashing thighs, and nipples pressed against her sweater.

I decided to be honest before it was too late.

"I'm already looking for Scupper McKay."

"You are?" She blinked, apparently amazed by the coincidence. Gorgeous she was, and passionate, but maybe not a great actress. "May I ask for whom?"

"My next door neighbor. Scupper's brother, Scooter McKay. Scooter took the picture you liked. He owns the newspaper."

The brothers McKay were opposites in every way two men could be.

Scooter was steady. He was my age, a large fellow, prone to extra poundage. He had started working for the *Clarion,* delivering papers, when we were 2nd graders in Newbury Prep, had married young, fathered lovely children, and still adored his wife. He had a voice loud as a foghorn.

The missing Scupper, five years older, had dropped out of school, ran away from home, and joined the Marines. He would show up in Newbury on occasion when Scooter and I were kids, tell tales of women in far off places–New York, London, Dublin, Shanghai–share a bottle of wine, and disappear. He was a wiry little guy, with the strikingly handsome chiseled features that only improve with age. His voice was so soft you had to lean in to hear him, but lean you did because you didn't want to miss a word.

"Perfect," said Nina.

"What's perfect about me already looking for a Scupper?"

"We don't have to sit around your office while you take notes. We can discuss the big picture over lunch at my place. I'm staying in the Bell's cottage." She gave me a look. Newbury gossip credited the Bells' weekend visitors with unplanned offspring nine months after visiting that famously romantic guest house with a fireplace in the bedroom and a collection of antique pier glass mirrors artfully positioned around the four poster, which had a mink bedspread.

"It's secluded. Wolves could howl and no one would hear."

"I don't mix business and pleasure Ms. Russell."

"Why not?" she asked, baffledly wide-eyed as if I had proclaimed that the sky was not blue.

"If you hire me, I'll give you my all."

Big smile. "I can hardly wait."

"All my effort as a detective. I'll do my best to earn my fee. That means keeping a clear head."

Her smile got bigger. "That's exactly the kind of head I want from you. If we leave behind the distractions of your office, I'll give you clear undistracted head. You'll give me clear undistracted head."

"What big picture?"

"The picture we'll paint by sharing what we know. I'll tell you secrets that I know and you'll tell me secrets that you've learned and between us we'll figure out where Scupper is hiding."

"And where he hid your piece."

"Like I said, perfect. You get your man. I get my antique."

"We don't we get started right here in my office?"

She swept to her feet in a ballet of sinuous motion, scooped the cat off the floor, and put him back on the chair. I had never seen that cat allow anyone to move him.

"Do you have any anchovies?"

"Anchovies?" Shapely tongue, full lips, come-home-with-me smiles, sincere sounding compliments, "positions," bed, undistracted head, and now anchovies.

"I have some leftover porterhouse. I was going to make a Caesar salad to put under it."

Call me healthily paranoid, but it sounded like she had done the kind of research on me you don't find on Google. A Caesar salad propping up slices of porterhouse steak was my favorite lunch.

"And I've got a gorgeous Argentine Malbec to go with it."

If she said it was a Taymente Malbec, I would be wise to bring a gun.

"A Taymente," she said.

Well, I wasn't really going to bring a gun, but at least I knew why Nina Russell had bothered to research me. She had known I was looking for Scupper before she walked into my office. "Lunch sounds great. But I will bring a notebook."

"Don't forget your GoPro."

I must have looked puzzled. Why bring a camera?

She laughed. "I have an exhibitionist streak. Video me tossing your salad, or something."

"Business," I repeated, staunchly. "Not pleasure."

"I can't seem to restrain myself. I really should be spanked."

Soundly, thought I. "I'll get the anchovies."

On the laptop in my kitchen that I use to check the weather, I googled "Nina Russell" and "American Empire antique furniture." Darned if she wasn't selling a bunch of it on eBay.

I agreed to ride out to the Bells' in the hot red GTI she had parked in front of my house, rather than follow in mine. People talk freely in cars. Maybe she would tell me what the hell she wanted from me that she couldn't get by simply paying me to track down Scupper McKay. She unlocked it with a fingerprint she moistened with her tongue.

"Can I ask you something?" she asked as we climbed in. "Do you find me ugly?"

"Not even slightly. Why do you ask?"

"Are you seriously saying there's no chemistry between us?"

Before I could repeat that I didn't mix PI business and pleasure, she answered herself, saying, "It's nuclear—Hey, wait a minute. Oh my gosh. Are you gay?"

"Yes," I said. That should shut her up until I found Scupper. But just then a very attractive woman passing by in her Jaguar, stopped it abruptly in the middle of Main Street, and lowered her window to call, "Hi, Ben!"

I said, "Hey, Rita. You're back."

Rita raked Ms. Russell with eyes of ice, snarled, "Later," to me, and sped away.

Nina Russell laughed. "If you're gay, you forgot to tell Ms. Glower."

"Okay, I'm straight. But I don't mix business with pleasure."

"Never, ever, ever?"

"Real estate business I'll mix with pleasure," I said. "Not PI."

"You're making me crazy." She reached across and laid a hand on my knee. The car was still at the curb. She hadn't even started the engine yet. "I came here for legitimate business. Then I took one look at you and I thought, I want that. I want that now—and I have to tell you, Ben. This isn't the usual me—I'm not saying I would kick a good looking guy out of my bed, but I'm usually demur about it."

She started the car and drove. As we passed the General Store I recognized the hapless U-haul parked out front by the white scrape of flagpole on its side. I had been wrong about Florida. It had New York plates. But he didn't get that suntan in New York. Tanning parlor? Just then he stepped out of the general store. I got a closer look. His hair was bleached in the washed out way when sun combines with salt water and sand, and I knew I definitely did not want to go to Nina's cottage.

I said, "Making your crazy to take me to bed makes me either the luckiest man in Connecticut, or you are running a number I can't begin to figure out."

"Just go with it."

"Stop the car," I said, reaching for the door. "I don't want to go to the cottage with you."

She pulled over to the curb and reached under the dashboard. Like I said, I knew a femme fatale when I saw one. But I'd devoted so much energy into dodging her wiles that I failed to pay attention to what was really going on, and I was suddenly looking down the barrel of a smallish automatic that fit her hand snugly.

There are some things you never forget. Taught, even though pretty long ago, how to take a gun away from someone pointing it at you, the moves stay with you. You may not be as quick as you were back when training, and probably not as smooth. But muscle memory, drilled a thousand times by short-tempered SEAL instructors, is a reliable friend.

Brain memory, however, reminds you that your instructors dubbed such a move. Do or Die and recommended not trying it unless your adversary's eyes had gone dead and he was already squeezing the trigger. The problem, they explained, is the gun is very likely going to go off and someone is going to get shot. Maybe the bad guy, more likely you, but in either case, they taught us to ask, Do you really want to go to the blood option?

I said, "Ms. Russell, you do seem to feel strongly about me not leaving your car."

"Do I finally have your attention?"

"Undivided."

"Any more questions?"

"Same question. What do you want? And don't say, 'you.' Because you don't want me. You want something from me and it ain't love."

She got sulky. "I'd settle for sex. No-holds-barred."

"Why are you jerking me around?"

"How can you say that?"

"You're selling a bunch of stuff on eBay."

"What's wrong with that? I'm selling American Empire so I can buy 18th Century Connecticut."

"Anybody can put up an ebay site. There's not your stuff. Just pictures. I recognized one from Scupper's website."

She looked abashed. Or at least, embarrassed. "Okay, you got me. I just wanted to make you believe in me."

"If you're not a dealer and you're not a collector, what do you really do?"

She hung her head. "I design cat toys."

"All right, don't tell me."

"Don't believe me?"

"I'll admit my cat thinks you're the cat's meow. He took to you like I've never seen him take to anyone. But for all I know you rubbed chicken liver on your boots to turn him on."

"Check me out, Detective Abbott. Google CatThrills." She gestured with the gun to use my phone. I googled CatThrills. It was an elaborate site–videos and all—not cobbled overnight. The videos featured enthralled cats playing with a variety of strange toys that resembled pinball machines, but were made of ordinary materials like cardboard and plastic, and sold for under twenty bucks.

"Very impressive. How do I know it's yours?"

"Click Contact Us."

And there was a picture of Nina—close to X-rated in a very skimpy cat suit with thigh-high boots, ears, whiskers, and a long tail that looked like something owned by a dominatrix—and an email address.

"What?" I asked, "do these cat toys have to do with Scupper McKay and your seeming bottomless desire for me?"

"A girl's got to make a living. Cat toys are a sideline, like you and houses."

"What do you do when you're not selling cat toys?"

"I'm a bounty hunter."

"That would explain your gun."

"The gun was for you. I don't need it for bounty hunting."

"Fugitives surrender in exchange for greatest night of their lives?"

"No! What kind of person do you think I am?"

I looked her in the eye and she looked back, mildly indignant, and apparently unaware that another of her sweater buttons had slipped its button hole revealing an up swell of breast that would have sent Rubens straight to his brushes. I answered, "Different?"

"I find stuff. Not people. Not fugitives. Stuff. Things. Valuable things."

"You recover stolen goods. So the antique Scupper has that you won't tell me about belongs to your client who is paying you to get it back."

"Sort of."

"If I'm going to work for you, I have to know how 'sort of?'"

"All you have to do is find Scupper."

"So it's small piece. Something he can carry on him. Jewelry? A watch. He likes watches."

"No," she said. "It's not at all small. He couldn't have it on him. But he'll know where it is."

"I can't take the job if I don't know what it is. What if he stole your stash of genuine antique cocaine? Finding it could have repercussions."

Tongue. Lips. A deep sigh. "Okay... Do you know what a highboy is?"

"A highboy?"

"You know what they are, don't you?"

"I've got one upstairs in my guest room. It's basically a chest of drawers sitting on top of a lower chest standing on legs. Highboys are so common in New England you'd think our colonist forebears had little to do with their time but build highboys."

"I can't say without seeing yours, but—"

"Come back to the house. I'll show it to you."

I was not all that surprised that she slipped the gun back in its secret compartment, pulled a u-turn, and drove back to my house.

We went inside. I let her lead the way up the stairs and the view was just wonderful. How could a woman look both slim and round at the same time? She looked over shoulder and gave me a smile that almost knocked me down the stairs.

She stood in the doorway of the guestroom and stared at the highboy, which was painted a sort of off white. Then she sat on the edge of the guest bed and smiled up at me.

"Your highboy is a perfectly respectable Boston factory-made piece that your great-grandmother probably bought in a Bridgeport furniture shop; it will fetch as much as eight-hundred dollars if you find a dealer drinking wine."

"I always thought it had a particularly graceful lines. Most highboys are pretty clunky. I mean it's a beautifully proportioned piece."

"Lovely. The factory obviously copied a good one. Carefully remove that whitewash and it could take your breath away. But the highboy I am talking about is a one of a kind museum quality piece built by a cabinet maker so meticulous that he finished very few pieces, of which even fewer survive."

"A highly valuable highboy."

"Orgasmic."

"Priceless?"

Nina looked me in the face. "There are buyers who will pay almost anything for orgasmic. I would if I could afford it."

"How much is the one you're looking for worth?"

"Depending on which hedge fund heroes' wives talked them into bidding for Eighteenth Century Connecticut antiques, anywhere between two and eight million dollars at auction."

"How much did your client pay?"

"One-point-five."

"Paid it or promised it?"

Nina hesitated. I saw her eyes turn inward, slightly, as if she was not sure. "Honestly?"

"A nice basis on which we could work together."

"You'll take the case?"

"Paid or promised?" I asked again.

The client *claims* he paid Scupper."

"Up front? The entire sum?"

"That's what he claims."

"Do you believe him?"

"I would, except the hedge fund manager is on the lam."

"Where'd you run him down, the Caymans?"

"How did you know?"

I surprised her by reaching out to stroke her cheek with the back of my fingers. Her skin was hot. The flush was sunburn.

"An educated guess," I lied. "The Cayman Islands were a favorite lam-ation resort back when I was on Wall Street. A safe place to stash your dough before the tax man pounces, while you sunbath on the beach. I presume it still is as the charms of a sovereign state that welcomes financial criminals are timeless. So what does he want with a highboy in the Caymans? It's a lot drawers for a bathing suit and tee shirt."

"He's broke."

"If he's broke, where did he get the one-point-five for the highboy?"

"He got lucky with a money transfer mistake."

"Aha. He saw his chance and took it." Banks serving hedge funds made money transfer mistakes all the time. When the bank is shifting billions daily, odds are the occasional fat-finger key stroke will accidentally send an extra couple of million. It's no big deal and the hedge fund sends it back.

Nina said, "He figured to triple the money by investing in Scupper's highboy, pay the bank back, and keep the rest."

"Did he admit that when you tracked him down there?"

"Gosh no. You should have heard him." She threw her arms wide, like a hedge fund crook protesting his innocence, minus firm breasts pressing a sweater. "'Your bank's accusations are ridiculous, bordering on laughable. They're maligning my character.' Etcetera and blah, blah, blah. Except, earlier, he had emailed the bank: 'Don't panic, I'm dealing with this.' He knew exactly what was going on."

In the course of this conversation, I stepped closer to the bed. "Just to be clear," I said, "He's not your client. The bank that made the wire transfer mistake is your client."

Nina's gesturing hands floated to a soft landing around my waist. "Right. The bank wants the highboy or the money, preferably the money. If it were me I'd want the antique and make a lot more at auction."

"Now we're getting somewhere," I said. "You want the antique. I want Scupper."

Nina gave me her best smile yet. She smiled. "First, I want you."

I had a brief opportunity to step away. I failed to seize it. Her hands joined behind me, and instead of stepping away I bent down and kissed her mouth. Then hands were going—mine cupping firm hips to help her up from the bed, hers loosening my belt—and clothes were lifting—my shirt, her sweater, her skirt. I traced bikini lines along beautiful curves front and back. She pressed hard against my fingers, and we returned to kissing, eyes wide open and locked tight.

She said, "Why don't we go to the cottage?"

"Later."

"If you keep doing that with your fingers," she whispered. "I will explode."

Not only did I not stop doing it, I did it faster.

She said, "I am not going to explode alone." My belt, button, and zipper went by the boards. She wrapped both hands around me, one high, one low. Still kissing, she explored with fingers light as feathers, then set them into motion.

The one thing she had not lied about was the chemistry.

Some long time later I became vaguely aware that a private investigator and his beautiful client were sprawled, partially clad, on the floor beside a highboy in what appeared to be my guestroom. Eventually, I got a towel and dried us off.

Nina laughed. "Don't you feel like a couple of eighth graders?"

"I feel convinced that the handjob is a vastly underrated art form."

"Any chance of becoming grownups at the cottage?"

"Let's get back to business."

"Can we at least have lunch?"

"I'm starving."

We were back in her car, driving down Church Hill and just entering the Frenchtown section, where my wrong-side-of-the-tracks cousins live, when I said, "Pull into that gas station. I gotta talk to a guy."

"I thought you're starving."

"It'll just take a second."

The Chevalley Enterprises gas station and repair shop had seven bays going strong. In one of them was a big, red dump truck full of sand. I found my cousin Pinkerton Chevalley, an enormous man in a tight black tee shirt that said, "Deploy! Destroy! US Marines," waited for him to finish frightening a mechanic, and said, "Pink, do me a favor."

Ten minutes later, Nina and I got to the Bells' guest house, which was deep in the estate and truly far enough from anywhere to not hear wolves howl. Nina strolled through the kitchen and partway into the bedroom where the gas flames jumping in the fire place were reflected in a dozen mirrors.

"Lunch?" she asked. "Or should we work up an appetite?" She had one thumb hooked in the waist band of her skirt and other toying with her sweater buttons. Her beautiful mouth was filled with a smile, her eyes were hot, her breath coming short, and I knew that if I was reading this whole thing wrong, I would regret what I was about to say for the rest of my life.

"I'm starving."

She worked up the Caesar dressing in the bottom of a big maple bowl. I washed her Romaine leaves and sliced her beautifully grilled cold porterhouse. She asked me to open the Malbec and I had just decanted it to get some air into it where her cell phone rang.

She snatched it up and listened briefly. When she put the phone down, she looked troubled and could not meet my eye.

I said, "Let me guess what that was about. As soon as you got me out of my house, a suntanned fellow—what is his name?"

"Randy."

"Randy parked a moving van in my driveway, entered my house, which is never locked, and went up to the guestroom. He began to disassemble the highboy when suddenly he heard a racket in the driveway. He looked out the window and saw this huge red dump truck full of sand blocking his moving van. Not only could his moving van not get out of my driveway, he couldn't even open the door to load the highboy."

Nina Russell looked very unhappy.

I said, "So he ran downstairs and told the driver to move the truck. The driver refused. Then what happened?"

"He threatened the man in the dump truck."

"I have one more question. Is your friend in jail, or pressing ice cubes to a black eye in the nearest bar, which is the White Birch Tavern."

"He's not a friend. It's strictly business."

Another guy who recognized femme fatales. "Is he in jail, or pressing ice cubes to a black eye?"

"He's in the White Birch."

"That makes things a little simpler."

We drove to the White Birch, a busy biker bar in Frenchtown. The suntanned broke hedge funder was sitting on a barstool, pressing ice to his left eye and right ear, and dabbing blood from his nose. My cousin Pink, who is not a bad sort for such a large and violent man, had bought him a beer.

I said, "Thanks Pink."

"I'm outta here," said Pink. "Randy, you take care." He gave Randy a friendly goodbye slap on the back that nearly knocked him off his stool, and lumbered out the door to the great relief of a gang of chopped-Harley riders who were maintaining close eye contact with their beers in hopes Pink wasn't looking for a fight.

Nina asked Randy, "Are you all right?" in tones that said she didn't much care.

Randy said, "I realize now it was a mistake to threaten him without a gun in my hand."

I said, "The last guy who tried that ended up eating it. I have one question: How did you know the highboy was in my house."

"I'm not answering any questions."

"I have one question before I turn you in to our resident state trooper for breaking into my house. How did you know the highboy was in my house?"

"Scupper didn't like anybody in this town except his brother and you. He said that you had a saying: Everybody's got to make a living somehow."

"So?"

"I took it to mean you weren't judgmental about stuff like stolen property."

"I do not stash stolen property. That highboy wasn't stolen."

Nina said, hotly, "The hell it wasn't. He stole it from me."

"You didn't own it. He didn't take your money."

"He took mine," said Randy.

"As I understand it, he took the *bank*'s money."

Nina rolled her beautiful eyes.

I said, "To echo my cousin Pink, I'm outta here."

I headed for the parking lot, figuring to walk home if I needed to. Nina followed.

"I would like my retainer back."

"I left it at the house."

"I'll drive you."

We drove back to Main Street. She broke the silence as we rounded the flagpole.

"Ben? How did you know?"

"You got sunburned in a bikini tracking a guy who got his suntan in the Caymans."

She neither winked, nor grinned, but I thought could hear it in her voice. "Is that why wanted to get my clothes off?"

"I thought I saw the burn on your face, and your cheek felt hot. So it seemed worth going to the trouble to confirm it."

"Trouble? Okay, I deserve that. Listen, all the bank wanted was their money. I thought if I could sell the highboy for more than Randy owed them, the profit was mine, fair and square, right?"

"Everybody's got a make a living somehow."

"I wouldn't have done it," she said. "Except the best cat toy I ever made just got counterfeited by the Chinese factory I paid to manufacture it. Instead of hitting the big time, I ended up broke. This just seemed to like an incredible opportunity to get some back with a minimum of damage. Do you know what I mean?"

When we got to the house, I tore her check in half and gave her the pieces.

"Would you mind?" she asked. "Could we go upstairs?"

"What for?"

"I would like to see it one more time."

I followed her up to the guestroom. She feasted her eyes on the highboy. That was the other thing she told the truth about. She really loved antiques.

"You were right," she said. "Gorgeous lines." She laid a gentle hand on it, and caressed the wood. "Scupper should be shot for whitewashing it."

"He got the idea from the Tibetans. They paint their art black to hide it from Chinese invaders."

"Why did he bring it to you?"

"He knew it would be safe."

"Where is he?"

"I wish I knew."

"Not exactly case closed, is it?"

"Not until I find Scupper. And figure out who really owns this thing. Did he buy it? Did he pay for it? Did he lift it... If he owns it and he's dead, Scooter's his heir, not that he needs the dough."

"Ben, I couldn't have done it if I already knew you."

"Don't worry about it. It's worked out fine. You and I have wrapped up our business. I can get busy on Scupper with new leads, thanks to you. And you can go back to designing cat toys."

She said, "I don't know what to say."

I said, "I do."

"What?"

"Take off your clothes."

ABOUT THE CONTRIBUTORS

Although he is the author of several books, including the private eye novel *All White Girls*, two-time Derringer Award-winning writer **Michael Bracken** is better known as the author of more than 1,100 short stories. His crime fiction has appeared in *Crime Square, Ellery Queen's Mystery Magazine, Espionage Magazine, Flesh & Blood: Guilty as Sin, The Mammoth Book of Best New Erotica 4, Mike Shayne Mystery Magazine,* and in many other anthologies and periodicals. He lives and writes in Texas. Learn more at www.CrimeFictionWriter.com and CrimeFictionWriter.blogspot.com.

Max Allan Collins has earned an unprecedented twenty-one Private Eye Writers of America "Shamus" nominations, winning three times, including his Nathan Heller novels, *True Detective* (1983) and *Stolen Away* (1991). In 2012, his Nathan Heller saga was honored with the PWA "Hammer" award for making a major contribution to the private eye genre. His graphic novel *Road to Perdition* (1998) is the basis of the Academy Award-winning Tom Hanks film. His other comics credits include the syndicated strip "Dick Tracy"; his own "Ms. Tree"; and "Batman." He has created a number of innovative suspense series, including Mallory, Quarry, Eliot Ness, and is completing a number of "Mike Hammer" novels begun by the late Mickey Spillane (*Kill Me, Darling*). His tie-in books have appeared on the USA TODAY bestseller list nine times and the *New York Times* three, including *Saving Private Ryan, Air Force One, American Gangster* and the CSI series. Collins has written and directed four feature films, including the Lifetime movie "Mommy" (1996); his produced screenplays include "The Last

Lullaby" (2009), based on his novel, *The Last Quarry*. He lives in Iowa with his wife, writer Barbara Collins; as "Barbara Allan," they have collaborated on eleven novels, including the successful "Trash 'n' Treasures" mysteries (*Antiques Swap*).

Cuban born, Miami Beach- based **Carolina Garcia-Aguilera** is the author of ten books as well as a contributor to many anthologies. She is primarily known for the seven novels that feature Lupe Solano, a Cuban-American private investigator that lives and works in Miami. Her books have been translated into twelve languages; One Hot Summer, her seventh novel, was made into a film for Lifetime Television. Garcia-Aguilera, who herself has been a private investigator for over twenty-five years, has been the recipient of many awards, including the Shamus for best novel, and the Flamingo.

Ted Fitzgerald is the vice-president and former general awards chair for the Private Eye Writers of America. He has published stories in collections edited by Max Allan Collins, Mickey Spillane, Ed Gorman and Marty Greenberg but this is his first story for a collection edited by Bob Randisi. It's better than Viagara!

Parnell Hall is the author of the Stanley Hastings private eye novels, the Puzzle Lady crossword puzzle mysteries, and the Steve Winslow courtroom dramas. Parnell is a past president of the Private Eye Writers of America, a three-time Shamus nominee, and a former private eye. His current Stanley Hastings private eye novel is *Safari*. His next is *A Fool for a Client*.

A reformed newspaper reporter and ad man, **David Housewright** won an Edgar Award from the Mystery Writers of America (*Penance*) and three Minnesota Book Awards *(Practice to Deceive, Jelly's Gold,* and *Curse of the Jade Lily).* His 17th novel - *Unidentified Woman*

#

15 - will be published in June 2015 (St. Martin's Minotaur). He also has published a volume of short stories called *Full House*.

Housewright was elected President of the Private Eye Writers of America in 2014.

Jerry Kennealy has written twenty-one novels, including ten featuring private eye Nick Polo. Jerry has worked as a policeman and real-life private investigator. He has been nominated for the Shamus for the best P.I. Novel twice, and has served as the vice president of PWA. Jerry lives in San Bruno, California with his wife Shirley.

Terrill Lee Lankford is a novelist and filmmaker. His novels include *Earthquake Weather, Blonde Lightning* and *Shooters*. He most recently worked as a writer and producer on the TV series, BOSCH.

Dick Lochte's most recent novel, *Blues In The Night*, was short-listed for the Shamus Award. His *Sleeping Dog*, which won the Nero Wolfe Award and was named one of the 100 Favorite Mysteries of the Century by the Independent Booksellers Association, and its sequel, *Laughing Dog*, were recently re-released in new trade paperback and Kindle editions by Brash Books. Lochte, who lives in Southern California with his wife and son, is also an award-winning drama critic and has written screenplays for such actors as Jodie Foster, Martin Sheen and Roger Moore.

John Lutz is the author of more than forty-five novels and 250 short stories and articles. Awards include the Edgar, Shamus, and the Short Mystery Fiction Society's Golden Derringer Award. He is past president of MWA and PWA. Two of his books have been made into movies. His latest book is the thriller *Frenzy*. He and his wife Barbara divide their time between St. Louis, MO, and Sarasota, FL. Following the sun.

Christine Matthews is the author of the "Gil & Claire Hunt" series, and over 60 short stories. Her current novels are *Sapphires Aren't Forever* (Dagger Books, 2015), the first novel in her Jewelry Designer series, and the stand alone suspense novel *Beating the Bushes* (Crossroads Press, 2015). She is also a member and officer in long standing of the Private Eye Writers of America.

Fifty Shades of Grey Fedora

Warren Murphy who lives in Virginia Beach has won a dozen national awards as novelist and screenwriter. His Destroyer series -- with sales of 60 million books -- is now being readied for a film in Hollywood and his next project, besides the Destroyer series which continues on and on worldwide, will be *Bloodline*, a fictional history of the New York City crime families. Murphy swears this will be his last book... but he has lied before.

M. Ruth Myers won a Shamus in 2014 for her novel *Don't Dare a Dame*, third and most recent in her Maggie Sullivan series. The series follows a gritty woman P.I. in Dayton, OH, from the final years of the Great Depression through the end of World War II. Ruth also has written ten books in other genres.

V.I. Warshawski, **Sara Paretsky's** ground-breaking detective, has practiced serial monogamy from the start. Despite her many lovers, some dozen over the course of 19 novels and 32 years, her sexual activity is left to the reader's imagination. One of Sara Paretsky's career goals is never to be shortlisted, let alone win, the "Literary Review Bad Sex in Fiction" award. For this reason, all of her writing about sex is as oblique as George Eliot's, so writing a story for *50 Shades of Grey Fedora* was a stretch.

Born under a bad sign, **Gary Phillips** has kept writing to get out from under ever since. His latest work includes the graphic novels *Big Water*, about greed, lust and that most precious of resources and *The Rinse*, about a money launder (optioned for Fox TV), and just out is *Hollis, P.I.*, six short stories of a character he first created in comics. Please visit his website at: gdphillips.com.

Robert J. Randisi is the author of the "Miles Jacoby," "Nick Delvecchio," "Gil & Claire Hunt," "Dennis McQueen," "Joe Keough," and "The Rat Pack," mystery series. *The Honky Tonk Big Hoss Boogie* (Perfect Crime Books), the first book in the Auggie Velez Nashville P.I. series, appeared in 2013. *Upon My Soul* (Down & Out Books, 2013) is the first book in the "Hitman with a Soul" Trilogy. The second book is *Souls of The Dead* (2015, Down & Out Books). His recent novel *McKenna's House* (Crossroad Press) has been called his best book yet by several reviewers. He is the editor of over 30 anthologies. All told he is the author of more than 600 novels. His "Housesitting Detective" series will begin appearing from Dagger Books in 2015, with the first book, *Dry Stone Walls*. He is the founder of the Private Eye Writers of America, the creator of the Shamus Award, the co-founder of Mystery Scene Magazine, the American Crime Writers League, and Western Fictioneers.

JUSTIN SCOTT was nominated for the Edgar for Best First Novel and for Best Short Story. His novel *The Shipkiller* is honored in the International Thriller Writers' *Thrillers: 100 Must-Reads*. Scott writes the Ben Abbott detective mysteries set in small-town Connecticut. He co-writes the early-20th Century Isaac Bell detective adventure series with Clive Cussler. *The Assassin;* their latest Isaac Bell debuted March 2015. Scott's main pen name is Paul Garrison, under which he writes modern sea stories and, for the Robert Ludlum banner, *The Janson Command* and *The Janson Option*.

If you liked this, consider other mystery/thriller titles by Riverdale Avenue Books:

Camden's Knife: Volume One of the Macroglint Trilogy
by John Patrick Kavanagh
http://riverdaleavebooks.com/books/5144/camdens-knife-volume-one-of-the-macroglint-trilogy

Of White Snakes and Misshapen Owls: The Charlotte Olmes Mystery Series
by Debra Hyde
http://riverdaleavebooks.com/books/4101/of-white-snakes-and-misshapen-owls

Transition To Murder
By Renee James
http://riverdaleavebooks.com/books/4109/transition-to-murder

Cobra Killer: Gay Porn Murder, The Manhunt to Bring the Killers to Justice
by Peter A Conway, Andrew E. Stoner
http://riverdaleavebooks.com/books/4106/cobra-killer-gay-porn-murder-the-manhunt-to-bring-the-killers-to-justice

Made in the USA
Middletown, DE
24 November 2019